WHEN the de la Cruz Family *DANCED*

Praise for

When the de la Cruz Family Danced

This extraordinary novel illustrates a family's long journey toward making peace – with the world, with the family, and with individual selves. Miscolta is a pitch-perfect prose stylist and a passionately empathetic creator: she savors sentence-making and attends to the all-important nuanced moments between people. This chronicle of a family is beautifully observed and heart-rendingly told, and these characters will linger long after you've closed the book. I feel blessed to have met this family and made the journey with them.

– Antonya Nelson, author of *Bound*

A smoothly written debut that sways between the Philippines and the U.S., between the present and past, and between the secrets and hard truths of its compelling characters. This is a complex story of immigration and loss that packs an emotional punch.

– Cristina Garcia, author of *The Lady Matador's Hotel*

When the de la Cruz Family Danced introduces a wise, warm, funny, and big-hearted writer to the world. This book is a delight.

– Rebecca Brown, author of *American Romances*

In her deft debut novel, Donna Miscolta presents a clarifying vision of post-immigration America. Longings acted upon or stifled, secrets disclosed or withheld, connections made or frayed – Miscolta shows that the extended de la Cruz family is a mirror of the things that bind us and keep us apart. *When the de la Cruz Family Danced* may be one particular family's aching story, but the novel also has a largeness that encompasses the evolving formal history of the novel, the history of family life in America, and the continuing story of how immigrants carry the burdens of the past into the strange present. Miscolta's novel is intricate, tender, and elegantly written – a necessary novel for our times.

– Rick Barot, author of *Want*

When reading *When the de la Cruz Family Danced,* you feel like the story is already familiar – not that it's been told before, but that its words have the flow of memory, of having been there standing in the de la Cruz kitchen or sitting at the dinner table where there is the nostalgic talk of family meals, of family tragedies, of the heartfelt things left unsaid that are later recalled or written down in letter sent through the mail or watched in a home movie. We, as readers, aren't a part of this life or this history and yet by reading, we see ourselves just standing at the edge of the frame in a de la Cruz family portrait. We're family.

– Shawn Wong, author of *American Knees*

When the de la Cruz Family Danced is my kind of book – characters I fell in love with, prose that made me swoon, dialogue that rang true. Donna Miscolta did something wonderful here: she created a world that I didn't want to leave.

– Noël Alumit, author of *Talking to the Moon* and *Letters to Montgomery Clift*

WHEN the de la Cruz Family *DANCED*

a novel

Donna Miscolta

SIGNAL8PRESS

Hong Kong

When the de la Cruz Family Danced
By Donna Miscolta
Published by Signal 8 Press
An imprint of Typhoon Media Ltd

ISBN: 978-988-19895-9-8

Typhoon Media Ltd: Signal 8 Press | BookCyclone
Hong Kong
www.typhoon-media.com
www.bookcyclone.com
www.signal8press.com

Cover design: Clarence Choi
Author Photo: Meryl Schenker
Interior design: Alex Jeffers
Set in Adobe Garamond, Helvetica, and Bodoni 72 OS

For my father
Jose Tiongkiao Miscolta
Wish you were here.

1971

A MONTH IN THE TROPICS

Johnny de la Cruz stood in the main lobby of the Manila airport, waiting. He gripped a suitcase in each hand as he searched the crowd for his brother-in-law, Romulo, whom he only knew from photographs. He felt a slight embarrassment at his inability to discern among the faces around him. Though the plane had been packed with Filipino families, though his American neighborhood back home was sometimes referred to as Little Manila, being in a whole country of people like him - yet not like him - was disorienting. A man who could be Romulo approached, and Johnny set down his suitcases to prepare for a greeting. A handshake, as it turned out. Johnny knew at once that his tie to his family in the Philippines – his father and sister, his long-dead mother – was as tenuous as Romulo's grasp was strong.

Romulo carried both suitcases to the car, though Johnny protested. Despite his empty hands, he felt weighed down – by the fifteen hours of flying, the lack of sleep, and now as he followed Romulo through the automatic glass doors, the dizzying tropical heat.

In the days leading up to his trip, Johnny had gone bent-kneed with indigestion, for which Tessie spooned Pepto-Bismol into his mouth. The smooth, sticky taste nearly made him gag.

Tessie massaged her own temples as she told him not to worry, that she and the girls would be fine. But going back worried him. He feared heat and mosquitoes and sleeplessness. He feared being a stranger. He had a suspicion that his daughters would not miss him, and he tried to ignore the thought that he might not miss them.

They were all there to see him off. His daughters were silent and outwardly bored, though he sensed their giddiness about his departure. When he hugged them each clumsily in turn, he felt a pang of sorrow and unease. He had never been on a plane before. What if his plane went down in the ocean? Would they grieve for him? Only Tessie dabbed at her eyes.

As Romulo drove through the crowded city that gleamed along the boulevards and grew coarse down side streets and alleys, he pointed out landmarks, some vaguely familiar to Johnny, though too often at odds with the version that had lived in his head during all his years in America – in Kimball Park, a smudge on a map of southernmost Southern California. He had not been back since leaving in 1946, not even when his mother died. But he had written regularly, though the intervals had increased over the years, and he had always sent money, and every so often photographs were exchanged. It had always been apparent how much they looked alike – he and his father. Years ago, when they would stand side by side, Johnny felt the redundancy in his long face, big ears, and wavy hair. Whenever his father, angry at some insolence or other, demanded that he look him in the eye, Johnny was too distracted by the similarities to focus just on his father's black irises, which, after all, were Johnny's as well.

"Rizal," Romulo said, nodding his head in the direction of the famous park.

Johnny understood from his brother-in-law's vigorous turn of the wheel, the way he thumped the switch on the air conditioner to blast full force, that hosting a Filipino who lived in America was a matter of pride. Johnny offered Romulo a cigarette, and they smoked in silence. Even when the car filled with fumes from their Camels, Johnny could sense the clammy swelter of tropical smells pressing against the roof and glass. Johnny lowered his window a crack. The violent heat stung his eyelids.

Manila had sprawled to its outlying towns and villages. There was no countryside anymore – just more houses and stores and traffic, and suddenly a driveway.

"Home," Romulo said, by which Johnny was sure he meant his, Romulo's, home.

"Welcome," Romulo added.

Again, Romulo insisted on carrying Johnny's bags. Before they reached the porch, the front door opened and his sister Nora came running toward him. He was startled by the welling of his smoke-irritated, sleep-deprived eyes. He was aware of Romulo edging past them, laden with luggage; of two small children tugging at his hands and elbows, his trouser thighs; of being gently shuttled into the house and then falling to his knees at the chair that held his father, a withered stick of a man who patted Johnny's back over and over as his bony chest heaved.

◈ ◈ ◈

In the first week of his month-long visit, Johnny was overwhelmed, embarrassed, and secretly pleased by the attention. There were visitors nearly every day. They pressed gifts into his hands, and he, in turn, doled out the things Tessie had tucked in the crevices of his suitcase. When all of these had been offered – the movie magazines, fountain pens, Avon products, and key rings – he gave his own belongings – his watch, a cigarette lighter, a belt – as he remembered was the custom.

There was a game of poker one afternoon and *mah jongg* on another that lasted far into the night. There was a fiesta to attend. He was nearly swept into a procession as he stood on the sidewalk, self-consciously waving a crepe-paper Philippine flag someone had thrust in his hand. At night in bed, he lay exhausted and wide awake in the bungalow-style house that was open and airy, accessible to lizards and scorpions and mosquitoes. He pulled the net tight around his bed. He thought of these people whose house he was occupying, the pleasant stranger who was his sister Nora, her deceptively placid husband and their well-mannered children, and his fragile, shrunken father, who hardly resembled the man who once put him on a ship to America.

Johnny had left the Philippines in the aftermath of the war, when the Japanese occupation had been replaced by American ships in the harbor and sailors in the cantinas. He had spent his testosterone-fueled, risk-taking adolescence running messages, pesos, and the occasional grenade through rice fields for the local band of guerillas. When the war was over and he was back in school, the classroom could not contain him, so he spent his days roaming the villages and beaches, pleasantly idle, if sometimes bored. His plans for the future consisted only of waiting for Bunny Bulong to turn sixteen, when she would be allowed to date him. But he was on a ship a week before Bunny blew out the candles on her birthday cake. His father had added a year to Johnny's age to make him eligible for the U.S. Navy. The lie was eventually corrected, though there still remained the occasional muddle with official documents. Nevertheless, it made for a good joke whenever someone asked his age. As for Bunny, he made himself forget her, just as he made himself forget the Philippines, retaliation for having been sent away.

◈ ◈ ◈

In the second week of his visit, Johnny and his father sat quietly in the shade on the narrow slab of patio, the emotion of their meeting that first day absent, as if it had evaporated in the heat. Behind them an electric fan rotated with a steady murmur, a backdrop to their conversation, intermittent as the buzz of mosquitoes. Despite the fan, a layer of sweat sealed his clothes to his body, and Johnny shifted often in the bamboo chair. In the pauses in conversation, while his father squinted upward as if trying to locate something in the hot blue sky, Johnny watched his sister's children play. The girl, Trinidad, tossed a rubber ball, aiming it at the stick her little brother, Pablo, held and swung too late. The ball bounced behind him and rolled between the feet of the old man. Johnny watched his father lean down to pick it up as Trinidad approached slowly, hands behind her back. When the old man held it out to her she ran, smiling, to take it from him.

Johnny wondered if his father remembered confiscating his marbles until everything he'd won clacked heavily in a burlap rice bag – a sackful of wrongs. Skipping school, forgetting chores, arriving home late. Talking back.

The whir of the fan was a never-ending sigh between them.

His father said, "Tell me about my granddaughters."

Johnny was surprised at how much he could tell, how from this distance he could see his daughters more clearly than all those times they had walked past him in his own kitchen. He described their appearance, their resemblance to this or that family member, and he talked of their interests: Laura's competitiveness and her good effort but middling success at sports; Josie's compassion for scabby, ill-tempered strays; Sara's penchant for craft-of-the-week projects, which hung gracelessly in the bathroom or kitchen before someone consigned them to the garage. All were infinitely more endearing in the telling than they ever were at home.

Johnny thought of his daughters, who were probably not missing him much. He had never been present enough to earn being missed. Johnny wondered if his father could somehow know this. He glanced at his father perched at the edge of his chair, eyes on some distant object, his head nodding at Johnny's words.

"And Tessie? What does she like?"

"She likes her garden. And she collects..." Johnny struggled for the word akin to *knick-knack*. He used his hands as he described little ceramic ducks and roosters, and his father grinned with comprehension.

"Do you remember your mother used to collect shells?"

Johnny didn't remember and he panicked momentarily, so he said what he knew must be true: "She liked pretty things." His father smiled, and Johnny felt a flash of pleasure, almost a sense of accomplishment at having reached across the wide ocean of their separation.

But then it was just the fan between them again. It was Johnny's turn to ask a question. *Tell me about yourself,* he wanted to say. *Tell me about* ***myself.*** Before Johnny could speak, his father cleared his throat – a long rumbling space-filler that vanished into the drone of the fan as he fell asleep.

Johnny turned from his sleeping father to watch the children play, and they drew him into their game. Sometimes the ball bounced Johnny's way, and when he caught it, the children clapped in approval. If he missed, they raced each other to retrieve it and place it in his palms like a gift. Then they ran to the far end of the yard and called to him to throw the ball. He wound up his arm like a baseball pitcher and the movement fanned the air around him. He released the ball, sending it in a high arc against the bright sky, and the children danced back and forth, their arms outstretched, anticipating its fall.

Now Trinidad came to sit near Johnny. She was attentive,

unlike his own daughters, and almost adoring as she leaned toward him with concern. "Are you hot, *Tito*?"

"I'm not used to it."

"If you stay, you'll see the rains."

"I have only two weeks left." The little girl took his hand, as if she could hold him there with her wistful grasp. But the truth was he was ready to go back. The heat was oppressive, the mosquitoes unrelenting, and the food at times unfriendly to his stomach. He was homesick. He didn't want to see the rains.

He hadn't been away from Tessie and the girls since his years in the Navy. He had hated the Navy. He had hated being at sea. Once he was there, the isolation grew on him; when he returned, the separations seemed in the end less painful than the awkward reunions on confetti-strewn docks. The squeals, the leaping embraces, and the prolonged kissing other families displayed made Johnny self-conscious. He was not given to such expression, but once, struck momentarily with an impulse, he attempted to swing Tessie in his arms. Laughing with embarrassment, she kept both feet on the ground, and Johnny only succeeded in pulling her off balance. While Tessie straightened the corsage on her shoulder, Johnny patted the heads of his daughters and dropped a piece of candy into each hand.

Despite the prospect of another awkward reunion, he was homesick. He wanted to go home. He didn't want to see the rains.

"What time is it, *Tito*?" Trinidad's question brought her brother running to her side.

Johnny played the game they had played nearly every day since his arrival. "What time do you think?"

The children laughed and pulled Johnny to his feet. They left his father bent in sleep and walked down the street in this town that Johnny barely remembered. Streets were paved, and many had sidewalks – though they were narrow and cracked by the exposed roots of trees – coconut, banana, acacia – that wove their leaves and branches through an uneven network of telephone wire. The children, still holding his hands, skipped at his side, causing his arms to swing unnaturally, against the rhythm of his stride. Yet he was unwilling to pull back.

When they were within sight of the *sari sari*, the children broke away and dashed to the entrance, where they waited for him beneath a faded Coca-Cola sign. Inside, it was dim after the bright light of the sun and slightly cooler from the fans that rotated in a lazy spin from the ceiling. The air was thick and musty with the smell of incense, bamboo, dried goods, and sweets. The old woman behind the counter greeted them and began to bag the rice candy that had become their custom to buy. The children ran to the aisle where the toys – mostly cheap trinkets – were shelved: plastic tea sets, rubber balls in a variety of sizes, paper fans.

"Choose something," Johnny told the children. Trinidad chose the tea set, white with blue flowers painted along the rim of each imitation piece. Pablo was undecided. Johnny spotted a bag of marbles. He weighed them in his palm. "How about these?"

But the boy shook his head, picked up instead a lunging action hero made of hard plastic. Johnny let the marbles slide from his hand back onto the shelf. He patted Pablo's head and paid for the toys.

◈ ◈ ◈

That evening there were guests for dinner. "You remember Bunny?" said his sister, when he came into the living room, feeling hot and sticky despite the shower he had just taken.

"Of course he does." The woman stood to embrace him. She wore a white sundress bright with fancy birds; her black hair was knotted at the side of her head; orange toenails were on display in backless high-heeled sandals. She hugged him close. The knot of her hair pressed against his nose, and he smelled coconut and hair spray. For the first time since he'd arrived, he felt a connection to the life he had left behind.

"Bunny Bulong, Miss Sampaguita 1946," he said, remembering how the announcer's voice had gone mushy with the news. She was fifteen – precociously glamorous and keenly aware of her appeal.

"Bunny Piña, now," she said.

"Piña," Johnny repeated dumbly.

"This is Carlitos, her husband," Nora said of the handsome, smiling man standing off to Bunny's side.

"Carlitos," Johnny said, appalled at his inability to do nothing but echo the names announced to him. He extended his hand to Carlitos and they shook, Johnny gripping hard.

"Enjoying your visit?" Carlitos asked with a grin that was affable enough, if quick to fade.

"Yes," Nora answered for Johnny. "He finally made it back to us."

"Yes," Bunny said, "finally."

"Yes," his father repeated softly.

Over dinner, the talk at first centered on Johnny and his impressions of the town after his long absence, but he made a poor focal point with his brief, unembellished answers to their proddings. Johnny felt their annoyance at his insubstantial answers. But what could he say? Life had gone on without him, and now this place that was once home was as unfamiliar to him as the sound of Bunny's last name. He was glad when Bunny took charge of the conversation, offering her own assessment of the changes she had witnessed over the years, changes that ultimately drove her to Manila proper.

"When a small town tries to be big, you might as well go live in the real thing."

"Lucky for me she did," Carlitos said, placing his hand over Bunny's, before withdrawing it to allow her to bring her glass of wine to her lips, shiny from lip gloss and *pancit*. When she set her glass down, she put her hands in her lap.

"More *pancit*, Carlitos?" Nora asked, pushing the plate of noodles toward him.

After dinner they sat in the living room, and Romulo played American jazz on the stereo. Carlitos tapped his foot. Nora brought out a photo album in which she had collected pictures Tessie had sent over the years – school pictures and faded Polaroids of the girls. Bunny commandeered the photo album and made Johnny sit next to her. When she crossed her legs, he could see a light blue vein run across the curve of her calf. She propped the album on her knee, and as she turned the pages with her graceful orange-tipped fingers, she made Johnny answer questions about his family. It didn't take her long to recognize and name each of his daughters. She was quick to notice the feature that united them – prominent, long-lobed ears, a lamentable de la Cruz trait that was only partly offset by large eyes.

"Those eyes are your saving grace," she teased.

Bunny closed the album and set it on the coffee table, her calf again visible to Johnny.

"You'll have to come visit us in Manila before you leave," Bunny said.

"Yes, go to Manila, see the sights," his sister urged him, just as she would a tourist.

"Yes, the sights," Carlitos chimed in, and though his nod was amiable, his voice was flat, airless.

"Romulo goes next week on business," Nora said. "You can go then."

With that settled, Bunny announced, "Time to dance." She went to Romulo's collection of records and slipped one onto the phonograph.

Carlitos stood up, summoned from his daydream by Bunny's command. They were a practiced pair, their turns smooth, their flourishes unforced. Romulo and Nora danced, too. Then the four of them traded partners. Johnny did not dance. They knew and remembered this about him, so they did not invite him, saving him the humiliation.

"Bolero," said his father, who did not know how to dance any dances either, but could at least name them. Johnny watched the measured, dreamy movements of the dancers, the rise and lift of their torsos with the sweeping slow step, their graceful decline with the quick-quick rock of the foot on the next two beats. Where did people learn such things? His father kept the tempo with a nodding of his head, and Johnny pretended to do the same. He tried not to look at the heightened curve of Bunny's calves as her toes gripped the insoles of her sandals, tried not to watch how her movements electrified the birds painted on her dress, tried not to blush when he found Carlitos's gaze.

In the third week of his visit, Johnny went to Manila. Romulo negotiated the traffic, weaving in and out of four – sometimes five – lines of cars that crowded a highway marked for three lanes. At intersections, where heeding traffic signals was regarded as optional or advisory at best, cars pitched forward in spurts. Ragged children, ignoring the clamor of horns and shouts from drivers, darted among the cars, running up to those stalled in traffic and offering for sale fried peanuts, mangoes on a stick, or *bagoong*, the salted shrimp that Johnny liked but resisted now. The small street hawkers amid the tangle of cars made him nervous. He held a package in his lap, a gift for

Bunny and Carlitos, and he gripped it tighter now as Romulo veered into a gap in the next lane and then maneuvered down some side streets.

Romulo left him at the door of a small apartment house squeezed between a bar and a butcher shop. It was not the kind of place Johnny imagined a former beauty queen would live. Of course, it had been only a local pageant. But Bunny's regalness had extended beyond the tiara woven with *sampaguita* petals. Her straight posture and the angle of her chin made her imposing despite her small stature. Bunny's presence always improved her surroundings, he remembered as he pulled open the splintered door.

The hallway was hot and musty. A gecko was fixed to the ceiling. He knocked on the door that said *Piña*, barely readable in the dimness caused by several burned-out bulbs. He heard heels clacking, and then Bunny was at the door, more subdued in her dress and make-up than she had been the other night at dinner. Her hair was loose and fanned at her shoulders, her lipstick a soft coral, her dress flowing rather than clingy. The realization of what would occur once he stepped inside the door took him by surprise. As soon as he saw her, he knew that Carlitos was not at home. His impulse was to turn away, back down the airless hallway and into the gritty heat of the street, but his feet remained planted, obeying some other desire, which had everything and nothing to do with Bunny.

She held out a hand to greet him, and Johnny, flustered, handed her the package. Bunny smiled and led him to a small living room. It was cramped with worn furniture and dense with pillows, but Bunny's elegance bested the clutter. She opened the package, and her delight seemed genuine at the hand-painted ceramic candle holders, which she set on the coffee table already graced by a cheap sake set. Music played from the stereo, something light-hearted that made Johnny feel easy about taking a seat on the couch and accepting the glass of sake that Bunny handed to him. Bunny sat down too. They were side by side, just an inch of space between them. Bunny didn't cross her legs like she had the other night at dinner, which nevertheless made him think of the vein in her calf, that fine blue line beneath her skin.

He could think of nothing to say and waited for her to begin the conversation.

When she opened her coral-painted mouth, the words she spoke came out of the blue, without context.

"Do you remember my sister Odette? She has no children either. She says you get used to it."

The sake burned in his throat.

"There's still time for you," Johnny said, silently calculating her age. Thirty-nine. Old, but not too old for having children. He was embarrassed at how easy it had been for Tessie to become pregnant, how she finally went on birth control pills after Sara was born, despite the Catholic Church – because, after all, they had already defied the Church.

It was not just the memory of the abortion that prompted his next action, but some larger sense of desire and regret and loss that had seemed to coalesce in him since his return. He put his hand on Bunny's knee and slid it up her dress. There on the narrow sofa, they made awkward, indecorous love, careful not to upset the sake glasses on the table. He kept his eyes closed and breathed in the reckless scent of orchids and the tropics that came from Bunny's skin.

In his fourth and last week, Nora took him on a trip to Nayong Pilipino, a theme park consisting of the country in miniature, the various regions condensed into an instant Philippines tour, the geography abbreviated in replica volcanoes and rice terraces. A jeepney took them to the different regions – Bicol, the Visayas, Mindanao and Sulu, the Cordilleras and Ilocos.

"Small world," Johnny joked.

He bought souvenirs. A tray inlaid with mother-of-pearl for Tessie, brushes with ox-bone handles for the girls, and for himself a picture postcard of the park, the abridged version of the Philippines further reduced to a small rectangle of glossy paper.

A few days later he packed these things carefully in the middle of his suitcase. He straightened out the room he had occupied for the last four weeks, adjusting the lampshade, arranging the mat so it was square to the bed, moving the vase of dried flowers back to the middle of the small table where he had stacked the American newspapers he read each evening. Then he sat on the bed next to his open suitcase and waited for his party to begin.

Guests crowded the house for a farewell feast. The smell of garlic and fried foods mixed with colognes and sweat, and inside the cocoon of well-wishers, Johnny felt something catch in his throat. He accepted backslapping from the men and kisses from the women, and everywhere around him were hearty, insistent, unfailingly polite words.

"So little time to know you."

"You mustn't stay away so long next time."

"At least you will miss the rains."

His father, sitting on the couch, nodded at him, knowing what Johnny knew – that he would not come again. Johnny wished then for an obliterating, torrential downpour.

At the airport he was escorted to his gate by a dozen relatives and their friends who had made a caravan to see him off. He had observed the occasion by wearing a suit, despite the heat, the cooling rains still weeks away, and he had loosened the tie a little and carried the jacket in the crook of his arm. On the stairs that led down to the departure gate, they posed for a picture, arranging themselves five tiers deep, with Johnny in the middle. Later, when his sister sent him a copy of the black-and-white photograph, he saw how obviously he stood out from the others. At first, he told himself it was because of his suit. But then admitted the suit had nothing to do with it.

As the plane left the tarmac, Johnny watched the distance open up between him and the land below. For a short time, they were over the archipelago, its islands a jigsaw of sizes and shapes that defied piecing together. Then it was just ocean.

1990

I

SPECIAL EFFECTS OF HOME MOVIES

Johnny de la Cruz was the center of attention – a place he'd never sought and seldom been. Though he was not particularly comfortable there, he knew there was no way out.

His daughters, three anxiously bored women, were seated around him in the living room, an uneasy audience to the wheeze in his chest, the chafing of his limbs, his tendency to suck air in the space where he had ceased wearing two of his bottom teeth. Here for Sunday dinner, they had recently taken to leaving their spouses and children at home to spare him the clutter of too many bodies at the table. Now they sat surrounding him with their careful silence. He let a fart escape him. They pretended not to notice.

He looked away from them, and his eyes found the swan, the coffee-table eyesore that spilled tendrils of fake ivy from a hollow in its glazed ceramic back. He had always been accepting of Tessie's décor, but now found it dime-store depressing. He wanted to sigh, but knew it would cause him to cough.

No one had said he was dying. And though no one had assured him he would recover, no one had said he would not. This lengthy illness that had rendered his bony frame even bonier, his blood thick as yogurt, his lungs diminished as leaky balloons, had earned him this fear of Sunday dinners.

Of course, it was really his daughters he feared. Eventually, he would get the nerve to talk – really talk – saying things he had never said before. Eventually, they would have to answer back, wouldn't they?

"Are you thirsty, Dad?"

He looked up. Laura adjusted her designer glasses at him. He, in turn, took off his own, which Laura had fitted for him at a discount. He set his gaze in the direction of his out-of-focus daughters. As babies, they had come in quick succession. He had been at sea during each of the births. He would come home on leave and Tessie would offer him the new bundle to admire and hold, and he would gingerly stroke its cheek and be amazed at its simple, unfathomable responses. It was the closest he ever felt to them and it shamed him to admit it.

"Yes, a little," he said, though he wasn't, not a bit. But it sent Laura out of the room and now he was not so outnumbered.

"Should we turn on the TV?" Josie asked.

Sara answered okay.

As if she were the one who had been asked, he thought, until he put his glasses back on and realized that she had been.

He receded into his chair, his sharp bones finding the gaps in the abundant pillows. Tessie had prepared the chair for him after his most recent release from the hospital. She had cushioned the already fat upholstery with thick bath towels and inserted pillows inside of each armrest. Unless he burrowed into it, he rode atop the padding, and the possibility of a human avalanche presented itself.

◈ ◈ ◈

"We have a surprise for you, Dad."

They had just sat down to the chicken adobo and rice Tessie had made for Johnny and the tacos she had made for their daughters. Johnny, whose appetite was never hearty these days, felt his stomach constrict at Laura's announcement.

"Make that two," Josie said.

Johnny looked at Sara, fearing a third surprise, but she was busy unwrapping submarine sandwiches from the SubClub franchise she and her husband had recently acquired.

"Okay," he said, feeling guilty already for the false pleasure he would show.

"No, dear, after dinner," Tessie said, and he was grateful for the reprieve.

Platters of food shoved up against each other in disproportionate abundance to the five of them seated around the table. With Johnny's unpredictable appetite, Tessie never knew how much to cook, except on Sundays, when she could divide any leftovers among their daughters, none of whom had developed more than passable cooking skills.

He himself had been an involuntary student of the kitchen. As a steward aboard ship, consigned to the galley and mess hall, he had learned about table setting and service, about cooking in quantities, about the infinite uses of Worcestershire sauce and the tricks for folding fruit into Jell-O. It was one of his failings that he had not passed this knowledge on to his children. Though he must have taught them other things. If pressed, surely he could name them.

Steam from his rice and chicken clouded his glasses, and as he ate, temporarily half-blinded, the conversation went on around him – his daughters repeating the latest Dan Quayle jokes from Johnny Carson, and Tessie noting the newly painted front door of their neighbor Hector Cabrera. The color of yams. A surly color, she said, and Johnny wondered at her use of such a word.

"More rice, Dad?" Josie was offering to spoon a second helping on his plate.

He remembered that she had been the one as a teenager to volunteer at the retirement home, feeding the old and the helpless. He imagined her silently coaxing peas past a patient's clenched dentures. Now she fed and watered doomed dogs at the Humane Society. He waved the spoon away and, rebuffed, Josie reached for another taco. Johnny wanted to make it up to her, to invite her to serve him another mound of rice, but it was too late for him to be believable.

He pushed his chair back. Laura dabbed at her mouth with a napkin and Sara began rewrapping the SubClub sandwiches, which no one had touched.

◈ ◈ ◈

Johnny was not one to inspire imaginative gifts from his daughters. For Father's Day, Christmas, and birthdays, they kept him supplied with tube socks, undershirts, and ties in quantities to last well past his expected lifespan, his cancer aside. Sometimes, though, they would surprise him with useless trinkets – a zodiac sign key chain, coffee mugs with cartoons and funny sayings about marriage and children, a flashlight that was also a transistor radio.

Now he wondered what was inside this package, wrapped in blue tissue paper and tied with ribbon. It was the size and shape of a videotape.

Maybe they got it right this time. Maybe it was one of those classic war movies. He had been a teenager during the war, hiding in rice fields, smuggling grenades, and awaiting MacArthur's famous return. He wouldn't mind watching again how John Wayne or William Holden had fared. It would help him pass the time during the week, when Tessie was busy.

Lately, she routinely disappeared on errands, only to return an hour or so later with just a quart of milk or a can of soup. Once she had come home with an empty paper bag. He never asked for explanations. He envied these little escapes from him and his illness. He did wonder though if she really thought he didn't notice the measly results of her outings, if she thought that somehow his illness had rendered him an idiot.

He opened the package, slowly, sliding the ribbon off, running his finger along the seam of the wrapping to break the adhesive and uncovering, yes, a videotape, something homemade with the wistful title *When We Were Young*.

"We had all those old home movies of us converted to video," Laura said. "Before the film on those old reels faded away."

Johnny thought it was part of the natural history of memories to fade. Let sleeping dogs die, as Tessie would say.

"The video is great," Laura assured him. "All in chronological order and with titles." She held out her hand. "Here, let's play it."

With a shrug he knew his daughters would interpret as embarrassed gratitude, he accepted this gift as he had the tube socks and ties and undershirts.

"We had music added to it," Laura said, handing him the remote.

Johnny adjusted the volume on a sentimental piano tune that he recognized from a pharmaceutical commercial.

While the pace of the music never matched the action on the screen, it still made it cheerfully nostalgic, so that scenes of Laura steering her child-size car over the tail of the neighbor's puppy, of Josie careening on training wheels, of Sara gyrating furiously to keep a hula hoop above her hips were excruciatingly, sweetly funny. Once in a while, the camera found Tessie, who shielded her face with one hand and made shooing motions with the other. And of course, there was no sign of him, since he held the camera.

At first, his daughters were pleased with their guileless selves, with the delight they took in being observed by the camera. Eventually, though, they quieted as if they were in a movie theater watching actors in a story other than their own. That was the problem with moments captured on film, Johnny thought. Too often, they looked better than the lived experience (or at least the memory of it), leaving you with an alarming sense of loss.

He punched the button to stop the video, freezing on the screen for a moment Sara's open-mouthed glee at some off-camera wonder. Then the image was gone, the screen blank, a mocking reminder of the mystery of what had induced Sara's happiness, which must surely have belonged to them all.

So the family sat, stunned by the distance between then and now.

Tessie cleared her throat, and Johnny remembered there was a second surprise. He looked at Josie, but her hands, locked in combat with each other, held nothing, which made Johnny more nervous than the prospect of another gift.

"Well," she said, "you know, Gabe's out of school next week and David wants to take him on a road trip to visit his folks in Texas – kind of a bonding thing before Gabey turns thirteen. So we're going to have the house painted this summer while they're gone. And I'm going to move in here for a while so I can help out and give Mom a break when she needs one and – you know, keep you company."

He knotted his own hands, his fingertips pressing into the valleys between his knuckles. He felt a cough rising. "Oh," he sputtered. It came out as acquiescence and he was glad, since he had meant to say no and he knew that it would've been wrong.

◈ ◈ ◈

He sat alone in the living room, the knick-knacks and artificial plants his only company now. And *Columbo* – a rerun. He liked the rumpled detective with his outward bumbling and inward deftness, and he appreciated mysteries, even unsolved ones. Especially unsolved ones. Let sleeping dogs die.

He watched Columbo scratch his head, fumble in his raincoat for a pen, and add up clues behind a wrinkled forehead. Johnny touched his own forehead. His daughters had kissed him there before they left. They had lined up at his chair and one by one put their feathery breath to his skin. It was their occupations he smelled on them – the flinty smell of optical machinery on Laura, the reek of old dogs on Josie, and the stink of mayonnaise on Sara. Or maybe he had just imagined the smells, or remembered them. Imagining and remembering seemed to him much the same thing these days.

Johnny was restless. Tessie was finishing up in the kitchen, humming in her preoccupied, slightly off-key way. Before the show was over, before Columbo revealed the murderer, Johnny slid from his chair and wandered in to sit at the table. Tessie was washing dishes as if it were a favorite pastime, some recreation that required the yellow sweat suit and white sneakers she wore. Johnny stared at Tessie's back and jiggled his leg, making dull slaps against the stiff overhang of the vinyl tablecloth. Tessie turned from the sink.

"Can I get you anything, dear?"

It was a question she had asked him almost daily over the years of their marriage. Routine and rote, yet now different.

"Nah," he said.

Tessie had already turned back to the sink, back to her humming over dirty dishes. She was humming the music from the pharmaceutical commercial, now the background melody to their daughters' childhood.

He went outside to the front yard. He could get around on his own, which he often did when there was no one around to fuss over him, or when Tessie forgot. He lowered himself carefully into one of the faded redwood-stained chairs on the little square of lawn. Plastic deer grazed around him and ceramic squirrels posed in mid-scamper. Orange monkey flower, red geraniums, and something yellow and bitter-smelling struggled from bulky planters that tilted on a jagged quilt of rocks – white, gray, and baby-girl pink. A hibiscus next to the driveway twisted on itself with unpruned growth. Down near the sidewalk, a small tree dangled its thin limbs that shed sticky red filaments on passersby. He and this anemic garden were enclosed by a chain-link fence, flimsy protection in a neighborhood that had grown vulnerable over the years.

When they had chosen this home, the tract was new and each single-story three-bedroom with patio and two-car garage sat orderly and unassuming on its small unlandscaped parcel. The houses were white or tan or gray. Theirs was white with beige trim. On one side, only a few feet separated it from the neighboring house, but on the other was a lot, wide and dusty and empty where the city would plant a park with playfields and picnic tables. He had quit the Navy then, because this was where he wanted to stay, to buy a house for Tessie to decorate, to raise his family, to sit in the front yard on summer evenings.

But with the park had come litter and graffiti, and, soon enough, teen beer parties, blaring boom boxes, drug deals inside the slow prowl of cars with tinted windows, the occasional fistfight. Once, bullets flew, one straight into their kitchen where it ricocheted in a cupboard, exploding coffee cups in its zigzag path.

Johnny still liked to sit outside in the evenings, though. He had watched the changes over the years from this chair with its dusty plastic cushion, replaced each spring, a hopeful ritual on a street that had tried its best to dress itself up. Except for Hector Cabrera, who only painted his door, people had covered the colorless exteriors of their houses in fancy crayon shades – turquoise, sunflower yellow, ripe peach. Johnny had painted his home pistachio green, trimmed in white.

But the colors clung to the stucco like mud, and the jumble

of hues did not lend a picturesque effect. The houses were made heavy and morose, their torpor further weighted by the iron bars that had been erected over windows and across screen doors to ward off intruders. The colors of the neighbors themselves had gradually homogenized with the influx of immigrants from the Philippines, mostly Navy families, active or retired, all eager to embrace life in America here in Kimball Park, this diffident collection of neighborhoods, fast food restaurants, and car dealerships that went unnoticed from the freeway in the ceaseless back-and-forth traffic between San Diego and Tijuana.

It surprised him even now, the flood of Filipinos. He lived in America surrounded by Filipinos, and yet he lived apart from them. He had practically rid himself of his accent. His children spoke like Americans, their vowels flat and wide, their consonants hard, and their grammar correct. They did not confuse *learn* and *teach*. He had heard one of Hector Cabrera's children say to eight-year-old Laura, "My father learned me to play checkers." "You mean *taught*," Laura had responded. Johnny had been smug that Laura knew the difference. Ashamed, too. Not that Laura would correct their neighbor's child, but that the need existed for her to.

One thing that hadn't changed in the neighborhood was the saunter of Little Leaguers in front of his house on the way to the ball field. He liked watching them go by in their uniforms, glove tucked under an elbow, their baseball caps at an earnest tilt. They never looked over at him. If they had, he would've smiled or waved, maybe shouted a bit of encouragement: *Go get 'em, hit it out of the park.*

He had played baseball as a boy with a bamboo stick for a bat. His mitt was a rubber sandal folded in half that he clamped shut to trap the small rubber ball, its skin flaked away from overuse.

Now he felt less generous toward the Little Leaguers, and if one of them were to look in his direction now, he might show indifference, might even turn away. No one looked, so he just sat, and as dusk began to fall he remembered how he had once tossed a baseball in the air, his nonchalance forced as he walked the path that led to the rice fields, his saunter studied but brisk enough to carry him to his destination before curfew. He had found the ball among some weeds, its canvas cover loose, flapping now as he tossed it. He would take it home and fix it somehow. A real baseball.

He caught the ball with quick swipes, the dull slaps against his palm loud enough to warn of his approach. To be sure, he began to count out loud the number of times he caught the ball. He counted in Japanese as far as ten before needing to start again. He hadn't learned the numbers higher than that, having dropped out of school to protest the use of the language that supplanted his own. With each toss and each catch, he shifted the weight of what he carried hidden in his shirt. He tried to slow the beat of his heart to make it steady, like the up-and-down motion of the ball.

At the end of the path he saw no one. He began to think that the sentry was not there tonight, but then saw him emerge from the rice field where he had undoubtedly gone to pee. The soldier, his cap askew, his rifle hanging at his side, seemed uninterested at his approach, and Juan knew this could be either a very good sign or a very dangerous one. He continued to toss the ball, but only a few inches into the air, so that now the up-down of his arm was jerky and strained.

Suddenly, the soldier shouted something, and Juan stopped in his tracks, the ball dropping at his feet. He looked at the soldier, his outstretched hand, his fingers shaped to catch the ball. Juan leaned down to pick it up, and the objects in his shirt squeezed against his chest. He tossed the ball to the soldier, who pitched it back to him. The soldier motioned to Juan to throw the ball again. They went back and forth this way several times, maybe a dozen. The soldier threw hard, firing at Juan's knees, or skimming a grounder at his feet. Juan scurried each time to capture the ball and return it to the soldier with a wary deference.

Finally, the game was over. The soldier kept the ball, tossing it in his own hand while he looked Juan up and down, assessing him with eyes narrowed to suspicious slits. He shouted something in Japanese, his voice harsh and his hand open and demanding.

Caught off-guard, Juan was ready to surrender what was hidden in his shirt when he remembered his pant leg. He pointed there, and the soldier used the tip of his rifle to probe the rolled-up cuff and expose some cigarettes, a handful, bent but mostly intact. The soldier motioned to Juan to hand them over. He pocketed the cigarettes, then held the ball out to Juan. As Juan stepped forward to accept the trade, the soldier turned, tossed the ball in the air and whacked it with the butt of his rifle, sending it in a high arc over the rice field. The soldier laughed and taunted him to go after it. Juan did, running hard, an arm protectively across his ribs. He ran without stopping, running right past the ball that lay in his path, its canvas cover completely torn off, the core small and skeletal. When he got to the other side of the rice field, he paused just long enough to give the two grenades he had been carrying to the waiting guerrilla, and then he continued to run all the way home.

The next night, he hid on the beach as Japanese soldiers rounded up the young boys in the village in retaliation for a grenade attack. He lay among the driftwood, one cheek pressed against the sand. He listened to the sounds of the night, the rustle of palm leaves, the slap of the surf, the breeze that came from across the sea.

All these years later, it wasn't the threat to his life that he saw and felt most vividly now. It was the baseball.

That night, another Sunday dinner behind them, Johnny lay in bed next to Tessie, her face cold-creamed, her hair in spongy rollers, her feet in tube socks borrowed from his lifetime stash. It was never dark in their bedroom, just spookily gloomy from the tall candle on the shelf. Tessie had taken to keeping it lit, and it always grew so large in the night. In the quiet half-dark, when his breath sounded the loudest and he could almost feel the crawl of the disease in his bones, he felt the aloneness he had always felt. But now he found it was not altogether unwanted. He remembered then that Josie was coming back to live with them. He turned to Tessie, whose oiled face shone in the candlelight.

"Is something wrong between Josie and David?"

Tessie sighed heavily. "She feels like something is missing in their lives."

She turned on her side, away from him, so all he saw were her sponge curlers. Her sigh lingered between them, so he turned on his side too. Over the years – and more recently, since he'd been sick – they had talked of the things they lacked: a vacation home, dinners out at fancy restaurants, hired help. They said these things jokingly, because they couldn't bring themselves to say what had really been missing: a son.

2

PACKING BUNNY'S THINGS

After Winston Piña's mother died, his Aunt Odette came twice a week to tidy the house, water the fuchsias, and discreetly pack away some of his mother's things. After each of Odette's visits, Winston would go into his mother's room to see what remained of her belongings, which seemed to suffer in her absence. Who would wear Bunny Piña's well-maintained shoes, her tailored pantsuits, and the occasional hat – now idle and abandoned? Of course, Odette was right that the clothes should be packed off to charity. Winston had already picked out the few things he would keep – her house slippers, a silk flowered scarf, and the wedding ring she ceased wearing the day they left Manila for America, two years after Carlitos had left *them*.

It was after Odette's last visit that Winston found the letter. He had shoved aside a stack of shoeboxes in the closet and there on the floor lay the envelope. It was addressed in Bunny's small script, her name Benicia Piña in the corner, the name and address of a Johnny de la Cruz in the center – with what Winston considered more than her usual brandishing of curves and curlicues. There was no postage. Beneath its mustiness, the envelope was faint with lavender, a scent Winston had almost forgotten to associate with his mother, because she had smelled chemical and malignant those final months.

Two weeks before Bunny died, as she lay swaddled on the sofa and banked by stiff pillows, she had a sudden false burst of energy. She lifted herself from her reclining position and stretched her fingers the way Winston did when he warmed up to play the piano. Winston had recognized the sign, but hesitated, given his mother's debilitated state.

"Scissors," she commanded. Winston scurried off as urgently as if she had said *morphine*, but by the time he had retrieved them from her dresser, she was slumped back into the womb of blankets, hard asleep, her face tight with suffering.

His mother had always cut his hair, even before she trained at the Anaheim City College School of Beauty, even after she had risen from associate cutter to manager and eventual owner of Bella, attracting clients from L.A. to San Diego, minor celebrities with capped teeth and tanned society wives with calves honed from tennis and power yoga.

For the funeral, Angelo, his mother's top stylist, had tactfully offered Winston his services. Winston had just as tactfully declined, and as he stood at the pulpit in church reading the words he'd written about the inimitable Benicia Piña, his hair hung like the black mantillas he recalled the women wearing on Sundays in Manila when he was a boy.

Now, six weeks after delivering the eulogy at Bunny's funeral, nineteen-year-old Winston held the fragile envelope, seal side up, in his palm. He curled his hand so that the envelope buckled, but the seal did not break. As he stared at the unopened letter that his mother had written to a man he had never heard of, he ran his other hand through his uncut hair, droopy in the early summer heat.

◈ ◈ ◈

"How would you like it?" asked Stormie, the stylist who stood behind his chair at Kwik Kuts. Winston watched her in the mirror as she tufted strands of his chin-length hair, her lanky fingers light against his scalp. Her own hair was short and hard from dyes. Her chin bounced to a tune on the pop radio station that played over the speakers. Mariah Carey *ooh-oohed.* Winston shifted under the blue plastic cape.

He wasn't sure how he had ended up here in the cheap seats, so different from his mother's salon whose windows opened to a balcony garden of potted azaleas and birds of paradise. If Winston had paid attention only to the spiky blonde and black twisps that sprang from Stormie's head, he might have abandoned his Kwik Kuts chair and cape without pause.

Winston looked away from Stormie's barbed hair and her bored blue eyes, and saw her hairstylist license – her picture underexposed and unsmiling – taped to the corner of the mirror. Below it was a picture of a squinty-faced little girl with a defiant slouch that matched her mother's current posture.

"Well?"

Stormie had her hands on her hips, her thumbs digging inside the waist of her jeans and exposing a belly that was not firm but not unattractive. She must have been about thirty-five, a mother making her living cutting hair. The way Bunny had.

"Whatever you think looks best," he said out of habit.

She shrugged, and he regretted his lack of decisiveness.

She squirted him down with a spray bottle and then began to comb and snip. The sound of the scissors working reminded him of Bella, whose reputation for flair and style was Bunny's as well.

Winston had been awed by his mother. He had told this to the mourners from his place at the pulpit where he could see that their heads, lowered in grief, also showed to great advantage the newest hair fashions, elegantly combed and coiffed as if to honor Bunny.

Sometimes Winston had been afraid of his mother. This he

didn't say to the mourners, though he wondered if any had also at times taken cover from her indomitable presence.

Winston bowed his head as Stormie placed her hand at his nape.

"So your name's Winston."

He nodded, causing Stormie to snip air.

"Yeah?" She gathered up the escaped strand. "Like the cigarette?"

"Yes," he had to admit. It had been his father's favorite. And a lifesaver during the war, coming in handy for bribes and barter. Winston had been lately missing his father, a man who had been an idea, an abstraction, ever since as a boy of seven, Winston waved goodbye to him as he boarded a jet to Europe, to train for and eventually be placed as a manservant somewhere in the British Isles – a temporary situation, of course, until his economic circumstances stabilized. But Carlitos Piña had never returned to his wife and son in Manila, vanishing – as much as a brown man could – into the Anglo-Irish landscape.

"Where're you from?"

Winston knew Stormie didn't mean his neighborhood two miles from Disneyland, but his country of origin. Still he answered, "Here. Anaheim."

She looked at him with narrowed eyes. "Me, too," she said. "The place sucks."

"Yeah," he agreed, though really he had no complaints. Neither had Bunny.

Bunny had been a woman determined to make the most of opportunities, wasting little time on regrets, and always looking ahead while never failing to stop and smell the *sampaguita*. When it was clear that her husband did not intend to return to the Philippines, she had set her sights on America. Visas were secured and arrangements made for them to join Bunny's sister and brother-in-law, who had arrived years earlier in the

Golden State. Bunny showed Winston travel brochures of orange groves and beaches, immaculate shopping malls and cheerful neighborhoods, and, of course, Disneyland. And unlike the calendar pictures of castles and countryside that had so enamored Carlitos, these pictures showed people in them – which proved that the places were real and accessible. From the moment they landed at John Wayne International, their lives were ordered by Bunny's plans and her timetable for seeing them through.

They stayed with Odette and Felix no more than six months before moving into their own cramped apartment within sight of the Matterhorn. Eventually, they moved to the split-level that Bunny was soon able to decorate with smartness and elegance, the same traits she used to grow her reputation over the years as one of the best salon owners south of Los Angeles.

Winston tried to imagine Stormie among the stylists at Bella. She stood in front of him now, bent at the waist, her elbows jutting out as she angled her scissors above his face. Her breath was on his forehead, her breasts directly in his line of sight. A bead of sweat rested in the hollow of her collarbone.

"Hot," she said huskily into his eyebrows.

"Yes," Winston agreed. He swallowed. It sounded loud.

Stormie stepped back and eyed him. "AC's on the fritz," she said. "This place is a dump."

"It's not so bad." Though it was pathetic, really, in contrast to Bella with its plush chairs, gilded mirrors, and cotton caftans for the clients instead of plastic capes. Winston looked around for something redeeming. His eyes found the picture of the little girl.

"Cute kid," he said.

"My daughter. She's in Hawaii on vacation with my ex." Stormie tugged on a hank of hair and worked her scissors across it near his scalp. "And his girlfriend," she added.

Winston looked again at the saucy girl in the photograph. "She misses you, though," he assured her.

Stormie snorted, "Bet you're in college, Mr. Know-It-All." But she smiled as she massaged gel somewhat roughly into his now much-shortened hair. Winston closed his eyes.

He was to start his second year in the fall, though for the first time he realized that this wasn't necessarily guaranteed. People died; they abandoned one another; nothing was certain.

Bunny had begun arranging her funeral service and wake as soon as she felt the lump in her armpit. It was left to Winston to carry out her plans, which is how he had found himself at the piano, singing "What a Wonderful World," while guests held plates of cold cuts, deviled eggs, and fried *lumpia* on their laps in the living room of Odette and Felix Ocampo rather than her own, since she would not be there to supervise the cleanup later.

"She loved that song," someone whispered.

And when Winston's voice cracked with the last note, sniffles and sobs filled the air, noses were blown, handkerchiefs wrung, and he knew that she loved that too. Being missed, being loved. Because she could not get enough of it to make up for her husband having left. Never mind that she had not truly loved him, as she had once let slip to Winston.

"Okay, college boy." Stormie handed him a mirror and swiveled his chair in a slow circle.

Winston looked at himself, at the graceful shape of his head revealed with his hair shorn on the sides, a small bed of spikes at the top, his face startlingly visible and bereft. When Stormie released the cape fastened at his neck, and her fingers lingered there on his skin, he turned his head slightly so that his earlobe touched her pinky.

◈ ◈ ◈

At home, he checked the phone messages. There was one from his aunt telling him to come for dinner that evening. There was one from Junior Tamayo, who had moved their belongings out of a dorm room at UCLA and into a nearby apartment complex with a game room, pool, and sauna, telling him to get his Filipino ass up there. The last message was for his mother, someone wanting to "pressure wash her driveway, patio, walkways, and more."

Yesterday when a vacuum salesman called, asking if he could please speak with Benicia Piña, Winston had answered no. "And why is that?" asked the salesman in his pushy friendly salesman's voice. "Because she's dead," Winston said. He had wanted to shock the salesman. He wanted to shock himself, because in the days after Bunny's dramatic exit (she had emitted a long note of pain before a last whooshing breath), it seemed he had been abandoned by his grief, and he was as lonely for that as he was for Bunny. Maybe more so.

He took the envelope from his pocket and smoothed its creases between his hands. He ran his thumb across the back, found a gap in the seal, and lifted the flap open. He slid the letter out, and as he unfolded its onion skin, he steadied himself to read it quickly, to feel the sting all at once and be done with it. But that proved to be impossible. The letter was in Tagalog. It had been years since he had read anything but English.

He took the letter to Bunny's desk, took a fresh sheet of paper from her stationery, and scratched his head with his pen as he reckoned with idioms and long-neglected conjugations until finally he had translated Bunny's words. Even in his upright, unadorned handwriting, the words and their tone were unmistakably Bunny.

Dear Juanito,

I'm sure you thought you would never hear from me again. At least, I'm sure that was your hope, since you so gallantly made your escape from my couch that afternoon. We each had our reasons for what happened – reasons that were self-serving and callous, though, of course, we were not aware of them then.

You should know that I'm living in the States now, not 100 miles from you and your family. Your sister gave me your address. What will your mestiza wife who speaks only English think of this letter written in Tagalog on perfumed paper?

You should also know this: I have a son. His father abandoned us for his own life. He's a beauty. The son, not the father. A smart boy with only a little of his father's dreaminess. You remember Carlitos. Too much a dreamer, that man. And you, not enough of one.

Be a good husband, Juanito.

Always,
Miss Sampaguita
Bunny Piña (née Bulong)

After Carlitos left them, Bunny never remarried and had only a few harmless romances. Winston had not been naïve enough to believe it was out of loyalty to Carlitos. Still, it stunned him to know his mother had cheated on his father, and he wondered if this was what had driven him away.

He wondered, too, why the letter was still here rather than in the hands of Johnny de la Cruz. Had she forgotten to send it, or changed her mind? Had she run out of time? The letter wasn't dated and there was no clue in the message as to when she might have written it.

He took the letter back to the living room and sat on the couch to ponder his next move. He was about to put his feet up on the glass-top coffee table, but thought better of it. Still, this was his house now. He had looked forward to leaving it, if only as far as up the freeway. He had chosen UCLA for his mother's sake, to be near her. Now the obligation no longer existed. He could apply to Notre Dame like the nuns had encouraged him to do in the first place. He could quit school. He could travel.

One thing he could not do though was cook. He pocketed the letter again and headed out the door to his aunt's house.

◈ ◈ ◈

He parked his motorcycle on the far side of the driveway since Odette disliked seeing it, having criticized Bunny for giving it to Winston. She was plucking dead leaves from the geranium box on the porch. She looked at Winston's head, but didn't mention his haircut. He knew it would come later. Odette always saved her opinions until after dinner. It was important to her that everyone eat. It was less important that they digest.

Winston bent down to hug his aunt, he being taller than the average Filipino and she shorter than average, especially since she had never shared Bunny's love for high heels. Her scalp showed through her thinning hair. Bunny had been the glamorous sister, the tough competitor, the shrewd businesswoman. But Odette, in her sweat socks and tennis shoes and K-Mart outfits, was the steady one, and bossy in a different way than Bunny. She nudged Winston towards the house.

"Go see if Felix needs help."

Inside, Felix, still in his car-salesman clothes, was setting the table. He wore a yellow tie on a green shirt above rust-colored pants. He looked like some woodland creature that belonged among the plastic flamingos and deer that adorned many of the yards in the neighborhood. He grinned gently at Winston.

According to Bunny, Felix and Odette had always wanted children. "They'll want to spoil you," she told Winston on their arrival from the Philippines when they took up temporary residence with his aunt and uncle. Felix and Odette never did spoil him, though; in fact, they never came close. It was as if they believed their inability to have a child of their own entitled them neither to indulge nor discipline another's child. So they offered their love and concern as if across some invisible fence. This situation had been complicated of late by Bunny's death, and Odette in particular had ventured more than once into a parental role. Inevitably, though, she drew back.

Felix liked to greet Winston with a high five, but when Winston went to slap him heartily, Felix's hand went limp, and the touch of their palms made a thin sound.

When Winston was thirteen, he had a rare moment of rebellion against his mother's benevolent dictatorship and stuffed a backpack with his belongings. It was Felix who had tracked him down at the airport, sitting across from the British Airways counter, frustrated at his inability to purchase a ticket. Before Felix drove him home to Bunny, they stopped at a Denny's, where they ate BLTs and milkshakes, and at one point Felix laid his skittish hand upon Winston's, resting it there until Winston relieved them both by knocking over his shake.

Winston helped Felix put the food on the table. Then Odette came in and served, heaping the largest portions on Winston's plate. "Eat," she commanded.

Bunny's rule at dinnertime had been that they have conversation. Mandatory items of discussion included a positive anecdote, something new that had been learned, and a compliment to the other person, as well as some constructive criticism. There were, of course, many nights when they did not observe the rule, when they didn't have dinner together because Winston was at one of his high school activities, or when Bunny had tickets to a play or the symphony, courtesy of one of her clients, or when neither could pay the other a compliment and had only criticism to construct.

There were no rules of conversation at Odette's table; in fact, there seemed to be no expectation of it. Eating was the only purpose for sitting at the dinner table. Winston ate his fish and rice and vegetables, taking the seconds that Odette layered on his plate. When he had finished and Felix had untucked the napkin from his chin, revealing once again his awful tie, and Odette had drained the iced tea in her glass, he finally spoke.

"Auntie, who's Johnny de la Cruz?"

Odette stared at her empty glass. "We knew a boy by that name, your mother and me. Juanito. So many girls liked him – Bunny too. But he was shy, and a bad dancer." She sighed. "No rhythm. So unlike a Filipino." Here she patted Felix, whose other talent aside from selling Cadillacs was the waltz.

"So what happened to him?"

Odette squinted her small eyes to see that far back into the past. "During the war the young men disappeared, taken by the Japanese or hiding in the hills with the rebels. Johnny was a survivor." Then she shrugged. "After the war, he did like so many others. Joined the American Navy and never came back. Married a mestiza." Odette's nose wrinkled with her last comment, but her flat nose could not carry off the look of disdain. She merely looked on the verge of a sneeze.

"Why do you ask about Johnny de la Cruz?" Odette looked at him sternly.

"I found a letter." Winston's hand went to his pocket. He had no intention of withdrawing the letter, but when Odette held out her hand, he complied, just as he would have with Bunny.

She frowned at the name, turned the envelope over, and saw the broken seal. "Do you think your mother meant for you to have this?"

Winston wondered if Odette guessed at the contents of the letter. The possibility made him go silent with unease.

Felix came to the rescue. "What was his mother's is his now."

It was rare that Felix asserted an opinion that did not coincide with Odette's, and on such occasions, Winston saw his aunt pleasingly startled at the opposition. This, of course, did not guarantee that Odette would yield any ground. For now, she merely got up and went to the kitchen to fetch dessert, leaving Felix and Winston together to wait. The letter lay on Odette's woven bamboo placemat.

"What will you do next?" Felix asked.

"Go see him. Johnny de la Cruz." Until that moment Winston hadn't known.

He was unencumbered by responsibility (he had no job), by his studies (school was out for the summer), by parents (since now he had none). Bunny's lawyer had settled her estate, and Winston had been granted a more than modest allowance. He would go see Johnny de la Cruz, this man his mother called not enough of a dreamer. Which had she disdained more? The man who did not dream enough or Carlitos who dreamed too much? Winston recalled the tone of Bunny's letter – seemingly forgiving, but really not.

Odette came in with bowls of Neapolitan ice cream, a cookie garnishing the side. She handed round the bowls and set her own on top of the envelope. Both Winston and Felix avoided looking at it and at the brooding expression she wore. Again, they ate in silence. Odette was the last to put down her spoon.

"Winston, your mother, would she have approved of that haircut?"

Winston knew he was not expected to give an answer, only to recognize the correct one. He tried not to think of Stormie's fingers at his neck.

"Your mother may be gone, but she still lives here." Odette

reached across the table and tapped Winston's chest, and he flinched a little at her sharp finger.

When she thought she had made her point, Odette said, "Winston, you may clear the table."

As Odette and Felix watched TV in the living room, Winston cleared the ice cream bowls from the table, wiped the placemats, and put them away. The only thing left on the table was Bunny's letter, which he slipped back into his pocket.

When Winston left Odette and Felix to their evening game shows, he pointed his motorcycle in the direction of Kwik Kuts, arriving just as Stormie was coming out the door. The sequins on her denim jacket and the earrings that swung against her slim neck flashed in the white light of his headlamp. She posed in the spotlight, one hand on a jutting hip, the other shielding her eyes from the glare.

Winston removed his helmet and clenched the handlebars as Stormie sauntered toward him, thumbs inside the waistband of her low-slung jeans.

◈ ◈ ◈

One of Stormie's Doc Martens rested on the coffee table, her pale leg jutting from its loosely laced high-top. She lit a cigarette in a room where none had ever been allowed.

"It's okay, isn't it?"

Winston handed her a coaster to catch the ashes as he imagined Bunny on the sofa next to Stormie, a pained look on her face.

"Nice place." Stormie sent smoke in a circle around her head as she twisted in her seat to survey the living room. Bunny's house, unlike Odette's, had nothing that was cane or bamboo; nothing embroidered, woven, or beaded; no caribou carved of wood; no rice paper lamps. Bunny's furnishings were modern and spare, with sleek, simple lines, from the long-necked floor lamp to the mosaic tile coaster on which Stormie was drizzling cigarette ashes.

"So, do you live here alone?"

"Yep," Winston said, and he put a leg up on the table next to hers.

"Really? Why don't you show me around."

On their way to his bedroom, Winston pointed out the dining room, the den, the patio, the bathroom, walking past the closed door to Bunny's room where inside her belongings were sorted and boxed.

There was no preamble to their lovemaking, apart from the haircut in the afternoon. Stormie removed her tank top with one hand, ruffling the rough ends of her hair as she pulled the remarkably small garment over her head. Winston stuck his thumbs inside the waistband of her jeans, skimmed his thumbnails across her hip bones and in the soft hollows. As they moved easily to the bed, Winston marveled at himself, at the indifference he felt as he imagined Bunny's horrified reaction to someone like Stormie here between the sheets Bunny herself used to change each Wednesday.

Winston's sexual experience, though not vast, was superior to most sheltered Filipino boys who had attended all-male Catholic high schools. It was the generous instruction of Eva Velasco that rescued Winston from the beat-off parties and porn videos so many of his classmates relied on. Eva was cousin to Bunny's master stylist Angelo and a pet among the salon's clientele. When Eva dropped in to hang out at Angelo's station, no one complained. Eva was a senior in high school, a year older than Winston when they met. She had sized him up with a long sweep of her false eyelashes; she had made a project of him. They used Angelo's apartment for Eva's Lessons for a Catholic Schoolboy – pithy advice like "Don't maul" or metaphoric admonitions like "Remember, there are two people doing the tango here." These were things Winston knew instinctively, though he didn't mind being told.

Winston and Stormie lay side by side, the bedside lamp further tinting Stormie's dyed blonde head. He stroked the coarse bristles, a disagreeable sensation that was addictive. She smoked a cigarette, tapping ashes onto the back of a small picture frame that rested on Winston's stomach. He had grabbed the nearest object to serve as an ashtray. Now Stormie overturned the photo onto his chest, spilling the ashes and streaking them across his ribs. He pounded his chest like Tarzan, and Stormie whooped. The silence that followed seemed louder than their voices had been.

"Wow," Stormie whispered. "It can get real quiet in here."

He'd noticed it more and more as Odette had gradually packed away Bunny's things. Bunny's clothes and cosmetics and small decorative cases that housed jewelry, hairpins, aspirin, small change, and her favorite rosary were as colorful and bold as she was. Now that they were tucked out of sight, the house was subdued.

"Wow," Stormie said again, her mouth at his ear, and Winston was suddenly aware of a sourness that came from her breath, or maybe her skin, which looked sallow against the sheets. "Sweet," she cooed.

Winston turned his head sharply toward her to discourage this endearment. But she was looking at the photo in her hand – a picture of Winston, age seven, with his parents, all dressed in Sunday clothes. It was a studio portrait and had been airbrushed so that no lines or blemishes showed on his parents' faces, and his own face was velvety and artificially rosy.

The glass was smudged a bit from the ashy residue on Stormie's thumb. She took the end of the sheet to wipe it clean, but Winston stopped her, pulled her long knobby fingers away. He set the photo back on the nightstand. The lamp gave the smear on the glass a sheen that blurred the faces in the picture.

"It's fine," he said.

Stormie tapped the side of Winston's head with her open palm, playfully, he thought. Later he conceded it might have been a slap.

3

PICTURE IMPERFECT

In the quiet de la Cruz kitchen, the walls seethed with yellow paint, but the surfaces – the bronze-colored appliances, the rust-colored floor tiles, the cupboards and counter in oak veneer – gave a muddy cast to the room. There was no breakfast conversation, just the sounds of chewing and swallowing.

It was early, only five-thirty, but Josie had to leave for work at six. Johnny was usually up at this time after a restless night, and Tessie would come to the table to sip a cup of weak coffee with him. Sometimes she woke when he tossed and turned in the night, but sometimes she herself was unsettled and talked in her sleep. He listened there in their darkened bedroom to the words, fragments with no apparent context. Once, in the throes of a dream, she had flung an open hand from the sheets, catching him on the cheek; he lay silent on his side of the bed, stunned by her harshness.

Josie finished her cereal and toast, and Johnny listened to her drain her orange juice. She seldom drank coffee, a non-habit that he found vaguely irritating. Josie carried her dishes to the sink, tossed a banana and some cookies into a sack, and headed out the door, off to her job of caring for dogs – abused, unwanted, or just plain old, feeding and watering them until it was time to either process adoption papers or stroke their heads while the vet slid a needle into a tense and knowing muscle.

"Be careful," Tessie called out, because she harbored fears that Josie would be bitten and contract rabies, or she would have the flesh torn from an arm or leg, maybe an ear ripped away. Tessie had read of such things, seen them reported on TV, true-life horror. Such silly fears she had.

Johnny's concerns about Josie's vocation were common sense. He had never liked pets, didn't believe in them, and couldn't understand caring for discarded ones. He thought Josie should be doing something better – an office job, maybe, with her own cubicle. She should have learned to type.

"More coffee, dear?"

Johnny let Tessie fill his cup. He watched her hesitate before she poured herself a second cup, barely half full. They sipped in silence until they heard the thud of the newspaper on the porch.

"I'll get it," Tessie said, unnecessarily.

This morning he went straight to the crossword puzzle. As soon as he inked in the first answer, Tessie said. "Well, dear, I think I'll go back to bed for a little while."

He should've assured her that it was okay, told her to get some rest, but he kept his eyes on 13 Across, looking up just in time to watch the back of her faded blue robe disappear down the hall.

It was on board ship that he had begun the crossword puzzles. He found a book of them while wiping down tables in the mess hall. Someone had left it on a chair. He brushed the crumbs from it and tucked it in his apron; later, in his bunk, when he opened it and looked at the list of words, he wondered how he would ever fill in the blank squares. Eventually, though, he did. And with the new (if sometimes useless) words and phrases came the opportunity to try out the sound of them. Each new word he learned in those early days, he said to himself repeatedly to achieve the correct pronunciation. He was determined to train his jaw to encompass the short and long sounds of English. He practiced saying *big*, not *beeg*, *ham* and not *hum*, *invisible* instead of *inbisible*. He adopted sounds nonexistent in his own language. By the time he met Tessie, the sound of Tagalog in his speech was practically extinguished. He could say *I love you* with perfect inflection.

◈ ◈ ◈

Johnny awoke to Tessie's humming. He had fallen asleep on the couch, his knees pulled up so his feet would not dangle over the edge. Wincing at the ache in his legs, he unfolded himself slowly, flexed his feet as he lowered them to the floor, and then marched them in place while he sat, his fists digging into the cushion for balance.

"Cramps again?" asked Tessie, shaking her head as if in reprimand, perhaps at the offending cramps, perhaps at Johnny. She wore mint green sweatpants, a sleeveless top that showed the loose skin on her upper arms, and her all-purpose sneakers. She knelt down in front of him and massaged his calves. Tessie's hands were ugly and strong. Although her grip brought relief, he was glad when she released his thin legs.

"I need to get some vegetables for dinner. Want to come along for the ride?" Tessie stood up and looked down on him. "C'mon," she wheedled, as if he were a child.

He followed her to the door. He was supposed to get out of the house for brief amounts of time. It was good for him, he was told, and he tried not to sulk.

Before he got sick, Johnny had never occupied the passenger seat, except when he was teaching his daughters to drive. Now Tessie drove him everywhere. He watched her foot, her leg tensed, ready to move to the brake. Tessie drove as if she expected something to go wrong – a blown tire, an oncoming car crossing the center line, a sudden pothole. Johnny jiggled his leg, bumping his knee against the glove compartment. He wished he could smoke a cigarette.

Life looked different from the passenger seat. There was more opportunity to feel the bumps in the road, notice the weeds in the cracks in the sidewalks, read the graffiti on storefronts and tree trunks, realize that as he had become older and frayed at the edges so had Kimball Park, this inconspicuous little city that, though he did not love it, suited him just fine.

Tessie pulled the station wagon into the parking lot of a corner produce stand, where a dusty canopy protected the rows of fruits and vegetables from the midday sun. "I'll just be a minute," she said, taking the keys from the ignition and dropping them in her purse.

Johnny nearly followed Tessie out of the car, but she was already too far ahead. He sat and watched her long loping strides, the forward lean of her torso as she headed for the business of picking out onions. Johnny watched her chat with the cashier, a Mexican man in his fifties who seemed to know her. Tessie laughed her loud, pleasant laugh that was too large for such a small transaction as vegetables, no matter how fresh, Johnny thought.

Was this where she came when she went on errands alone?

He wondered what small talk passed between them, if their comments on the weather were in English or Spanish. Tessie's Spanish was bad, malformed in grammar, deficient in vocabulary. Even Johnny, who knew no Spanish, could hear the hesitations, the stumblings, the endings swallowed to disguise mistakes. When he met her, it was one of the things he understood about her – the ambiguity of who she was and who she did not want to be. She was Filipina *and* Mexican, both and neither.

When Tessie got back in the car she handed Johnny the bag,

as if that's what he was there for – to hold the vegetables. He looked inside.

"I thought you might have bought green beans," he said.

Tessie was silent a moment. "Well, dear," she said finally, "I'm not a mind reader."

Johnny acknowledged this with a disappointed nod. "It doesn't matter," he said. But it did matter, because some couples knew such things about each other. He knew it was his fault that he and Tessie did not.

"My fault," he admitted, too late. Tessie was already getting out of the car. When she came back and handed him the beans, he could not bring himself to say it again. He looked out his window as Tessie nosed the big car onto the street.

After a lunch of soup and crackers, Johnny sat ensconced in the padding of his living room chair, and Tessie was clattering away in the kitchen when the telephone rang. The phone never rang for him, unless it was a salesperson who was always told, no, there was no Johnny de la Cruz at this number. He listened as Tessie ceased her kitchen noises and picked up the phone, and he braced himself for one of her long gossipy ramblings with her sister or one of the women she used to work with at the Shop Smart before she had retired to take care of him.

Tessie had a nice phone voice. If her grammar had been better, she could have passed as one of those professional recordings. In person, her voice tended toward a trill, but the physics of the telephone wire moderated it. Johnny knew she was coming across to the caller as someone polite and in charge.

"Yes," she said several times. "No, he's not available. Yes. I'll tell him you called."

Before Tessie could resume her clang of dishes and utensils, Johnny asked, "Who was that?"

Tessie poked her head around the doorway from the kitchen. "Do you know anyone named Winston?"

"Winston?" Johnny repeated, doubtful.

As he shook his head to say no, he didn't know any Winston, he tried to think whether he knew a Wilson or a Whitsett or a Plimpton because Tessie usually got names wrong. "No," he confirmed.

"Okay, didn't think so." Tessie went back to the kitchen and set the dishwasher to rumble, and Johnny, alone in the living room, wished he did know a Winston.

◆ ◆ ◆

When Josie came home from work, Tessie gathered up her keys and purse. "Going out for a while," she called from the front porch, where flies tended to buzz at the cat food Josie had begun leaving for strays.

"Where?" he asked, casually, determined not to whine.

"It's my support group."

"But that's on Tuesdays."

Tessie appeared in front of him. "And Thursdays."

She had changed from her sweatpants into a skirt. The muscles in her calves flexed slightly from the lift of her narrow-heeled sandals, which had become her costume for her group meetings. He wondered what compelled women to dress up to talk about their troubles.

"It's all right, isn't it? Josie's here if you need anything."

Johnny waved his hand in front of him to chase a fly, and then Tessie was gone.

"How much support do you need?" he grumbled as he thought of Tessie sitting in a circle of strangers, listening to their stories, waiting for her turn.

Johnny himself had been encouraged to join a group. People feel less alone, the doctor said. But Johnny had never been a joiner. He had always declined the invitations by his neighbors to join their Filipino social clubs, their bowling leagues, their *mah jongg* foursomes. No, he had never joined anything. Except the Navy.

◈ ◈ ◈

Go *to school or else,* his father had said to him. He had dropped out of school during the war and had learned other lessons – how to sharpen bamboo to points, pulverize chili peppers to mix with sand for makeshift spray guns, thread ropes through vegetation to trap an ankle. But the war was over and he was back in the same old classroom. That is, when he wasn't on the beach.

It was midday, the sun high and hot. He stood near the water's edge where the sand wouldn't burn through the rubber thongs on his feet. The blue bay churned with the purposeful engines of bancas and ferries. He dropped the book he was holding onto the wet sand and then flopped himself down beside it. From the cuff of his pant leg, he pulled out a cigarette and lit it with the silver lighter he'd stolen from Mr. Balagot's store. He leaned back onto his elbows, his right hand holding the cigarette, his left thumbing the pages of his history book as he stared out at the bay and beyond to the horizon.

It was humiliating to be in the same grade as his younger sister. And Bunny Bulong. Flirtatious Bunny who hinted that she would go out with him when she turned sixteen: "I like older boys." How many times had she said it as he slumped in his desk trying to make himself inconspicuous among the younger students? But it was his father's voice that he heard now. *Go to school or else.*

Juan stood up and flung the book into the air, watched it fly open, its white pages fluttering before landing face down in the bay. He sat down again. His cigarette lay in the sand, slowly burning itself out. He leaned back, stretching his legs so the water just licked the bottom of his feet. He closed his eyes and felt the tug of the water around his legs, and the sand trickling away beneath him. A motor boat roared and then a wave slapped over him, filling his mouth and nose with salt.

◈ ◈ ◈

In Leoncio's pick-up, the seats were hot, and the breeze that blew through the windows barely cooled the three of them squeezed in the cab. Though slight himself, Juan was keenly aware of the advantage of height and muscle he held over his father wedged in the middle. Yet his father had this power to decide his future for him. Juan looked out the window as the truck bumped past fields of sugar cane and stands of coconut trees. He turned his head to watch a pair of gray and saggy water buffalo yoked together at the side of the road. The wind pushed their thick, sharp scent into his face.

As they approached Manila, the road became busy with cars and trucks, with donkey-drawn carts clattering along the sides. Inside the city, there was the heave and groan of packed buses, taxis, and pedicabs all jostling for space with street vendors. The air smelled of diesel and fried foods.

Juan opened the sack his mother had thrust into his hands. He found a mango and a banana, as well as a generous piece of *buko*. As he reached for the slab of coconut flesh, his fingers found something else – a photograph of him at seven on his first trip to Manila with his father. They had eaten churros and chocolate at an outdoor café, and later his father had bought him a blue-and-white spinning top at a toy store. In the photograph, two thin, stiff figures stood against a seawall; the smaller one, a physical repeat of the other, held a toy top.

"Do you remember that?" his father asked.

Juan looked up to nod, remembering how he had spun the new top too close to the edge of the seawall. Both he and his father had lunged to save it, but it whirled into the bay. Then he saw that his father was talking to Leoncio and pointing at something out the window. Juan put the photograph back inside the sack.

The truck wound its way through a one-way arterial, then spilled onto a wide boulevard. They traveled its length along the bay, where Juan saw American naval ships, massive and authoritatively gray. When they reached the dock, Leoncio stopped the truck but kept the engine running. He leaned over Juan's father and gave Juan a friendly punch to the shoulder. It was a manly farewell, with even a parting joke about blonde American women with big breasts. His father prodded him out of the truck. Together they walked to the check-in station, and when Juan had to sign his name to a roster, he handed his father the sack to hold. It was only when he passed through the gate that he realized he forgot to reclaim the sack from his father's hand.

Johnny had hated the Navy, hated the sea, the close quarters of the ship, the galleys where he was assigned to work with the cooks, waiters, pantrymen, dishwashers, custodians – all stewards, all Filipinos. He came to hate the smell of steamed vegetables, the bags of chicken parts stacked shoulder-high in the walk-in freezer, the giant cans of tomato sauce.

But he learned a lot. He learned to make biscuits and gravy, scalloped potatoes and meatloaf. He learned how to stuff a turkey, garnish canapés, and make radish flowers with deft maneuvers of a paring knife. He learned to fold a napkin to look like a rose. He learned how to live in exile by becoming an American with children who didn't know a word of Tagalog and were happy not to.

If he hadn't joined the Navy, he wouldn't be here today in this house. His house, where he sat in the living room on this hot June afternoon, his company Tessie's ceramic fairy folk and plastic bromeliads. Dying, if that in fact was what he was doing, was a tedious occupation.

Josie was all moved in, but so far had not acted on her announced intention to keep him company. What a relief, he told the elf that sat cross-legged on the end table next to a glass of soda water gone flat. When Josie came home from work in the early afternoon, she busied herself with little tasks like collecting the drinking glasses he left scattered throughout the house. She would wipe the water stains from the coffee table or the bookshelves or the top of the TV, and he would make an effort to leave new stains as quickly as she erased the old ones.

"Call me if you need anything," she would say before disappearing to another part of the house. He thought he could hear her drumming her fingernails.

He resisted an urge to snap the hat off the jaunty elf or the neck off the swan. He was really beginning to lose patience with these silent inhabitants of his house. But then he remembered his resolution to be more accessible to his family – in fact, to be the one to make overtures. He picked up the elf and repositioned it on the table, pushed himself out of his chair, and went in search of Josie.

He had barely turned the corner to the hallway when he nearly collided with her holding a camera. He recoiled, afraid she intended to point it at him. She had taken a photography class one summer and had built a portfolio of uninteresting portraits, always missing the moment, never making art.

"What are you going to do with that?" he asked.

"I thought it would be fun to take some pictures."

"Of what?" He had never liked having his picture taken. Even before he got sick, when he had been only thin and not gaunt, when his hair still covered all of his scalp, when his ears had not seemed so excessively large, he had shied from the camera.

"Of all of us. Kind of document our everyday lives. Anyway,

with David and Gabe away most of the summer, I thought I'd send pictures of what's happening here."

"What's happening here?" he asked sharply, wondering what he was missing, what was being kept from him.

Josie held the camera to her chest as if he might try to hijack it. "I mean just ordinary moments."

Johnny said nothing, thinking that she couldn't help but capture the ordinary.

As if reading his mind, she said, "There's beauty in the ordinary." It came out defensive, almost a question, as if she needed convincing.

Her voice was wobbly. He saw that he could come to the rescue, so despite his dislike of the camera, he volunteered himself for a picture, offered her an ordinary, everyday moment to capture. She squinted hard, and he felt a pinch in his throat.

"The light's bad in here," she said. "Let's go to the sun porch."

Josie waited for him to lead the way. They always did that – made him walk in front. It made him self-conscious, and he moved cautiously, as if guarding against the loss of fragments along the way, avoiding any need for them to catch the pieces.

The sun porch was a small extension he had built at the back of the house. Into it Tessie had squeezed a white wicker loveseat, a pair of matching chairs, ferns and ivy in claustrophobic profusion, and a canary. Dirt regularly blew in through the screen, leaving everything gritty. He lowered himself onto the wicker loveseat, its warped weave tilting him. Josie clicked the shutter, afraid, perhaps, that he would disappear from the viewfinder if she waited for him to get his balance. But she seemed content with the shot, and Johnny decided it was not such a hard thing to do – offer something of himself to his daughter.

"What's going on?" Tessie stood at the threshold, barefoot, carrying her shoes, their high heels swinging freely.

"Josie's documenting the ordinary moments of our lives," Johnny said, looking at Tessie. Her roughened, unpretty feet were perversely attractive. Wanting to extend this moment of giving to his daughter, he motioned for Tessie to join him on the loveseat.

Tessie sat down. She was strong and solid next to him, and she nudged his sagging posture upright. She smelled of dried sweat and her hair looked windblown. Josie, one eye closed behind the viewfinder, offered no comment on Tessie's disheveled look, so neither did Johnny. When she cued them, Tessie was already grinning, and it occurred to him then that Tessie was also one to normally dodge cameras.

"Look over here, Dad."

Johnny stared into the lens, searching.

4

CAFÉ CHA CHA

Felix had insisted on the Cadillac.

"Used," he said, "but in tip-top condition." He stroked the hood and placed the keys in Winston's hand.

So Winston found himself behind the wheel of the gleaming Seville with the gold exterior, butter-colored upholstery, and white hubcaps. He could not refuse this extravagant, unnecessary, frill-laden car because he could not disappoint Felix.

Odette had packed a cooler of sandwiches and soft drinks and installed it in the passenger seat, provisions for the journey, as if his destination required a week's rations.

"Don't chase a wild goose," she had warned earlier. But now she stood silent next to Felix on the curb. They waved as he pulled away.

Winston almost wished they had tried to stop him. It would have given him a chance to reaffirm his decision out loud, perhaps even understand it. But they only watched him drive away in the sandwich-stocked Cadillac. They didn't approve of his going in search of Johnny de la Cruz. Odette's pursed mouth and Felix's creased brow told him so. Even with Bunny's passing, although they might criticize, they would not interfere. So Winston had gone from the constant reach and sway of

Bunny's influence to being essentially on his own – a startling and bracing prospect.

He felt conspicuous in the Cadillac and wondered whether the dark glasses he wore helped or hurt the situation. He decided to leave them on, and he turned the radio loud as if to hide in the hard funk of Prince.

As the Cadillac glided beneath him, making his departure quiet and effortless, he remembered his father's leave-taking years ago, another quiet event, also effortless. He and his mother had seen his father off. They had helped him pack, though none of them was sure what a stay in Ireland required. Dress shirts, for sure, so they folded his best *barongs*. And then, along with a few pairs of trousers, they packed short-sleeved T-shirts, because that's what he owned. They hoped that was enough. When they waved goodbye to him at the airport, Winston felt his arm part waves of sticky heat. For a moment, his father shimmered there on the tarmac. Then he was gone.

Soon after he arrived on the Emerald Isle, Carlitos sent a note – not a letter, but a small scrap of paper torn from a child's tablet – that explained he was making a new life for himself. Winston took his cue from Bunny and didn't blink an eye. They seldom heard from Carlitos after that, except when once in a while out of guilt or maybe a moment of recalled affection he sent a postcard glossy with castles or sheep. Sometimes, a small package would arrive – biscuits shaken to crumbs, chocolate melted to a lump, or a wool scarf useless in the tropical heat. Winston wondered if packages still arrived from Ireland to their old house in Manila, never to be claimed.

As he sailed south down the interstate on cruise control, Winston hardly thought of his destination and Johnny de la Cruz. His mind was on his father, who seemed to have fastened himself in Winston's head since Bunny's death, and even more so since the discovery of the letter. Carlitos had always been the scenery to Bunny's show – and to Winston's, for that matter. Maybe Winston's most of all. Winston was aware of his gifts, the ease with which he won spelling bees and geography honors, the speed at which he covered a basketball court or cross-country race course, the rhythm that lived in his body and found expression in agile piano fingers, a liquid tenor, and any number of dance styles. But no matter how dexterous, quick, and accomplished Winston proved himself, Carlitos seemed only politely impressed.

Winston remembered his precocity at sports. Even in grammar school, long-limbed and sure-handed, he glided to the basket for layin after layin, sinking shots from the perimeter, swishing free throws. He remembered catching glimpses of the fist-pumping crowd, and seeing how within that ecstatic mass sat Carlitos, immobile, with a detached half-smile floating on his handsome, passive face.

Just as Carlitos's reaction to Winston's exploits was muted, Winston was only mildly hurt by his father's congenial indifference. He was mostly surprised and puzzled, like someone finding a blank strip of paper inside a fortune cookie, wondering what it meant.

Then there was Bunny, whose love and attention had been more than enough to compensate. She, too, though, had tempered her enthusiasm with regular reminders to Winston that he could only take credit for so much. "You are blessed with..."

"Luck," Carlitos always interjected.

Bunny smoothed the silky knot of black hair at the back of her Nefertiti-like head, features she was proud to have passed on to Winston in masculine form.

"Genes," she said.

"Genes," Winston said out loud inside the Cadillac. Now, for the first time, he asked, "Whose?"

◈ ◈ ◈

Winston stopped in a beach town about ten miles north of where Johnny de la Cruz lived. He pulled the Cadillac up to the registration office of the Beachcomber, a relic of the Fifties motel boom that consisted of two rows of units facing each other across an asphalt parking lot. In the middle, there was a small rectangular swimming pool whose water glittered chemically blue.

He paid for two nights. In order to write his license plate number on the registration form, he had to first peer through the window at the Cadillac, flamboyant in the late morning sun.

"Nice car," the man behind the desk said. "Yours?"

"It's a loaner."

"Uh huh." The man was stocky and over-muscled and tanned to his subdermal layers. He danced a key on the counter, his eyes traveling from Winston to the Cadillac and back again to Winston.

Winston placed his own lean brown fingers on the key and waited for the man to release his grasp. As Winston walked away, key in hand, it struck him that this unruffled posture in the face of intimidation was not unlike his father's stillness in the midst of a bleacher full of yelling fans. Winston had learned tolerance from Carlitos, and this surprised him. Because Bunny's influence had been so immediate and obvious, Winston had never considered that he might have received something of substance from his father, particularly when those gifts from Ireland arrived broken, melted, or otherwise useless. Now that he connected this gift of tolerance to his father, Winston had to wonder what it was his father had tolerated so well.

In his room, Winston spread himself out on the bed and turned on the television. He didn't bother to surf, just stared inattentively at a string of commercials. Now that he was here, he needed a plan. He reached over, took the letter from his backpack, and set it beside him on the bed. There was an intimacy about the way Bunny's delicate script formed the man's name, gave a precision to the street numbers – insurance against any misreading of the address. It would not be hard to find. Winston got out the map on which he had marked the route to Johnny de la Cruz's house. It seemed too easy, just down the freeway, exit a thumbnail's width from the Mexican border, and then a few turns to Acacia Street.

Winston pulled the phone book from the nightstand. It would be best to call first, he decided. A woman answered, her voice telephone-polite. He turned down the theme music of a soap opera that was starting, and asked for Johnny de la Cruz. "Please," he added.

"May I ask who's calling?"

On the TV screen, an attractive middle-aged woman was stroking the hand of a handsome young man.

Winston said his name, first and last.

"I'm sorry. He's not available at the moment. But I'll tell him you called." Then she hung up.

Though the woman's voice had sounded agreeable, Winston was not so sure that she *was* agreeable, and he began to doubt her assurance that she would tell Johnny de la Cruz of his call. She hadn't even asked for his phone number.

Winston stared at the TV as he pondered his next step. The woman on the screen bit her lip as she revealed some awful truth to the young man that sent him bolting from the room. Winston snickered at the melodrama. He switched off the set and jumped off the bed. He knew what he would do. He would go to Johnny de la Cruz's house, meet him face to face. And her, too, the woman on the phone. Forget the preparatory niceties. He scooped the keys from the bureau and made a soap opera expression in the mirror before heading out the door into the bright chlorine-scented air.

❖ ❖ ❖

Winston's Cadillac was not out of place in Johnny de la Cruz's neighborhood, where a deVille or a Fleetwood was displayed in more than one driveway. One or two Cads crept along the nearly treeless streets, music pounding against the tinted windows, an almost visible bouncing of the long lines of the chassis keeping the rhythm. When Winston rolled down the street and then up again to locate the right house, he was certain he did not attract undue attention; when he parked along the curb at the scruffy park that bordered the de la Cruz's faded green house, he felt as good as camouflaged.

While he sat in the car rehearsing his introduction, he observed the street. Despite the showy cars, the area was the opposite of upscale. In Johnny de la Cruz's driveway an old green station wagon made an ugly match with the popsicle hue of the house. The front yard had a disorderly appearance despite the neat sections of decorative rock and the deliberate placement in twos and threes of container plants interspersed with ceramic or plastic wildlife. It seemed that the residents tried too hard or not at all at landscaping, since the other houses either mimicked the de la Cruz clutter of ornamentation and scraggly blossoms or were bare except for a meager yellow lawn. A rooster squawked from behind someone's house. A ragged cat crept along the fence and then slid beneath the gate into the de la Cruz yard.

"Hi," said Winston to the steering wheel. "You don't know me, but you knew my mother."

It struck him now that Johnny had known his mother the way Winston in high school knew Eva and a few days ago knew Stormie. As he fought off imagining details, he saw a woman emerge from the house. She appeared to be about

Bunny's age. With a motherly firmness, she gathered up the cat that had earlier slunk inside the yard and tossed it back outside the fence. Then she took long enthusiastic strides to the Buick in the driveway, and as she paused to unlock the door, Winston noticed her bad perm and her discount department store clothes – the cheap, heeled sandals and the lavender skirt that was made of something synthetic and staticky. Not that he made any judgments. As the son of Bunny Piña, he just *noticed.*

The woman started the car, which thundered with too much gas. Winston watched her back out of the driveway, swinging the car in a wide arc onto the street. The car jerked forward, a giant frog making a spastic hop, and then she was off at a scrupulously slow pace.

Winston watched the car signal a left turn well before it reached the corner. It paused for passing traffic, then swung right. Without quite knowing why, Winston found himself steering the Cadillac around the same corner. The Buick was easy to tail, and he followed it past an aged shopping mall, then a string of small Filipino restaurants and markets interspersed with taco stands. He began to feel hungry, but would have to settle for Odette's mayonnaise-heavy sandwiches, which still sat in the cooler next to him. He didn't want to lose sight of the Buick.

He followed it into a residential area where the homes were older and smaller, with peeling paint and drooping porches and bare yards with no pretense at landscaping or fake garden fauna. Winston had to slow down considerably since the Buick was at a crawl, but after a few blocks it turned onto a quiet business area of old storefronts – a *panadería,* an insurance agent, a beauty salon, a few small stores with the word *boutique* in their name, a small café. The Buick jerked toward the curb into a parking spot. Winston drove past, careful to look straight ahead, though his peripheral vision caught a glimpse of the woman checking her lipstick. At the corner, he searched his rear view mirror and saw a swatch of lavender disappear into a doorway.

He parked his car, then crossed the street and sauntered casually past empty shops until he was opposite the place where he had seen the woman enter. The sign painted in swirls of red and gold made the letters *Armida's Dance Studio* flash in the sun. Through the storefront window, Winston could see a dozen or so people, middle-aged and older, milling about, the lavender woman among them. Except for Armida's name painted on the glass, there was an unobstructed view inside the studio, and, of course, out. He ducked into the doorway behind him and found himself in a tiny café, empty except for two old men slurping coffee over a game of checkers at a table near the back. Neither man looked up when Winston came in, but one of them, without moving a muscle, called out gruffly, "*Caridad!*"

Winston, who had studied French rather than Spanish in high school, wondered if he was being addressed. But then a woman emerged from behind a curtain, a laminated menu under her arm as she wiped her hands on the apron not quite wide enough for her figure.

"Table for one?" she asked, holding up her index finger.

Winston nodded and gestured toward the window to indicate his preference.

"Sit, sit," she said, shooing him toward the table that gave him a clear view of Armida's.

She set the menu in front of him. Despite the smears on the plastic, the choices on the menu appealed to him. He thought guiltily of Odette's sandwiches as yet untouched in his car. Winston ordered *carnitas* and a Coke, and after the woman had removed the greasy menu, he leaned his elbows on the sticky table and looked across the street.

The dance students had paired up, the lavender woman with a tall, big-shouldered, slightly paunchy man, who in his younger days might have been the high school second-string quarterback. In the midst of the couples was a woman clapping them to attention. Her short, twirly skirt showed off curvy dancer legs, and the lithe contours of her form continued right up to her high sweeping ponytail, the end of which curled at her nape. *Armida,* Winston thought as he watched the woman's hips demonstrate a rumba.

Winston had learned the rumba in seventh grade. And the fox trot, the paso doble, the two-step, and, of course, the waltz. His mother had insisted on the lessons. Every man should know how to dance, she believed. Carlitos had been an adequate dancer, but Bunny often was impatient with his lead, finding it plodding and unimaginative.

"Dance starts here," Bunny told Winston, and she placed her palm across her belly. "You feel it in your guts. A man who doesn't have the music here will not be a good leader." Winston winced at Bunny's use of the word *guts*, as if dancing were something of courage and command rather than rhythm and pleasure.

Dance came naturally to Winston. Bunny liked to show off his dance skills – and her own – at weddings and other gatherings, where they often upstaged the guests of honor. "What a beautiful couple you make," people would say, which made Bunny glow and Winston blush.

After Armida's demonstration, she cued her pupils with a clap of her hands, and the couples began to slink and wiggle to the music that surged in volume, escaping into the street and entering the café. The old men playing checkers moved to the beat in their chairs and Winston tapped his fingers on the sticky tabletop.

The couples took their rumba around the room a few times until Armida stopped the music to demonstrate a new combination. Armida beckoned to the lavender woman and walked her through the steps. When the music started, their hips and shoulders made one sinuous sway.

Caridad set a plate of *carnitas* in front of Winston. "A little spicy, *verdad*?"

Winston's eyes went from the two hip-swaying women across the street to the sizzling dish in front of him. When Caridad saw his confusion, she wiggled her aproned hips to give context to her comment. Winston, embarrassed, thanked her for the food and began to eat, eyes on his plate as he scooped the pieces of roasted meat with a tortilla.

By the time he swept up the last shred of meat and salsa with the last piece of tortilla, the dancers had moved on to the cha cha, and the lavender woman was being chased by the big-shouldered man. He tapped her on the back and she responded with a half-turn into his arms.

Caridad was standing in the open doorway moving through the cha cha on her own. Winston looked back at the men still playing checkers. Though they acknowledged the music with some foot-tapping and head-bobbing, their focus remained on the red and black discs in front of them. Winston wiped his hands, rose from the table, and approached Caridad from behind. He tapped her on the shoulder, and with her feet still miming the steps of the dancers across the street, she turned around. Winston, feeling the music in his guts along with the spicy *carnitas*, pulled her smoothly into step with him. They cha-chaed in the tiny café between the tables, Winston expertly directing Caridad and her wide hips back and forth, then side to side as the men at the checkers table whistled their approval.

She smelled of cilantro and onions and now sweat as her face shone with the exertion of dancing. When the music ended, Caridad collapsed happily into a chair, and Winston scrambled to bring her a glass of water. She took only a few sips before she sprang to her feet. "*Aquí vienen los dancers.*"

Winston looked over and saw that the dancers were leaving Armida's and straggling toward the café. "They come here? All of them?"

Caridad was busy gathering menus. Winston slipped out the door while the dancers were still crossing the street, glancing at them long enough to notice that a lavender skirt was not among them. As he made his way down the block, he saw her up ahead, scampering to her car. Behind him, someone called "See you next week, Tessie." The woman turned and waved, and Winston froze, out on the sidewalk, entirely conspicuous. Too late to drop nonchalantly to the ground to tend to a shoelace or spin around in the opposite direction for a suddenly remembered errand, he just stood, watching, hoping she wouldn't notice him.

Perhaps the small pause he detected in her wave was an artifact of his own anxiety; it was him blinking his eyes or holding his breath that made it appear as if she, for an instant, had taken him in with a measuring glance. Quickly, she got behind the wheel, checked her mirrors, and pulled her large, awkward car away from the curb with a squeal.

Although Winston worried she might have spotted him, he felt alone at her departure, especially now that he knew her name. He stood for a minute in the quiet midday of this unfamiliar neighborhood. Then he got in Felix's Cadillac and headed back to the Beachcomber, Odette's sandwiches at his side.

5

OBLIGATION

On Sundays Tessie woke filled with obligation. There was church in the morning, her daughters at dinner, and in all the other spaces of the day there was her husband, sick and slowly getting sicker, but not dying. Not yet. It was just one of those things she could feel inside of her, like when she was pregnant and knew whether she was carrying a girl or a boy.

Johnny slept in on Sundays, as he nearly always had, only a twice-a-year churchgoer. Tessie listened to him gasp and shudder as if tormented by some demon, but she knew that was just the way his sleep sounded these days.

Tessie believed in consequences. When she was a girl, her mother had warned her and her sisters that if they played cards at night, the devil would pull their hair. Probably just a ploy to get them to go to bed, but you really couldn't be too sure when it came to the devil. She found herself issuing this warning to her own children when they were young, but they only laughed at her. She had laughed too, so they wouldn't think her foolish.

At least she could make them go to church back then. But who listened to her now? Tessie felt these breaches deeply. How did such things happen? She was overwhelmed. There were too many people to pray for, and only her to do the praying.

She slid out of bed, careful not to disturb Johnny, though she suspected he might not really be sleeping. Sometimes he lay awake, but with his eyes closed, quiet except for the low rumble of his breath, and she wondered what he might be thinking. She wondered, yet she wasn't sure she wanted to know. It had been too long since they had really shared their thoughts about anything that mattered, and until she stopped working at the Shop Smart, she had been willing to not notice.

In the bathroom, she washed her face and then sealed it with moisturizer, patting extra into the creases at her eyes. She looked young for her age, but she could see the parching and shrinking happening at the edges. It didn't matter, she told herself. She didn't want to regret getting old. There was already enough to mourn. A sigh fluttered across her lips. The small gust of breath that made a faint cloud on the mirror made her think of the candle, and she hurried back into the bedroom.

On the shelf was a glass container etched with the image of the Virgin of Guadalupe. Inside it, the tall pillar candle Tessie had placed there six days ago had shrunk to just a few inches. She glanced at the calendar on the night stand and congratulated herself once again on how closely she had estimated the candle's burn time. She reached under the bed for a fresh candle, which she purchased by the dozen. She transferred the flame from the nearly extinct candle, which she removed from the glass container, and slipped the newly lit one in its place. She had become an expert at this ritual.

Johnny turned on his side, and the smell of his medicated body rose above the blankets. It was like bug repellent and indistinct from the smell of mothballs that came from the open closet. The sliding door was jammed open. Something was misaligned, off track – the way she and Johnny had always been. No, not always. But for a very long time. She nudged the door gently and felt its resistance. She didn't like things to stay broken, but she didn't know how to fix them. She could get Rey to come over, but there was Johnny to consider. It pained him that Rey was older, had really done nothing different than Johnny, each of them smokers since childhood and weekend beer drinkers almost as long. But it was Johnny whose body was being eaten by cancer. Given the ten years Rey had on Johnny and all other things being equal, shouldn't Rey be the first to go? Shouldn't Gloria be the first to tend to a sick husband? But all other things weren't equal. Rey was quiet and unperturbed, while Johnny had always been quietly perturbed.

As she sorted through her small collection of outdated dresses and skirts that hung with Johnny's unworn slacks and shirts in the broken closet, Tessie reminded herself that life wasn't always fair. Rey, who had paced himself to Gloria's hyperactivity, her talkativeness, her penchant for giving orders, could very well outlast Gloria. Wouldn't *that* be a joke? Tessie was ashamed at such an uncharitable notion toward her sister, especially on Sunday. She resolved to give herself a penance at church today, and she would do it at St. Michael's whose mass Gloria always insisted was better. Tessie would give up St. Agnes, which she had attended alone all these years. She was tired of going to church alone.

As she slipped off her bathrobe to change, Tessie turned to see if Johnny was awake and looking at her in her bra and half-slip. She couldn't remember when they had ceased dressing and undressing in front of each other. Johnny was still turned away, and Tessie slipped the cool rayon of her dress over her head, feeling its softness hug her breasts and her hips, and swish her wrinkled knees.

◈ ◈ ◈

Tessie walked quickly down the center aisle of St. Michael's all the way to the second row, where Rey and Gloria knelt in prayer. She scooted in beside Gloria, who lifted her eyes briefly to Tessie before bowing her head again. Rey leaned across Gloria and winked at Tessie, who hid a smile and busied herself by making the sign of the cross and falling dutifully into a prayerful pose.

After a few minutes on her knees, Tessie discovered, as she so often did, that prayer would not come to her, overwhelmed as she was with the burden of praying for so much. Her mind wandered, her eyes strayed, and her lips did not move with silent Hail Marys. Tessie shifted on her knees and glanced around guiltily, as if someone might guess at her waywardness. Next to her, Gloria's head was bent and her eyes closed. Tessie closed her eyes as well, leaned her forehead against her clasped hands, and thought hard. She could at least ask forgiveness for her sins, which nowadays were unquestionably minor.

She hadn't been to confession in years. Couldn't bring herself to do it, despite the anonymity of sitting in the dark, speaking in low tones through a screen, the priest just a shadow. But her sins of the past had surely been atoned for by now.

They never spoke of it – her abortion, their abortion. It belonged to them both, she always insisted to herself, but she knew it was more hers. He could never know what it felt like, could never feel the loss the way she did. What else could they have done, though? When they married, they refused a formal wedding to save the expense, they told her parents, told each other, and took themselves to the judge at city hall. Later, when their children came, each time a girl, Tessie knew they had paid. Tessie believed in consequences.

And what were her sins these days? Only a harmless deception, playing hooky from her support group. Anyway, her dance class was like a support group, and she stifled a giggle as she thought of Manny, her dance partner, and his slab of an arm balancing her in the dramatic sweeping dip at the end of a Jobim tune.

She felt Gloria move away from her to settle back onto the bench. Tessie murmured a quick apology toward the altar for her secret dance lessons and then slid herself next to her sister. Rey sat as well, as if it was some gentlemanly thing to do to finish his prayers only after the women had finished theirs. He leaned over and whispered, "How's Johnny?" Gloria shushed him and then asked in her own much louder whisper, "Is he feeling better?" Tessie nodded to keep them from talking further. She didn't approve of talking in church. She had instilled the "no talking" rule early in her daughters. A look from her could silence them in a moment, but she could not use her look on Rey – and certainly not on her older sister.

She was saved though by the sudden eruption of organ music and the entrance of the priest, solemn and splendid. The sun, filtering through the stained-glass windows, flung color on the shimmer of his chasuble. She knew without looking that Gloria had become rigid with focus, ready to follow the mass, her missal open in her hands, her lips poised to utter *Amen* at all the appropriate moments. As a girl, Tessie had mimicked her sister as the mass went on around her in a mystifying haze of incense and Latin. Though she had gradually learned to adopt an attitude of earnest reflection and worship, it was as if she had now reverted to that little girl befuddled by the ritual before her, straining her eyes and ears for its meaning. But there was no longer Latin to blame, and that was a crying shame.

Tessie's mind wandered during the scripture readings, the gospel, the creed, and soon everyone around her was extending a hand and she had to put hers out and mumble the requisite *peace be with you*. She didn't like this part of the mass, this audience participation. She was not the kind of person to clap or sing along at a concert. Once when she and Gloria had been given complimentary tickets to be part of a live studio audience for a local TV show, they had been instructed to shout "Good morning!" to the host when the cameras flashed on. Tessie could do no such thing, and she had caught herself in the monitor, lips pursed in an embarrassed smile as Gloria's mouth opened wide to join the chorus. Now, as the congregation was turning this way and that to take the hand of first one neighbor and then another in the sign of peace, Tessie could hear Rey with his accent turning the greeting into "Piss be with you." Tessie, who had never laughed in church, laughed now. And Gloria turned a chilly look on her.

Tessie went to her knees and closed her eyes to study the calming and hypnotic swirl of orange dots that floated behind her eyelids. Feeling far from a state of grace, Tessie decided she would not take Holy Communion that morning. But then Gloria nudged her, and without thinking, Tessie rose and stood in line. When the priest handed her the wafer, she took it gingerly in her hand and then transferred it quickly to her mouth. As she did so she realized that this was how Johnny took his medicine: gulping, and hungry for transformation.

Outside after mass, Tessie stood with Rey and Gloria in blinding sunshine that bounced off the sidewalk into their squinting eyes. Gloria greeted a stream of fellow parishioners, her voice shrilly friendly as she asked after their health because she was on familiar terms with many of their ailments. Then she would introduce Tessie as "my sister from St. Agnes" as if it were another country, far away and not as civilized.

Finally, Father Ramos made his way toward their little group, and Gloria waved him over as if he were a taxi. She introduced Tessie. "Her husband has cancer," Gloria informed the priest, who had begun to sweat beneath the sun, his face glistening as brightly as his garments. It seemed unpriestly to sweat, and Tessie lowered her eyes as Father Ramos murmured, "I will pray for your husband," before moving on to another knot of parishioners.

Gloria looked triumphant. "Maybe we should come by and see Johnny," she said, as if she might already be able to see the effects of Father Ramos's prayers.

"Come for dinner," Tessie said, surprising herself, since she did not cherish the ritual of Sunday dinner as everyone supposed. Still, she thought the company would be nice.

"It's too much trouble for you," Rey said.

"Nonsense," said Gloria. "Tessie always cooks a lot on Sundays."

"Not today," Rey insisted. Then he winked at Tessie. "We'll bring Chinese."

Tessie left St. Michael's feeling mildly blessed.

◈ ◈ ◈

When Tessie got home from church, Josie was in the front yard aiming her camera. "What are you doing?" Tessie asked, though she saw that Josie was taking a picture of the garden chairs, which looked vacant and stark in the hot sun. Everything – the lawn, the lanky flowers, the colored rock – looked wanting.

Josie pressed the shutter. "Still life," she said.

Tessie didn't trust Josie's motives for taking pictures of her front yard and did not believe she had flattering intentions. She watched her daughter guardedly. She didn't look like a woman in her late thirties with a son nearing adolescence in size fourteen sneakers. Maybe it was her lack of grown-up work that made her seem almost adolescent herself. The way she bit her lip as she sized up her subjects for the camera did nothing to give her small face the seriousness of adulthood.

Tessie, who seldom volunteered herself for a photo, went over to sit in one of the empty chairs. "Take a picture, now," she told her daughter. Josie snapped just as Tessie, suddenly feeling wilted, saw Hector Cabrera peek from his open garage at the goings-on.

Tessie went in the house, leaving Josie to survey the yard for further inspiration and nosy Hector to wonder at the sanity of her family. Tessie shook her head. It made no sense to take pictures without people in them.

She found Johnny in the living room lying on the couch, no comforter to cover the pajamas that fell loosely around his bones. His skinny feet were bare and the skin that never saw sun was white and shiny as an onion. His head rested on a bolster, his flattened hair making his large ears appear unevenly placed. He raised himself slowly, bringing his legs in their baggy pajamas to the floor.

"You're home."

Tessie tried not to look startled at his words, remarkable for their near-genial tone. Early in his illness, Tessie had coddled her husband, and like a spoiled child, he had soon come to expect the constant attention. But no amount of attention could quell his anger at and fear of the disease, which one afternoon resulted in his throwing across the room the bowl of soup she brought him as he sat stretched out on the living room couch. She had to peel wet noodles from the carpet and scrape bits of chicken from the TV screen. She completely overlooked the flecks of green onion that were camouflaged among the plastic foliage, and for weeks afterward a dried, green sliver would drop to the coffee table like something shed.

"How was church?"

"Good," she answered. "Did Josie fix you something to eat?" she asked, ready to berate their daughter if she hadn't, given Johnny's sudden affability.

Johnny pointed good-naturedly to a spill on his pajama top as evidence that he had eaten. All his meals were marked by blots of food or drink on his clothes, the result of a spasm in his arm or shoulder that often sent his spoon into his lap or ribs. Tessie hated these smears that were reminders of her husband's condition.

"Do you want to go for a drive," she offered, so that he would feel the need to change into a clean shirt.

"Nah. The baseball game's coming on." He patted the couch for the remote control. Tessie went to retrieve it where it lay at his feet. He made his slow way to his chair, where the pillows would hold him in place for nine innings. When he had settled into its cushiony hold, Tessie draped an afghan over Johnny's shoulders, bringing the edges together to cover the dried oatmeal that sprawled like a misshapen hand over his heart.

"Rey and Gloria are coming for dinner," Tessie said as she fluffed and fitted a pillow under his feet and a towel over them. "They're bringing Chinese."

"Good," he said, and as he clicked the remote, crowd noises sprang into the room, echoing his approval.

She went to the bedroom, switched on the fan, and kicked off her shoes with a little dance of gratitude for tiny miracles. She made up the bed and then sat on the edge, reaching for the phone with one hand and with the other, aiming the remote control at the portable TV perched on the dresser. Johnny called "Strike!" from the living room. Tessie nearly dropped the phone, but she recovered with a quiet giggle. There was something pleasurably secretive about shopping by phone, placing an order for a piece of merchandise that was there on the TV screen before her eyes. But before she could give her full attention to the QVC Channel, she was distracted by movement outside her window.

Tessie leaned across the bed and pulled back the curtain to see Josie absorbed in shifting the yard ornaments, apparently composing scenes to photograph. Josie stood the ceramic gnome in one of the redwood chairs, placed the squirrel in the other. Click. She put the gnome and the squirrel together in the same chair. Click. She laid the gnome on its back on the shriveled grass, on the sparkly pink rocks, on the cracked cement sidewalk, and stood above it, her camera at a bird's-eye view. Click. Click. Click. She picked limp flowers and laid them at the gnome's feet. Click. She threw the plastic fawn into the mix.

"Josie!" Tessie yelled through the screen.

Click. "What?"

"Put everything back where you found it."

Josie, her concentration broken, sighing the sigh of the misunderstood, squinted to see Tessie on the inside of the screen.

"When you're done," Tessie said.

"I know," said Josie, tightly.

Tessie drew the curtain and turned the volume up on the TV so she wouldn't hear Josie tampering with the yard ornaments – Tessie's garden art, thoughtfully chosen and placed, which she was one hundred percent certain Josie would not remember to put back correctly. Tessie focused furiously on the QVC Channel.

At the end of an hour, Tessie had bought a stretch bracelet, silvertone with blue beads hung with angel charms; a reversible cat's-eye pendant necklace, white glass on one side, scroll design on the other; and a genuine jade earring, necklace, and watch gift set. She switched off the TV, and she could hear Johnny's snores mixed with the baseball noises that still played in the living room. Then she heard clicking. Josie's camera was now busy in the bedroom across the hall.

She lay back on the bed, her head propped against the headboard. She picked up a magazine from the nightstand, and studied the pages of celebrities, resisting the urge to see what kind of peopleless pictures Josie was making now.

When Josie had proposed moving in with them while she had her house painted, Tessie hesitated, nearly sputtering a *no* just as she knew Johnny had meant to when presented with the offer. But then Josie explained coolly, "If I were here, then Dad wouldn't be alone when you went to your support group – or wherever it is you go."

Tessie, fuming inwardly at this, told her, "You're welcome here anytime," thinking that if Josie wanted to pretend she was having her house painted, that was her business.

She had always found it difficult to talk to her daughters, Josie in particular. Anyway, it wasn't as if any of her daughters wanted her advice. She didn't forget how mean they were to her when they were adolescents: snippy and sullen, with their eyes narrowed and mouths rigid with conceit, convinced that they were smarter, better, and destined for a life that would surpass their parents' in every way. Which is what Tessie had wanted for them. And now was it her fault that their lives were as ordinary as hers?

Tessie looked at the photos of Hollywood stars. What perfect teeth! Such lovely bodies! Tessie had been lovely once. Of course, she had never been silly enough to believe she could be famous for it. Tessie, in fact, had never held aspirations beyond marriage and family. In the tenth grade, she had been required to write an essay on her plans for the future. She had just finished reading a book on Clara Barton, and, inspired, Tessie wrote how she too would like to provide comfort in times of crisis, tend to the sick, deliver life-saving supplies, be called an "angel." But not long after high school, Tessie married and then became a mother, Clara Barton all but forgotten.

Now she thought how handy it would have been to be a nurse, able to heal her children's wounds. She did her best by them, giving enemas when they were constipated, taking temperatures when they were feverish, filling hot water bottles when they ached. Now here was Josie, all grown up, married and with a son, and Tessie wanted to tell her that whatever else she was missing, at least she had a son.

Tessie remembered entering the labor room after the birth. Josie was propped against a pillow, sweaty and exhausted, hollow-eyed and dazed. She had refused drugs – a needless heroic, thought Tessie, who had learned that children brought enough pain as it was – no need to deliberately subject yourself to it as they fought their way out of your body. Josie held the swaddled Gabriel.

"A beautiful name," Tessie said, though she thought the baby should have been named after Johnny.

"I thought I would have a girl," Josie said, a sigh escaping her. A sigh of fatigue, of astonishment at the miracle of birth, but surely not a sigh of disappointment, Tessie thought. "Do you want to hold him?" Josie asked, tilting the bundle toward Tessie. Tessie had shaken her head and only stroked the baby's cheek, the way Johnny had when their daughters were born.

A son. Where had this expectation come from? What commandment or instinct? Did she require one as a symbol of her own fruitfulness, a desire to please Johnny? Did she even need a reason? Surely, a brother would have been good for her daughters. Surely, they too suffered this lack.

She put down her magazine and went across the hall to Josie's room. She paused outside the door and could hear no rustling around, no clash or bump of objects to indicate the staging of more still lifes. Tessie knocked and entered just as the camera flashed at Josie, who sat cross-legged on the bed, her back pressed into the corner of the wall. Her brooding face turned angry at the interruption. Tessie looked at the camera perched on the shelf near the door, its large round eye inert. She could think of nothing to say.

"We're having Chinese tonight."

"Okay."

Tessie moved to the bed and sat on the edge, her hands on either side of her for leverage as she stretched her legs in front of her. Her calves had become toned with her dancing, though beneath her dress her thighs were slightly thick, a little flaccid. She remembered the time when her daughters were adolescents, suddenly taller and stronger than she; she remembered thinking that in a physical fight with any one of them, she would surely lose.

"Josie, is there anything I can do for you?"

Josie tilted her head questioningly. A perplexed puppy, like the homeless ones she groomed daily, Tessie thought. She wanted to reach out and run her hand through her daughter's thick hair, but it was held back in a braid. It would be too reckless a gesture to loosen it.

The phone rang then, and though its repetitive jangle penetrated the closed bedroom door, Tessie ignored it, wanting to finish this moment. Now Josie was annoyed. "What are you talking about?"

The phone stopped ringing and she could hear Johnny's voice, gruff and mumbling down the hall. She wanted to strain to listen, but Josie's peevishness distracted her.

"I'm here for you and Dad," Josie reminded her.

"Yes," she told Josie. "Thank you." Then she moved to the door, but Johnny had hung up the phone.

6

FORTUNE COOKIES

"You should have a girlfriend," Reynoso Bacaycay told Johnny as they made their way along the seaweed strewn beach.

Johnny shrugged. He thought of Bunny Bulong, who was not his girlfriend back home. She might have been had he stayed, but he was here in America now and he wanted a girlfriend. "How did you meet Gloria?"

"At a wedding. All the Navarro sisters were there." Rey chuckled. "Gloria was a bridesmaid, but she outshone the bride."

"But how did you meet her? What did you say to her?" he asked.

"Nothing." Rey smiled.

Johnny was annoyed at Rey's secretiveness. He was annoyed at being at the beach, annoyed at the sand filling his shoes. At least it wasn't the kind of day that required him to shed his long pants and shirt. It was hazy, with a chill in the air, barely spring. A picnic at the beach seemed an impatient and too-hopeful thing to do.

Johnny followed Rey to a picnic table, where two young women – sisters – were arranging sandwiches. Their black hair was brushed away from their faces, spilling thickly into the space where the neck curved to the shoulder. Lipstick brightened their mouths, full like Rita Hayworth's, and their dark eyes slanted only when they laughed.

They looked up, showing identical smiles and sounding alike in their high-pitched, almost shrill hellos to Rey. Closer up, Johnny saw the differences. One was slimmer, thin actually, and the fullness of the lips, eyes, and hair all seemed exaggerated on her, making her more noticeable. But not more beautiful, decided Johnny, giving that honor to the second sister, whom he was now hoping was not Gloria.

He grinned widely when the thin one stepped up and took Rey's arm. "It's about time you got here," she scolded him with a laugh that wasn't really a laugh. "We've been here an hour. Isn't this a great spot? You should have worn your light blue shirt."

"Say hi to Johnny," Rey told her.

She saluted Rey, then brought her arm down smartly against her thigh, skimming the hem of her shorts, below which goose bumps ringed her knees. "Hi, Johnny. Say hi to my sister Tessie," she commanded in return. Then Gloria and Rey wandered off, she chattering, he contentedly silent.

"Would you like a sandwich?" asked Tessie, whom Johnny noticed had had the sense to wear longer pants that revealed only her calves.

Johnny said yes, not because he was hungry, but because he could think of nothing else to say. He sat down across from her and accepted the sandwich, touching her hand briefly. Too shy to look at her face, he watched her hands as she poured coffee from a thermos. She passed it to him, and again his fingers touched hers, which were not long and tapering, but of a uniform thickness that made them appear short. The nails were closely trimmed. No polish. The knuckles were prominent and divided by veins in inky blue relief against her brown skin.

"If you don't like ham, there's chicken."

Johnny looked at Tessie who nodded at his sandwich still in its wrapper. He unwrapped the sandwich, and when a breeze threatened to steal the paper, Tessie fastened it beneath the thermos. He began to eat, and Tessie clasped her hands on the table, her fingers woven together like the bottom of a well-made basket. She made light conversation, posing questions kindly and with interest – nothing deep or difficult. After a while he remembered to ask, "And what about you?"

She smiled and began to talk of herself, hurriedly, as if her answers didn't matter. But Johnny listened carefully. She was in high school – a senior. Gloria had just graduated. There were two younger sisters, Ruby and Lydia. She thought she would like to be a nurse. Johnny imagined her hands, strong and devoted, rolling up a sleeve to press her fingers to a pulse.

"What are your plans?" she asked. "You know, for the future?"

Johnny was astonished to realize he had thought so little about the future, and was astonished again when he heard himself say, "To own a house."

Then she asked, as if it followed logically from her last question, "Are you a citizen?"

"Yes," he said. He told her how it had happened, how he stood in the third row, close enough to see the bead of sweat at the corner of the officer's nose. It was hot in the small room where two hundred and fifty Filipino sailors – the cooks, stewards, and valets of the ship – in dress black lined up in tight formation. They stood at attention, while the officer paced back and forth, ceremoniously solemn, delivering in a slow monotone the rights and privileges of citizenship. When the officer stopped his pacing at last, he was out of Johnny's line of sight; when Johnny raised his right hand, it was at the behest of a disembodied voice. Johnny repeated the pledge in the fluent English achieved from the months of self-imposed practice – reading aloud the labels on soup cans, reciting the week's menu or the list of supplies needed to replenish the shelves. Now the sounds of the new language glided smoothly over the oath of citizenship. At the close of the oath, the officer gave a signal. Immediately, hands were raised and hats thrown into the air, and amid much congratulatory backslapping, plans were formed. Men who had wives in the Philippines would bring them over; men without wives would marry; they would all have American-citizen children. They would buy houses and have lives more prosperous than if they had never left their towns and villages to become Navy stewards.

Though he told her all this without hesitation, what he didn't tell her was that the act itself, his very presence and participation in the ceremony, was filled with hesitation. When offered this chance at citizenship, he did not clamor with glee or breathe deep with relief, nor furtively wipe away a tear of gratitude. He merely followed his shipmates to the assembly room because he did not want to be left behind.

He felt surprisingly expressive as he described the event (minus the hesitation part). Still, he wondered if he was conveying it right, since Tessie's smile, though lovely, seemed distant. It occurred to him that Bunny Bulong would have understood.

◈ ◈ ◈

Now, as he sat on the sun porch, he thought of Bunny – Bunny who was supposed to have been in the Philippines all this time. He had always imagined her there – tropical, colorful, fragrant nearly to excess. Somehow he felt deceived. Bewildered. He thought of the phone call that had come earlier that day and how this time he had answered and not Tessie, who did get the name right that first time. Winston. It was a pleasing name with alarming intimations. Bunny's son who wanted to see him. Johnny had not said yes right away, but neither did he give the matter long deliberation. How could he see him? How could he *not* see him?

Now the significance of what was to come sent a flutter through his veins. Anticipation and dread roiled in his stomach like the brew of medications he ingested daily. He patted the sweat at his temples.

The air was heavy with late afternoon heat and the smell of tobacco on Rey, his best friend, his only friend. Given to frequent naps in his old age, Rey had dozed off in the middle of a sentence, a syllable suspended in his throat until it was delivered, faint and garbled, in a loud exhale that pushed his chin to nestle in the plaid of his shirt. His mouth was smashed into a smile. The tomato he had been talking about rested in his curved palm.

Johnny looked at the tomato, red and plump, ready to burst. If Rey's fingers were to unfold, it would slide from his hand to the precipice of his knee. But for now, except for the soft rumble of exhalations, Rey was perfectly still – a quiet, instructive presence, the way he'd always been, ever since their first encounter that Sunday afternoon on leave.

Johnny had joined several other sailors at a pool hall downtown where they came upon another group of Filipinos. All of them sailors, all in uniform – black, because it was the cool season. Together they drank beer and smoked Camels and played Eight Ball. The pool hall swarmed with their gang. The stale air made them lethargic and heedless of the growing impatience of the other patrons at their presence, but they lingered on, even after they were bored with playing pool– except for Rey. Though Johnny had only just met him, he paid attention to this man not because he was older or because he had more rank. Johnny just sensed that he knew how to live in this world. So when Rey – a short, handsome man who was quiet, but not out of shyness – suggested they leave the pool hall, Johnny and a few of the others did, mimicking his stride that was a dignified retreat.

Listening to Rey's slumbering breaths, Johnny felt a swell of emotion, and he brought his sleeve to his eyes. He was wearing a fresh shirt over his pajama bottoms, and he still felt the touch of Tessie's fingers on his chest earlier that afternoon when she had buttoned the shirt for him. She had run a comb through his sparse hair, his scalp tingling from the plastic teeth. She handed him a washcloth and he wiped his face. When she held out her hand to take the washcloth, he intertwined his fingers with hers. For the seconds that she squeezed back, he felt gratified, optimistic. But as their hands came apart, the image of Bunny and the idea of Winston amplified the separation.

Johnny had told Tessie then of the phone call from Winston, who he was (the son of an old friend), and that he wanted to visit. He made his voice casual, matter-of-fact: "His mother died. He needs someone to talk to."

"Why you?" Tessie asked.

"We're from the same hometown," Johnny said, which somehow seemed an intimate thing for him to say. But Tessie was too American to feel threatened by anyone or anything to do with a place so distant and foreign.

Rey snorted but did not wake, and Johnny turned his gaze elsewhere. Josie had appeared in the backyard, her camera slung around her neck. He watched her move slowly along the path, paved unevenly with bricks that made a rectangle around a rash of geraniums. She sat on her haunches and looked around her, taking in the limited scenery from ground level. The stray cat that had taken up residence in their yard brushed against Josie's ankles, then slithered out of reach. Josie rose and stood, hands on hips.

Skinny girl, he thought. *Woman,* he corrected himself. When had they grown up, his daughters? All skinny. None of Tessie's curves. Skinny like himself. Josie was wiry with small muscles and ropy tendons conspicuous in her lank limbs due to the miles she ran and the weights she lifted, routines she devoted herself to, and he wondered at this daily striving to accumulate strength. He heard her sometimes in her room, the panting that came with the strain of curling dumbbells to her chin. Sometimes it made him clench his teeth for her.

Josie's camera had settled on the toolshed, zooming in and out to capture it in pieces or in its ramshackle entirety. It had been a playhouse once. Johnny had made it, with built-in benches on three walls and a table in the middle, big enough to fit three little girls. Tessie had sewn curtains. But he had made only two windows, which proved to be inadequate: inside it was airless, and sometimes Sara's nose would bleed from the trapped heat. After a while, the playhouse was abandoned to the spiders that laced the doorless threshold with their webs, and it became a place of threatened exile. When Tessie lost patience with the girls for their bickering or when she became helplessly enraged at their insolence, she would yell, "Keep it up, and I'll put you out in the playhouse." Except she never did and the girls knew it was an empty threat.

The playhouse eventually became the repository for all things broken and superfluous, mostly rusted garden tools, cracked planters, coils of old hoses, and crumbling statuary. The curtains had come down long ago. It was a toolshed. But Johnny knew that in the dusty corners and in the cracks in the floorboards were lodged a tiny Barbie shoe or a peeling rubber ball or some other long-discarded relic of childhood.

He watched as Josie, satisfied with snapping exterior shots, took her camera inside. He caught glimpses of her elbow through the little playhouse windows as she angled her camera this way and that, and Johnny imagined the pictures she would make. The dirt-clotted teeth of a rake, the chipped and pocked bowl of a birdbath separated from its pedestal, a pile of rubber sandals whose straps would disintegrate to the touch.

Josie emerged from the playhouse, and when she was done slapping dust from her shorts, she looked up and saw Johnny on the sun porch. She came forward and peered through the screen. "What are you doing there?"

He might well ask her the same thing, he thought, but he was determined to be friendly. "Just sitting," he said, and beckoned her in.

Josie opened the screen door and joined them on the sun porch. Though she tiptoed out of consideration for the dozing Rey, she allowed the door to swing shut on its own and Johnny winced at its long squeal. Josie, apologetic, folded herself onto a wicker stool.

"I was just taking some pictures," she said, fingering the camera strap at her neck.

Johnny was tired of her camera and didn't want to encourage conversation about it, so he kept silent.

Josie cracked her knuckles. "Can I get you anything?"

That question again that had become rote, tossed at him like feed to a pigeon. Before he could summon the courage to say something kind, something to break the triteness of this call and response, Josie was on her feet.

"Hey," she said, "How about if I get a picture of you and Uncle Rey?"

"He's sleeping," Johnny said, pointing his hand in Rey's direction, thinking he might try to shield him if necessary.

"That's okay. That's what makes a picture real." Josie was squinting one eye at Rey, pondering an angle.

Johnny looked over at Rey, pleasantly napping, soft snores ruffling his lips that were still pushed in a smile, his hand still cradling the ripe tomato. For once, the idea of a picture appealed to Johnny. He sat up straight and tried not to smile as Josie brought the camera to her eye and pressed the shutter. Rey blinked awake with the flash of the camera and the tomato teetered on his fingers a moment before it skittered down his knee to the floor.

Rey spewed a curse, and Josie, giggling, reached over to pick up the tomato, which now sat slightly flattened in her hand.

"Sorry, Uncle. I'm taking candid shots of the family." Josie held out the tomato to him. "See, it's fine."

"It was perfect before, wasn't it, Johnny? Fine is no good." Rey pronounced *fine* with a P. His accent was thick, and his children and Gloria often made fun of him. He took it in good humor. That was Rey – endearing, in a way that Johnny knew he himself was not.

"The taste will be off," Johnny said, taking Rey's side, wishing the tomato had broken and splattered so Josie could see what ruin her camera had wrought.

Rey shrugged and smiled. "Plenty more," he said, and held up the paper sack next to him. "From my neighbor's greenhouse."

"Here," Josie said, "I'll take them to the kitchen."

"Make sure you *p*eed them to this guy," he said, patting Johnny's knee. "They're *p*ull of *b*itamins."

Johnny saw Josie smile at Rey's words. She leaned over and kissed her uncle. They enjoyed each other, Josie and Rey. Johnny waited until that moment between them had passed, waited for Rey's attention.

"You're lucky you see your children," Rey said. "My kids are too busy, all the time busy."

Rey's daughter was married to a lawyer and lived in one of the wealthy neighborhoods to the north. They had a swimming pool and a live-in nanny, and Linda played tennis while her children attended classes at their private schools. Rey's son was manager of an electronics store in Tustin, and spent his spare time writing screenplays that never sold.

Wait till you're dying, then they'll come, Johnny wanted to say, thinking of how he had been beset by his daughters since his illness, how it both gratified and alarmed him.

Gloria poked her head out onto the sun porch. "Time to eat, you two." She held the door open as Rey and Johnny filed in and Johnny sensed the slightest recoil as he passed her. Gloria did not like sickness, but she did have a curiosity about it, which she satisfied by collecting second-hand accounts of other people's illnesses and using these as the basis of her expertise on a variety of infirmities. Because he was often subjected to Gloria's advice, Johnny made up horrible details about his doctor visits and hospital stays when she asked how he was. Not all of it was untrue. Plenty was real. But so much of it was the same – the invasiveness, the indignities, the loss of control – so Johnny added textures and colors. The ache in his arms felt like gravel scraping his veins, he told her. Once he said his blood in a test tube was the color of canned beets. Another time he compared its thickness to melted chocolate. Gloria hated to have the parts of the body likened to food.

When she had greeted him earlier, she had patted his arm. Her hand lingered over the bone for a moment, as if she were both drawn to and frightened by the vanishing of him. When she had kissed the air near his cheek, he heard the little smack her lips made, like a tiny insect flitting past his head, something to swat away.

At the table, Tessie – unduly occupied with passing food around the table – ceded command of the dinner conversation to Gloria, who veered randomly from subject to subject, her ramblings predictable only for their frequent return to news about her children: Linda's new car, Sonny's promotion. The speed with which the words skimmed off her lips fascinated

Johnny. With his insides gone awry, he had become more aware of the body's external parts. He watched the slow action of Rey's jaw as he ate, the flexing of Josie's fingers as she worked her chopsticks, even the slight tremor of his own wrist as he brought a spoonful of wonton soup to his mouth.

"How do you like that? They only gave us four fortune cookies," Gloria sniffed, indignant at the oversight.

"Go for it," Josie said.

So Gloria took one and passed the plate around.

Rey snapped open his cookie first.

"What's it say," Gloria said, impatient to read her own, which she liked to do after everyone else had read theirs.

"*A financial reward awaits you.*" Rey grinned. "Time to go to Las Vegas again."

"Hah, jackpot," Johnny said. "*Your health will improve,*" he read out loud, too loud, shrugging and making a joke of it, not wanting to show how much he wanted to believe the little strip of paper.

"You see," Gloria exclaimed, "It's Father Ramos's prayers working already. Okay, Tessie, what does yours say?"

"*You will attend an unexpected social event.*"

"Here, let's see," Gloria said, reaching for Tessie's fortune as if to verify the words, because it was Gloria who loved social events. "Well, I wonder what that could mean," she said, handing the fortune back to Tessie and at last pulling out her own to read. "*Dream lofty dreams, and as you dream, so shall you become.*"

She frowned.

"Gibberish," Josie said, while shredding the fortune Tessie had scooted in her direction as if it were a coupon, transferable and redeemable.

"Well, it means *something*," Gloria insisted, though she

dropped her fortune onto the table, where it soaked up some sweet and sour sauce.

Josie rose to clear the dishes. Over the clink and scrape of plates, Johnny could not be sure he heard Tessie's casual announcement, but she repeated it for Josie, who had stopped her clattering to ask, "Huh?"

"Johnny's going to have a visitor," Tessie said.

Rey leaned forward, curious, and Gloria seemed to have forgotten her disappointment in her fortune cookie.

"A boy named Winston Piña," Johnny said, the words sending a shiver beneath his skin. "A young man," he corrected himself, remembering the voice on the phone and wondering how old, how young.

"Winston as in the cigarette?" Josie said.

"His mother was a friend of Johnny's," Tessie said.

"Remember I told you about Bunny Bulong?" Johnny said to Rey.

"The beauty queen? Miss Sampaguita?"

"Beauty queen?" Tessie and Gloria said it together. Johnny was reminded of the time he first saw them, how they were nearly indistinguishable to him.

"And Bunny, where is she?" Rey asked.

"Dead," Johnny said. "Just recently. Of cancer."

He seldom said it out loud, his disease. But it had been Bunny's disease too. *What a strange thing to have in common all these years later,* he thought, vigorously rebuffing the idea of that other thing they might have in common: Winston.

7

THE VISIT

It was Winston's fourth day at the Beachcomber, longer than he had intended to stay. He could've found a better motel, or he could've gone back to Anaheim and taken Bunny's letter back with him. Odette had warned him about not chasing a wild goose. But he was still here.

He had called Odette and Felix the first night to let them know he had arrived safely. She had inquired about the sandwiches. Had he eaten them all? Had she put enough mayonnaise? Yes, he told her as he stared into the open cooler on the floor by his bed, a couple of sandwiches drowned in the melted ice. Felix asked about the car. Any problems? None, Winston said. "That's right, none," came his uncle's knowing reply. "That Cadillac will take care of you."

Now, as he sipped a beer purchased with the fake ID Junior had given him for his nineteenth birthday, Winston had to agree that the Caddy had been a comfort, if a conspicuous one. Its quietness was reassuring; its spaciousness gave him the sense of openness and possibility. Winston wondered if these thoughts were his own or if he was just remembering one of Felix's sales pitches.

The Cadillac had been practically an accomplice in his so-far-tentative attempt at meeting Johnny de la Cruz. He felt uneasy about having followed Tessie that afternoon – not just because she might have seen him, though that did weigh on him. He wasn't sure why he had followed her, except that it delayed an encounter with Johnny de la Cruz. Procrastination had never numbered among his faults, but now – rudderless without Bunny, and with Carlitos's long absence haunting him – he was lately given to hesitancy and self-doubt. And, he had to admit, he was a little squeamish about meeting his mother's one-time lover.

The last few days, he had spent much of his time at the beach body surfing, and then, exhausted from sun and salt water, sleeping in his bed at the Beachcomber or lounging in the deck chair right outside his door as the sun went down. He would watch the pink sky turn indigo and think of Bunny, a bright flaming color gone dark. These were desultory days, much removed from his previous purposeful, habit-filled existence as Bunny Piña's dutiful son. The truth was he didn't want to go back to Anaheim yet, and he wasn't ready to join Junior in Los Angeles. Bunny's letter had disoriented him, left him unmoored.

Until he found the letter, he had never thought of his mother as having any secrets. Now he thought it unfair of Bunny, since Winston felt that she had known everything about his life. Of course, that couldn't be true. How could she have known that the modesty he showed at being selected valedictorian at St. Augustine High was really guilt at having cheated, if only mildly, on his physics exam? How could she have known that he lost his virginity on an afternoon when he was supposed to be at debate team practice? She couldn't, of course. Yet Winston believed that somehow she *did* know or could guess such things. Now it was Winston's turn to know something about Bunny.

He set down his beer and reached for the phone and dialed

Johnny's number. He was taken aback when a man's gruff *hello* strafed his ear. For some reason he had expected a woman – Tessie – again.

Fearful that a gradual introduction would be cut short by a dial tone, Winston blurted, "I'm Bunny Piña's son."

There was a silence, then a cough before the man said, "Why are you calling me?" It was a quiet question, with hardly an inflection, yet it jarred Winston because he had not really articulated the answer to himself.

"Because," Winston said, knocking over his beer, "you were a friend of hers – my mother."

"Yes. I knew her."

Winston winced at the words. It was audible, the sound he made, gargly and phlegm-like. He swallowed and blurted, "Bunny's dead."

He listened to the silence on the line. "Cancer," he added.

He heard nothing on the other end and wondered if Johnny was still there.

"You were a friend of hers," Winston said again. "I'd like to meet you."

There was more silence. Then Johnny was saying Monday afternoon and giving his address, and Winston, though there was no one to see, pretended to write it down as if the number and street were not already chiseled in his memory.

◈ ◈ ◈

Restless, Winston grabbed a towel and his sunglasses and headed out the door, making his way to the beach on foot.

The beach swarmed with bodies slick with tanning lotion, and the ocean breeze carried the smell of coconut oil and hot dogs. Boom boxes, scattered like driftwood, pounded out overlapping rhythms. Winston stripped off his shirt and sunglasses and zigzagged his way around oily sunbathers to the water, where he threw himself into wave after wave, riding each brief surge until it disappeared beneath him.

When he was seven, Bunny and Carlitos had taken him to the beach. Bunny wore a yellow bathing suit and yellow beach slippers, and the straw hat on her head had a yellow and white striped ribbon woven into its brim. Bunny looked like sunshine. She arranged herself in a cabana chair with a movie magazine in her lap and shooed Carlitos and Winston toward the water: "Okay, you two, have fun."

It was Carlitos's job to teach Winston to swim, but Winston already knew how. Benjie Bayani's older cousin Leo was a lifeguard at one of the city pools, and he would allow Benjie and Winston to sneak past the admission booth. At first, they just splashed in the shallow end, but when Leo was off duty he showed them how to stroke their arms and turn their head to breathe. It was not long before Winston was swimming laps well ahead of Benjie, who not long after that stopped inviting Winston to sneak into the pool.

When Carlitos demonstrated the crawl stroke, Winston pretended to flail and sputter. Carlitos guided Winston's arms as they stood on shore. "That's it," Carlitos said. "Now try it in the water." Winston stroked tentatively at first, his arms chopping at the surface. "Reach," Carlitos instructed. So Winston reached, and soon he was slicing cleanly through the water, gliding with dolphin ease, and Carlitos was sidestroking beside him cheering him on, excited at his own success as a teacher.

"Good work," Carlitos said, when they both ceased their stroke to tread water side by side. Winston liked the way the back-and-forth motion of their legs and arms mirrored each other.

He thought they would swim together for a while, maybe race to the dock or play a game of tag. But Carlitos only smiled at him. "Stay near the shallows," he said as he stroked to shore. He sat in the wet sand, water lapping at his feet, and set his gaze on Winston, who obediently swam back and forth. Eventually, though, he realized that Carlitos was not looking at him, but somewhere off in the distance behind him.

Winston dove beneath the surface and swam under water for as long as he could, his eyes wide with the effort. When he had scared himself with his need for air, he kicked to the surface and burst through with a gasp, only to find that Carlitos had never even missed him.

They had stayed at the beach all day, eating the picnic lunch Bunny had brought, but having dinner at the beachfront café owned by a friend of Bunny's, a man with a vigorous mustache and a hearty laugh. After their meal of fried squid, Bunny suggested they go back to the water's edge and watch the sun set. No, not the three of them, just Carlitos and Winston. She would stay behind and chat with her friend. So Carlitos and Winston sauntered through the sand and sat side by side at the tide line. The water swished at their feet; sea birds circled and squawked. Otherwise, the silence between father and son was the loudest sound. Carlitos, who liked ballads, began to hum. And even though it was the sun that was on the horizon and the sea across whose expanse they stared, "Moon River" was the tune that came from Carlitos. Then he sang the words, measured and lugubrious with an achy resignation. *I'm crossing you in style someday.* He nudged Winston to join him, so Winston did, and it was one of the few things they ever really did together.

◈ ◈ ◈

Back at the Beachcomber, full of sun and the burritos he had bought from a boardwalk vendor, Winston fell asleep to dream of Bunny and Carlitos swimming underwater looking for him while he drove Felix's Cadillac across the sand in slow and meandering pursuit of a green station wagon.

◈ ◈ ◈

On Monday afternoon, Winston arrived at the de la Cruz residence exactly on time. He parked in front of the house, just out of the drop zone of a tree that sent a shiver of red needles to the ground without provocation. Winston looked at Bunny's letter, which had been riding in the passenger seat next to him. Not a companionable presence. He thought about Bunny's words slanting gracefully across the page. *You should know this: I have a son. His father abandoned us for his own life.* Winston, bewildered by Bunny's infidelity, wanted to see the man to whom his mother wrote, but failed to send, the chiding, wistful letter, which he now shoved in the glove compartment.

Even through the screen door, he recognized Tessie. She was dressed in white slacks and an aqua short-sleeved blouse that, though becoming, made Winston think of the synthetic color of the Beachcomber pool. For now, her clothes were all he could observe; the murky interior made it difficult to ascertain her expression behind the screen. He knew though that its mesh allowed her a sufficient view of him. He introduced himself, made himself talk confidently to the screen as if his sureness and control might erase any recall she might have of seeing him before. There was a pause on the other side before Tessie opened the door, and when he saw her face, he could not help but feel that she had prepared the expression she wore – polite, smiling, and without a trace of recognition.

"I'm Tessie," she said. She did not offer her hand to shake, but took it to her hair, though there were no strands loose or out of place. Her hair was dull from too many perms and clumsily styled, but he saw that she had been pretty once. Still was, he supposed, for her age. He remembered Odette's wrinkled nose as she minced the word *mestiza*. Tessie's face did not conform to the kind of beauty that belonged to Bunny. There was no flamboyance, nothing of the floral grace or vivid hues of a former beauty queen.

He felt her looking at him the way Bunny had in the occasional delirium of her last days, when he had appeared to her as a complete stranger and he watched her eyes strain for something familiar. But then he saw only politeness in Tessie's face and decided he had imagined the rest. He followed her into a small foyer wallpapered with an embossed gold pattern that, despite its geometry, had a chaotic effect. A plastic Grecian statue, holding a bowl of ivy that sent itself in feeble tendrils to the floor, did nothing to mitigate it.

"My husband is in the living room," she said. Her own words seemed to give her pause, to make her reconsider their interaction thus far. "If it comes up," she said, "my husband might wonder why you happened to see me that day. Anyone might, you know."

"Yes," was all he could manage before Tessie led the way to a room darkened by wood paneling. A man sat on a couch as if he had been propped there. He wore a white shirt and tan slacks, colors that neutralized him into the fabric of the couch.

"Well, here he is, honey. Here's Winston," Tessie said, pointing him out as if he were among a crowd of visitors in their living room.

Winston stepped forward and around a coffee table that held more ivy, this time artificial and trailing out of the hollowed back of a glossy ceramic swan. He extended his hand. "Nice to meet you, Mr. de la Cruz."

The man, obviously ill, rose, and Winston could see how thin he was, how his belt was pulled to the last notch and still the tan pants sagged. He noticed the man's gaunt face that made his red-veined eyes protrude like dark marbles and his ears appear as large as hamsters. Winston could not tell what effect his presence had on this man who seemed drained of all expression. When they shook hands, Winston felt as if his grasp was holding the man upright.

"Call me Johnny," he said, sinking back into the couch, his feet grazing the raised swirls of the carpet. He wore the kind of athletic shoes sold in large bins in parking lot sales. Winston was aware of his own clothes, casual but well-made khakis and a linen shirt, organic breathable fibers.

"Have a seat," Johnny said.

Winston looked around him now. Aside from the couch, where Johnny seemed tenuously balanced, there was a matching love seat and a chair with a thicket of pillows. Winston walked around the coffee table to sit in the love seat. Next to him on an end table was a cluster of framed photos, but everywhere else – on the coffee table, on shelves, on and around the TV – were figurines, colorful blots that did not quite brighten the room.

"Well, Winston, can I get you anything?" Tessie asked. She was already sitting down next to Johnny, so Winston said no, though he would have liked a drink of water. His mouth felt dry and there was a faint odor in the room that made him wish for something clear and cool against the roof of his mouth. He wondered if there were household pets or if perhaps there was mold in the soil of the houseplants. Most of the greenery was artificial, though. Maybe it was aging plastic that he smelled. Whatever the smell, it seemed to be embedded in the fabric of the house, or maybe in its occupants, who sat across from him with rigidly polite expressions.

Winston cleared his throat to thank Johnny for seeing him, but Tessie spoke again: "We're so sorry about your mother."

"Thank you," he answered, embarrassed that the condolence came from Tessie.

They were all silent then, as though some business between them had reached its conclusion. Winston searched the room for some topic of conversation, his glance occasionally landing on Johnny and Tessie side by side, though not quite touching, on the couch, and he tried to imagine Bunny on the other side of Johnny. He thought of the letter in the glove compartment, how he could utterly change this moment with the mention of it.

"And your father? Where is he?" Tessie asked.

"My father?" Winston repeated blankly, oddly unprepared for the question and recovering too late to observe any reaction in Johnny. "I don't know," he said. "I mean, he's in Europe. My father lives in Europe."

"Oh, how interesting," Tessie said, clearly impressed with this news.

Winston did not elaborate, though he would have if asked, conceiving details on the spot, weaving a neat and credible narrative the way he had in the impromptu rounds at speech tournaments in high school.

"We've never traveled." Tessie sighed, and she shifted her position on the couch as if to protest their stationary lives. "Only Johnny traveled when he was in the Navy. Where'd you go, dear?" Tessie touched her husband's arm and he teetered toward her slightly. "Japan, right? Austria, too, I think."

"Australia," Johnny corrected, a barely audible growl.

"And then there was your trip back to the Philippines." She turned to Winston to explain. "Not with the Navy. He was out by then."

"Oh, when was that?" Now she put her hand on Johnny's leg and Winston could see the looseness of the pants fabric around it. "Nineteen seventy-something."

Seventy-one, Winston thought, his mouth even drier now, his throat full of pebbles. He had calculated June, nine months before his birthday. He looked at Johnny, waiting for him to say the year, the magic number, but Johnny's eyes were fixed on Tessie's hand on his leg as if it were some sort of restraint. Or lifeline.

The sound of the front door opening made Tessie call out in a voice that went suddenly shrill. "Josie, come in here, we have a guest."

Winston, frustrated at the interruption, forced a smile as he stood to greet a youngish woman who brought the musty smell of animal fur into the already burdened room. She smiled Tessie's large-toothed smile, though there was something transitory and skeptical to it, prone to retraction. Her handshake was unduly firm – overcompensation for the thinness of the arm that extended it.

"You're Winston," she said.

He felt accused.

Josie lowered herself cross-legged on the floor in a posture that showed remarkable flexibility and made her seem almost adolescent, though he guessed she was somewhere in her thirties. For a moment he thought of Stormie and hoped the blush creeping up his neck was not visible in the dim room.

"That your Cadillac out front?" she asked.

"Oh," Tessie said, looking amused, "you drive a Cadillac?"

"It's my uncle's," Winston said, glad he could disclaim ownership. He ran a hand through his short hair, aware of Josie eying him. "And my Aunt Odette's," he added as if lining up allies. "My mother's sister."

Winston was aware of how his voice had grown loud with the words, how the words turned the dark living room quiet. In the long pause, Josie looked at her father, turned back to look at Winston, then at her mother, and then they all seemed to turn their attention to the swan on the coffee table, except for Winston, who was stealing glances at each of his hosts in turn: Tessie's tenuous smile, Johnny's contraction of himself into the furniture, Josie's long elastic limbs knotted around each other. He sensed his role as intruder, but rather than making him uncomfortable, it infused him with a kind of power – the kind that Bunny had exercised over her employees, over rooms full of partygoers, over complete strangers when she walked into a restaurant, and over him, heir to her command and charisma. Early on, Winston had been made aware of his gifts. In Manila, Bunny's friends clucked over his looks, calling him a Filipino Elvis. Bunny dismissed such nonsense. George Chakiris, she declared. That's who her son resembled – the mambo-dancing gang leader in *West Side Story*, her favorite movie. "You're a Shark!" she would tell him.

He looked around the room more boldly now, not impolitely, but with the confidence of a guest on a TV talk show whose very presence assures viewer interest. He felt their curiosity keenly. Their disquiet, too.

His eyes fell on the line of photographs on the table next to him. "You have three daughters?" he asked, addressing Tessie, though including Johnny in his gaze.

"Yes, three," Tessie said, congratulation in her voice, as if Winston had taken this fact like a rabbit from a hat. But there was something else in her voice. Apology. As if her total number of offspring were deficient in some way.

"Laura's our oldest. She's an eye doctor."

"Not a doctor, Mom, an optometrist."

"Sara's the youngest. She and her husband run a restaurant."

"Fast-food franchise," Josie clarified.

"Well," said Tessie, "I'll let Josie tell you what she does for a living."

"Animal technician," Josie told him, and then to Tessie she said, "It's my actual title."

"So, what do you do, Winston?" Johnny asked. They all turned to look at him, as if he'd only just materialized.

"I'm a student at UCLA." Winston said. "Pre-law." This wasn't strictly true, since he hadn't declared a major. It *could* be true, he reasoned to himself, ignoring his disinclination for argument, which he thought to be a consequence of Bunny's authority.

"Well," Tessie said, "isn't that nice."

Winston saw approval in her eyes. Then he looked at Johnny and saw it there too, made more affecting by his withered looks.

Even though Johnny soon took his gaze away, Winston knew that he would be invited back to the de la Cruz home. There followed ten minutes of small talk, in which Winston did most of the talking. He chatted about his life, starting with Bunny's ambition for herself and her dreams for him, which brought them from Manila to Anaheim, where he was given Catholic schooling, lessons in dance, music, and sports (all of which brought nods of approval from Tessie). He told of how he had worked at Disneyland during summers to save money for college. He said he was a dancer in the Main Street parade. He had to wear tights, he said, grimacing as he pretended to recall his chagrin. He said it modestly, with self-deprecation, offering himself up for friendly sarcasm to show he was a good sport.

"A dancer," Tessie noted, and Winston blushed. Johnny scowled.

Josie asked if he had had to wear make-up.

"Of course he did," Tessie said.

When Winston spoke about Bunny's success as a salon owner, he saw Tessie's hands go to her perm; when he told them about his aunt and uncle, he saw Johnny look up again at the mention of Odette's name. Then Winston stood to indicate his departure. Though he had received no offer of refreshment, he thanked them for their hospitality. They all rose, even Johnny.

"Well, come back anytime," Tessie said.

She said it as a courtesy, the way people slung *have a nice day* at each other. Winston looked to Johnny, who asked, "Going back to Anaheim?" A question unencumbered by suggestion or overtone, it seemed to Winston.

"I'll be in town for a while," he said, and he thought he saw something like welcome in Johnny's otherwise drooping posture. But just in case he might be imagining Johnny's signals, he decided to make his intentions clear. "I'll be in touch," he said, feeling confident, in charge.

As he made his way down the driveway to his car, Winston heard Josie call his name. He turned around to find a camera pointed at him, and he couldn't help it – he smiled.

8

SHELTER

Josie disposed of the last of the dogshit.

It was how she started the day. There was something quite expurgatory in shoveling shit early in the morning, especially as she prepared to follow it up by hosing down the kennels. At this hour, there was still a blanket of fog. The spray that blasted from the nozzle roiled the mist, which with the rumbling gutturals of the dogs made for a pleasant kind of eeriness.

These were her first chores of the morning, commenced with great energy after having a cup of hot chocolate with Troy, the security guard. On her way to work, she always drove up to the Winchell's window and ordered two large. Josie knew it would be polite to also bring a cup of chocolate for Lyle, her co-worker who tended the cats. Somehow she never managed to do so.

Josie steered a broom around to direct water into the floor drains. Already her feet had begun to sweat inside the rubber boots she wore, and so began the accretion of grit and odors that by the end of the day would make her feel laden and clumsy and disheartened by the plight of homeless animals. Still, she found the work suited her. On her rounds to fill water and food dishes, the dogs greeted her with thrashing tails and clamoring yelps; when she scratched behind an ear or beneath a chin, their needy eyes went grateful with love. But then their fawning joy became too much for her and she was glad to sternly order them into a corner. They were too compliant, and though that was what life in a kennel induced, there was something unappealing about this behavior. Nevertheless, it allowed her to distance herself from them, and she was coolly efficient as she doled out dog chow.

It was a transient population, so she tried not to get attached to the animals, though she knew all their names and personalities. She conversed with them daily – about the weather, the morning headlines, her own personal worries or triumphs. Josie tried not to have favorites among the dogs, but there was always one that she talked to more frequently, shared more than the passing news about the latest celebrity scandal. This morning when she came to Jackson's cage, she had plenty to tell him. Jackson, a black shepherd mix whose gentle frown and one cocked ear seemed particularly suited to her ramblings, looked up from the back corner he favored for sleeping. When she opened the gate, he got up and came forward to greet her, not in spastic excitement or timid obeisance, but in calm, matter-of-fact cordiality. This was one of the things she appreciated about Jackson, even admired. She scratched Jackson under his chin and he closed his eyes with satisfaction. When Josie pulled her hand away, Jackson didn't clamor for more, but quietly padded back to his corner to watch Josie fill his water and food bowls. Josie took her time. She liked being in Jackson's cage. When she spoke to him about her personal issues, he sat objectively, sometimes indifferently (all the better, really), and she rambled freely. For the past two weeks she had been updating the dog on Winston's now-routine visits to her father.

"So, Jackson, guess what? My father has a new best friend. Yep, you guessed it. Don't be sad, Jack. You were never in the running for that position. My father is not a dog lover. He's not exactly mad about Winston, either. Still, they're spending a lot of time together. Weird, huh?"

Jackson swished his tail politely.

"I'll tell you one thing, though. That Winston is scarily handsome." Way more than his share of lucky stars, she added under her breath as if this opinion should be kept even from Jackson. She gave him a friendly pat to make up for the slight.

"Okay, Jackson, have a nice day. Just another hour before the looky-loos come by."

Josie was always wary when the potential adopters stopped at Jackson's kennel, worried that someone unworthy would claim him as a pet. But Jackson was generally overlooked, since he did not fawn and work himself into a frenzy of indiscriminate affection. It was just as well. There was no need for disappointment when it came to expectations of love.

Sometimes as she went about her work, she was reminded of the times when as a teen volunteer she was assigned to meal times at the old-folks' home. At first, they had scared her, the withered, shapeless people with slack jaws and few teeth. She spent more time scraping food off chins than spooning it into mouths. The smells were terrible and relentless: urine, dentures, apple juice, peas and carrots and squash, boiled, strained, pureed, steamed. The first few times she walked into the building, the stench made her gag. She could smell it before she stepped through the front door.

Several times a week, she was asked to take a couple of the patients outdoors to the terrace for some sunshine and fresh air. First, she would wheel one old man into the elevator, backing the chair in so that he faced the elevator doors. Then, keeping the doors open with a piece of masking tape, she would back in the second wheelchair with another old man in it. Once, one of the old men reached out a wobbly hand and angled it up her candy striper pinafore. Shocked, she turned around, pushing the cold bony fingers back at their owner who was by now grinning widely, saliva dripping from his lower lip. But she got used to it all – the reek of bedpans, the drool and mucus, the gnarled, probing hands – because sometimes life stank.

◈ ◈ ◈

As the morning wore on, Josie felt a coating of pet fur accumulating on her body. She scratched frequently, her ragged nails scraping across her clothes and underneath to her dry and roughened skin that smelled of disinfectant, dog food, and (only faintly) the aloe lotion she had rubbed into her hands before coming to work. She went to the storeroom to get plastic chew toys from the clean bin. She emptied the sack of dirty toys she had collected from the kennels into a bin of soapy water, hurling suds in all directions.

"Easy there." Lyle had come in. Josie tossed a stray toy into the bin for an extra splash.

Though a few years younger than Josie, Lyle was an old-timer, having worked at the shelter since he was a teenager. His tenure at the shelter added up to almost fifteen years, and he tended to flaunt his seniority over Josie's mere two years. Josie suffered his smugness in silence, keeping private her degree in zoology to save the trouble of having to explain her present employment, which she had yet to explain to herself.

Early on, Josie and Lyle discovered they had attended rival high schools. Though they were both in their thirties, with presumably more interesting events in their lives than reminiscing about the past, Lyle's first question to her when they met had been "What high school did you go to?" Lyle was fond of recalling his high school days. He spoke of the "extra-curricular activities" with a wink that made Josie cringe. He listed them on his grubby, cat-scratched fingers: smoking dope, keggers on the weekends, make-out parties. It galled Josie that they now shared the same job classification.

Josie didn't believe that Lyle really cared about animals. They were just inventory to him. More interesting than ball bearings in a warehouse or soup cans in a grocery store, but inventory just the same. When he held a cat, it might as well have been a loaf of bread.

The second question Lyle had asked was "Nervous?"

Josie stared at him, but Lyle seemed amused at her indignation. Then she realized she had been tugging at the ring on her finger, and her annoyance heightened at his mention of this nervous habit that meant absolutely nothing.

◈ ◈ ◈

The morning's work went at a moderate pace. When it was too slow, Josie could feel the lethargy of the animals, their desperation. Today the non-urgent demands allowed Josie to be equitable in her care, grooming each dog and allotting a dozen brisk strokes per animal. She answered patiently the questions from the would-be adopters as they strolled past the cages appraising their choices, waiting to fall in love. And she helped process two newcomers – a frantic chihuahua and a beagle of opulent girth. Each, she predicted to herself and to them, would be claimed by their owners. Josie could always tell the lost from the abandoned. She thought of Winston, who sometimes seemed *both* lost and abandoned…though other times, he seemed perfectly convinced of belonging wherever he happened to be – often the de la Cruz living room these days.

At lunchtime she walked to the taco stand down the street. Lyle was already there, sitting at one of the outdoor tables shaded by faded green umbrellas, the special – six rolled tacos for $2.99 – in front of him. He had three tacos bunched in his fist and was making quick work of them, his Adam's apple bobbing busily. As she went inside to order, Lyle waved at her and gestured to an empty chair at his table. She gave him a noncommittal look, but ended up bringing her tacos outside to his table after all. He was licking his fingers where hot sauce had trickled, and she wondered if he had washed his hands of cat before eating.

"How many adoptions you get this morning?" he asked. Lyle was competitive that way.

"Three," she told him.

"Ha," Lyle slapped the metal table. "Five cats." He held up five fingers, wiggling them in triumph.

It irritated her that he beat her. There were two euthanizations scheduled that day. They were always in the afternoon in case there might be a reprieve – a last-minute adoption – which never ever happened.

"It's not a contest, Lyle."

He disputed her words with a grin. Josie turned away from his smugness and concentrated on her tacos.

"Hey, I hear your husband's on some kind of trip."

Josie sighed at her own indiscreetness. She had mentioned it in passing over hot chocolate one morning with Troy.

"Road trip with our son," she told Lyle now.

"Male bonding," he said knowingly, and Josie, remembering his claims of fraternity and high jinks in high school, scoffed inwardly.

"So how's your dad?"

Josie was surprised at the sincerity of his concern. Even though he worked at the shelter, she had always suspected him as someone whose surely delinquent past included dipping pigeons in paint or dangling cats from freeway overpasses.

"Better these days." It was true.

"That's good," he said. He tapped dirty fingernails on the table.

They were quiet for a while. Josie felt self-conscious about the crunch of her tacos and the grease on her lips. Then Lyle announced that he had just bought a new stereo system, and soon was narrating in great detail all the features. As she pretended to listen, Josie watched Lyle, his bony face with the sparse mustache that gave it a dirty cast, his floppy hair with the frayed ends, his rangy limbs, and then she thought of Winston's beauty. How hard it was to turn away from.

Often she would come home from work and find Winston there with her father. Sometimes they would be talking, though the topics seemed peculiar, outside of the expected realm of interest or fluency of her father – the habits of geckos or the nesting behavior of sparrows – as if by some agreement their conversation was technical, emotionless. Or so she thought, since their conversation often ceased when she showed up. Then the two of them sat and watched TV together, only a few words passing between them. Josie noticed that unlike the silences that were so typical of her family, their silence was comfortable. It was not without its tension, but it was a tension that again seemed by contract, which was the thorn in Josie's side. Barring the recent and rather occasional stabs at niceness from her father, the tension that she shared with him was the kind that existed between strangers.

"Do you invite him here?" she asked her father once.

"He's welcome to come." He shrugged his shoulders as if he didn't care, and Josie shrugged too, as if she didn't care either.

Though Winston's visits often made Josie's presence superfluous, she didn't wholly resent them. She could conveniently blame them for her lack of opportunities to bond with her father, which, in truth, she hadn't vigorously pursued. Nevertheless, she had complained to Laura and Sara of Winston's frequent visits, but could only elicit mild concern.

"Let's wait and see," was Laura's useless advice.

Sara added her own expendable opinion: "Yeah, it's not as if he's some scoundrel after the family fortune."

Now, as she pretended to listen to Lyle blathering on about amplifiers, she felt herself scowling and wondering – if not the family fortune, then what?

◈ ◈ ◈

After work she stopped at her house to check the mail. Among the bills were two postcards, one from David and one from Gabriel. Gabe's was a picture of the Alamo. *This place is puny. So's the gift shop. Did you know there's a Hooters on the Riverwalk?* David's card was a picture of the Riverwalk, a part without the Hooters. *It's been a long, hot drive. A/C broke down. Looking forward to the coast.*

She and David had made that road trip once, before Gabe was born. They had stopped at the Alamo then too. They watched a group of re-enactors in the courtyard and rooted for the Mexicans. They tried on coonskin caps in the gift shop and were asked to leave because of their too-loud jokes about roadkill. Then they walked across the street to the Crockett Hotel and made love.

She tossed the postcards on the coffee table along with the ones of blazing blue skies in Yuma, Tucson, and Las Cruces. Their destination was Corpus Christi, where David's mother lived. There, he and Gabe would be fed hand-made tortillas every day, *pozole* on Wednesday, and *menudo* on Sunday to compensate for the deprivation they suffered at Josie's hands. Nowadays, she never seemed able to feed them enough.

Gabe had become this hulking teenager whose capacity for food seemed boundless. His grown-up size and deepening voice often startled her when he excused himself from the breakfast table and rose from his chair, leaving behind a plate with only a streak of egg yolk or a smear of bacon grease escaping the demolition done by his appetite. Though she felt a mother's pride in having produced this imposing boy, she found that she was shy with him sometimes, even a little afraid.

Next to the vibrant glossiness of the postcards was the plant David had given her before he left. Josie hated houseplants. They were tricky, temperamental things and she was disinclined to care for them. Wasn't this something a spouse should know after sixteen years of marriage? Why had he given it to her? For company? From guilt? As a test?

The plant was limp and brown at the edges. When she picked it up, it was light as a sponge, all the water in the soil having evaporated. Was it worth saving, she wondered. She took it to the kitchen sink to let it soak for a while. She would take it with her and nurse it back at her parents' house. She sat at the table, taking in the emptiness of the stingily constructed house – the cramped rooms, narrow hallway, the plainness of its unpainted walls. David and Gabe took up so much space in the house that even when they were gone, the space did not seem to belong to her.

She decided to shower while she was there. The sight of the limp plant in the sink made her feel wilted herself. Plus, she smelled like dog.

◈ ◈ ◈

When she arrived washed and feeling new at her parents' house, she noticed that the station wagon was gone, but Winston's Cadillac sat in front, sunlight bouncing off its windows and mirrors. Inside, Winston and her father were at the kitchen table playing cards. Her father, as usual whenever Winston visited, was wearing a shirt and slacks rather than pajamas. He was studying his hand and didn't look up. Winston smiled his celebrity smile at her. He had alarmingly straight teeth.

Josie cared nothing for cards, found the games tedious, and barely paid attention to any conversation remotely related to the subject. Still, she asked, "What are you playing?"

Winston mouthed the word *poker*.

Josie mouthed *oh* back at him. She guessed that the mints from Tessie's candy dish that were scattered on the table were the poker chips. She stood leaning against the wall to make herself unobtrusive to her father. He was squinting at his cards, the muscles in his face retracted upward, deepening the lines at his eyes and across his forehead. Even so, the gauntness in his face was less pronounced and he looked far less cadaverous these days. Josie remembered the moribund plant she had left in her kitchen sink. It would at least collect the slow drips from the leaky faucet she'd been meaning to have fixed.

Finally, her father played his hand, and Winston threw down his cards in defeat. Johnny gathered the mints to his side of the table. "You're going to owe me that Cadillac soon if you're not careful," he said.

"You hate Cadillacs," Josie reminded him. "We all do," she explained to Winston. "Nothing personal."

Winston smiled forgivingly.

Josie knew she had irritated her father. He was making a mess of the mints. He looked at the clock on the wall. Although it hadn't been wound in ages, they were all in the habit of looking there for the time, which was forever 9:05.

"Where's your mother?" he asked her.

Now Josie was irritated. "At her meeting?" She deliberately made it a question. After all, shouldn't he know?

She saw Winston begin to collect and stack the cards, taking great pains to align them.

"Yes, her meeting." Her father seemed satisfied, and for some reason Josie felt compelled to disrupt his composure.

"She's late." Josie showed him her watch. "It's almost four. Her meeting ended over an hour and half ago."

"Errands, maybe?" Winston suggested.

"You're late, too," Johnny said.

"I stopped at home to check my mail." She wished she hadn't forgotten the plant so she could produce it as evidence.

"Any news from the guys?"

Johnny liked to refer to David and Gabe as *the guys*, as if the three of them together were all part of some brotherhood. But while David and Gabe were close and shared an easy, joking rapport, their relationship with Johnny was somewhat stilted. Her father tried too hard to be one of the boys. Josie suspected he was trying to impress Winston.

"More postcards," Josie said. "Same old *wish you were here* stuff."

"How's the housepainting coming?"

"Oh, that," Josie said.

But then Tessie was at the door, and they all turned to greet her as she appeared, looking hot but pleasant-faced, her purse swinging lightly off her shoulder.

"Sorry I'm late," she said a little breathlessly. "We went overtime."

Josie stared at her mother, but Tessie was showing great interest in the poker game. "Well, dear, I see you've won again." Then she scooped one of the mints from Johnny's win pile and popped it into her mouth.

"Go ahead, keep playing. I'm going to start dinner. You staying, Winston?"

Josie thought she saw something flash between her mother and Winston, not anything indecent like a wink or dire like a raised eyebrow, but still something implied and acknowledged.

"Josie, you look a little tired."

"No. I'm not," Josie told her mother, but turned down the hall to the bedroom anyway.

◈ ◈ ◈

She lay on the worn rug, looking up at the ceiling and remembering how badly she used to want to grow up, leave this room, and be someone wonderful.

At age twelve, she had wanted to be a veterinarian. She announced this to her parents, and they smiled indulgently. Her ambition waned by the time she got to college, but she enrolled anyway as a zoology major. She pursued her studies conscientiously, but without passion. There was something missing for her, but she couldn't think what, so she doggedly continued on her path.

After college she had wandered from job to job – a pain research lab where she cataloged facial responses from videotapes of dental patients, a museum where she cataloged small rodents with their tiny snouts and large teeth, a science library where she cataloged her own boredom.

Now she was married and a mother.

Now she shoveled dogshit.

She got up and went to the closet and reached for a folder in the corner. She emptied the folder and laid out on the bed the photographs she had recently taken. The picture of her parents on the sun porch; the picture of Rey asleep; of her mother and Gloria self-consciously sisterly; of her startled, angry self; of the garden art in the front yard and the playhouse in the back. There was also one of Jackson and her together, which she had taken at the shelter one morning. She had knelt beside him, raised the camera to arm's length in front of her and snapped. The result was a foreshortened view of her nose and Jackson's snout. Stark and grotesque, or just plain cheerless?

Then there was the picture of Winston – a photo that could easily rival anything in Tessie's movie magazines. "Pretty thing," she said out loud, though surprising herself at her lack of nastiness, especially given the equivalent of a secret handshake she had just seen between him and her mother. That was the aggravating thing, when admiration, grudging as it was, outweighed jealousy. She placed the photo in the center of the others. She couldn't decide whether it made the other pictures look better or worse. So she left it. For now.

9

ODDS, MEANS, AND ENDS

Winston woke to the small click of metal blades, like the snip of scissors in his hair, and his hand went to his head first before he thought to pull the curtain aside near his bed. He saw a close-up of his new landlady decapitating dead roses inches from his window. Bev waved the glinting clippers at him and smiled, showing breakfast bits in her dentures and multiplying the wrinkles across her cheeks. A flutter of dyed blonde hair peeked above and below her pink Nike-swooshed visor.

"Beautiful day," she said. Her voice, husky from a daily habit of vodka and cigarettes, carried easily through the closed window.

Winston gave a thumbs-up and closed the curtain.

He had abandoned the Beachcomber and was now cozily installed in a narrow but clean and pleasantly furnished room with a hot plate, mini-refrigerator, bathroom, and private entrance. He had answered an ad for a "quiet, responsible tenant willing to play a few sets of tennis on occasion with spry landlady possessing a maniacal forehand."

Since moving into Bev's "classic rambler with 60s charm," Winston had had several opportunities to confirm that, yes, she did have a maniacal forehand that sent the ball whizzing out of bounds, not to mention a backhand that was absent and a serve that almost never made it over the net. "I'm not as good as I used to be," she shouted from the baseline as another one of her serves landed at her feet.

"Can't take much satisfaction in beating a seventy-year-old woman, can you, now?" she asked after each game that Winston tried desperately to lose. "And a widow at that," she added. "No need to feel guilty, though."

Winston gathered that Bev enjoyed her widow status. His mother hadn't been a widow, but she allowed people to believe that she was. "Gone too soon," Bunny would say in reference to Carlitos's absence.

"I'm sorry," they would say, sympathy in their eyes. And Bunny would bravely smile.

"I'm sorry," Winston told Bev.

"Never apologize for winning," Bev admonished. "My late husband never did."

So Winston remained respectfully silent until Bev chided, "Some people might say back, *There's no shame in losing.*"

"Did your late husband say that?"

"Are you kidding?" she snorted. "I'm just saying *some* people might say it."

"There's no shame in losing, Bev."

"You're a sweetie."

◈ ◈ ◈

Bev liked him, as did most women. The notable exceptions were the de la Cruz women. Josie for sure, Tessie, maybe. The others, a good bet. He had only met Laura and Sara a few times, when they had dropped by the house – seemingly with the sole intention of scoping him out – during one of his visits with Johnny. They came in the middle of the workday on some improbable errand. The first time, they came together, Laura in her white optometrist's smock and Sara in a yellow SubClub T-shirt. Laura brought lens cleaner for Johnny's glasses.

"Here, let me see those," she said, lifting Johnny's glasses off his face. She squirted cleaner on them, wiped them with a small cloth, and held them up to the light – which happened to be in Winston's direction – and peered at them through her own glasses.

"That should do it," she announced, settling the glasses back on her father. "That should help you see better."

She smiled at Winston. "So what have you two been up to?"

"Just reading the newspaper," he told them. "Watching Court TV, drinking iced tea in the front yard. That sort of thing."

"I see," Laura said, looking hard at Winston.

Johnny had been silent during this interrogation. Sara had leaned toward Winston and said, as a sort of aside, "If he doesn't talk much, don't take it personally." Winston suspected that *she* took such things personally.

He saw them each again separately. One morning Laura was there when he arrived. She was reading the newspaper to Johnny. Another day, Sara stayed to watch Judge Judy with them after dropping by with a box of day-old cookies, which the SubClub had been unable to sell at half price. Later, after Sara had gone, Johnny insisted Winston take the cookies home with him.

Winston took his bowl of cereal outside. The door to his apartment opened to the side yard of Bev's bungalow, and Winston sat down near her bucket that contained the dead heads of roses. Many more still lingered on the bush, but Bev was nowhere in sight. She was a slapdash gardener, abandoning tasks minutes after beginning them. It was not from fatigue or fragility. Bev was an unusually fit septuagenarian. "Life is short," she would say, leaving the lawn half-watered or the planter box only partially plucked of weeds, dashing off to some other more pressing matter.

The day was already warm. The milk from his cereal was sticky in his mouth. The smell of dying roses crept inside his nose. The air was still, no breeze to carry the ocean to Bev's house today. On days like this one, Winston felt defeated in his pursuit of Johnny de la Cruz.

It was true they had reached a kind of accord, circling around each other in conversation, their dance of words a simple do-si-do. They spoke first of things in Kimball Park – the new freeway that roared through the middle of it, the proliferation of noodle huts that threatened to outnumber taco stands, the graffiti everywhere, even on swatches of earth.

"It's no Disneyland," Johnny would say, a joke that would lead them to the topic of Anaheim. Winston would duly share mundane aspects of his life there, incorporating references to Bunny a little at a time, but – sensing the undeclared boundaries – never making her the focus.

Winston was the one who always initiated their meetings. Despite Johnny's gruff manner and few words, he displayed little resistance to Winston's overtures, which were after all modest and measured. At times, Johnny seemed to welcome his presence, even when they did little more than watch TV in silence. But Winston couldn't help wondering if Johnny was merely tolerating him.

When Johnny fell asleep, sometimes Winston closed his eyes too and thought about Bunny, wondering just what she had meant to Johnny, and he to her. Inevitably, though, thoughts about Carlitos intervened, and Winston had to wonder too what his father and Bunny had meant to each other.

Sometimes he sought Tessie out. She was always polite, but distant. He wanted Tessie to like him, wanted her to know that he could be trusted not to mention his seeing her at Armida's.

He liked her, liked her laughter which seemed charged with music, bouncy like the Barry Manilow tunes she hummed. He liked her mispronunciations and mangled idioms, and often gently baited her so he could hear her describe the local news anchor as a drip in the bucket. She always asked him how he was doing, and before he could answer, told him to help himself to anything in the refrigerator. He made small talk while she peeled potatoes at the counter or stirred soup at the stove. The radio played softly in the kitchen, and when something fast and rhythmic came on, Winston thought of her at Armida's studio. He was tempted to ask her to dance, but despite her show of friendliness toward him, this thing called Bunny came between them like the sliding glass pane at drive-up bank windows.

On days when Tessie wasn't there, he wandered the house, taking note of the old Book-of-the-Month Club selections on the undusted bookshelf, the packaged foods that lined the kitchen counter, the mail piled on the table in the hall. And every so often Winston thought of Bunny's letter, still stowed safely in the glove compartment of Felix's car. It could stay there forever, or for as long as Johnny was willing to do-si-do.

Bev came around the corner wielding her tennis racquet, slashing the air with her forehand. She laughed when she saw Winston's face. "Relax, kid. I've got a tennis date with someone else."

"Who?" Winston asked, relieved.

"Well, wouldn't you like to know?" she teased, pirouetting in Lycra tennis togs, the tanned wrinkles at her knees and elbows waggling as she danced. Bev had flossed the breakfast from her teeth, applied untidy streaks of color to her lips, and dusted her cheeks with pre-workout spots of pink. She smelled lemony, the citrus of household cleaner.

"It's the Seniors Mix and Match at the tennis club," she confessed. "With any luck, I'll draw a partner with a killer backhand and a weakness for unnatural blondes."

"Go get 'em, Bev."

"Hey, you have fun today, too. You going to see your friends again?"

Winston nodded. *Friends*: the word he had used to describe the de la Cruzes to Bev. He waved, and Bev swatted the air with her racquet. It made a sound like a giant scoffing sigh.

◈ ◈ ◈

At the mini-mart gas station, he filled his tank, checked his tires, and bought some butterscotch candies that he knew Rey and Johnny liked. He tossed the candy in the glove compartment and looked at his watch.

"Come on Tuesday morning at eleven," Rey had said.

"Make it ten," Johnny said.

A few days earlier at Johnny's, Rey had come by with a jar of pennies, and the three of them played a few hands of poker. Both of the older men took the game seriously. They were silent and glowering with concentration, and Winston was glad when each of them won a game. Rey pulled his pile of pennies toward him and stacked them in little towers. He grimaced at the unimposing effect.

"Johnny, you should get this boy to take us to the casino. We can win some real money."

Winston had laughed it off, thinking it was just a joke. But here he was, keeping his ten o'clock date and hoping it really was a joke and they would laugh at him when he walked in the door.

Rey's car was parked in front when he drove up, and it was Rey who came to the door. Though the sight of him made Winston stifle a laugh, he realized Rey's appearance meant the casino was a serious proposition.

"You're prompt. I like that," Rey said, and turned around and led the way into the living room where he sat down beside Johnny.

Winston looked at them, side by side, dressed in what might have been their Sunday best, had church been a Saturday Night Fever discotheque for aging Filipino men. Rey wore a white *barong* with pants the color of lime sherbet. Johnny was similarly decked out in baby blue pants and a blue and white print shirt of an indeterminate pattern, perhaps clouds or treetops. Between them rested a paper grocery sack and a straw boater with a green feather – Rey's accessories, Winston guessed.

"You sure you're up to this?" Winston asked Johnny.

"No worries," Rey said. "He took his medicine already. We'll take blankets and pillows so he can rest on the way." He pointed to the chair where they were stacked.

Winston hesitated. He wondered if Tessie knew about the outing, wondered if he should ask. He dreaded keeping another secret. "Is Tessie around?"

"No," Johnny said, his face going dark above the placid blue of his shirt. "Why?"

But Rey was already on his feet and pulling Johnny to his, so Winston picked up the blanket and pillows and led the way to the door. He waited for the two older men to shuffle past him, first Johnny in blue and then lime-sherbet Rey, now with the hat on his head and the sack tucked under an arm. Rey paused to tap Winston lightly in the chest.

"Sure you're up to this?" He didn't wait for an answer, just chuckled as he accelerated his shuffle to catch up to Johnny.

While Rey scooted himself and his grocery bag into the back seat, Winston settled Johnny into the front passenger seat, arranging a pillow at his back and side and a blanket under his sneakers. Then Winston checked his mirrors, checked his passengers, slipped on his sunglasses, and started the engine.

"Here we go, guys' day out in a Cadillac," Rey said, and when they pulled away from the curb, Johnny let loose a whoop that nearly caused Winston to brake.

Rey laughed. Johnny patted Winston's shoulder. "You okay, son?"

Winston went light-headed at the remark and barely managed a yes.

After Rey had directed him to a shortcut to the freeway, Winston heard the fizz of a soda can, and then Rey was thrusting a ginger ale between the front seats. Johnny took the can, spilling a fat drop on his pants.

"Napkins in the glove compartment," Winston said, but Johnny was looking out the window, watching the ugly freeway scenery – large colorless buildings, oversized signs missing letters, ragged palm trees.

"I've got coffee, too," Rey said. "You want coffee?"

Winston checked his rear view mirror and saw Rey pulling a thermos from the grocery bag. He imagined the upholstery of Felix's car dappled with stains from Rey's sack lunch.

"Need any napkins back there?"

"Don't worry, son, just drive."

So now Rey had called him *son*, too. A figure of speech, a casual address, nothing more. Winston turned his eyes to the road.

◈ ◈ ◈

There was little conversation for most of the trip. Johnny was content to look out the window, while Rey rattled on about what he might do with his casino winnings. Every so often, one of the old men dozed off, but when both men fell asleep, Winston felt a panic rise inside him and he drove faster, the sooner to arrive and wake them. At least the snores indicated they were still breathing.

Like children, they woke up as the car neared its destination. Winston leaned across to flip open the glove compartment and extract some candy. He turned onto the reservation and started the Cadillac on the winding climb to the casino. They all sucked on butterscotch as they looked out the windows at the haggard hills, occasional house or trailer home, a listless dog panting in the shade of a rusted truck.

As the road narrowed and steepened, Winston had to slow down behind one of the casino buses that brought senior citizens from the city for an afternoon of gambling.

"When we're old, we'll have to take that bus, eh, Johnny?" Rey joked.

Winston took a cue from the casino bus and stopped to unload his passengers at the curb to save them the walk from the parking lot. He waited while Rey transferred the peanut butter sandwiches from the grocery bag to his jacket pocket. When both men were safely on the sidewalk, Winston, nervous about leaving them unattended, hurried away to park the car. When he returned, Rey and Johnny had already headed inside, wanting to keep up with the group of seniors that had disembarked from the bus and were now making a creeping beeline to the gaming hall. Rey and Johnny were making surprising progress with their shuffling steps. Fearing a sudden tumble forward or backward and a pile of blue or green polyester on the carpet, Winston jogged to catch up to Rey and Johnny. He walked close behind them, his hands at the ready.

They were men on a mission, keeping a slow but steady pace down the long corridor bright with chandeliers and mirrors. Finally, they reached the gaming hall, where the ambiance abruptly changed. The room was dim, lit mostly by the flashing lights of the slot machines. Music seemed to come from everywhere – Motown hits piped in overhead and tinny tunes emanating from the different banks of machines, each with its own theme of has-been TV sit-coms: *I Dream of Jeannie*, *The Munsters*, *Bewitched*.

To Winston's surprise, Rey and Johnny settled themselves at the slot machines rather than head to the poker and blackjack tables in the middle of the room. They hoisted their pastel bottoms onto the deeply padded stools meant to invite long periods of sitting. They spaced themselves apart, with an empty machine between them, and that's where Winston seated himself to watch. Rey and Johnny immediately went to work, playing twenty dollars' worth of quarters at a time. At first he tried to pay careful attention to their results, hoping to track their losses, so that he might cover them if he could. But this required him to lean quite a bit – first one way and then the other. The back-and-forth crane of his neck made a conspicuous seesaw.

Rey stopped his lever-pulling to look at him. "It's not a spectator sport, you know."

"Just taking in the atmosphere," Winston said. He swiveled his chair to survey the glittering machines that lit the washed-out faces of the people hunched in front of them. Most were senior citizens, some in wheelchairs, some with aluminum walkers parked at their side. There was a scattering of middle-agers, probably playing hooky from work, or out of work and trying to extend their unemployment benefits. Across from them, a man in a plaid vest and bow tie balanced a cigarette on his lip as he studied his machine, squinting through his own smoke. Every so often his ruddy face went a deeper red with fits of coughing that required him to temporarily remove his cigarette.

Winston watched his charges carefully for signs of breathlessness or fatigue, but his surveillance was often interrupted by the gofer duties – fetching water or coffee, making change – Rey and Johnny had assigned him. They were unwilling to budge from their seats, fearful that abandoning their machine would only prove lucky for the next person.

Once, when Winston accidentally leaned his hand against Rey's machine, it clanged to signal three of a kind. For the next few rounds, Rey required Winston to touch his machine before each pull of the lever. But the superstition didn't last long, and Rey told Winston to never mind. "Not such a good luck charm, after all."

After a while, Winston said, "Hey, you guys want to take a break and get something to eat?"

Neither of the men looked up, but Rey pulled the sandwiches, smashed and soft, from his pocket. He handed one to Winston and shoved the other past him to Johnny. As they continued to push buttons and pull levers, Rey and Johnny grazed at the flattened slices of bread glued by peanut butter, washing it all down with the water and coffee Winston kept provisioning. Just when Winston wondered when they would need a bathroom break, Rey turned to Johnny, "You want to go first?"

Johnny got up slowly, and Winston got up to accompany him.

"No!" Johnny and Rey shouted together.

"Sit there," Rey instructed Winston, and nudged him toward Johnny's machine.

Winston sat but swiveled to track Johnny's trek to the men's room and stared at the door until Johnny emerged some long minutes later.

"Okay, my turn," Rey announced. He patted his stool. "Take over, kid."

Winston took Rey's seat but had lost his patience. Rather than watch Rey shamble down the aisle of slot machines, he turned to Johnny, who remained riveted to his game. The lights from the machine played on his face, making his cheeks stark and skeletal. He was in a rhythm, punching his bet, pulling the lever, watching the pot grow or diminish. A certain energy flowed from his fingers to the machine and then back again, fueled by the possibility that one more pull of the lever would deliver the big prize.

"You think we ought to be getting back soon?"

Johnny tapped the display screen a few times before looking up. "No, Winston. Do you?"

"I just thought…" Winston didn't finish, since Johnny didn't seem to be listening. Besides, Winston didn't know exactly what he *did* think. Just when he believed himself to be on the verge of a small breakthrough with Johnny, he found himself playing chauffeur to two senior citizens in unspeakably bad clothes. He had never been with Johnny outside of the de la Cruz home, and he missed the safety of that tedious – but now familiar setting – where across the kitchen table from each other, or side by side in front of the TV, they had established a tenuous connection.

Rey came back and nudged him off his chair. "Nothing for you to do here. Go play on your own." He made a shooing motion like someone chasing a hungry dog from the kitchen door.

When Johnny didn't offer an invitation to stay, Winston got up, feeling rather harshly dismissed. "Okay, I'll meet you back here in half an hour." But his words seemed lost on the two old men absorbed in their machines. He would give them fifteen minutes, maybe twenty, then he'd be more forceful and take charge. After all, he was the chauffeur, he told himself grimly.

He wandered until he found himself at a blackjack table. There were only two people playing, sitting at opposite ends of the table. Winston stood behind an empty stool in the middle and watched. The dealer, a young woman with dark roots and heavy makeup, looked at him occasionally as she flicked cards onto the green baize. When her eyes were lowered, he could see her painted lids and the gummy blackness of her lashes. A lamp hung above the table, illuminating her powdery face and the frowns of concentration on her customers. Standing behind the chair, Winston had meant to stay out of the lamplight, but the dealer pointed her deck of cards at him.

"You in or out?"

She wore a nametag that said Mandy, and Winston thought of the Barry Manilow tune and then of Tessie, and then of the fact that he had brought Johnny to a mountaintop Indian casino probably without her knowledge.

The two other players looked at him.

Winston sat and plunked down money for tokens, which Mandy pushed toward him with the professionalism conferred by her fake velvet dealer's vest. The game moved quickly, Mandy's hands flitting smoothly across the table as she delivered cards or swept them back into the deck. Winston's mind moved just as quickly, placing his bet, adding up his cards, opting or not for another. He could always perform under fire, and his stack of tokens grew. And while a steady stream of people came to the table, only to leave a few rounds later with little or no gain, Winston stayed and grew his stacks. Of course he had setbacks, but they were small, and he was on a streak. He was winning, because winning was what Winston did. Mandy broke her professional demeanor a few times and smiled at him, but Winston never blinked, until over the music and through his concentration, he became aware of a spasm of activity somewhere in the background.

"Someone's down at the slot machines again," Mandy said. "Probably another heart attack." She flipped a card onto the table in front of Winston. But Winston never looked at it, tumbling his stack of tokens in his haste to sprint from the table.

"Hey," Mandy called. "You forfeit to the house."

As he pushed his way past a circle of onlookers, Winston feared a larger forfeit than the one at the blackjack table. He saw two people crouched over someone splayed out on the floor. Winston gasped with relief when he saw that the man on the floor wore neither sherbet green nor baby blue pants. It was the man, once ruddy and now colorless, who had been playing opposite Rey and Johnny. Winston looked around. Rey and Johnny were nowhere in sight.

Winston approached one of the security guards who had come over to disperse the crowd. "Have you seen two old guys? They were sitting right over there playing the slots."

The guard eyed him as if Winston might somehow be responsible for men keeling off gambling stools. "Hey, look around. There are old guys everywhere."

Winston stepped back, craned his neck, turning in a circle, squinting through the dimness and smoke, hoping for the glimmer of a *barong*, a glimpse of blurry blue shapes on a shirt. Sweat skittered from his armpit past his ribs to his waistband. Medics were lifting the man on the floor to a stretcher, and Winston stared at him one more time to make sure that it wasn't Rey or Johnny, almost wishing that it was so at least he would have located one of them.

Winston hurried to the men's room, but there was only one occupied stall beneath which a pair of cowboy boots was visible. He ran to the gift shop, but there was only the clerk idle and bored at the cash register. Winston felt an ache at the roots of his hair as he rushed back out to the game floor, where the music stabbed at his scalp. He jogged the aisles, looking up and down the banks of slot machines, until finally he was in an aisle whose path was lit by small beckoning arrows. Winston raced down it and was delivered at the end to the entrance of the casino restaurant. Here everything was illuminated and the smell of steamed vegetables, oily salad dressings, and garlic bread hit his nostrils. He headed to the salad bar in the middle of the restaurant and scanned the room. When he saw them sitting side by side in a booth – Rey cleaning the meat from a drumstick with his teeth, Johnny wiping soup from his chin – he felt his chest unclench. As he moved forward on rubbery legs, he stuffed his hands in his pockets to keep his anger in check.

"Where've you been?" Rey practically scolded as Winston approached in a forced saunter.

"I've been looking for you," he told them, trying to curb the scold in his own voice.

"Well, here we are." Rey waved his naked drumstick at himself and Johnny.

Winston felt the anger threatening to escape him and spill upon the two old men and their buffet lunch.

"Didn't Ernie tell you?" Johnny asked.

"Who the *hell* is Ernie?"

Winston saw Johnny and Rey exchange looks at his outburst. Part of him wanted to take it back; part of him wanted to utterly let loose on them.

Rey shook his head. "I knew we couldn't rely on that guy."

"Yeah," Johnny agreed, "Mr. Plaid Vest." He and Rey chuckled at the mention of the man's tacky apparel.

"Oh, jeez," Winston breathed.

Rey and Johnny were staring at him. He wanted to tell them that Ernie was unconscious on the gaming floor, his plaid vest ripped open so medics could pound his chest. He wanted to tell them it could have been either one of them on the floor. He wanted to punish them for abandoning him and making him look for them.

"Sit down," Johnny told him.

Winston remained standing, uncertain, flustered.

"Eat," Johnny said. "We ordered the special for you."

"A thank-you for guys' day out," Rey said.

"Sit," Johnny said again, gesturing at the extra plate of food.

It was a club sandwich with fries and a salad. Winston sat down, and even though the fries were cold and the salad was soggy with dressing, he ate, voraciously and with vast relief. Rey and Johnny looked on, pleased at his appetite, pleased with themselves.

"You want dessert?" Rey asked. "It's on us."

"Anything you want," Johnny said.

Winston, his stomach roiling with grease, hiccups threatening his esophagus, now knew that he had won them over. Even as they all indulged in the hot fudge sundaes they ordered, traces of whipped cream at the corners of their lips, he felt just the slightest unease. He plucked the cherry that decorated his ice cream dish and popped it into his mouth. *Don't apologize for winning*, he told himself.

◈ ◈ ◈

On the way back, Johnny wanted to ride in the back seat. He immediately fell asleep. Though Winston was anxious to get him home, he did stop once on a whim at a gas and food mart. "I'll just be a minute," he told Rey. He returned with a sheaf of lottery tickets. "For you and Johnny," he said. "I think it's our lucky day."

Rey, who was sucking on a butterscotch candy, held out his hand.

IO

UNINVITED

Johnny sat bolstered in his chair, his back cradled by a hot water bottle, the soft edge of a blanket pulled across his chest and tucked under his armpits. It was a cool morning, with fog softly pushing down on the world. He was glad to be bundled up, though he knew that despite the fog, there was the threat of sudden awful heat. For now, he nestled into the cushions and drew the blanket to his shoulders, leaving exposed his feet sheathed in white tube socks that were baggy at the toes.

Johnny remembered the ride in Winston's Cadillac, how smooth it was, how the leather seats welcomed him. He had always had a disdain for flashy cars and was annoyed at his neighbors who cherished them. "Just like a Pinoy," Tessie would say, as if Filipinos were the only ones who drove a Seville or DeVille or a Fleetwood. But now that he had ridden in one, he had to admit the Big American Dream Caddy really was a classy car. Winston was a classy fellow. A graceful young man, accomplished, with good manners and social ease. The kind of son he had always imagined for himself. And that was the trouble. He could only imagine such a son, because how could someone like himself have produced such a young man? Johnny was not ignorant of his own shortcomings, especially when he saw them repeated in his daughters – the awkwardness and hesitancy with which they stumbled from childhood through adolescence to confused adulthood, in constant anticipation that life would begin to happen at any moment, but fearful at heart that it had already happened without them.

Of course, he had done the math over and over, even before Winston's first visit, but there was nothing in Winston's features to suggest that he could be Johnny's son. Johnny picked up one of the framed photographs on the table beside him. He took off his glasses and peered up close at his reflection in the glass, which offered back unnecessary details – the lines and pouches below and the puffy lids above his eyes, his mouth reshaped by partial dentures and missing teeth.

Johnny tried to recall what Carlitos looked like, but he had only a vague recollection of a man whose good looks were due more to an aggregate pleasantness than to any one feature of note. He had paid little attention to Carlitos when he met him and he cursed him now for not being at the apartment that afternoon.

After his visit to Bunny in Manila, he had never attempted to contact her. He had wanted only to forget that afternoon, and apparently she had too. He'd never heard from her, not even through Nora. When he left the Philippines that second time, it was with a sense of leaving everything behind…but now here was Winston, chasing him like a lost puppy after a lap to rest on. Johnny was willing to give him only that, a temporary place to settle himself, to gather his thoughts in the aftermath of Bunny's death. Johnny wasn't sure what Winston knew – or thought he knew – about him, but he didn't seem a malicious young man. Johnny blamed Bunny – for not staying in the Philippines. It was where she belonged. For him, anyway.

◈ ◈ ◈

Johnny sat without his glasses on and looked around him at the indistinct shapes. Nothing had boundaries: objects blended one with the other; dimensions barely registered.

He heard footsteps on the carpet and turned to see Tessie approach from the hallway. He could make out the dark blur of her head, the yellow splash of fabric at her torso marred by a muddy blob, and, astonishingly, her nakedness from the waist down. He had lately begun to believe that he had had some small triumphs with Tessie, flashes of tenderness, a touch prolonged for just a second, a meeting of the eyes. But not even in their younger years, when they were both more or less in brisk form, had Tessie been so bold as to walk the halls half-naked. She stopped in front of him and he squinted shamelessly.

"Are you okay?" Her hands went to her brown hips. There was something wrinkled and misshapen about her thighs.

Johnny remembered he didn't have his glasses on and felt foolish. He put them on now and saw Tessie in full focus. She was not half-naked. She was wearing brown shorts and the blob on her T-shirt was the SubClub logo. Sara had given them store logowear. Johnny never wore T-shirts with advertisements.

Tessie began tying a bandanna over her hair as she headed for the kitchen.

"Where are you going?" Johnny asked, because he wanted her company.

"To the Bahamas."

She came back with the broom and dustpan in her hands. "What are your plans for today?"

Johnny wanted to make her laugh. He scratched his head and pretended to look thoughtful. "Let me check my calendar," he said.

"Well, you did go out the other day with Winston and Rey."

"Just for a drive in his Cadillac," he said, trying to sound casual.

"So you said." She headed to the sun porch, humming "Copacabana."

Tessie hadn't been home when Winston brought him and Rey back from the casino. Exhausted, he had allowed Winston to help him change into pajamas. Even his shirt and pants looked spent, draped over a chair. He fell asleep before Winston left, despite the deep ache in his bones. When he woke hours later, it was dusk outside and darker inside, and Tessie was sitting on the bed beside him.

"Where did you go today?" she asked.

Johnny thought about the times Tessie left the house on a supposed errand, only to return rejuvenated, as if she really had been to the Bahamas.

And then he had a spasm of pain in his arms and legs, and though it was only a small spasm, he winced. Tessie began massaging his limbs, dutifully though somewhat recklessly. She seemed unaware that her blouse was unbuttoned. He could see the sway of her breasts as she bent over his thin legs.

◈ ◈ ◈

He had taken his glasses off again to see the pattern in the carpet diffuse into amoeba shapes when he heard Tessie scream, not once but a succession of screams strung together by frantic gasps. He groped in his lap for his glasses and when they were on his face, he groped again, trying to find his way out of the blanket that now seemed like a straitjacket around him. Finally, he had his feet on the floor, and after nearly tripping on the extra length in his socks, he hurried to the sun porch to find Tessie. She was standing on the wicker loveseat, her broom held in front of her and aimed at the corner, where a snake lay uncurled and tensed.

"Why is a snake in our house?" she demanded, laughing nervously.

Johnny stepped forward slowly and motioned for Tessie to give him the broom, which she surrendered reluctantly. "Where's Josie?" she whispered, now mimicking Johnny's stealth.

Johnny ignored her. If Josie were here, she would take the side of the snake. He continued his advance. The snake twitched and then began to slither along the wall, and then without warning it accelerated straight at him.

"Get it!" Tessie screamed.

Johnny had only meant to guide it out the door, but Tessie's cry spurred him to combat, and he beat the snake into retreat with the slap of broom bristles, a tactic that inflicted little damage though it caused a shiver in Johnny's forearm. The snake, though perfectly still, seemed angry and disoriented.

"It's playing dead," Tessie said, accusation in her voice, not taking her eyes off it, determined not to be taken in by its trickery.

Johnny, now bent on finishing off the snake, also refused to be taken in. He flipped the broom in his hand so that now he was pointing its end like a spear at the snake.

"That won't work," Tessie hissed. She pointed to the loveseat she was standing on. "Under here."

Tessie kept a baseball bat stashed near each entrance to their home, in the event of intruders. Johnny lowered himself carefully to his knees, grabbed the bat, and then planted the fat end on the floor to help raise himself back to standing. He panted for breath. His forearm tingled with the weight of the bat as he lifted it, aimed, and brought a direct hit to the tiny skull – which sent a searing stab along the length of his arm. The snake convulsed and then went limp. Tessie screamed at the violence. Johnny fell to the floor, holding his arm, weakened from disease, and now smashed to pieces with his questionable heroics. He squeezed his eyes against the pain, curled his legs to his chest, and rocked from side to side.

◈ ◈ ◈

Paramedics immobilized his arm, dosed him with a painkiller, and strapped him onto a gurney. They wheeled him through the house and out the front door and into the stark sunlight which had burned away the fog and made the air heavy with heat. Tessie stood beside him on the driveway, holding his good arm, apologizing, telling him everything would be okay.

The paramedics lined the stretcher up to the waiting ambulance and Johnny could see the waves of red that the flashing light on the roof threw on their faces. He could sense a small crowd gathering and could hear their concerned and curious inquiries. He was glad that the businesslike paramedics asked them to step back and that Tessie was too distraught to acknowledge any of the neighbors. No one needed to know he had shattered his arm swinging a baseball bat at a snake.

The paramedics were about to lift him into the ambulance when the shriek of tires skidding to a stop made them pause. The paramedics, Tessie, and the crowd of onlookers turned their heads. He heard running footsteps, and then Tessie let the world in on Johnny's plight: "Winston, Johnny broke his arm. There was a goddamned snake."

Winston leaned across the metal rail of the gurney so that his face was up close, closer than Johnny had ever seen it. There were Bunny's long lashes and well-shaped, expressive eyebrows.

"It's okay, Johnny," Winston said, and for a moment Johnny thought he was being forgiven for something. But no, they were words of reassurance, of promised harmony, and he thought he should return the sentiment.

As the paramedics started to slide the stretcher into the

ambulance, Winston gave Johnny's good hand a squeeze, then released it so quickly that Johnny wasn't sure if he had squeezed back.

◈ ◈ ◈

The doctors wanted to keep him in the hospital for a few days. His bones were fragile. They required observation. He looked at the cast that held his arm together. He had broken in it three places, the fissuring occurring during the swing of his arm; the snapping, on impact.

Tessie sat in the chair beside his bed. She was still in her brown shorts and mustard T-shirt. Winston stood at the foot of the bed underneath the ceiling-mounted TV. Tessie was calm, almost cheerful now.

"Are you still in pain, dear?"

"No, I don't think so," he said, though he knew his answer didn't make sense. You either hurt or you didn't. Either way, you knew.

"Not exactly pain," he tried to clarify. A loss of feeling, a numbness, he thought.

"More like pressure?" Winston asked. "I broke my arm once too."

Johnny felt himself brighten at this revelation that someone so composed and in command of his body could have suffered a similar mishap.

"How did it happen?" Tessie asked. "Playing tennis?"

Johnny wondered why Tessie knew Winston played tennis. Winston had never mentioned it to him.

"Well, not exactly *playing* tennis. I jumped over the net after a match and my shoe caught in the webbing. Came down right on my arm."

Johnny appreciated Winston's generosity in confessing such a blunder.

Tessie smiled.

Now Johnny wondered if this dialogue had been staged for his benefit, wondered if they had plotted together as they drove to the hospital in the Cadillac. Johnny felt a little jealous that now Tessie had ridden in the Cadillac, too.

But then she turned to Johnny, her eyes watery. "Thanks for killing that awful snake." She leaned over and stroked his cast. He watched the back-and-forth movement of her fingers, which were deeply creased at the joints. He put his good hand over hers and held it still, feeling the weight of both their hands on his cast. When she leaned over to kiss his forehead, the SubClub logo on her shirt brushed against his glasses; when she drew back, there was lint on his lenses.

It was quiet in the room except for the click of the minute hand on the wall clock. Johnny looked up and was surprised to find how much time had passed since sitting in his chair that morning. The sun was still bright outside, but the chill of the hospital room isolated them from its heat. At home, it would be penetrating the sun porch, becoming trapped there so that everything absorbed it: the cushions on the loveseat, the drowsy philodendron in the corner, the baseball bat in the middle of the floor, and the dead snake against the wall. Josie would be heading home soon, and she would find it there. He didn't want her to stumble upon the awful sight of it. But more than that, he didn't want her to mourn the snake more than his broken bones.

"It's still on the sun porch," Johnny said.

"Oh, God," Tessie shrank in her chair.

"I'll take care of it," Winston said, stepping forward, ready to be of service. Johnny was relieved to see him out from under the drop zone of the TV.

Johnny and Tessie watched him leave. Afterward, Tessie hummed awhile to make up for Winston's absence, then suddenly stopped, a question on her face.

Johnny sipped from the glass of water on the bed tray. It tasted of dust and sanitizer.

"So what was Bunny like?"

He heard both curiosity and unease in Tessie's voice. She had never really asked about Bunny before – even after that first phone call from Winston. Bunny was just someone from his hometown, someone from a long time ago, someone who was now dead. Johnny knew Tessie couldn't imagine him interested in a girl from the islands. She had always considered the girls "back home" as foreign, far from her American ways, not worth asking about. Until now.

Johnny shrugged and the water in the glass swirled over the rim onto the sheet. "She was just a girl when I knew her."

"You never saw her when you went back again?"

He couldn't recall ever having lied to Tessie – except for small things, like telling her no, the meatloaf wasn't too dry, or that he liked her new hairdo, when in fact he hated the stiffness and overly sweet odor of it.

"Briefly," Johnny said. "At Nora's house. With her husband."

"What was he like?"

"Quiet," Johnny said. "Polite."

"Like Winston," Tessie remarked, as if such a thing were hereditary, coiled neatly in one's genes.

Tessie hummed again. It made Johnny edgy – even edgier when she broke off.

"It would've been nice," she said.

"What?" He wished she hadn't stopped humming.

"To have had a son."

They hadn't said such a thing out loud in years. He felt as if she'd crossed a boundary, broken a pact, invited heartbreak. He groaned softly.

She touched him lightly above the cast. “Does it hurt?” she said.

He didn’t know what to say. He wasn’t sure what she was talking about. The possibility that Winston *could* be his son did pain him – and elated him, though he had hardly acknowledged either feeling, keeping them at arm’s length the way he had always kept his daughters. Even Tessie.

“Yes,” he told her.

“At least it’s only a few days here,” Tessie said. “Do you want to watch some TV?” She handed him the remote, and they both stared at a man in a flowered tie giving the weather report.

◈ ◈ ◈

He woke up to find Tessie gone, tried to find a trace of her scent in the aseptic room, but found none. It was dinnertime, he knew without looking at the clock. The smell of food steamed to death that always filled hospital corridors at mealtimes filled his nostrils. He straightened his glasses, which had slanted off his face while he slept, and looked over at his bed tray. There was his dinner. He lifted the plastic lid. Rice with bits of vegetables and soft shreds of gray meat. A dish of applesauce on the side. Pudding for dessert. A packet of instant coffee and a tea bag next to a cup of hot water.

A *Gilligan’s Island* rerun played on the TV. He turned the volume down and watched the Skipper chase Gilligan around a coconut tree. He took off his glasses and saw only wavering splotches of color. On his tray, the food was a smear of browns and yellows. He switched to a news station and ate his squishy food while he listened to the day’s miseries and triumphs – genocide in Yugoslavia, starvation in Somalia, a twelve-year-old boy granted a divorce from his parents, slogan-shouting picketers at an abortion clinic.

He knew the screen was filled with protesters holding signs aloft with pictures of babies and fetuses that looked as though they were pleading. He had seen such footage many times before and had never let it inside his brain, but lately his brain had been vulnerable to ambush and assaults from the past. He stared at the blurry images on TV and kept his glasses off, as if the memory of the abortion could be softened by his poor vision.

◈ ◈ ◈

Johnny had borrowed Louie Sebastian's two-toned Mercury, silvery blue and white, with a guarantee that he would return it waxed and polished on the outside and free of lint and odors on the inside. Johnny had already meticulously groomed the car when he drove to Tessie's house, honking the horn as he pulled up, alerting the entire block to his arrival. Tessie, her face lit with a smile and rouge, loped down the walkway in her long stride, the soft fabric of her skirt folding around her thighs as she moved. Ruby and Lydia followed on her heels, elbowing each other for the lead. Johnny got out of the car, came around to the passenger side, and leaned, arms crossed, against the fender as the girls admired the car.

"Take us for a ride," Ruby pleaded, working her eyelashes too sexily for a fifteen-year-old.

Tessie aimed a look at her sister. "No, we'll be late for the movie."

"Just around the block," Lydia insisted.

Johnny uncrossed his arms and stood up straight as Tessie's father banged out the front door, scuttling toward them with his bowlegs, and puffing on the stub of a cigar. He motioned for Johnny to get in the car. "Take me to the store. I need some cigars."

"*Y leche*!" Tessie's mother called from the window. She eyed the car suspiciously.

Ruby and Lydia jumped in the back seat, and Johnny drove off, leaving Tessie standing at the curb. He saw her in his rear view mirror, saw the wind lift her hair away from her shoulders and press her skirt against her legs.

"Go three blocks and turn right," Mr. Navarro said, pointing with his lit cigar – which was filling the car with its smoke.

Lydia opened her window and leaned her arm out, her bracelets swinging against the car's finish. "I hope someone sees us."

Johnny pulled up at the HiHo Market, and Mr. Navarro and Lydia got out. Ruby climbed over the front seat, the heels of her shoes sliding over the upholstery. She smiled at Johnny. "I'll wait with you."

She was wearing pedal pushers, so the lower half of her legs was exposed. She crossed her legs and let the shoe on her top leg dangle from her toes.

"So what movie are you and Tessie going to see?"

Johnny couldn't remember the name of it. He wasn't fond of the movies Tessie liked. "The one at the Roxy," he told her, hoping that would be enough.

Ruby smirked

"You're lucky my parents let Tessie go out without a chaperone now. Gloria convinced them." She swiveled the rear view mirror to apply lipstick from a grimy tube she pulled from her pocket. "I think they're wrong." She smacked her lips. "Very, very wrong."

Johnny returned the mirror to its correct position. Ruby was not a good girl, he decided. Bad things will happen to her. Ruby looked out the window and hummed as she twirled a strand of hair around her finger. "If you want to marry her, you have to be good," she said. Then she swung herself over the back seat, and Johnny turned his head so her hip wouldn't graze his temple.

As Mr. Navarro and Lydia emerged from the store, he glanced

in the rear view mirror at Ruby, who smiled at him. "This is a really nice car."

When he drove them back to the house, Tessie was sitting on the steps, her knees and ankles together and tilted to one side. She leaned back on her elbows so that her breasts, outlined in her sweater, jutted forward. It was almost natural, her movie-star pose.

Mr. Navarro, looking stern, held the door open for his daughter, and Tessie offered an obedient smile as she moved past him to slide into the front seat. Ruby caught Johnny's eye and mouthed, *very, very wrong.*

He was relieved when it was just the two of them in the car, although his hands sweated on the steering wheel. They sweated some more in the movie theater while Jane Powell or Rosemary Clooney (he could never keep them straight) sang on a starlit terrace. He held a box of popcorn, and every so often Tessie dipped her hand in daintily, never taking her eyes off the screen. His hands were still sweating when he pulled her from her seat before the start of the second film of the double feature. As they made their way in the dark to the exit, he felt a hesitation in her step. He'd already made his move, though. He saw no way to undo it.

Back in the car again, his hands were dry now, though he felt the residue there on his palms and between his fingers. He drove around, partly from giddiness, partly because he didn't have a plan of where to take Tessie now that they had left the movie.

"Have you ever been to the Point at night and seen the lights of the city?" she asked.

So Johnny, who had been heading in the opposite direction, turned the car around and climbed a winding road. There were turnouts along the way, tourist viewing points, and Johnny drove past several before he found one unoccupied by other cars. He shut off the engine, and when he set the brake, it made a sound of complaint that reminded him of Ruby's smirking warning, *very very wrong*. He turned to Tessie, ready to suggest that they return to the movie or maybe go bowling, but she was occupied with the glittering skyline in front of them. Everything seemed promising and right.

"It's like the movies," Tessie said. "Only it's real."

That's when Johnny lowered her onto the front seat of Louie Sebastian's Mercury.

Two months later Johnny borrowed Louie's car a second time. They drove to a doctor in Tijuana, someone Tessie's cousin knew. He waited in a small room with green linoleum floor tile and metal folding chairs and a Coca-Cola machine in the corner. He was the only one in the room, which made the wait terrifying. He was holding his head in his hands, digging his fingernails into his scalp, squeezing his eyes shut, when someone tapped him on the shoulder.

The doctor was an older man – gray mustache sagging at the corners of his mouth, bags slouched beneath his eyes. "Everything's going to be fine," he said.

Johnny wanted to sink to his knees. But he couldn't move, except to clasp the doctor's white coat in gratitude.

"Don't worry," the doctor said, gently removing himself from Johnny's grip. "There will be other babies."

II

WALTZ

What did a snake signify?

Tessie was not superstitious, at least not overly so. She had to admit to certain beliefs, though. When making a bed, she avoided interrupting her work, for fear of spending a restless night. And she did believe in the luck of a four-leaf clover. As for black cats, she always turned her back to them so that they could not walk away from her and take her luck with them. These were precautionary practices. Many people engaged in them: her sister Gloria, for one, and Gloria could name a dozen more.

Tessie had never seen a snake in her yard, much less inside her house. The intrusion gave her the shivers. Snakes were hideous, sinful things. *Trespassers beware* was her motto, despite Josie's lament at the senseless massacre. "A garter snake, for God's sake," Josie had said over and over, as if everyone should realize its harmless, defenseless nature. Tessie had imitated Josie when she related the whole episode to Gloria on the phone.

Gloria was sympathetic in her know-it-all way. "They bite, you know." And then she offered the tragic and true tale of her neighbor's cousin's daughter who was bitten by a garter snake (though Gloria pronounced it "gardener snake," giving it a purposeful occupation, which made its demise seem harsh after all). The bite became infected, horribly swollen, and painful with pus. "They almost had to amputate the arm. Can you imagine?"

In the heat of the afternoon, Tessie shivered at the thought of no arm, and felt guilt again at Johnny's broken one. Perhaps she could have shown more restraint. Tessie was skipping her dance class today, missing out on her rumba with Manny – a self-imposed punishment for precipitating the broken arm disaster. As she drove to the hospital to visit Johnny, she tried to think of other ways she might make up for her hysteria. It weighed on her, this outburst. What would she have done if Johnny hadn't been there? She would have picked up the baseball bat herself. But then what? She cringed at the thought of slamming the fat end of the bat into the tiny head of the snake. But neither could she have coaxed it out of her house, shepherding it intact out the door. Maybe she would have just run from the room, surrendering it to the snake. Then what would have kept it from slithering to other parts of her house? Still, she should have done something other than scream for Johnny.

She had always been accustomed to having Johnny take control of situations. His illness now required her to take charge of some things. Like driving, which she didn't mind for the most part. She tried to ignore how he pressed his own foot to the floor when she braked, how he clenched the door handle as if he might need to escape.

As she brought the old station wagon to a stop behind a late-model sedan, Tessie noticed how obsolete her car was. Why did they still have this station wagon? It wasn't as if they still had a carload of kids or groceries. When the light turned green, she gave the car extra gas, changed lanes, and passed the sedan. Just as she suspected: the windows were rolled up. Air conditioning – something her station wagon lacked. How had she tolerated such a deprivation for so long? She merged aggressively onto the freeway.

Lately, Tessie had been mulling over the idea of Bunny. She really had not been more than that – an idea, an abstraction. She did not even exist as a photo. Tessie had no physical image of Bunny and this lack made her aware of the power of the unknown. More and more, Bunny grew in Tessie's mind as someone irrefutable. Winston was the proof of her existence: a beautiful son with charming manners and an eagerness, almost an obsession, to please.

Last night Tessie had pulled down the box of loose photos from the top shelf of the linen closet. They were pictures from when she and Johnny were young and dating. She was so slender then, and her hair, thick and bouncy at her shoulders, often appeared romantically windblown. She sorted through the pictures of them at the beach, on the grass in front of her parents' house, on a downtown street where they leaned against a borrowed car. There were pictures of Johnny with his Navy buddies, their sailor hats tipped at a sexy angle, their smiles aiming to be sly and boastful. There were pictures of their early years as parents – of christenings and first birthdays, the requisite baby-in-the-bathtub shots. She picked through them until she found what she was looking for – three photos, each of a different young Filipina woman wearing the traditional butterfly dress. One stood under an archway of flowers; another held a straw hat in her hand; a third sat on the grass, legs tucked under her, her dress pulled over her knees. Tessie turned each photo over to read the inscriptions. *Just a simple memento to my friend. Just a simple souvenir. A simple keepsake.* It must have been the customary message of the times. So simple and proper; so deceptively coy. Tessie was sure that each of them had hoped Johnny would return to the Philippines to take a wife. They were all pretty: Ising, Nating, and Violeta. None of them was Bunny.

When Tessie arrived at his room, Johnny was sitting up in bed. The newspaper was spread across his lap and the TV was on, but he was staring into space. His face was alert, almost tense, but as soon as she entered the room, his facial muscles slackened into his everyday expression.

Tessie stood at the foot of the bed. "What were you thinking about?" she asked, though she really wanted to know *who*.

"Nothing," he said, his voice solemn, his eyes wide as if surprised by the question.

Tessie bit her lip and fussed around the room a little, rinsing out his water glass and filling it up again, tossing tired bouquets into the trash, wiping down the bedside tray with a damp paper towel. After a while, she flopped down in the chair beside his bed and watched his profile as he scanned the sports page. How large his ears had become, the lobes long and papery. His face had shrunk, the skin pulled taut so that his cheekbones were knobs. She wanted to touch them.

Johnny looked up. "What are you thinking about?" he asked.

"Nothing," she said, reflexively. She added, "We should trade in the station wagon."

He squinted at his paper, sending bands of wrinkles to slant down his face.

"I want air conditioning," she said in the air-conditioned hospital room where the hairs on her arm stood on goose-bumpy flesh.

He nodded. "You're right." He said it gently, agreeably, and Tessie tried to remember when he started to be like that. Was it before or after Winston showed up in their lives?

A nurse came into the room on thick rubber soles: Aurora, the day nurse, a tiny Filipina with an abrupt manner, whose thickly-accented speech Tessie pretended to understand. If Tessie asked Aurora to repeat something she'd said, Aurora looked at her sharply, her glasses slipping down her nose even as her face tilted upward. So Tessie nodded or made unintelligible sounds of assent if she thought an affirmative response was expected. Then, when Aurora was out of the room, Tessie asked Johnny, "What in the world did she say?" which seemed to offend him, even though she could tell sometimes he could not decode Aurora's words either.

There were a lot of Filipinos on the staff – nurses, lab technicians, food service, housekeeping. They spoke Tagalog to each other as they passed in the corridors or rode together in the elevators. Often when they giggled, Tessie wondered what was funny, wondered if she were the joke. She had never gotten over it – a sense of superiority spoiled by an irksome feeling of being left out. She was proud that her diction was unencumbered by either a Filipino or Mexican accent. Let those others jabber in their foreign language. See who would understand when they tried English.

It was clear, though, that Aurora was dedicated to her profession, seeing to Tessie's comfort as well as Johnny's, fastidious in the performance of her duties, and remembering to add a smile to her bedside manner whenever she visited the room. Aurora's smile made her look like a rodent, but Tessie always enjoyed her smile and looked forward to those moments when Aurora retracted her lips to reveal her little teeth.

Aurora's visit now was merely social. Tessie watched as she picked up Johnny's hand in both of hers and patted it. "How is Mister Johnny today?" Aurora never engaged Johnny in conversations in Tagalog, and Tessie felt excluded for him, though he rarely spoke the language and had given it up like a bad habit.

"Ebryting okay?" she asked.

Johnny gave a half-smile, and Aurora showed her small animal grin.

"He's a tough one, eh, Tessie?"

Tessie smiled in agreement, watching Aurora let go of Johnny's hand and reach behind him to fluff his pillow. It was nice to have someone else see to Johnny's needs, while she could just sit in the chair nearby or not be there at all.

"Dare you go," Aurora said. It took Tessie a moment to filter the accent. *There you go,* Tessie thought as Aurora squeaked out of the room in her nurse's shoes.

"Isn't today your support group?" Johnny asked.

Why did he remember these things? Surely with all that had been happening, it would be natural to forget.

"I'm not going."

It occurred to her that she really ought to go. That would be her real punishment, on top of missing dance class. She'd gone to the first few meetings, but found she could not speak. Where was the comfort in announcing your anger to a roomful of strangers? Because it was anger she felt, anger at Johnny for getting sick. And now she was angry at Bunny for being dead. And Winston, too, for – well, for being Winston. How would all that sound out loud in a support group?

Tessie turned on the TV, a local talk show, and they watched together for a while. The stiff-haired co-hosts, a white man and an Asian woman, each possessing the standard attractiveness of local programming, engaged in unimaginative banter before introducing their guest, a pet psychic. The psychic claimed an ability to communicate with any kind of animal: dogs, cats, horses, mice, ferrets.

"You name it, I've spoken to it," said the woman, middle-aged with a long, graying braid draped over her shoulder and oversized hoops through her ears.

"Parrots?" joked the male co-host.

"Snakes?" asked the woman co-host with mock horror.

The psychic looked at her hosts and the television audience with knowing, spiritual eyes and assured them, "Every creature has a story."

Tessie turned off the set, but before she could worry about snakes again, Winston came into the room bringing gifts – a game of Scrabble, a deck of cards, and a couple of milkshakes.

When Winston saw Tessie, he smiled. "I was hoping you'd be here." He held out one of the milkshakes. "I bought you one just in case."

Tessie wasn't at all convinced. She took the milkshake anyway. It was vanilla. She preferred chocolate.

"How's the arm?" Winston asked, holding up Scrabble in one hand and the deck of cards in the other for Johnny to choose. Johnny raised his cast to point.

Tessie sipped her shake as she watched them play Scrabble. She never said the name of the game out loud, because her mouth always produced *scramble*, and this in turn produced a correction from Johnny. *Scramble* was a much better word, she thought as she looked at all the tiles spread across the inside of the box. She watched Johnny line up tiles on the board to spell *sippet*. She wondered if that was really a word and if Winston was going to let him get away with it. Winston gave an admiring whistle and tallied up the points for the fake word.

Tessie finished her milkshake, grazed Johnny's cheek with sticky lips, and left him and Winston to their game.

Tessie sat in her car down the street from Armida's. The class had just finished; she watched them dance their way to the café. Manny held the door open to let them all pass through before him. Manny the gentleman, the gentle, competent dancer. They rotated partners in class, but Tessie always managed to start and end class with Manny. She had never socialized with the group after class, always going straight home – except for once, when the last dance with Manny had gone exceptionally well and she had wanted to prolong the rapport she had felt in the dance. She had gone across the street with the others to the café to sample the *carnitas* and guacamole. When she reached inside her purse to pay her share of the bill, Manny put his hand over hers to stop her. "My treat," he had told her. Only after he took his hand away, she realized it was the first time he had touched her outside of class.

◈ ◈ ◈

Tessie stood in her front yard, looked around, and felt dissatisfied. Something was lacking. Harmony, maybe. Or more contrast. Texture? It didn't help that the colors were faded. The brightness of the sun overwhelmed the flowers, and they looked tired and peeved. The garden statues had a layer of grime. She uncoiled the hose and aimed the spray at each one in turn – the gnomes, the deer, the squirrels, the pair of chipmunks. The force of the spray knocked over one of the chipmunks, sending it into its companion and toppling that one too. She set the hose down on the bed of rocks and stooped to restore the chipmunks to standing. When she stepped backward to assess her work, her foot pressed down on the hose, sending the nozzle up into her face. She screamed and lost her balance, ending up in a heap on the rocks, the nozzle from the hose leaking water at her feet. The rocks were hard and unforgiving, but she didn't pick herself up. She unscrewed the nozzle and let the water run in a soothing stream over her hand. She lifted the hose above her head and closed her eyes, feeling the water wash over her until her clothes were indecently wet against her body.

◈ ◈ ◈

When Tessie answered the knock on her screen door, she was wearing dry clothes. Her hair was still wet, beads of water balancing at the tips. Winston was on her front porch. She stood mystified at his presence. He was dressed up, and the scent of aftershave wafted through the screen. His hair, longer now than when he first came to their door weeks ago, was also freshly washed, and held comb marks. "I came to take you dancing, Tessie."

She remembered that particularly exhilarating lesson, when she had danced with Armida; later, practically skipping to her car, she had turned around to see this startled young man, guilty and innocent, vulnerable and troublesome all at once.

Tessie opened the door. "It's about time," she said.

They had dinner first, a seafood restaurant that Winston had found by driving along the San Diego harbor. Tessie hadn't been out to dinner in a long time. Even when Johnny was well, they seldom went out, so her dress-up clothes consisted of the few skirts she alternated for her dance classes. Armida disapproved of slacks, and encouraged stilettos for dancing. Stilettos were for showgirls. Tessie was reluctant at first to wear such steeply heeled shoes, but eventually she bought a pair on one of her pretend shopping errands. This evening Tessie boldly wore her dance shoes along with her twirly lavender skirt.

They weren't seated near a window, so Tessie had to look over the heads of other diners to see the sun staging a flamboyant exit. They made small talk over most of dinner. Now she had only a few curls of fettuccine and no scallops left on her plate, and Winston's lobster shell was nearly picked clean. It was time for some real talk.

"Why were you there, Winston – in front of Armida's that day?"

Winston looked up slowly from his plate. "I was lost."

Tessie was not prepared for the tragic picture he made with his yearning eyes above the lobster carcass.

"Tell me about your father," Tessie said gently, though it was really Bunny she wanted to know about.

"There's not much to tell." He pressed the thick restaurant napkin to his buttery lips and drank from his water glass. "I was seven when he left. He never came back."

Tessie took her fork away from her mouth, the fettuccine still dangling from it. "I didn't know." She sipped her water now too.

"Even when he lived with us, it was kind of like he lived apart from us. You know?"

Tessie, chewing on a piece of ice, nodded – and had to make herself stop nodding. She swallowed, but the scrap of ice lodged momentarily at the base of her throat. Winston was looking into his glass of water, where the half-circle of a lime floated like a grin. Tessie studied his face: the girlish lashes (were they Bunny's or Carlitos's?), the cheekbones that made him look both resolute and fragile, the artistic mouth that still had a remnant of lobster butter at the corner. She often studied her daughters like this, appraising their features, wondering at their thoughts; when they looked up and caught her, they would say, "What?" their voices defensive, annoyed.

Winston looked up at her. "Dessert?"

After dinner they went upstairs to the lounge and dance floor. The band was taking a break; recorded tango music oozed from the overhead speakers, lulling the patrons into a swaying, wistful silence. Tessie watched as Winston showed the waitress his ID. In the semi-dark of the lounge, the waitress squinted at the card, then at Winston, then at Tessie, who pretended interest in the specialty drinks menu.

"Okay," the waitress shrugged.

Winston ordered a beer, and Tessie, who didn't drink, surprised herself by ordering a flavored martini.

The waitress set something green and syrupy in front of her. It tasted like cough medicine, and Tessie contained the urge to spit it out.

She remembered a time when Josie was small, barely three years old, and obnoxious with a cough. Tessie was pregnant – due any day – and running low on patience. The constant rasping was driving Tessie crazy. She was trying to get some cough medicine down Josie, less for Josie's sake than for her own, but Josie had shut down, her hand clamped over her mouth and her eyes squeezed tight for good measure.

Tessie had abandoned cajoling: "Open your mouth if you know what's good for you." But Josie called her bluff, so Tessie abandoned threats too, this time issuing a simple, teeth-clenching order: "NOW." She heard the anger in her voice and saw how it scared her daughter.

Eyes still clenched, Josie moved her hand away and opened her mouth, just barely. Tessie slid the spoon between Josie's teeth and tilted the medicine into her mouth. She saw Josie's eyes open wide, her throat constrict, and her lips contort… and she should have known to shield herself. Josie spat the medicine right into Tessie's face, into her eye and the corner of her outraged mouth. Tessie saw her hand fly out and slap her daughter, this small child whose nose was now spurting blood. And Tessie was angry at that too, because somehow she knew then that her baby was not a boy.

Winston raised his glass. "To Johnny's health."

Tessie touched her green martini to his beer and then forced down another dose of its cough-medicine flavor.

The four-piece band took the stage again and opened with a rumba. It was too loud for conversation, so Tessie and Winston just sat, their hands clasped around their drinks, and watched a few couples bob self-consciously. It was not a dance floor you could hide on. If Tessie and Winston were to dance, they would be easily observed by any of the patrons sipping cocktails. Normally Tessie did not like to call attention to herself. She worried that her hair was out of place, or her lipstick was smeared, or her skirt clingy from static. Just walking from her table to the ladies' room made her feel conspicuous. But dancing was different. Despite the slight bulge at her midriff, and the softness that was showing on the underside of her arms, Tessie was confident in her body on the dance floor. It was something she had only recently discovered. She and Johnny had never danced much. Johnny simply lacked the ability, so Tessie had taken to the sidelines with him. On New Year's Eves, they watched Rey and Gloria cavort at the VFW Hall. At each of their daughters' weddings, they stumbled through the one requisite dance and then smiled from their seats for the remainder of the reception, Tessie tapping her foot, sometimes both feet.

She hadn't meant to forsake her support group for dance lessons. She was driving to the community center where the group met. An accident on the road forced her to detour, and when she tried to find a shortcut back to her normal route, she ended up circling in an unfamiliar neighborhood. When she pulled to the curb to ask for directions, there she was, in front of Armida's. It was as if Armida was beckoning her inside as she moved her hips and shoulders in a rumba – although at the time Tessie could not identify the dance. Now Tessie could not only name a whole repertoire of dances, she could execute them as well.

Tessie wondered if Winston had suddenly gone shy. He had been so bold earlier when he announced he was taking her dancing; now here they sat, mere spectators to mediocre dancers. But it was a rumba, and it would have been obscene to wiggle her hips with Winston the way she did with Manny – though wasn't that obscene too, in a way? The way she felt the music play beneath her skin, threading through her muscles and in the brilliant turn of her hips?

A waltz came next. Just when she thought she would have to exercise her motherly standing and order Winston off his chair, he set his glass down, appeared to gulp, then rose and held out his hand to her.

Before they even reached the dance floor, they were in step with the music. Winston guided her around the floor, expertly avoiding other pairs of dancers, none of whom glided as agreeably as they.

She wondered how such a young man could be so polished. She was aware that people around them were beaming, the way they beam at a mother and son, and Tessie, turning, turning, and turning again, felt how right this dance was.

12

FAMILY FOURTH OF JULY 

They had resurrected it only in the past few years – the annual Fourth of July picnic at the beach. It was Laura's idea: "To give our own kids the kind of memories we have." Josie was skeptical; in fact, she couldn't imagine anything worse.

"Let's make new memories," Sara said. As if it were a crafts project, Josie thought, remembering Sara's macramé phase and the hideous creations that had once adorned her bedroom walls, and even the family bathroom until the steam and careless spatters of shaving cream and toothpaste made mush of all the knots.

Memories aside, there had been concern about bringing their father out to the beach, about his ability to sit for hours in a flimsy beach chair. But despite his never caring much for the beach, despite his distaste for picnic food, despite his arm still trapped in a cast, Johnny declared himself ready for the Fourth. So Winston called ahead and made arrangements with the Parks Service for use of a special drop-off point nearest the picnic shelter.

"If he needs to go home early, I can drive him," Winston said.

Good boy, thought Josie, deciding to herself that she would be the one to take her father home early if necessary.

So here they now were, the Bacaycay and the de la Cruz families and Winston, spread among three tables and assorted beach chairs at a picnic shelter near the listless bay, where swimming was no longer advised. They had arrived early to stake their claim on the shelter nearest the restrooms and the footpath leading to the ocean. Actually, it was Rey who had risen at dawn to sit in a line of cars at the gate, hours before the park opened. The rest of them had straggled in at various intervals, so that by ten o'clock they were nearly all assembled. Only Linda and her family had yet to arrive.

"Oh, they're always late," Gloria said, her complaint carrying a hint of pride about her daughter's habit.

"They live so far," she said by way of explanation. "Way up there."

Way up there was not just an allusion to distance, but to social status. *Way up there in the rich neighborhood* was what Gloria meant, though no one gave her the satisfaction of a response.

"Here they come now," she said triumphantly.

Linda was striding down the path, her pedicure on display in ropy sandals, her figure shown to best advantage in a halter top and sarong. A breeze fluttered the newly trimmed ends of her shoulder-length hair. She wore a straw handbag slung from one shoulder, and she hugged a volleyball under her opposite arm. Although Josie hated volleyball, she always found herself participating against her will – invariably bruising a finger, most often her own, but sometimes mangling the pinky of one of her teammates as well.

Linda's husband strolled behind her, carrying his laptop. He always spent family gatherings sitting apart from the others, the computer balanced on his lap, his fingers making earnest clicks on his keyboard. "He's a workaholic," Linda sighed – but more than once, Josie had spied Solitaire on his screen. His name was Walker, which they had all had fun with until the novelty wore off.

More cherished, of course, were the twins. Fraternal look-alikes except for skin and eye color, Madison and Mason were an intriguing sight. Madison was dark like her mother; Mason bore her father's green eyes, and though not as fair-skinned as her father, she was nevertheless several shades lighter than her sister. Side by side, one was the photographic negative of the other. They were the center of the universe even if their names were, according to Rey, not even real names.

Gloria blamed the children's names on their father. "They like those kinds of names." She referred to Walker in the plural as if he were a conspiracy.

She lowered her voice to explain. "Hydrogenous names."

But it was really Linda who favored the androgynous names. Strong and distinctive, Linda said. *Self-important and trendy,* Josie thought.

If their names were genderless, the twins were nothing if not miniature images of their mother, their eight-year-old bodies wrapped in their own little sarongs and halter tops. They walked on either side of their newest nanny – a college girl, probably, slim and serious with limp auburn hair and a modest case of freckles. Over the years, there had been an assortment of non-family members – boyfriends, co-workers, best friends of the moment – attending the family Fourth, but Linda was the only one who ever brought hired help.

"This is Wren, our nanny," Linda said as the twins pulled the redhead by the hand into the circle of beach chairs.

"Wren, like the bird," they said. It was a practiced chirp, as if they made this clarification often.

Wren smiled and greeted them. She was quiet but not at all uncomfortable, which made Josie glad. She felt Linda was too pleased with her role as employer of domestic help.

In the posh, mostly white neighborhoods of North County, cinnamon-skinned Linda had made a place in the world. Once an ace secretary – typing, filing, and organizing with great efficiency and command – she was now the stay-at-home wife of a successful attorney, applying her talents to the scheduling of housecleaners, poolman, landscapers, and a succession of nannies with whom she also negotiated light laundry duties.

Linda tossed a no-look pass to Sonny who caught the volleyball with one hand. Josie knew they would be high-fiving each other on their side of the volleyball net later on. This is what she really envied about Linda – this brother-sister bond she shared with Sonny, full of a teasing affection, different from the sniping rivalry between sisters.

Linda spotted Winston, whom she hadn't yet met, but had surely heard about from Gloria. Linda leaned across the picnic table and extended her hand. "You must be Winston."

Josie saw the look of approval and curiosity in Linda's eyes as Winston, ever congenial, returned the greeting. Josie was determined to claim him for the de la Cruz side of the volleyball net. Maybe this year they would win. *That* would make a new memory.

◈ ◈ ◈

Johnny hated the beach, was not fond of tradition, and had never been a holiday reveler. He tolerated the Fourth of July picnic. It was one of the few things they had done as a family over the years, so he participated with a sense of obligation, lugging coolers and picnic baskets, bags of groceries, charcoal briquettes, blankets, beach towels, inflatable mattresses, collapsible chairs, and always forgetting something – a spatula to turn the hamburgers or a pump for the water toys.

The tradition had begun with the Navarro sisters. Gloria was engaged to Rey, Tessie and Johnny were a steady item, and the younger sisters, Ruby and Lydia, were anxiously awaiting their own turns at love. Gloria, who wore a bathing suit well, as, in fact, did all the sisters to varying degrees, favored the beach and jumped at any opportunity to spend time posed prettily on a blanket. She was the one who inaugurated that first Independence Day family gathering in 1949. Even the Navarro parents, Concha and Fredo, who hated sand and the smell of seaweed, joined in on these occasions – Concha to tend a pot of frijoles and a pan of empanadas over an open grill while sipping a bottle of beer, and Fredo in the background, a straw *bracero* hat shading his face, a cigar clamped in his teeth, watching over his daughters.

Over the years, the tradition of the family Fourth waxed as the family grew and then waned as it grew apart. The Bacaycays and the de la Cruzes started their families. Then Ruby moved away, eloping to Nevada with a saxophone player, and later Lydia married and moved with her husband to a little Midwestern town, which apparently lacked reliable mail or telephone service since they seldom wrote or called. Concha believed the Midwest was overseas and was therefore forgiving of their slight.

But the ritual continued without Ruby and Lydia, and later, after their passing, without Concha and Fredo. Rey was the cook, with Johnny assisting, leaving Gloria and Tessie free to scream warnings at their young children. None of the Navarro sisters had ever learned to swim. "We were too poor," Gloria explained. Their rise to the lower middle class, however, did not result in children that could swim. Despite swimming lessons at the municipal pool, neither the de la Cruz children nor the Bacaycay children had ever learned to do more than a few yards of a belly float with a frantic flutter kick before their toes struggled for the bottom of the pool. There was something inherently unbuoyant about them, and Johnny took the blame for that. There was also something deeply ingrained in them: fear. He blamed that on Tessie and Gloria.

They had always scared the wits out of their children. There was the fear of drowning, of course. The solution was to keep them out of the water – even at the beach, a senseless endeavor. They were allowed to wade waist-deep but were always corralled closer to shore with a shrill *Not so far* whenever they ventured deep enough to be sprayed at the armpits from a cresting wave. Even when they remained obediently in the specified "safe zone," they were not really safe. There was the sting of a phantom jellyfish that could paralyze. There were the ragged edges of shells that could slice a toe. There were long ropes of seaweed to wrap around their ankles and pull them under water. Perils, everywhere.

Away from the water, there were other don'ts. *Don't swallow watermelon seeds.* They could lodge in their stomachs and sprout. *Don't eat so fast.* Did they want to choke on that hot dog and die? *Don't get so close to the fire.* They should roast their marshmallows away from the flame.

Surely, such parenting by alarm had left its scars. He should have done more than shake his head at it all.

It had been a relief to abandon the family tradition when their children at the height of their teenage loathing had declared the gatherings to be lame. But now they were back, and he didn't mind, really. Though it was amusing – daring, even: a family that couldn't swim, playing at the beach.

Johnny had never learned to swim as a boy. He was skinny, with long feet and sharp elbows – nothing to buoy him up in the water. Where he grew up, swimming was something children were expected to acquire merely as a result of contact with other children, through contagion like chicken pox, or imitation, or – if necessary – bullying. Parents trusted that somehow their children would learn to stroke their way across a river or cut cleanly through the surf. But Johnny didn't like the water, its unknown depths, how he had to struggle to stay at its surface. When his father first asked him if he'd learned to swim, he answered, "Not yet," because he had still meant to try. But the third time his father asked, Johnny lied and said yes because he didn't want to be asked again. "Good boy," his father said, though he never requested proof. *He really should have,* Johnny thought.

When he joined the Navy, there had been a swim test to pass. The new Filipino recruits were lined up at the dock. The boys who could swim made their way to the front of the line, eager to show they belonged. Johnny hung back with the others whose ability in the water was questionable. One by one, at the blast of a whistle, they dove or jumped into the green bay, their objective a platform fifty yards away.

Johnny watched as the strong swimmers skimmed the distance and lifted themselves easily onto the platform. He tried to memorize their movements, to will them into his body. But then the weaker swimmers made their way across, slapping the water, impeding their own progress with their slashing strokes. When they got to the platform, they hugged the edge like a long-lost friend before heaving themselves over the top, their chests visibly laboring. Johnny tried not to watch them; he did not want their struggle to mar the image of ease he had tucked away of the good swimmers. On the other hand, he was relieved to see that each of the marginal swimmers had made it, giving him hope that he would too.

As his turn approached, he could feel his heart bang around like a caged squirrel; he shivered from a breeze that swept suddenly at his back; his breaths came quick and short; his fingers folded into his palms. After the boy ahead of him dropped reluctantly into the water, Johnny clenched his toes to the lip of the dock, flattened his hands, bent his wobbling knees, and shot himself into the water, hoping to reduce as much as possible the distance he would have to swim. His outstretched arms found the water just before his belly did. Still, the impact on his torso stunned him, forcing out the air that he had saved in his lungs. He took one last life-saving breath and began to kick madly, propelling himself through the water with violent thrusts of his legs and long, frantic pulls of his arms. Each time his head bobbed out of the water, his eyes opened wide to take in the distance to the platform, and his heart thumped at the realization that he was closing the gap. He must have taken another breath or two by the time his knuckles scraped the platform, because he was sputtering air and water, his nose and throat achy with salt, his head dizzy with effort. As he dragged himself out of the water, his father's voice boomed in his water-plugged ears: *good boy*.

◈ ◈ ◈

Josie, her husband and son away on a buddy trip, was feeling lost and superfluous in the midst of this family gathering. She looked around her. The family separated itself by generations: Josie's cousins and sisters sat at one of the picnic tables; their children sat at another. Walker had isolated himself with his laptop on a stretch of sand occupied only by shore grass.

Laura's husband, Chip, and Sara's husband, Andy, were setting up the volleyball net. Over the years, such tasks had fallen to them. They erected and collapsed the beach chairs as needed, pumped the inflatable mattresses with air, and hauled in the coolers of beer, soda, and potato salad. Thank goodness for those sons of yours, Gloria always said to Johnny, and Johnny would blink with surprise until he realized she meant sons-*in-law*. "Yes," he would say, "thank goodness," and if they were within reach, he would clap them on the shoulder.

Chip, the manager at one of the city's recreation centers, was lanky and perpetually clad in shorts and a polo shirt. The flexibility and good humor he demonstrated on the job with riotous adolescents also served him in his family by marriage, as a few of its members (Tessie and Gloria, to be exact) had a tendency to pluralize his name and call him Chips. Andy was quiet, a small freckled man with a receding hairline who liked to tell jokes to an audience of one. He would circulate at family gatherings until he had delivered his punch line at least a dozen times. Now, as they pounded stakes in the sand to anchor the volleyball net, Andy related his latest joke and Chip cocked his head with its unflagging grin to listen.

Gloria and Tessie sat nearby, sipping diet colas, happy to no longer have children young enough to require their unrelenting vigilance. Every so often though they issued a high-pitched red alert to a grandchild – which did not have the same effect as it had years ago on their own children. They pretended not to care.

Rey was monitoring the progress of the coals, where he would later grill the hamburgers and hotdogs and reheat the store-bought empanadas. Frijoles were no longer part of the menu with Concha gone and no one willing to go to the trouble. Johnny was seated in a beach chair watching Rey watch the grill. He wore a baseball cap and sunglasses that attached to the lenses of his regular glasses. His windbreaker was zipped to his collarbone, its prominence visible through the nylon fabric. The sky was hot and blue, but the sea breeze was enough to chill someone like him. He sat tilted because one side of his chair was deeper in the sand than the other, a disequilibrium that he seemed to accept as part of this outdoor experience.

Winston lounged in a chair next to Johnny, looking as if he had always belonged there, always been part of these family Fourths. Both Johnny and Tessie had recently embraced him. Really embraced him – not the polite acceptance Tessie had shown before or the lethargic friendliness Johnny had begrudged him. *Still, no one had yet invited him to Sunday dinner,* Josie thought as she floated among them all.

She held her camera at the ready, trying to capture a candid moment but invariably alerting her subjects to her presence and getting clownish poses or self-conscious grins instead. Sometimes she felt it was impossible to capture real life. There was always somebody to spoil your efforts.

She thought about David and Gabe, who were probably fishing now off the Texas coast, Gabe with his size 14 feet resting on the rail of her father-in-law's rickety boat, and David pointing with his fishing rod at the Corpus Christi coastline, naming its landmarks for his son. Josie remembered that trip with David, when he had shown her where he had grown up, the high school football field where he had scored the winning touchdown, the swing he had pushed his first love in when he was seven and she was six, the tree limb that broke under his weight as he rescued a neighbor's cat. She had taken a picture of him at the site of each of these memories. Later, when she showed him the portfolio she had made, a silly grin sneaked across his face. "I made that stuff up," he said, snorting slightly as he tried to contain his ha-ha-gotcha laugh. That was her husband. That was the kind of thing he thought was funny. But then, she had laughed back then, too.

◆ ◆ ◆

Johnny leaned into his collapsible chair that sat slightly off-balance in the sand. Another reason he disliked the beach: everything underfoot sloped or bulged. But he set those dislikes aside for today, the Fourth of July, family picnic day. He wished he had shown more enthusiasm for the holiday when his daughters were growing up. He wished he hadn't complained about packing up the car, the drive, the sheer boredom of spending an entire day at the beach, the sand collecting in his socks.

Now he felt absurdly content. His felt his arm healing beneath its cast, though the fact of the cast, its rigidity and weight, was another thing that made him feel off-balance today. Other things seemed to be approaching a kind of equilibrium, though. Tessie was no longer startled by his random moments of warmth and had begun to occasionally respond in kind. For instance, lately, when she excused herself to go back to bed after their early morning coffee, she put her hand on his and gave a little rub. Johnny waited until she was out of the room to scratch the place where she had irritated the capillaries.

She hadn't raised the subject of Bunny since that time in the hospital, and she seemed to look upon Winston with a kind of protectiveness. The three of them existed in a careful harmony, derived of restraint and circumspection, wordless like the songs Tessie hummed, and always hard to name. It remained only for his daughters to join in and add their voices. But for now, he was content to watch the goings-on around him – his family and friends at leisure at the beach.

Winston, athletic in his shorts and flimsy T-shirt, was helping Rey light the coals in the barbecue pit. As soon as the grill was hot, Rey wanted to tend to the cooking alone, so Winston headed to the empty chair next to Johnny. Johnny watched Winston's calf muscles flex as each foot sank in the sand and emerged again. He sat down, his arms and legs stretched out to the sun. Only Johnny's hands were exposed to the elements. His windbreaker was zipped to his Adam's apple, his face was shaded by the visor of his baseball cap, and no gap existed between the cuff of his pants and his shin-length socks.

"You warm enough, Johnny?" Winston asked. "Need a blanket?"

He was fine, actually, but it was a thoughtful gesture, too thoughtful to pass up.

"That would be perfect," he said.

◈ ◈ ◈

Linda's nanny was taking the twins to play in the surf. Gloria called after them, "Don't go too far into the water!" No one turned to acknowledge her, though, not even the nanny. Josie got up to follow them, signaling to Gloria that she had it covered.

Josie walked a little apart from them, since the twins were bossily possessive of their nanny. Every so often though, Wren would turn and offer bits of pleasant small talk about the *awesome* weather or the *fabulous* ocean breeze. She was a nice girl, confident and seemingly comfortable in her surroundings as she shepherded her brown-skinned charges along the path.

The park was occupied mostly by brown and black families, in contrast to the beaches to the north. For a few years the family picnic had taken place in La Jolla as a result of a teen rebellion led by Linda.

"The beaches are better there. Cleaner," she insisted, to persuade Gloria.

"Grassy areas, not just sand," Laura told Tessie.

The men grumbled about the drive, but acquiesced. They cooked their hot dogs where sand could not be blown across them, walked the beaches supposedly unmarred by broken shells, and waded into the ocean, where long-haired surfers splashed past them, boards tucked under their arms. All around them it seemed were blond, bronzed people. Of course, they weren't all blond. Just a preponderance of them.

This is where the action is. This is where it's happening, they thought to themselves as they tried not to notice that they did not quite fit in. It wasn't just the color thing. There were other differences: sunglasses, for instance. There seemed to be a particular style that was in vogue, just like swimsuits, beach towels, flip-flops, even Frisbees. In subsequent summers, they were careful to choose their beachwear in the more fashionable discount stores. Eventually, though, even the right clothes at the good beach could not sustain the annual family Fourth. The teenagers were restless. The parents were tired. They took a holiday from their holiday. Now they were back.

With the ocean in sight, Wren and the twins raced in ankle-deep to test the water. Josie sank cross-legged onto the sand near their discarded towels. The sun on the sand and water gave a white-blue gleam to the atmosphere that gave even the uncomely bodies bulging from bathing suits an airy grace.

Josie leaned back on her elbows and looked around her. Some people had brought their dogs, even though they were not allowed at the beach. She thought of Jackson, who had recently been adopted by a retired librarian. She hoped the librarian talked to him, hoped she was not a shusher. The adoption had taken place on Josie's day off. Lyle broke the news to her. "Love at first sight," he said, which did not reassure Josie: she was skeptical of his ability to recognize such an emotion.

Josie didn't believe in love at first sight, not even between a mother and her newborn. It was amazement at first sight. Love came later…if only moments later. The *realization* of love could be sudden, but falling in love happened gradually. So did falling out of love, she supposed.

She sighed and pressed her eye to the camera, finding Wren, who was splashing in the surf with the twins. Wren looked back and gave a tentative wave, but it seemed to be directed behind the camera. Josie turned and was so astounded at what she saw that she failed, as a good photographer would not have, to click her shutter.

Winston was maneuvering a wheelbarrow through the sand and around sunbathers. Earlier, it had been used to transport the cooler full of raw hamburger patties, grocery sacks of picnic supplies, and a couple of striped watermelons. Now it was being used to bear her father to the ocean. He was wrapped in a blanket, his knees pulled to his chest to protect his cast, the hand of his good arm clinging to the side of the wheelbarrow. Winston's Hawaiian shirt was undone and sweat streaked his chest. His windblown hair whipped across his face and plastered itself like a stain on his forehead. *Old country peasants,* Josie thought. *Refugees from a flood or famine or coup. A Filipino Joy Luck Club.* An impression Josie was sure her father would be loath to convey. But there he was, looking like a kid on a ride at Disneyland.

◈ ◈ ◈

Being trundled in a wheelbarrow was not in any way dignified, but it was fun, Johnny decided. A folded blanket beneath him and another one around his shoulders made him feel cozily tucked in. Then there was the beach ball under his knees for support and shock absorption. Now that they had left the pavement and were hindered by sand and the labyrinth of bodies on beach towels, the fun began to fade. He began to wonder if he should have gone with his first instinct and declined Winston's offer to "take him for a spin," but the invitation had been made with a hint of conspiracy and hijinks, which appealed to Johnny in this outdoor environment. It was breezy and clear, with only the wispiest of clouds high in the sky – a day of possibility. So with Winston's help, Johnny had climbed in, and he was surprised that he did not feel like an invalid or a feeble old man who had to be wheeled a short walk from picnic shelter to beach. He felt like a jaunty traveler. He had enjoyed the ride, was enjoying it still, and only for a brief moment when he saw Josie's astonished stare did he feel a little silly. But his pleasure rebounded, because he wanted her to see him this way, having fun – even if he looked a little ridiculous.

"Well," Johnny said to his daughter when Winston brought the wheelbarrow to a stop. "Aren't you going to take a picture?"

He sat up straighter and motioned for Winston to lean down so the lens could capture them both. Wordlessly and obediently, Josie took the picture.

"I suppose the easy thing to do would be to dump me out," Johnny joked.

"Actually, that *is* a good way," Winston said. "I could slide you right out onto your feet."

"Really?" Johnny said.

"Careful," Josie said.

Winston slowly tipped the wheelbarrow until Johnny's feet touched the sand. His bottom slid onto the beach ball that had previously supported his knees, and the momentum of the ball rolling to the ground pushed him to stand; he never had to take the hand that Josie held out to him.

"*Ta da*!" Winston sang.

Johnny, pleased with himself, took a bow. Again, he had to cue Josie to take a picture. It wasn't the same, though, re-enacting the moment, posing, trying to recapture the fleeting delight. Useless, really. He grimaced as he realized sand was seeping into his sneakers.

"Dad, why don't you take off your shoes and socks?"

If he did, his white feet would be exposed. They were bony and veined, with long toes. People might stare, or turn away in disgust. But hadn't he just ridden in a wheelbarrow, not caring who might gape at the sight? Anyway, his feet were no less attractive than the many beer bellies and hefty thighs on display around him.

"Yes, please take them off," he said. Josie bent down to untie his shoes while Winston supported first one leg and then the other. Johnny allowed his bare feet to sink into the sand. The sensation, so rare and yet so familiar, impelled him toward the water.

"I'll walk down with you," Winston said.

"No," Johnny said, "I'll go on my own."

"Are you sure?" Josie asked, but Johnny had already started to amble away. "Be careful," she called, but the beach breeze lobbed her words back at her.

Johnny knew that both of them were watching his every wobbly step. He did feel a little unsteady in the breeze, but the gentle gusts also made him feel unfettered. Despite the crowd of sunbathers, the world felt open to him. He hadn't realized how small his world had become – not just as a result of his illness, but before that, all those years when he declined to venture too far from Kimball Park.

He picked his way carefully around the near-naked brown bodies spread upon beach blankets. Meanwhile, the blanket he still gripped around his shoulders billowed out behind him like a cape. The sand beneath his feet was occasionally squishy, but mostly hard-packed and easy to walk on. He stood at the edge of the surf, just where the water touched his feet, making their whiteness glisten like fish. His pants cuffs were not rolled up and were in danger of submersion if he ventured farther.

Each time he felt the tug of the surf, that pull of sand away from his soles, the disequilibrium he had felt earlier in the day came back to him. He fought against it, pressing his feet more firmly into the ground. Closing his eyes, he gave the rest of his senses up to the sound of the ocean, the sun that penetrated his blanket and clothes, the breeze that carried salt to his lips and nostrils. Restored to some semblance of balance, he opened his eyes and was momentarily blinded by the sun on the water. He had the sensation that he was alone on the beach and a quiver of panic ran through him. Slowly the glare dissolved and the brown skin and colored bathing suits of the people clotting the shore materialized again. He found himself ankle-deep in water, and he heaved a great sigh. He remembered how he had survived that night on the beach. He remembered how for much of his life he had stayed close to shore, afraid to swim.

◈ ◈ ◈

Josie sat down in the sand, her eyes on her father's back, watching his blanket puff out behind him from the gusts that came from the ocean. He seemed oblivious to Wren and the twins just a few yards away. He seemed oblivious to everyone.

"Nice beach," Winston said, dropping down beside her.

"We like it." She thought that Winston seemed a little too smug about wheeling her father over like that, as if they were some sort of circus act together. Winston seemed to have dedicated himself at this outing to the wooing of the entire de la Cruz family.

"So this is a family tradition," he said.

"Yep." Josie pointed the camera at him and caught him at close range, the viewfinder framing him from eyebrow to earlobe.

"Did you have any?" she asked as she watched him blink, detected a muscle twitch in his cheek.

"Nah." He shook his head. He turned toward her, and his face filled her camera. "So, how's the house painting coming?"

"Huh?" She lowered her camera and studied the lens.

"Johnny says you're having your house painted."

"Oh, that," Josie said, thinking of her empty house, the walls gray from lack of cleaning, dust settling against the baseboards. "No, that's a lie." She didn't know why she confessed it.

"That's a funny thing to lie about."

"Well, it's not really a lie," she said, backtracking, playing down her admission, regretting her words, and then thinking that *his* words suggested there were some things it made sense to lie about. She turned to pounce on that, but he was standing, stripping off his shirt.

"Come for a swim?"

"You go. Our family doesn't believe in swimming."

He lingered as if expecting a punch line.

"We're waders," she told him.

"Oh," he said, laughing a little.

She waved him off and then watched him lope toward the water, past her father, never hesitating as he launched himself into an oncoming wave. She knew her father was watching Winston, just as she was. He made it look so easy, as if there was nothing in the world to fear.

As she watched Winston's aquatic grace, a thin, shaggy-haired man, shirtless and wearing shark-print bathing trunks, ran along the beach in front of her. A football sailed in the air behind him. He turned, backpedaled a few steps, and caught the ball. He cocked his arm, dodged some imaginary tacklers, and returned the pass, and as he whirled to go long, he caught sight of Wren. He stopped to ogle her stretched out on the sand as the twins dug holes at her feet.

"Hey, Lyle, heads up!" The ball bounced off his shoulder.

Josie shaded her eyes against this intrusion of Lyle into her life outside of work. She saw him signal to his throwing partner that they would plant their game of catch where they stood, rather than continue their traveling show. Lyle added spins and leaps to his technique of receiving a pass, but nothing seemed to draw Wren's attention from the twins' excavation project. When he dove onto the sand, arms outstretched, his fingers barely grazed the ball, tipping it away from Wren and in Josie's direction.

She looked down at the sand, hoping Lyle would retrieve the ball without spotting her.

"Hey," he called, and then he was plopped down in the sand beside her. "What are you doing here?"

"Family Fourth of July," she told him.

Lyle looked around. "You're by yourself."

"Not true. Those are my nieces over there. And that's their nanny you've been trying so hard to impress."

Lyle, embarrassed that he'd been caught, scratched his chest, sending sand to trickle into the waistband of his trunks.

"There's my father by the water," she continued, and then as if for good measure, as if to prove that not only was she not alone, but amid a collection of family members, she added, "and that's my brother in the water." The words startled her with their unexpected issue, their air of possession, even protection. Here was a lie that made sense to tell, to invent for herself a pretty specimen of a brother in front of Lyle, her pathetic co-worker who had the gall to try to flirt with her pretend brother's pretend girlfriend.

Lyle shrugged, and more sand shivered from his bony torso. He eyed Josie. "Hey, I didn't know you had a brother."

Now Josie shrugged. "Well, now you do."

Lyle tucked the football under his armpit. "Guess so." He gave Wren a last glance and trotted off.

The twins were burying Wren. They had covered her legs and were working on her abdomen. Josie went over to take a picture of the nanny. Sunglasses hid her eyes, but she wore a calm expression as she lay lovingly embedded in the sand, the grains sliding inside the curve of her navel, pooling at her collarbone.

Winston emerged from the ocean, and as he trotted toward her father to rescue him and his pants from further encroachment by the surf, water shimmered off him in beads. Josie wasn't quite sure why Winston was in their lives or how long he would stay. But as long as he was there, she would use it to her advantage. Who wouldn't want to lay claim to such beauty?

Later, when it was time to play volleyball, Josie pulled her sisters with her and they all lined up with Winston on the same side of the net.

13

SUNDAY DINNER

Winston was coming for Sunday dinner, and Sara had made it happen. She had dropped by her parents' house one day, for no reason, really. It was the middle of the afternoon. Sometimes it was just good to leave the restaurant, its smell of condiments and lettuce from plastic bags. She had even changed out of her SubClub shirt. Her father seemed to dislike it. The house was quiet, but not empty. Sara could always sense her father's presence. It was a mood or a color, she thought. Ocher.

She found him on the sun porch curled on the love seat, his gaunt cheek resting on a skinny elbow. His cast had recently been removed, and it made Sara nervous to see bone against bone. Winston was there sitting in the white rattan chair, a book open on his lap.

"I was reading to him," Winston whispered, and Sara nodded, wanting to see the title of the book.

Sara had tried reading to her father once. But he seemed bored and it panicked her to be boring, so she stopped and turned on talk radio.

Winston's reading had soothed her father to sleep with his lullaby voice, the way a parent read to a child. Sara couldn't remember ever being read to by her parents, though they must have once.

Winston rose and placed the book, still open, on the chair, and he motioned for Sara to follow him out into the backyard. He peeled back the screen door slowly so it wouldn't squawk, and Sara obediently tiptoed out, resisting the urge to flip the book over to read the title, as if doing so might be enough to disturb her father. She wondered, too, if she was afraid to intrude upon the privacy of her father and Winston.

Outside, there were no chairs or benches, so they sat on the pink bricks, hot from the sun.

"How's business?" Winston asked in a way that was different from the way her family asked, and she was happy to answer him.

"We're still getting the hang of it, of being business owners. It's fun," she said, suddenly realizing how true this was, even though sometimes Andy got on her nerves the way he insisted on telling jokes to their customers. Sometimes people just wanted to eat.

"Drop by anytime for a sandwich on the house," she told Winston.

As he thanked her, his eyes swept his watch, a barely noticeable movement, a graceful hint.

"You know, if you have to go somewhere, I can stay until Josie or my mom comes home."

There was reluctance in his eyes. "If you don't mind."

It was this consideration he showed that made her do it, his good manners that made her blurt, "Come for dinner on Sunday." She said it casually, as if it were an invitation that was extended routinely.

But he knew it was not. He was surprised, but clearly pleased. He rose and looked down at her still sitting on the hot bricks. "Thank you." He smiled his splendid smile.

She watched him go around the corner of the house with a

long, liquid motion; then she got up, out of the sun, to try to look at the title of the book without waking her father.

◈ ◈ ◈

There should have been some advantage to being the youngest. Wasn't it natural that she be the coddled one? But by the time she was six, Sara realized that no such status would ever accrue to her. This revelation was more curious to her than dismaying, and she held little ill will toward her sisters, who had received more of their parents' attention – a rather generous term for the detached parenting that Johnny and Tessie de la Cruz practiced. It was clear to the sisters that their parents had wanted a son. Laura was their first disappointment, but the letdown was forgivable because, after all, as Tessie often said, "there's something special about the first born." Of course there was no glory in being born second, but Josie had managed to gain negative attention with her brooding, neurotic ways, developed at least in part in response to Tessie's oft-expressed opinion of the first-born. It made Laura smug and officious, Josie maladjusted, and Sara more or less indifferent.

Sara was never one to make a scene. She had been the quiet baby, according to Tessie, and Sara believed this, not because Tessie said it was so, but because she remembered it herself – her reluctance to wail, her fear of imposition on others. Then again, Sara wasn't sure whether this was an actual memory or one manufactured from the memories of others.

Sara had never felt like the youngest. What she had felt was the faint but palpable perception that another baby should have come after her. None had, and she seemed always to be followed by a big empty space.

When Winston came into their lives, Sara finally felt that the phantom youngest child had at last arrived. She had gone with Laura to inspect the interloper, as Josie described him. There was something exotic about him. Or maybe it was just that he came from somewhere other than Kimball Park.

There was also something *familiar* about him, though she couldn't say what. He looked nothing like them. He was far prettier than they were, and naturally athletic, whereas they were athletic in a desperate, combative way, their thin arms wielding a tennis racquet or baseball bat as if their lives depended on it. They tried too hard at everything or not hard enough. He was effortless in all he did. He made everything and everyone around him look good, so they could hold no grudge or jealousy long. Instead, they wanted to embrace him, make him their own. Even so, Sara sensed her family's reluctance, as if they were afraid of rejection, so she took it upon herself to make the first move. Someone had to.

◈ ◈ ◈

It was an unspoken rule that Sunday dinner was for family only. It meant they never had to dress up or put on manners. It also guaranteed that Sunday dinner would be boring and tense. They ran out of things to say; they avoided eye contact; they knew by heart the floral pattern of Tessie's tablecloth. In the end, it was what they wanted: the comfort of the familiar. No surprises. Yet when Sara informed the rest of the family that she had invited Winston, there was only the slightest hint of hesitation before they each welcomed the idea, almost feverish in their assent, and a look of gratitude in her father's eyes.

Now Sara couldn't wait to see how things would unfold. There was a giddiness about the rest of the family. She herself felt calm. She could distance herself from things, view them like a movie. So when she felt emotion, that felt distant too. She thought of the home movies Laura had put on video, that frozen frame of her laughing, her mouth agape with silent glee against the ridiculous background music. Where had it come from, that glee? Where had it gone?

◈ ◈ ◈

For some reason, they had dressed in good clothes – nothing fancy, but not their usual casual, even careless, style of T-shirts and gym shorts. There had been no discussion or planning; they just all appeared in attire as fresh and crisp as the July temperatures would allow. They were all relieved when Winston arrived similarly attired, and they silently congratulated themselves on their good sense or good luck, whichever it might be.

Winston brought flowers: freesias, vigorous-stemmed and fat with color. But what to put them in? Josie hurried to the bathroom, made a small ruckus behind the door, and then emerged with their mother's glass jar of Jean Naté bath beads, minus the beads. It seemed natural that Winston would bring something vivid and intense that would send them scurrying for a vase that in its cheapness did not do the freesias justice. Later, when Sara flushed the toilet, she realized where the bath beads had ended up.

◈ ◈ ◈

The July heat was not burdensome that day. The air was light with a breeze. They sat outside, their parents in the two redwood-stained chairs, looking out at the neighborhood, at the activity in the yards similar to theirs, feeling satisfied at the scene in front of them. Sara sat with Laura on the cement porch; Josie loitered near the gate with the omnipresent camera around her neck. In their midst, perched on an overturned wooden planter gray with age, was Winston, unconcerned about dirt or splinters. He leaned on his hands, canted his torso forward, attentive to them all at once, his interest unfeigned. Behind him, the candle that Tessie kept lit in the bedroom shone through the window and illuminated his head. Conversation was easy. *Happy,* Sara thought. Though oddly, it consisted mainly of comments about the neighborhood, as if it were suddenly new to them.

Her father sniffed the air. "Somebody's barbecuing." They all inhaled deeply, the shared smell uniting them.

Tessie pointed out Mrs. Abayo's dahlias across the street. "Just look how beautiful." They all looked and murmured – the sound of people in church.

From the ball field, the cheers and urgings from the bleachers seemed a validation that all was right with the world.

But then Tessie made a small hiccup of annoyance, because there was that stray cat slipping under the gate and Josie on her knees beckoning to it. The cat, a slender black shorthair, slunk beneath Josie's hand and shot across the yard, skimming the space between Johnny's and Tessie's chairs, and twining itself among a clutch of ferns at the corner of the house. The cat blended into the shade, disappearing except for its unblinking yellow eyes. Tessie sighed and seemed to resign herself to its presence.

After a brief silence, when even the neighborhood noises seemed to fade away, Winston began rattling some rocks in his hands. He had picked them out of one of Tessie's beds of decorative rock, and now he was tossing them back and forth between his hands. Suddenly he was juggling them, ordinary objects that had taken on some magical dimension in his hands. There was no frown of concentration, no tenseness in his jaw or biting of his lip. Josie started snapping pictures, but Winston remained at ease. Sara got up and stood in front of him. "Teach me," she said. She meant the juggling, of course, but she also meant the ease and confidence he showed. Laura and Josie came over too, though Josie did not remove the camera from her neck.

"It's easier to start with balls," Winston said.

So they rounded up old tennis balls from the garage and soon the three sisters stood in a line in front of Winston.

"Start with one." He demonstrated and they copied. "Throw the ball in an arc. Eye level." He made his words a suggestion, his tone encouraging, a hypnotist's voice.

"Now two," he said. Josie extricated herself from the camera strap, and they all took a step forward, eager to show that this was easy for them, that they were ready to move on because they were anxious for the beauty and complexity of three balls in motion. Winston said, "Establish a rhythm." But already balls were dropping. "Throw the balls in an arc, not a circle."

Their parents watched, smiling.

Sara wondered what they were smiling at, what they were pleased about.

"Take your time," Winston told them. "Let your body memorize the movements." Laura reached for a third ball, so Josie and Sara did too.

"Okay," he said, but Sara could see that he was uneasy about their impatience. "But watch again first." As he juggled the three balls in a graceful easy rhythm, he spoke his instructions quietly, his voice as measured as the movement of the balls he kept in the air. The music of his voice was what they listened to, not the words, because in their eagerness to mimic him, they believed that it was all they needed to absorb this gift.

Winston had barely finished his demonstration when they began tossing their balls in the air, awkward and uneven, either too hard or too soft, never managing to have all their balls in motion. Soon, balls were rolling off a hand or dropping from mid-air. Laura held onto hers the longest, but she was desperately drifting and weaving, trying to track the wayward arc of a ball. Finally, when two of her balls collided at her chin, she threw down the third in frustration.

Their parents laughed and applauded, perhaps at their effort, but maybe too at their failure.

"Toss the ball in an arc, not a circle," their father said, making a sweep with his newly healed arm. "Stand straight, don't lean."

It sounded familiar, these instructions, and they realized it's what Winston had been telling them all along. Only they hadn't heard.

"It just takes practice," Winston said, retrieving the balls for them.

◆ ◆ ◆

The table was set for six. There had always been an empty chair opposite Sara and at her father's right hand. A gap.

"Sit there, Winston," Tessie said.

Tessie had made poached chicken garnished with mango sauce from a jar. There was a cucumber salad splashed in lemon and vinegar. And, of course, there was rice. It all sat prettily on the china that they never used. Sara had known better than to bring her SubClub sandwiches to the dinner table tonight. This was no potluck.

They ate the way they would at a restaurant, small bites, no clattering of forks, no dribbling of food from the serving spoon onto the tablecloth – cloth tonight and not vinyl. But there were still paper napkins, which they lay across their laps as Winston did, lifting them to dab at their mouths as appropriate.

"It's delicious," Winston said, and they knew he wasn't just being polite.

◆ ◆ ◆

After dessert – slightly underripe strawberries with milk and sugar to coax them to sweetness – they took themselves, full of food and restaurant manners, to the living room. Their muscles went slack inside the give of the furniture, which seemed friendly and familiar rather than outdated. They began to kid each other, gently, and no one took offense. They joked about Josie and her camera, Sara and her subs, Laura and the videotape she had made of their childhood. Even Johnny and his rangy ears did not escape the jests, which were, after all, affectionate.

Then Winston joined in, offering himself up for fun, volunteering a story about his trip down the interstate, something about the Cadillac, its deliberate pomp and flash, and his efforts to be inconspicuous behind sunglasses.

As they all laughed, something occurred to Sara. Without thinking, without knowing what motivated her, she blurted, "How did you happen to find us?" Because, really, his appearance in their lives seemed uncanny and serendipitous.

The question caught Winston by surprise. Color rose beneath the smooth brownness of his face, and his sudden loss of poise confused the family. Tessie fanned herself with a magazine. Johnny smothered a groan. Sara longed for more magic – juggling or a many-colored scarf pulled from Winston's short sleeve.

"The phone book," he said, finally.

And though Sara couldn't help but feel that the answer that had materialized from the air was not the answer to her question, she was relieved nonetheless.

"Of course, the phone book," Tessie said. She adjusted the vase of Winston's flowers and sent the fragrance of freesias around the room.

14

FLY AWAY, LITTLE BIRD

"I know all about you."

Wren had said this to Winston, in a kindly, confidential way. Of course, she didn't know *all* about him – only what she'd overheard from Linda and Gloria and even the twins, who were probably quite conversant in the hearsay surrounding Winston and the de la Cruz family.

"About your mother, I mean. And your father," she explained. "I think I understand your attraction to the de la Cruz family."

Winston was certain she didn't, but he appreciated her concern, her attention to him, her graceful limbs and pretty mouth.

After the Fourth of July picnic, he had met her again the day he read to Johnny in the sun room so stifling and monotonous with heat. He had picked a book from their dusty Book-of-the-Month-Club shelf. An unexpected assortment: *Valley of the Dolls*, *In Cold Blood*, *Rebecca*, *Portnoy's Complaint*. Except for Art Linkletter's *Kids Say the Darndest Things*, the books seemed hardly touched, their jackets clammy from the heavy air, adhering to each other and making little cleaving sounds as he removed one or another to sample its pages. He chose *Watership Down*.

"It's about rabbits?" Johnny asked, incredulous, after Winston had read a few pages. After a few more pages, Johnny's bafflement was eased by snores. Winston had been ready to make a quiet exit, but Sara stopped by unexpectedly, so he sat with her on the patio, curbed his anxiety, and made small talk. When he checked his watch with a glance meant to be casual yet perceptibly pressing, Sara urged him on his way. He went gratefully to Wren.

Winston had been aware of Wren's green eyes on him at the Fourth of July picnic. His focus had been on the family – the de la Cruzes and the others, too. He did not want to raise Linda's perfectly penciled eyebrows, nor excite the already piqued curiosity of the sharp-eyed twins, nor trigger gossip from Gloria. Still, he went to meet Wren that day after lulling Johnny to sleep. They drank beers in Bev's side yard where the roses were dropping their dark petals, their moldering scent a dizzying additive to the alcohol. But they did not lose their heads. Winston was circumspect. Wren was patient.

Sunday dinner had changed things. Before, there had been questions in the air, a cloud of gnats not quite within swatting distance. Now it seemed there was some tacit pact to take no notice of these nearly invisible nuisances. He had performed well, and Johnny and Tessie had applauded his juggling act. He had sat at the family dinner table; later, when Sara had asked out loud that question that could have ruined everything, no one had let it.

The next afternoon Wren came over again. This time, they left their beers out on the lawn, stepped over the growing mound of fallen rose petals, across the threshold of Winston's rented room, and into his borrowed bed. Later, Winston watched Wren sleep, her red hair spread across his bare brown chest, a color combination that he had to admit was not terribly agreeable. The red required the contrast of her own pale, delicately freckled skin. Winston peered down at her face, her closed lids sparsely fringed with straight short lashes, her nose that was a tad too long. Yet she was lovely, and her nakedness that should have made her seem vulnerable as she slept was instead both artless and composed.

He wondered what she really knew about him. He imagined that the gossip flowed rather freely from Tessie to Gloria to Linda and back again. For a brief unsettling moment, he wondered if Wren's interest was calculated, meant only to gain his trust and a trove of details about him. Wren shifted in her sleep, moved her head deeper into his chest, brought her long fingers to rest against his belly.

She had slipped her phone number into his hand that day at the beach. They were packing up the picnic food. As she passed him the Tupperware bowl with the runny remains of potato salad, he found a business card thrust into his palm. He tucked it into his pocket. Later that night, when he was shaking the sand out of his clothes, the card drifted to the floor. There was no business of any sort printed on the card, just a drawing of a small bird, a phone number, and her name. Wren Bailey.

Wren, like the bird, the twins had chorused.

Bailey – an Irish name. He wondered if Carlitos had a new family, an Irish one; if he had brown children with red hair.

◈ ◈ ◈

When Winston was in the third grade at Remedios Academy in a Manila suburb several neighborhoods away from his own, his teacher – an old nun whose face was deceptively kind – had asked the students to draw a picture of their family for Parents' Night. Winston liked to draw, and he had already filled many sheets at home at the kitchen table with portraits of Bunny. She was easy to draw. She made a good subject with all her colors. Even the scent of her seemed to transfer to the page. Carlitos was harder to put on paper. There was nothing that precisely or immediately defined him, like Bunny's hoop earrings or the gauzy red shawl that she wrapped around her shoulders in the evenings, or the high heels she wore whenever she left the house. Now, when Winston tried drawing them together, even though Carlitos was much taller than Bunny, somehow Bunny always took up more of the page. When Winston introduced himself into the picture, the spatial relationships went further askew, with himself and Carlitos appearing to be the same size.

Winston made dozens of attempts at portraying his family. Finally, he succeeded in rendering their relative sizes more realistically. He did this by drawing Carlitos first, then measuring off space that was smaller head-to-toe than Carlitos and fitting Bunny into the notch marks. He did the same for himself. But he found he had started too small with Carlitos and now there was too much unused space on the paper. It didn't seem right or fair. It hit him then what he lacked: a brother or a sister, or one or more of each, like Benjie Bayani who had siblings to spare, so many they were hard to keep track of. Winston wanted to see what his picture would look like with the spaces filled in. He drew in a brother, then a sister. To even things out, he added another sister, so now they were a family of six.

Though he knew it was wrong, knew that everyone would know that this was not really his family, he took the picture to school. When the teacher called his name to come to the front of the classroom, he held it in front of him and named each person in his drawing: his mother Bunny, his father Carlitos, his brother Salvador, and his sisters Pilar and Teresita. They were good made-up names, ones he was sure Bunny and Carlitos might have chosen.

Benjie Bayani, who earlier had been reprimanded by the teacher for having drawn a crowd of look-alike stick figures to represent his family, protested with a howl. The other children in the class pointed and laughed at Winston's new siblings.

Winston was made to apologize, visit the principal's office for a scolding, and then sit in the corner of the classroom to contemplate the wrong he had done. At recess, when the other children went to play, the teacher led him back to his desk, her cold hand wrapped around his wrist, and told him to draw another picture – one that told the truth about his family.

◈ ◈ ◈

He and Wren sat on the grass in front of the Kimball Park library, a small flat-roofed, one-story brick structure built in the Fifties. He had gone inside once to pass the time, to read a newspaper or flip through a magazine. It felt too cramped and outdated, the shelves chipped and carved with the initials of earnest adolescents, the books dog-eared and stained, the computers obsolete, the bathrooms accessible only with a pass from the front desk.

Sara had mentioned to him once that when they were children, she and her sisters would spend their Saturdays at the library. "After catechism class, we'd go across the street and take an hour to choose our books. Then we'd come out to the grass and read until my dad came to pick us up."

Now Winston imagined himself as a boy, reading a book on the grass, then turning at the honk of a horn to see Johnny waiting for him to get in the car to go home.

"That is so pitiful," Wren said.

Winston was relieved when he realized she was referring to the library. Together they stared at the faded brick building. He put his hand on hers. He liked that she didn't mind coming to Kimball Park, that she was indignant on its behalf. He wanted to see her in this environment of low-end tract homes, cheap strip malls, omnipresent graffiti, and a tumbledown library. She found it *interesting*. "Really," she assured him. She was a psychology major, one who drove her father's BMW to her part-time nanny job that was not at all essential to her survival.

◈ ◈ ◈

Winston was a scholarship student at Remedios Academy, because "you're smart," his mother told him. *Because you're poor,* some of his classmates taunted. One evening over a modest dinner of rice and fried fish, Winston asked his parents if they were poor. His mother's eyebrows rose ferociously. "We are middle class," she said.

Winston wasn't sure what his father did for a living, though Carlitos had told him once: *entrepreneur*. Carlitos pointed to his head. "I have ideas," he said.

Bunny worked at the cosmetics counter at the Ever Emporium, where she received discounts on all the makeup merchandise. She had hoarded her discounted purchases until she had enough to fill a tackle box. At first she toted that tackle box around the noisy streets littered with candy wrappers and cigarette butts on her very own neighborhood beautification project, lengthening the lashes of Cecilia Labao and putting color in the cheeks of old Mrs. Rojas. She made women ready for *work, play, and every day*. (Winston had helped think up the slogan.) It wasn't as if women hadn't already been wearing make-up. It was just that Bunny had a knack. She made thin lips look fuller and thick lips more subtle; she plucked and brushed eyebrows to arch their emotive best; she blended colors to accentuate the eyes, whether round, almond, or slanted; she created the effect of cheekbones on faces with no contour; she gave a lift to flat noses; she camouflaged pimples, moles, and warts. Soon, Bunny no longer had to tote the tackle box from house to house. The women came to her in the evenings and on the weekends, and sometimes before Bunny went off to her shift at the Ever Emporium cosmetics counter. Bunny was in demand. She was in charge. So if she said they were middle class, then it must be true.

⬥ ⬥ ⬥

Though Sunday dinner had signaled a new stage in his relationship with the de la Cruzes, Winston did not feel it prudent to disclose his developing involvement with Wren to the family. For her part, Wren had abided by his polite suggestion that they maintain their privacy. In the short time they had been seeing one another – a matter of days, really – they had been to the zoo, ridden the roller coaster at the beachfront amusement park, and browsed the swap meet. Each time, he had wanted to buy her something – a souvenir or gift, something meaningful, in exchange for her discretion. But nothing struck him as appropriate – a hand-crafted Zulu basket, a stuffed animal, a bootleg DVD. Nothing was right. He looked in the direction of the library as if behind the smudged window panes lay precisely the answer. He felt anxious that he had come up with nothing.

Wren tugged at his hand. "Come on, let's walk."

They wandered past tennis courts that had grass growing in the seams of the asphalt, a baseball diamond that lacked bases and tetherball poles without tetherballs. Under a tree, they stopped. She leaned into him and he kissed the top of her red head, and the sensation of his lips against her fruity-smelling hair made him think of food. He looked at his watch. "I have to go."

Wren tilted her head back and looked up at him, the length of her nose more pronounced at this angle. "Where?" she asked.

"Sara invited me to stop by the SubClub. She wants my opinion on something."

Wren stepped back altogether, allowing some space between

them, though she pressed her palm, fingers spread, against his chest. "I can come along if you want."

Winston was sorry that she was challenging the pact, that she was making him say no to her. "It's better if I go alone."

She sighed, her hand traced his sternum. "That family," she said, "you either belong or you don't. I have nothing to do with it."

"It's not that simple," he said, annoyed a bit at her ignorance.

She took his hand, but he let go, so she turned and strode away. She was already out of hearing distance when he called her name. *Wren.*

◈ ◈ ◈

The little brown birds were everywhere – in the rice fields of the provinces, on the telephone wires and rooftops in the cities, and painted on Bunny's paper fan. They were almost as numerous as the flies that lit on the runny noses of children, buzzed the street vendors selling papayas from bicycle carts, and drove patrons from sidewalk cafes. But the birds were not nuisances – not normally. They were so common that Winston had almost ceased to notice them. One day, though, he was walking on Fernando Street between Carlitos and Bunny, the three of them dressed in their Sunday clothes on a hot Saturday afternoon. Bunny kept a steady rhythm with her fan and the maya birds painted there moved madly in the humid heat. Carlitos dabbed at his temples with a handkerchief.

Suddenly, a cloud of maya birds whirled just overhead, stirring the steaming air, and Carlitos shook the damp square of cloth at the little sparrows.

"Too many birds," he complained.

"They're social birds," Bunny told him, "Like the Filipino people," she added in a near-reprimand of her husband.

Then one bird landed for a moment on Carlitos's shoulder,

which delighted Winston. He leapt up to capture it in his fist, but the bird eluded him: it flapped its wings against Carlitos's ear and disappeared into the fronds of a coconut tree, leaving a plug of greenish shit on Carlitos's Sunday jacket. Bunny covered up her laughter in a shrieky admonishment of the bird. Carlitos handed his sweat-drenched handkerchief to Winston and made him wipe away the mess as if he, Winston, were somehow responsible. When Carlitos was presentable, Bunny had composed herself, and Winston had blinked back the tears in his eyes, the three of them walked into the Fernando Street Studio for a family portrait.

◈ ◈ ◈

At the SubClub, tucked away in the corner of a strip mall, Sara greeted him with a pat on the back and Josie scooted to make room for him on the plastic bench. Laura nudged a glass of water toward him. The booth was small and he realized he had never sat so close to the sisters before.

They didn't look much alike, though they complained that people often mistook one for the other. He could understand that too. They were nearly the same height and shared more or less the same straight and lanky silhouette. Nevertheless, they were easy to differentiate. Laura with her fashion eyeglass frames, tailored blouses, and slacks with chemically sustained creases cared the most about her appearance. She wore a touch of lipstick, and earrings that dangled modestly. Josie wore shorts and an oversized polo that might have been her absent husband's or even her son's. Sara wore her SubClub T-shirt and apron over jeans. Neither seemed to have a clue about make-up. Both had their hair tied back, Josie's in a careless braid and Sara's in a low, neat ponytail.

Winston remembered his own long hair that Stormie had scissored and razored away. It had grown since then and could use some shaping now.

"We're all here," Laura said.

The words were inclusive and uniting, and Winston couldn't help repeating them. "Yep, we're all here." He felt happy to be part of this taste test.

It was near closing time in the middle of the week, when business was slow. Sara went behind the counter where all the breads, meats, cheeses, and mustards were arrayed. Sara's daughter Gina and Laura's daughter Mona were snapping lids on condiments and stretching plastic wrap across metal containers of sliced, diced, and minced vegetables. Winston nodded briefly to the girls. He always avoided them as much as possible. It bothered him that he was closer in age to them than to the de la Cruz sisters.

Sara came back with a sub cut in thirds. She lifted the top bun to reveal chorizo, avocado, pico de gallo, jack cheese, egg, and shredded lettuce. It was her invention – a new sandwich she was going to recommend to franchise headquarters as an addition to the menu. "Close your eyes and taste it," she instructed.

Winston obeyed. "Good," he pronounced after a single bite, but then wondered if he'd spoken too soon. He opened his eyes and saw Laura, eyes open, assessing both him and the sandwich she held in front of her face. Laura took a few discriminatory bites, her gaze now lifted to the fake Tiffany ceiling lamp as she contemplated her mouthful. Josie was packing fallen shreds of cheese back inside her bun. Winston felt foolish that he had been the only one to close his eyes.

"Who do you think will want to order this sandwich?" Josie asked, and Winston wished he had thought to ask some practical, clarifying question.

Laura took a sip of water, rinsing her palate with authority. "You know, there's the place on the other end of the mall that sells tortas. Are you trying to compete with them?"

"It might be a little imitative," Winston ventured.

Sara looked hurt. "I thought you said it was good."

All three sisters were looking at him.

"Yes," Winston said, trying to quell the defensive note in his voice. "I did." He decided to take the taste-test discussion back to Josie's question. "But is it right for the SubClub audience?"

"Audience?" Josie laughed. "It's fast food, not dinner theater."

Winston tried not to feel stung. He remembered that Benjie Bayani and his boatload of siblings always argued and said scornful things to each other.

"Well, it *is* good," Laura said, and Winston was relieved, and just a little bothered that no one seemed to have remembered that he had said it first.

"What do you call it?" Josie asked. "It has to have a name." She pointed at the menu board above the counter that listed the Tuscan, the Traditional, the Classic, the All-American.

"How about the Monterrey?" Winston blurted, inspired by the bits of Mexican chorizo and jack cheese that lay scattered on the plate. Under the table, he scrunched a paper napkin.

The sisters looked at him again. "Perfect," they agreed.

A half-hour later, when Winston drove away from the SubClub, he was pleased with the world or at least his small part of it. *Perfect,* he mused, echoing the sisters' assessment of him – well, not of him exactly, but still. He had been right to have left Wren out of it. After all, what did she know of Sunday dinners and juggling acts? Then the letter, its existence known only to him, intruded on his thoughts. He wanted to ignore it. It should've been enough that he was accepted as some sort of addendum to the family. It *was* enough, he told himself, determined not to glance at the glove box.

15

THE PRACTICAL CONSIDERATIONS OF LIFE

Tessie and Gloria were heading to the IHOP for lunch after a morning of shopping – but not at the feeble mall in Kimble Park, ignored for years by the locals in favor of the San Diego malls that glittered at the edges of the freeway. In recent years, a few miles to the south and east of their neighborhoods, mini-plazas of boutiques, drug stores, and family restaurants – along with the occasional Target or K-Mart – had sprouted on the hills, replacing the chaparral and black mustard. These nearby mini-plazas were more accessible to Tessie and Gloria, especially since they both were inclined to tension and panic on crowded freeways.

Gloria's constant stream of chatter didn't help matters. When Gloria talked and drove at the same time, Tessie could manage only the sporadic *uh-huh*, so busy was she watching the road for hazards Gloria would surely miss. It was worse when Tessie drove, as she did now. Although she only half-listened to Gloria, she also only half-concentrated on her driving and always ended up with a splitting headache. But the IHOP was not far, traffic was light, and at the moment Gloria was preoccupied with examining her purchases – rhinestone-studded denim purses for the twins and some lace bras for Linda. Tessie, who knew better than to buy underwear for her own grown daughters, came away with sports logo T-shirts for each of her grandchildren. Didn't all kids wear such things? She thought so. But sometimes she wondered what they really thought of the things she bought for them, what they really thought of her.

Tessie and Gloria never bought anything for themselves on these shopping trips, though today Tessie had been tempted by an emerald green dress on the sale rack, twenty-five percent off. "Going to buy that?" Gloria had asked. Tessie had already let the fabric drop from her hand, turning nonchalantly away from its sleek smartness. It was always there – that unspoken competition for selflessness. As mothers, even of grown children, they saw their role as putting their children first. Only on the rare occasions when she shopped alone did Tessie buy something for herself, as Gloria must. How else was she forever showing up in a new blouse or slacks? Like today. Tessie had certainly never seen Gloria wear *that* outfit before.

Tessie pulled into the IHOP parking lot, ringed by a Sav-On, a Jenny Craig, and a Baskin-Robbins.

"I'm starving," Gloria said, as they got out of the car. "Aren't you?"

"A little," Tessie said. "I had a big breakfast this morning," she said, wishing she really had.

"What are you going to have?" Gloria asked when they were seated in a narrow booth, laminated menus in hand.

*What are **you** going to have,* Tessie wanted to say back. "I don't know," she said.

She was trying to decide between the Lo-Cal special and the bacon cheeseburger and fries. The choices were illustrated with full-color photographs. The peaches in the Lo-Cal special looked overly orange and glossy.

When their waitress appeared with sloppy little glasses of ice water, Gloria ordered the Caesar salad. Tessie went with the

Lo-Cal plate. The peaches were bound to look better in real life.

Tessie sighed just as the waitress came back with their food and left the grease-spotted check at the edge of the table. She looked at her plate. The peaches, bathed in syrup, were indeed overly orange. She spooned them onto her napkin to drain.

Gloria nibbled at her salad. Gloria ate like a bird, and Tessie wondered if she still took appetite suppressants. Certainly, Gloria would never admit to such a thing, even if a foil packet of capsules were to fall in plain sight from her purse.

Over their meal, they talked as usual of their children and grandchildren. It was not a competition, Tessie told herself, though she suspected that Gloria exaggerated Linda's acquisitions and Sonny's celebrity acquaintances. Tessie, on the other hand, exaggerated the shortcomings and blunders of her daughters, and was overly modest on their behalf about any positive qualities. She didn't know why she did this.

"Linda said we should go up and use their hot tub while they're in Hawaii," Gloria said, chasing a wayward crouton around her plate with her fork.

"When do we ever go and sit in a hot tub?" Tessie said, laughing but appalled by the idea of exposing her thighs, even to her sister.

Gloria trapped the crouton at the edge of her plate and slid her fork underneath it. "Well, they'll be in Hawaii for two weeks. I tell you, that family loves to travel."

"Laura's going to Long Beach for an optometrist convention," Tessie said.

Gloria raised her coffee cup to her chin, pausing to consider Tessie with narrowed eyes, though just narrow enough to avoid showing the deepest wrinkles. "You need a vacation," she pronounced.

This was true, Tessie agreed to herself. "I don't know," she told her sister.

"It's stressful having a sick spouse. They tell you that in those support groups," she said knowingly. "Haven't they told you that?"

Tessie nodded, though she hadn't sat among the women in the support group long enough for them to tell her much of anything. The one time she had gone, there had been too many doughnuts and cookies on the table, and the women had adopted a tendency to take small bites of a cruller or an old-fashioned as they shared their grief, a tear sometimes rolling down a cheek and making a smear of the powdered sugar that had strayed there. It had made her throat clog with saliva – the raw grief amid all those sweets.

She'd never told Gloria about her dance classes. There were some things she would not confide to her, though she wondered if Gloria suspected. They were a family whose secrets often turned out not to be so secret after all – just camouflaged like a little rubber duck on the shelf blending into the daisy wallpaper.

"I don't feel right about leaving," Tessie said. Her reluctance had to do with the rapport that had been conjured between Winston and her family, not to mention the new dynamic between herself and Johnny – the touching of hands, the earnest looks and shy words. It was an almost tranquil place to exist, and she was afraid if she left, it would be like wrenching away one of the blocks near the base of a slim, precisely fitted tower. Yet she knew she could be convinced to go, because this almost tranquil place they found themselves in made her fearful, even expectant of calamity, and she did not want to wait around for it.

Whatever the situation, Gloria always knew someone else who suffered in the same way or worse. "My hairdresser's husband was sick. It was emphysema, oh, the coughing and the spitting, all that phlegm, I tell you. Anyway, he finally told her to go away for a weekend because he needed a break from *her*. Can you imagine?"

Tessie couldn't imagine Johnny suggesting she go away.

Gloria sipped her coffee and then stared into her cup, contemplating the muddy color. "You should come with me and Rey to Vegas on the senior bus."

It was a trip the couples used to take together. Even though Tessie and Gloria did not really consider themselves seniors, they nevertheless enjoyed taking advantage of the buses chartered by the Filipino Seniors Club: air-conditioning, free coffee and doughnuts, and sandwiches for $1.50.

"I don't know," Tessie said. "I don't know how much time is left."

"Tessie," Gloria said, setting her coffee cup down firmly, "it could happen while you're taking a long bubble bath in your own home with Johnny in the next room." Then she told of another friend whose husband was diagnosed with cancer, given less than a year to live: the wife had died first, hit by a bus. "And the husband lived ten more years. Can you imagine?" Gloria pushed her plate away in disgust at such trickery. "Some things are just out of our hands."

"It's just a weekend," she assured Tessie. "Anyway, Josie's there. And that Winston, too."

◈ ◈ ◈

When Tessie dropped Gloria off, Rey was dozing in a chair in the driveway, at his feet an overturned tackle box, its tangled contents sunbathing on the cement.

"He's cleaning out the garage," Gloria explained. She leaned over and honked the horn. Rey lifted his head and opened an eye.

"Talk to Johnny today," Gloria said.

Tessie turned the radio on low as she drove away, since the car was quiet now without Gloria's monologue. Gloria had talked again of illness and its consequences, inevitably bringing the conversation back to herself, always seeming to find relevance to one of her conditions – most often her hysterectomy, for which she still nurtured a sense of tragedy.

Tessie wondered what that felt like – to have that physical space inside of you emptied out. She had been intact all these years. Even into her mid- and late forties, there had always been the possibility of pregnancy, though they had stopped trying because they didn't want to risk another disappointment, another girl. It was a terrible way to put it. At a certain point in their lives, though, another pregnancy just would not do, at least not for her.

◈ ◈ ◈

A few months after Johnny's return from the Philippines, Tessie was late with her period. She told herself she had merely miscalculated the days. She would not panic, she told herself as she left work that evening, even when on her way out the door, she snagged her sales smock on a nail and ripped one of her pockets cleanly away, dropping used Kleenex tissue, a tube of lipstick and a few quarters in her wake.

When she got home, she took her place at the dinner table. Sara had heated the casserole Tessie had made that morning – but it wasn't heated through. When Tessie tasted the lukewarm noodles and the gluey coldness of the sauce, she dropped her fork and cried, silently at first, so her family didn't immediately notice.

"Food's cold," Josie hissed. Sara slammed down her own fork and began to retrieve the servings, sliding them back into the pan. She carried the pan, needlessly using a potholder, back to the oven. There was only a tattered salad on the table now.

Johnny decided to light his after-dinner cigarette before dinner. Tessie put her face in her hands and sobbed.

It's not a tragedy, she heard Laura say.

Tessie stood up, gasped incoherently at her family and then fled the room, Josie's whispered "jeez" making a small gust behind her.

She lay stomach-down on the bed in the semi-dark. She heard quiet talking in the kitchen, then joking and hushed laughter. Soon enough, she heard the oven door and then the sound of forks against plates. She couldn't help herself. She raised herself off the bed and went to stand near the door, so that when a loud knock came from the other side, she nearly jumped.

"You okay?" Johnny asked.

Tessie didn't trust herself to answer. She held herself still, so he wouldn't guess how close she was to the door.

Tessie watched the doorknob twist. She heard Johnny sigh at the locked door.

"You think you might be overreacting?"

She shook her head no on her side of the door. When she heard him walk away, his house slippers scuffling against the carpet, she quietly released the lock on the door and tiptoed back to the bed. On her stomach again, she slipped her hands beneath her to cradle her abdomen, massaging it at times, sometimes pinching hard.

She turned over to lie on her back, hands still on her belly, remembering the abortion – how when it was over, all she could feel was relief that they had undone what they had so recklessly done and could now get married as if nothing had ever happened. A clean slate. When she told her parents there would be no church wedding, Concha and Fredo Navarro at first had demurred, but not wishing to pursue the matter too vigorously for fear of confirming any unsettling suspicions, they stood as witnesses to the courthouse ceremony. Despite their religion, they were all attentive to the practical considerations of life.

She fell asleep, not waking until early morning. She was on her side, facing Johnny's back, his bumpy backbone visible through his white undershirt. As she lay in bed, she became aware of a dull pressure in her abdomen. She held her breath, staring at the knuckles of her husband's spine, counting them as if they were beads. When she was sure that the sensation in her abdomen would continue, she closed her eyes and waited until it was an ache. Then she rose quietly and moved to the bathroom where she removed her underwear and rinsed the blood from it in the sink, not once looking up to see herself in the mirror, not wanting to see the disappointment, refusing to see the relief. She reached in the medicine cabinet for an aspirin.

◈ ◈ ◈

At home Tessie put away the T-shirts she had bought. She wasn't sure anymore that her grandkids would like them. She could do without their disappointed looks. When would she learn that it was cash they wanted?

For dinner that evening Josie had bought *pozole* at the Mexican take-out. "No need to cook tonight," she announced when she came home from work that afternoon, though Tessie had in fact planned to make a soup herself. She felt like simmering something on the stove. Instead, they sat down to bowls of *pozole* that had been zapped in the microwave.

Tessie broke the sound of earnest slurping. "How was work today?" she asked Josie.

"Smelly."

Johnny, who was bent over his bowl, lifted his eyes. "Why do you stay at that job?"

"I like it," she said as she reached for a tortilla.

Johnny looked around the table sparsely laid with only their bowls, the tortilla warmer, and glasses of water.

Annoyed, Tessie got up to get the box of saltines. Josie had forgotten that Johnny didn't like tortillas, but it was a minor thing and there was no reason to call attention to it. At least Winston knew many of Johnny's dislikes and preferences. There was that to rely on if she were to go away for the weekend. So she said nothing to admonish Josie.

"What color are you painting your kitchen? I saw some curtains today that would look good in the window above the sink," Tessie asked, wanting to be nice.

Josie turned on her. "Mom, I don't need new curtains. Why don't you buy something for yourself when you shop?"

Tessie thought of the green dress with regret.

◈ ◈ ◈

Josie volunteered to do the dishes, which consisted only of their soup bowls and water glasses. Johnny zipped up his sweatshirt, gray with no logos, one that Winston had bought him, and shuffled outside to sit for a while and watch the summer evening fade. After a moment, Tessie followed and sat in the chair next to Johnny.

It was late July. Summer was going by fast. It would soon be over. She looked over at Johnny, who had both hands curled around the end of the armrests as if to keep from sliding off. His grip seemed strong.

There was no Little League game tonight. Still, there were kids on skateboards and on foot, a boom box hoisted on a shoulder or hugged at the waist. They were heading to the park to hang out and smoke. Cars rolled by, music blaring from open windows, occupants hunkered down in their seats, their eyes roaming the street for some action. Some of their neighbors were out in their front yards, watering lawns or snipping hedges, or, like them, just sitting inside their chain-link fenced yards.

Johnny was jiggling his leg. He had always had that habit. Usually she ignored it, the obnoxious, bobbing rhythm of it. But now she put her hand on his knee to make him stop.

16

THE RAINS, THE CAT, AND THE CANDLE

Unless he turned sideways, the Virgin was the first thing Johnny saw each morning when he sat up in bed. The paper Virgin of Guadalupe was glued to a clear glass cylinder that held a lit candle. The flame made the Virgin appear three-dimensional, movement flickering into her gold-flecked green robes and the yellow aura encircling her. At night, it was a spooky sight. In daylight, it was hard to distinguish the candle from among Tessie's knick-knacks.

Tessie had always burned a candle for some reason or other – each time a daughter went off to sixth-grade camp, took her driving test, needed a date for the prom, or some other exigency. All good and worthy reasons to petition for assistance, though Johnny scoffed at the ritual.

But here was this candle for him. Not one of those small votives, this one was a foot high, the wax poured to within an inch of the glass lip. And it didn't stand alone. Around the candle, Tessie had arranged a small throng of other saints – plastic statues or laminated holy cards propped up by whatever was handy, a half-empty atomizer or the plastic cap of a hair spray can, which seemed even to him, a non-believer, a rather unsacred thing.

From the beginning, since the day Dr. Lee delivered the

diagnosis, Tessie had burned a candle, never letting the flame die, transferring it to a new candle when the old one threatened to dwindle to a pool of wax. The candle had a life of six days, more or less. On the calendar, Tessie marked the day she lit a new candle. Then she marked the fourth day after that. On that day she began checking the candle at intervals, a nurse monitoring a patient's vital signs.

Yesterday, a Friday, was one of those days she had marked on the calendar with a little red exclamation point, a code of warning to herself to be on the watch for the candle's decline. Yesterday was also the day she left.

She had never gone on a trip without Johnny.

"Are you sure you don't mind?" She had asked twice, but not a third time. He just shrugged. So she went. Now as he lay in bed alone he could only wonder when his shrugs had stopped meaning anything but no.

Tessie would be back tomorrow, sometime Sunday night. *Too late,* he thought, looking at the candle which had burned down to illuminate the Virgin of Guadalupe right about the knees, putting a silly bend in her beatific pose.

◈ ◈ ◈

Today was the first time Winston was coming over because someone had asked him to – not invited him, but asked as a favor. Except for the recent Sunday dinner, all the other visits had been at Winston's initiative in response to Johnny's rather indifferently issued *drop by anytime.* Winston had become such a presence in their lives over the past weeks that something seemed off if they didn't see him for a few days. "Wonder where Winston is," one of them would say, casually, as if it were a matter of little importance. Then they went about adjusting the speed of the fan or turning up the volume on the TV to compensate for his absence.

When Tessie's impending trip became a given rather than a

possibility, she offered to call Winston, sure that he would be happy to check in on Johnny during the weekend.

"I know he will," Tessie said, and Johnny wondered at her certainty.

Even though during his social visits, Winston had taken on caregiver tasks – now and then slipping a blanket around Johnny's shoulders, bringing a fresh glass of water for him to wash down his pills, tucking a pillow behind his head when he dozed off – these were incidental to his being there. He had never been called on specifically to minister to Johnny.

There was no need, Johnny told her. It seemed too much to ask, a commitment too personal to expect from someone outside the family – even Winston.

"Besides, Josie's around," he added.

"Nope," Josie said. "Not on Saturday. It's our semi-annual adoption fair. And there's our spaghetti dinner fundraiser that night."

"Well, that settles it," Tessie said.

◈ ◈ ◈

He had expected to sleep fitfully with Tessie gone and was a little disappointed about his relatively restful night. Johnny glared at the shelf of saints.

Before leaving for Las Vegas, Tessie had cooked meals to last three days, stacked clean towels and linen, made sure that none of Johnny's prescriptions would run out, bought the latest *TV Guide*, and left a page of instructions in her egg-shaped handwriting taped to the refrigerator for Josie and Winston.

But had she checked the candle? Johnny opened his eyes and looked at it. It wouldn't burn out today. Sometime tomorrow, he figured. He thought of her returning home to find the candle extinguished, a hardened pool of wax.

The kitchen door slammed and then Josie appeared in the bedroom doorway sweaty and huffing, just back from a run.

Johnny noted the large circle of sweat at the neckline of her T-shirt. Johnny sweated from fevers, hardly ever from physical exertion anymore.

Josie panted. "Toast and oatmeal for breakfast?"

"Just oatmeal. Thin."

"I know. Mom wrote everything down," Josie said, already heading toward the kitchen doing cool-down lunges.

"Maybe not everything," Johnny called, not meaning to be heard, still hoping he would be.

He decided to eat in bed, but soon regretted it as he felt he had an audience in the saints lined up on the shelf. He stirred and slurped the lukewarm oatmeal that wasn't quite the right thinness. He slurped louder and met the flat, painted gaze of the saints. Though he could hardly tell them apart, he knew which ones watched over him.

Tessie had assembled them gradually, bringing in reinforcements with the same collector's zeal with which she added plants to fill dead spots in her garden or knick-knacks to unused surfaces in the living room. There was St. Christopher, patron saint of sailors. Not having been a sailor in years, Johnny wondered if St. Christopher's protection extended to the honorably discharged. There was St. Gabriel, patron saint of messengers – including, apparently, retired postal workers. St. Michael, the Archangel, patron saint of the sick, was given a place of prominence next to the Virgin of Guadalupe. On standby at the back of the shelf was St. Jude for desperate situations.

◈ ◈ ◈

Josie stood in the doorway, where a band of sunlight from the window made dust particles visible around her. The light muted the glow of the candle, which Johnny was doing his best to ignore.

"I'm going now."

He wanted her to stay, even if it was only to listen to the neurotic drum of her fingernails on the furniture, or the huff and puff of her exhalations as she did bicep curls, or the maddening shutter clicks from her camera. But he couldn't ask her.

He gave a limp wave, which made her lean inside to peer at him. She wore an *Ask Me About Adoption* button. "Everything okay?"

"Fine," Johnny said, looking hard at the button to keep from looking at the candle.

"Okay. See you tonight. Winston should be here in half an hour."

After she left, the anticipation he felt about the candle seemed to fill the house like a heavy perfume that numbed the nostrils and coated the tongue. It made him irritable and apprehensive about seeing Winston.

Not since their first meeting had Johnny awaited Winston's arrival with such quiet panic. The reason for Winston's sudden appearance had never been broached, and the unspoken questions had languished into something harmless and ignored like elevator music. It had been easy to ignore; in fact, it had seemed right to do so. But now, like the subtle persistence of elevator music, it had forced itself to the front of his thoughts. What did Winston want from him? What did he want from Winston? Their relationship so far had been a success – their time together easy and comfortably superficial. Winston had made all the effort. Johnny had accepted his overtures – had even welcomed them, to a point. But now he sensed they had trod the same safe ground too long. It could give way under their feet. Even so, his fear of such a collapse was outweighed by his need for company. So he tried to wait for Winston as though it were just any other day.

After flicking the TV on and off a few times, then marking

a few answers sloppily in a crossword puzzle, Johnny decided to get dressed and go outside to wait for Winston. When Hector Cabrera shuffled outside his front door at the same time Johnny did, they stopped and nodded to each other. They seldom spoke these days. They had never been friends, though they had been friendly once. The Cabreras had six children, three girls and three boys, in that order. Johnny had always wondered if he and Tessie had had one more child, would it have been a boy?

The Cabrera children had, one by one, left home to settle in some other state, each one moving farther than the one before. And when all six children had left the confines of the four-bedroom house, Hector's wife also left. Hector's explanation differed over the years.

"She's visiting her mother," he said at first.

"She's getting treatment for female problems," he said later.

"She left," he said, finally, an explanation given with such grim testiness that no one dared approach him about the noisy rooster he kept.

Hector and the other neighbors had seen Winston and his Cadillac coming and going. Is that your nephew, they asked. A family friend, he told them.

This morning Hector asked, "How's your nephew?"

"He's not my nephew," Johnny said. "No relation."

That was the end of the conversation, and as they both shuffled back inside their respective homes, Johnny started to wonder if Hector doubted him, the way they had all doubted Hector when he explained the whereabouts of his wife.

◈ ◈ ◈

Winston arrived wearing tennis clothes. The white cloth against his brown skin made him stand out in the yellow-gold monochrome of the living room. Johnny approved of

Winston's athletic appearance though it made him feel all the more frail.

Johnny's legs never saw the sun. Even when he had been healthy, he had never bared his skinny legs. So even on the hottest days, when he mowed the lawn or built the playhouse or laid the brick paths in the backyard, his legs sweated inside long pants. He hadn't worn shorts since he was a boy in the Philippines.

"Who do you play tennis with?" Johnny asked, realizing he never thought much about what Winston did when he wasn't here at the house.

"My landlady."

"She's young, then?"

"In her sixties," Winston laughed, but then he must have read the surprise and envy in Johnny's face. "It's a slow game. She barely gets it over the net."

Johnny wondered if that were really so. He wondered if Winston were sparing his feelings and, if so, he wondered at the motive behind it.

Winston looked around the room as if he'd never seen it before. His eyes landed on the stack of board games beneath the coffee table. "You wanna play some Scrabble?"

Johnny didn't. There was a listlessness about the day that made them both awkward and restive. Maybe it was Winston's tennis clothes, their incompatibility with the de la Cruz house. They watched TV for a while, channel surfing mostly, getting glimpses of sitcom lives, sinking putts, ballroom dancers, America's most wanted. Ballroom dancers. Johnny flipped back to the dancers in showy costumes performing showy moves. He watched them awhile, the women in heavy makeup, the men in makeup almost as heavy, their moves overblown, their smiles unreasonably big.

He snorted. "That's not how people really dance."

"They're professionals, Johnny. They're just adding a lot of fancy combinations."

Winston sprang to his tennis-sneakered feet. "Look, the basic step is easy."

Johnny watched Winston walk sideways and backward, sideways and forward.

"It's a box," Winston said, demonstrating again, his feet nimbly skimming the carpet.

Johnny knew it was a box. He wasn't stupid. He just didn't know how to match the box to the music.

"Listen," Winston said, his head cocked to the television. He began to snap his fingers and count.

Johnny nodded his head, the way he remembered his father nodding his head to the bolero.

Winston held out his hands. "Feel like giving it a try?"

Johnny remembered how Winston had tried to teach his daughters to juggle and how they had failed. Winston was pulling Johnny to his feet and Johnny did not resist. He felt small and a little silly inside Winston's grasp. His legs were unsteady, whether from weakness or unease, he wasn't sure.

"Follow my lead," Winston said.

Johnny, his eyes on the buttons at the V of Winston's tennis shirt, concentrated, willing his feet to move to Winston's count and the gentle nudge and prod of his hands. He was doing it. He was dancing.

He knew there was more to it, that you had to move the box around the room, but he found himself waiting for Winston's permission. Though he wasn't sure why, Winston's next instruction took him by surprise.

"Now, pretend I'm the woman. You lead."

He knew he should be imagining Tessie, but as he moved Winston carefully through the pattern, it was Bunny who came to mind, causing him to lose count and tread on Winston's shoe. Suddenly, annoyed, he let his arms fall to his side and stepped back.

"Tessie," Johnny said, and Winston looked around expectantly.

"She left some sandwiches in the refrigerator."

Winston went to fetch them. The two ate mostly in silence, and when they were done, Winston cracked his knuckles, which Johnny had never seen him do before.

"Hey, Johnny, mind if I wash my car?"

So Johnny sat out front, a crossword in his lap, while Winston sprayed the Cadillac with the garden hose, once or twice taking careless aim at the stray cat scratching at the base of Tessie's hibiscus. The cat's presence irritated Johnny, but so did Winston's half-hearted attempts to chase it away. He said nothing, though. In fact, not much passed between them for conversation, except that every so often, Winston would call out, "Johnny, give me a clue."

Sometimes Winston got the correct answer. Most of the time he didn't. That was no way to solve a puzzle. You had to sit down and look at it, see one answer give rise to another. Johnny surprised himself by finally saying so, more adamantly than he intended; Winston, looking diminished by the reprimand, released the trigger on the nozzle, pausing the flow of water over the Cadillac. "Sorry," he said.

But the ruefulness in his voice seemed disconnected from his words. Johnny did not want to retract his own words; nor did he want to temper them with others. He shrugged. He watched Winston pull the trigger on the hose again and continue rinsing the soap from his car. Johnny could see foam flooding down the driveway to collect in the gutter.

Winston was buffing the passenger door now, using slow meditative strokes. Johnny frowned at this meticulous attention to a car, but then he realized that Winston's focus was not on the Cadillac but on something inside it. As if provoked by a spasm, Winston yanked open the door and scuffled through the glove compartment with his hand. Johnny remembered the butterscotch candies Winston had stored there on the trip to Barona, and he wondered if Winston meant to ply him with sweets and for what purpose. But Winston emerged from the car and approached with an envelope which he held lightly, as if it were something fragile or dangerous. Johnny knew at once that this was the reason Winston had first set foot in his house.

Winston stood in front of him now and the envelope he held was level with Johnny's gaze. There was his name in the middle, and in the corner, Bunny's, the letters fastidious, intricate as dragonfly wings.

"Should we go inside?" Johnny asked, though he remained seated. Outside, he felt exposed, as if all the neighbors might see through their walls and guess not only at the words that would pass between him and Bunny's son, but at the words in the envelope as well. Going inside, though, would feel like bringing Bunny into his home.

"Or we can sit in the car," Winston offered and led the way.

He held the passenger door open and Johnny slid inside. The glove compartment was still slightly ajar. Johnny closed it, a belated, useless gesture. He thought about how he had ridden in this car to the casino. He wondered if Bunny's letter had been tucked there the whole time with the butterscotch candies and paper napkins.

Winston, in the driver's seat now, passed him the envelope. "I don't know when she meant to send it. Or if."

Johnny took it with shaky fingers, checking the front of the envelope to confirm the names and then turning it over. When he saw the open flap, he glanced up at Winston, who blushed at first. But then he recovered and met Johnny's question with the self-possession that had earned him the admiration and approval, even envy, of the de la Cruz family. Johnny unfolded the letter. The words in Tagalog pulled him back – to the sight of Bunny in a floral caftan, its wild colors hardly tamed by the black gloss of her hair, her toenails painted the orange of tiny fruits, and the lucent blue vein that traced her calf. And as he read, he felt the slap of Bunny's words for his escape from her living room, a rebuke he accepted readily and with a sense of relief. It was right that he be chastised. He read the taunt about Tessie, his *mestiza wife*, and forgave that too.

Then he came to the part that established for him that Carlitos was Winston's father. Although he did not want that burden, that proof of his infidelity to Tessie, he felt an inexplicable loss, as if something had been stolen from him. Finally, he came to the taunt he felt he did not deserve: Bunny's ridicule of his small dreams. How do you know if your dreams are small when you don't know how big you're allowed to dream?

"I wondered if you ever considered it. That I could be your son."

Winston's voice seemed to come from far away, though he was inches from Johnny.

"But you're not," Johnny told him.

Winston stared at him. "How can you be so sure?"

"It's in the letter. I know what she's telling me."

And though Johnny was utterly convinced of his words, it struck him – the possibility that they could mutually agree to believe it to be true – that they were father and son. It would be for him to say so. Hadn't they all embraced Winston, been buoyed by his presence, his good looks and grace? Didn't he have need of them somehow? It would be a congenial lie – a happy lie that would unite them, just as they were when he came for Sunday dinner. When he had enchanted them with his tricks.

Johnny looked at the letter again. He realized the absurdity of it, of claiming Winston for himself, for his family – his wife and daughters.

"Winston, when's your birthday? What month?"

Winston seemed taken aback at the question – a question so simple it should hardly require such a long pause, such a look of anxiety at the consequences his answer might bring.

"March," he said finally.

Johnny counted back the months on his still shaky fingers. "June," he said. "You were conceived in June. During the rains." He spoke quietly as he recalled the tropical heat, the stifling air, the longing for relief. "I never saw the rains."

He held up his fingers as if for proof. "It isn't me."

Winston's mouth slackened, moved wordlessly for a moment. He looked away and then he gathered himself, a pained smile on his lips.

Johnny folded up the letter and tucked it back inside the envelope, wishing that everything that had happened could be so neatly put away. He felt cheated and tricked, and yet he was responsible for Winston being there. Winston who looked stunned and stoic. Johnny felt moved to touch him, so he patted his cheek once – too hard, though, and Winston flinched. Disconcerted by his own clumsiness, Johnny wanted to be done with Winston for the moment, done with the letter. He released the glove compartment with his fist and tossed the letter inside. He opened the door and scooted himself out.

"Go now, Winston." Johnny gestured down the driveway, a brisk wave with the arm he had broken that summer.

He watched while Winston set the Cadillac in reverse to roll down the driveway. Just as Johnny was wishing he had done something to make up for his unintended slap, the screech of animal pain brought the car to a sudden halt. Winston got out of the car and Johnny joined him to inspect the rear wheel.

Together they looked at the ruins: the gape of the cat's twisted jaw, a paw pushed into the split halves of the ribcage, the tail hanging by a slippery tendon, the glob of viscera on the tire.

They decided to bury the cat – what remained of it. Behind the old playhouse, dust from the sandy soil floated up into Winston's face with each turn of the shovel. Johnny was seated on an old patio chair that Winston had unfolded from the debris stacked inside the playhouse and placed outside the dust zone of the burial site. It wasn't necessary for Johnny to be there; Winston could have handled the job without an audience or supervision, or a conspirator. In fact, the heat bothered Johnny and the dust was wafting toward him on the slow, heavy air. But he felt they were in this together, as if they shared responsibility for the cat's death and now its burial.

The cat was wrapped in newspaper, but parts of it – a bloody ear, a splayed paw – poked out of their shroud. A layer of grit had settled on Winston's tennis clothes. Johnny tasted dust on his tongue. He jiggled his leg to hurry the progress of Winston's shovel.

When the hole was just deep enough, Winston nudged in the newspaper-cloaked corpse with his shovel. Loose sand showered in after it. He replaced the rest of the dirt until it formed a small mound, then patted that down with the shovel.

"It's done," Winston said.

It was noticeable only if you really looked at that spot, and no one ever had reason to look behind the playhouse.

They went out front again, and Winston once more pulled out the garden hose, this time to wash cat tissue from his tire. They watched the residue slip down the driveway and into the gutter.

Winston's white clothes were damp and dusty; his face and neck were streaked with dried sweat. Although Johnny had not done the physical work, he imagined he looked as depleted as Winston, who took his arm and steered him back into the house, into bed.

"I'm leaving," Winston said. And Johnny, who wanted him to go but didn't want to watch, closed his eyes.

Johnny heard the brush of Winston's steps on the carpet, the suctioning of air as the front door closed behind him, and then the whisper of the Cadillac as it glided, newly washed, into the street.

◈ ◈ ◈

Whenever Johnny considered that hot, stifling afternoon with Bunny on her couch in that unlikely room in Manila, his eyes ached at the memory and his stomach fluttered with guilt. At the infidelity to Tessie, yes. But there was something else too: the insult to Bunny. After they had righted themselves and restored their clothes to their proper placement, Johnny had sat silent, head in his hands, elbows resting on his knees. Bunny sat for a while too, and then she stood up and collected the sake glasses onto the tray. When she carried the tray into the kitchen, Johnny left, closing the door softly behind him and walking quickly through the darkened hallway, nearly tripping on a torn floor tile. He walked out into the daylight on the busy Manila street, with its odors of diesel, dust, frying oil, and sickly sweet candies. Beneath the hot blinding colors of sky, and amid buildings painted cheaply yellow and orange, he felt disoriented and alone in a country he no longer belonged to.

◈ ◈ ◈

When the phone near his bedside rang, Johnny – emerging from a dream that already was slipping away – groped air, eyes still closed. The heel of his hand batted a cup of water and he heard the thwack of the plastic against the wall. He groped some more and skimmed his thumb against his glasses. He knocked the phone from its cradle and it landed on his flattened pillow and he could hear Tessie's voice repeating her hellos, calling his name, that small note of anxiety in her voice that stemmed from her distrust of machinery. Johnny lifted the phone slowly to his ear to catch Tessie in mid-sentence.

There were crowd noises in the background.

"What?" Johnny said. He reached for his glasses and put them on as if this would make him hear better.

"Did Winston come?"

Johnny couldn't answer.

"Can you hear me?"

Johnny took a breath. "Yes," he said. It came out loud, an anguished bark.

"It's a little noisy here. We're having a bite to eat."

Johnny knew that Tessie and Gloria loved the buffet table, all the choices available to them, the way they could fill their plates with little samples of mismatched foods and celebrate small victories or make up for losses.

"I won fifty dollars," Tessie said.

He sensed she had more to say. He waited, curious, hopeful.

"Johnny," Tessie said, excitement and disbelief in her voice, "Rey won the jackpot – over $2000, at the slot machine."

Johnny imagined the scene – the lights on the machine flashing, bells jangling, sirens screaming the good news, the miraculous appearance of five of a kind at the pull of a lever. "Lucky son of a gun."

They were both silent a moment.

"I'll be home tomorrow," Tessie said.

When she hung up, he laid the receiver next to his ear and listened to the dial tone, its pulsing regularity marking time.

He heard Josie come through the front door. When she came down the hall to check on him, he closed his eyes, the dial tone still at his ear. He was aware of Josie near the bed; he felt her standing over him, heard the click as she put the phone back on the hook. He took care not to tighten his eyelids when she lifted the glasses from his face. When she left the room, he put them back on and checked the candle.

◈ ◈ ◈

On Sunday morning, Johnny lay on his back, one arm draped across his eyes as he listened to Josie's exhalations as she lifted weights in the room across the hall. He had slept fitfully, waking often, each time seeing the light of the candle come from deeper within the glass, illuminating only the feet of the Virgin of Guadalupe. Now, as he prepared to look at the candle, the sound of Josie's breathlessness made his own lungs strain. He moved his arm from his eyes and slowly opened them. The flame had gone out. No one had saved it.

17

INSTEAD OF THE BULLFIGHT

Winston rolled down his window, and a hot breeze slapped him with the smell of scorched meats, overripe fruit, and sewers. He did not take offense. He nodded a greeting at the attendant, not venturing to speak, unsure whether he should try his limited Spanish. They were still on the U.S. side of the border, but over the last few miles on the interstate, the line between the countries had blurred, with billboards and business marquees in English bumping up against Spanish-language signs.

"Five dollars," said the attendant, who despite the warm morning wore starched jeans and a 49ers sweatshirt. The heels of his pointy-toed cowboy boots sank in the soft dust.

Winston handed over six dollars. When the attendant motioned them through, Junior leaned over the gearshift and threw a peace sign. Winston pulled away slowly, so as not to kick more dust onto the attendant's boots, and parked the Cadillac in the sloping lot. The car tilted on the driver's side, and when Winston opened his door, the thick yellow dirt rose to meet his sandaled feet.

As they wound through the spirals of the pedestrian ramp, Junior inhaled deeply. "So this is Tijuana. Smell that? Tequila. No fake IDs needed here."

Winston sidestepped a suspicious puddle. "It's not even noon. Besides, this ramp smells like piss."

Junior gave him a look. "Yeah. Whatever."

They hadn't talked much in the car, even though it was one of the few chances they'd had since Junior's arrival the day before. Winston had woken to a mad pounding on his door. "Open up! Police!" He lurched out of bed, his pulse quickening, his muscles springy, his conscience inexplicably guilty, only to find Junior's big-lipped grin on the other side of the door.

Winston pushed him off the step. "Asshole."

Junior went reeling back, landing on his backside, laughing his odd gargling laugh.

"That was stupid, man." But Winston laughed a little, too. The sight of Junior made him smile, the comic sprawl of his spidery limbs, his mouth a dark pink cavern, his eyes squeezed to disappearing. That's what was funny, not his stupid joke. He didn't come to Junior's defense when Bev came outside to berate him for impersonating an officer.

"I can report you for that. Don't think I won't."

Winston introduced his landlady to his best friend.

Junior, still on the ground, raised himself up on his elbows and made the grin on his face dissolve in the rubbery muscles of his cheeks. "Sorry," he said to the knotty finger pointed at him.

"Well," Bev said, pleased with herself. "Good, then."

Soon they were chatting like old friends, Junior showing off the backward bend of his double-jointed thumb and Bev countering with her wrinkled bicep.

Later that morning Winston had driven off to keep Johnny company, feeling an uneasiness about the day ahead. Junior's unannounced arrival had intruded upon Winston's careful concentration on Johnny de la Cruz and his family. When he had arrived at the de la Cruz home, he sensed a misalignment between him and Johnny. They had spent many hours together without Tessie in the house, but never when she had been out of town. Winston hadn't intended to show Johnny the letter. It had been an unthinking moment, an uncontainable thing. Now irrecoverable.

◈ ◈ ◈

The bottom of the ramp delivered them into a fenced area where they bunched up with other border crossers at a gate. They pushed through a metal turnstile, the way people entered amusement parks, and they were in Mexico. Immediately, cab drivers beckoned to them. "I take you downtown, señores. I take you see a show."

It was, after all, one of the things they had come for, one item on a laundry list of attractions: cheap eats, cheap souvenirs, cheap tequila, cheap women, and the bloodletting spectacle of a bullfight. They soon learned from one of the cab drivers that there was no fight scheduled that day. The driver persisted in his invitation to take them to see a show, enticing them with a flyer that pictured a woman in platform heels spilling out of a tiny leopard-print dress. But they had planned for such a show to be the capstone of the afternoon – the climax, so to speak, and not the foreplay. So they declined the offer and decided to walk into town.

They made their way past a throng of tourists already intent upon a bargain at tables of trinkets lining the cement wall that divided Mexico from the United States. Vendors at food carts waved skewers of stringy meat and mangoes on a stick at them. Winston liked the activity around him, and though he welcomed this little diversion across the border, he felt a desperate energy pervading it all. Junior, who had been trailing and gawking, vaulted over an underfed mongrel sniffing for scraps and caught up with him.

"This place is crazy, man." Junior had his grin on.

Small children advanced upon them, each thrusting chewing gum toward them with one hand and holding their free hand dirty palm up, small fingers curling slightly to cup anything that might be dropped into them. Junior trickled coins through his fist into the outstretched hands, and as they continued walking, the children followed, reaching, wanting.

"Cut it out, Junior," Winston hissed.

They walked faster to outpace the little gum sellers.

"Reminds me of the Philippines," Junior said.

"Yeah, you're the expert."

Junior had spent two weeks there one December holiday with his father, one of those weeks in the Manila Sheraton.

Tijuana, its colors and air laden with diesel and roasting meats, reminded Winston of the Philippines, too. And the Philippines reminded him of Carlitos – his faraway smile, his tentative pats on the shoulder, his matter-of-fact departure. Winston thought of his own series of departures – his and Bunny's from Manila, and then his alone from Anaheim, leaving Felix and Odette at the curb. His departure from Johnny's house yesterday had the greatest sense of finality to it, a sense of no return.

They were on a footbridge over a concrete channel that smelled faintly of sewage and gave a view of the corrugated metal roofs of the shanty towns. Children, surely inhabitants of those slums, lined the bridge at intervals – dirty, talentless children banging a drum or scratching at a fiddle while screeching a *ranchera* off-key, a tin can at their feet to collect change. Junior kept his hands in his pockets this time. It was Winston who, coming upon a legless man near the end of the bridge, loosed a spate of coins. The man's torso was planted on a plywood square nailed to four wobbly wheels. Bracelets for sale drooped in a tangle from one arm, and a dozen or so necklaces weighed against his chest. When Winston conferred his offering, nickels and dimes rolled off in every direction. The man nearly slid off his board as his arms, jangly with hoops, swam over the concrete to retrieve the runaway money. Winston, appalled at the spectacle his gesture had caused, hurried away.

On the other side of the concrete channel, where a wide esplanade offered canvas stalls of souvenirs and open-air eateries, the tang of sewage in the air gave way to grease and onions and beer. Winston waited impatiently while Junior lingered at a few of the vendor stalls, chuckling at a display of T-shirts with funny slogans about visiting Tijuana, then trying on a giant sombrero.

"You're not going to buy that, are you?" Winston asked.

Junior considered himself in the mirror fastened to the stall's canvas flap. "Later," he promised, lifting the oversized hat from his wild hair.

When they reached the main thoroughfare where Avenida Revolución clanged with traffic and swarmed with people, Winston was satisfied that later would not come. Among the tourists in shorts and T-shirts, a few sported giant sombreros and looked clearly ridiculous. There was a tacky festiveness that invited observation more than participation. Still, Junior did a funky dance step. "Wow, it's a party."

But the hosts were bored with their guests. Vendors sat behind counters or stood at the front of their store, their smiles automatic, their sales pitch flat-toned and weary as customers wandered in to finger embroidered blouses, wool blankets, or wooden flutes, or to try on flat-soled *huaraches* or high-heeled cowboy boots.

Winston and Junior walked aimlessly along the sidewalk for a while until they were conveyed by a surge of foot traffic into a shop. It turned out to be a warren of shops, with corridors that zigzagged, descended by ramp or stairs into airless little galleries. Winston suddenly felt compelled to buy souvenirs, as if passage out of the maze of shops depended on it.

He decided to buy something for Felix and Odette. He had been putting them off whenever they asked about his return. Though they never mentioned the Cadillac, Winston knew they were asking about that too. There was no longer any reason to put them off.

He found some unembroidered hand towels for Odette, something practical that she would actually use. Then he bought her a hand-woven shawl, blood-red roses splashed against a midnight-blue background, even though he knew that it was something Bunny, not Odette, would have worn. He wandered in search of something for Felix. Sidestepping a haggling tourist, he headed toward a wall where a line of men's shirts hung. *Guayaberas*, the sign said. Junior came up beside him. "Hey, they sell *barongs* here."

Winston fingered the front of one, the cool lightness of it, the sheerness of the fabric made for tropical climates, remembering when he had helped his mother pack Carlitos's *barongs* for his trip to Ireland. He saw the absurdity of it now. Not the part about helping him pack, but the part about ever expecting him to come home.

"They're *guayaberas*," Winston said. He bought one for Felix, not haggling over the price.

Junior, at a loss for what to buy from among the abundance of wares, came away with only a piñata, a black bull with yellow horns and hooves and red eyes – consolation for missing out on the bullfight. It dangled by its nose from a wire attached to a stick. Junior swung it over his shoulder and Winston ducked to avoid its pig-tailed rump.

When they emerged from the maze of shops, they found themselves on a side street. A woman in black stockings, teetering heels, and a purple lacy dress cut to reveal hefty breasts beckoned to them from a dark doorway from which thumped music, heavy with drums and sax. It was showtime, they decided, even though they had not yet had a drop of tequila to embolden themselves.

"*Pasa, pasa,*" the woman said in a voice that was more suited to directing traffic than proffering sex. She pointed the way down a dimly lit corridor, at the end of which another spike-heeled woman beckoned in a manner that, while more enticing, still had a rushed bossiness. This woman, not as chesty as the first one, gave them each a perfunctory caress before pulling open a musty velvet curtain. They were hit by the smell of body odor, beer, and cigarettes as they entered a small room with streaky mirrored walls. At the center of the room was a circular stage, upon which a few women in various stages of undress wiggled and gyrated. Strobes danced across the round white stage, throwing red, green, and blue spools of light upon the moving body parts of the women. There were blue breasts and red thighs, and when colors combined, there was a magenta face or a yellow hand. The stage resembled a large cake, topped with tragically melting decorations.

"Sit," a man dressed in a shiny black shirt told them over the throb of the music. He pointed to one of many vacant tables. "Sit. Sit."

Winston and Junior put their souvenir purchases on an empty chair, Winston's shopping bag first and Junior's piñata cozily slumped on top. Winston and Junior were so close to the stage that they soon found themselves leaning too, throwing their heads backward to view more than toes and ankles. Sometimes the strobes swept over them, coloring their skin and clothes.

A group of sailors a few tables away had made a game of the lights, each choosing a color and putting money on the table. The sailor whose color landed most often on a particular body part of the dancer in front of them won the money, a portion of which he stuffed in the dancer's cleavage. The winner of each round earned the right to call the next body part. *Left tit!* After several rounds, one sailor bored with the game wandered over to watch the dancer in front of Winston and Junior's table.

She had lowered herself to the scuffed floor of the stage and was writhing on her belly, her breasts smushed beneath her, her painted face turning from side to side, her spiky high heels dragging behind, making more scuff marks on the stage. All of her was awash in the back-and-forth sweep of the colored strobes. The music had become slow and slinky and the sailor was swaying his hips and clapping his hands off the beat.

Then the woman rose to all fours, and the sailor was inspired to grab Junior's piñata and dangle it in front of her. This new game drew his buddies immediately, all clamoring for a turn at puppeteering the bull. But Winston, driven to save the piñata, sprang from his chair, knocking both it and the table over as he seized the bull. There was an outcry and some tussling, and he found himself being propelled past the musty velvet curtain, through the dark switchbacks of the corridor and out into the street. When he whirled around, expecting to face his ejector, there was Junior, about to thwack him with the shopping bag that held Felix and Odette's gifts.

"What the hell was that about?" Winston demanded.

Junior howled. "You're asking me?"

Winston, feeling both foolish and heroic, handed the piñata to Junior. "Here's your bull."

Its tail was gone.

They looked around them. To the right was Revolución, but Winston went left, away from the chaos of the main drag.

"So where we going," Junior wanted to know.

"Nowhere." Winston walked faster, as if nowhere were an actual destination.

"Shit, Winston. What's going on with you?"

Winston said nothing as he led them for several blocks, stepping down and then up the steep uneven curbs into streets that were narrow and lined with small, faded storefronts. Winston was silently dismayed by his rudeness – but not enough to atone. After all, Junior was like family. Winston had known him since junior high school. The basketball players had always gathered after a game at Rudy and Myrna Tamayo's home, where there was always food and Myrna wasn't bothered by crumbs on the carpet or water rings on the coffee table. Rudy and Myrna were at every game. Bunny came when she could, but even after all the years of watching him play, she still didn't understand what a rebound was and couldn't be disabused of her notion that parents should be able to call time-outs. So it was nice to have the Tamayos in the bleachers as his loudest supporters, even though his consistently strong play often kept Junior on the bench. Junior, average athlete, average student, comic-book looks, was Winston's sidekick. Junior benefited from Winston's status as campus star, and Winston became an ad hoc Tamayo.

Winston stopped, unsure of his bearings. They were in a street of dilapidated buildings. Metal signs with bent and missing letters hung above doorways, many of them shuttered behind metal gates. A few people loitered in the doorways that weren't barred or at the sloping street corners. Winston was about to try and retrace his steps when Junior brushed past him.

"C'mon," he said, jaywalking across the street, an act which Winston at his most paranoid believed could land them in a Mexican jail, but which he now committed almost aggressively.

Winston followed Junior into a bar, a narrow space with the bar on one side and empty tables along the opposite wall. A jukebox at the far end played a whiny Mexican love song. The place was dim, lit only behind the bar and at occasional intervals along the lumpy plaster ceiling. Winston stumbled on Junior's heels, his forehead clashing with the rear hooves of the piñata.

"Easy, man."

They waited for their eyes to adjust to the murky interior and then skated with careful steps to the bar. A few feet away, the bartender poured consecutive shots of tequila for a woman with a heavily made-up face and a man with a mantle of gold jewelry around his neck. Their conversation was boisterous, almost combative, and in the spaces in between their peevish exchanges, the love song on the jukebox sighed and moaned. The couple, seeing Junior and Winston, retired to a table in the corner, taking the bottle of Cuervo with them. The bartender turned to his new customers.

"Hola, señores. What can I get for you?"

"*Dos cervezas,*" Junior said, holding up two fingers.

"Two beers," the man said. "I got it, amigo."

"Okay, amigo."

"Cut it out, Junior," Winston hissed when the bartender turned to draw their beers.

"Just trying to fit in," Junior said, setting his piñata on the bar.

When they had their beers in front of them, Junior took an earnest swallow, then turned to face Winston. "All right, so, talk."

Winston ignored Junior's Clint Eastwood impersonation, because he really did want to talk. He told him about the letter he'd found. That he had gone to Kimball Park to find out who Johnny de la Cruz was and had ended up playing Scrabble and poker with him, reheating his soup and sitting in silence with him in front of the TV – all this all summer long while the letter sat in the Cadillac. Even as he tried to sort things out for himself, the chronology was muddy: the picnic at the beach, guys' day out, dinner and dancing with Tessie…except for yesterday, when he had shown Johnny the letter, when he had killed and buried the cat.

"Stupid stray cat," Winston said.

Junior had been studying his beer, nodding as he listened, his forehead knit in sympathy, his fingers sweeping up the shreds of crepe paper Winston had been absently pulling off the piñata. He looked up now and signaled the bartender. "*Por favor, el Cuervo.*"

◈ ◈ ◈

Back on Avenida Revolución everything seemed too loud and bright, amplifying the tequila buzz in Winston's head. He wanted to get out of there, head back to the car.

"Hey, man," Junior said. "Know what we need? Food. We need *comida*."

Junior was right. Food would stabilize them and make their return through customs easier. They headed to a café in the plaza where earlier Junior had tried on the sombrero.

A waiter spotted them and made a beeline to secure them for one of his tables. He seated them at a sticky table abuzz with flies. Junior waved them away, though the waiter seemed not to notice either the flies or Junior's flapping arm. They ordered tacos and bottled water.

American rock music played over the speakers strung across the patio. A stage at the center of the patio was empty except for a karaoke machine. Dirty-faced Indian children approached their flimsy metal table with gum and bracelets to sell. By now Winston and Junior had learned to shake their heads, avoiding eye contact, pretending deep interest in their fingernails or looking off into the distance for the approach of a phantom friend.

They couldn't help but give a little of their attention to a woman who offered to tell their fortune.

"There's your chance, Winston."

"Ten dollars," the woman said. She was small and grave, wrapped in a black shawl from which she jutted an open palm. "Ten dollars," she repeated. "No lies," she assured him.

"No," Winston agreed, emphatic, but the woman took this answer as a rejection of her services and turned away with a scowl.

A microphone squawked. Someone had taken the karaoke stage and was emoting over an old Elvis ballad. People paid little attention to the singer, looking up only now and then whenever the microphone sizzled with static.

"Thank you. Gracias," the man – an American who appeared unfazed at the crowd's indifference to his performance – said when he ended his song to no applause. He then launched into another number. Even when his exhortations to the audience to clap along went unheeded, he continued as if they were as caught up in his singing as he was. Eventually the man took a break, setting the microphone down and stepping off the stage to a table where a woman sat with two margaritas.

"You're way better than that dude," Junior said. "Remember talent night?"

"Yeah, I remember," Winston said. It had been an unofficial contest, a hazing, really, an impromptu exhibition of talent by the freshmen on the team by order of the returning players after practice one evening. Junior walked on his hands from baseline to baseline, and Ricky Dixon stripped off his T-shirt and made his pecs dance. When it was Winston's turn, he stood on the St. Augustine Saints mascot painted at center court and sang in his clear, silky tenor a dazzling rendition of "Moon River," a song he had once sung with Carlitos. In the gym, he gave it a jazzy spin, hushing the players who only moments before had been rowdy with curses and awash with sweat. The otherwise-empty gym made a sound chamber for Winston's voice, enriching the already vibrant notes with a delicate echo, his very own backup singers. When he finished, the gym was silent, until the players, stunned with admiration, were roused from their stupor by the team captain who stepped up to high-five and chest-butt Winston. The rest of the team followed, leaving Winston flushed and bruised from congratulations.

Now in this outdoor café where the rusty-legged tables sat aslant on the stone patio, where patrons sipped margaritas and Coronas under umbrellas that were useless against the sun, where waiters pretended not to see the flies surrounding the food they served, and where no one paid attention to an American singing bad karaoke in the midst of it all, Winston was inspired to make a statement. He angled his way through the cluster of metal chairs and tables, past waiters and busboy carts to the stage. Only those sitting nearby, including the man who had preceded him at the microphone, noticed his appearance. He raised his margarita to Winston.

On the stage, Winston remembered the last time he had stood before an audience: in the pulpit of St. Augustine Church, when he eulogized his mother. The acoustics of the sanctuary had enriched his voice; its arched ceiling had held the sounds intact. Out here in the open air, in the cobblestone plaza, what would be the reach of his song? Who would hear him?

The man with the margarita raised his glass again, a question now. Was he or wasn't he going to step up to the microphone?

Winston stepped up. The mike was live; he could feel its electronic quiver in his face. He cleared his throat and heard the sound amplified around him. Some of the people at the tables looked up, briefly curious. Before he lost his nerve and their attention, he launched into song. He had taken the stage without knowing what he would sing, but now the words to "Moon River" again swelled from his chest, the same song he had sung with Carlitos, the same song he had made echo in the St. Augustine gym so that he sounded like a chorus. Here, it was his voice alone atop the plaza stage – Carlitos's voice long gone, and no walls to provide acoustic accompaniment. It was his voice alone that got lost beyond the first few rows of tables, that was accompanied by the clink of glassware and the scrape of forks against ceramic plates, and that, despite his earnest effort, garnered only meager applause from the few half-attentive listeners.

He felt only a little humiliation, but it was enough. He had exposed himself to the world's indifference and he had survived. Now he felt relief too, as if by humbling himself he had performed a penance. He replaced the microphone and he left the stage, wiping his hands, slick with sweat, on his pants.

"Tough crowd," Junior said when Winston returned to the table.

Crossing back over took forty-five minutes. They spoke very little as they shuffled along in the slow line through customs, and they were relieved to finally reach the dirt parking lot. Junior heaved an exaggerated sigh, making his piñata prance, and Winston had only a fleeting urge to yank it from its string and throw it under the wheels of the Cadillac, whose flanks – washed only yesterday in Johnny's driveway – were coated in dust.

18

NOT JUST ANOTHER TIJUANA SIDESHOW

Laura drove southbound on the interstate with a plan. Her tennis racquet was beside her and a new can of balls lay on the floor. She was headed to the practice wall at the local high school, where she intended to drill her forehand until the balls were pounded of their fuzz. In a few days, she would invite Winston to play a little tennis. Even if she couldn't win, she could at least show him that she was a competent player.

She had played on her community college team – admittedly, not a highly select squad. At tryouts, only the very worst players were not encouraged to come back. Still, Laura had been a collegiate athlete and Tessie made much of it, even though when Laura lost a match, which she invariably did, it was hard to explain to Tessie that she did in fact win some games – just not the match.

Laura felt that she could win at least a few games against Winston. She always beat Mona, which was hardly satisfying because her daughter was not a competitor. "It's about having fun," Mona would say sarcastically, as she watched one of Laura's cross-court volleys whiz past her shoulder. This was the trouble with raising an only child. There was no competition for resources, awards, or affection.

Mona was a dabbler, and she lost interest quickly in things.

Laura tried to guide her, to give her opportunities, but Mona yawned at her efforts, for which Laura blamed Chip's easygoing personality. Mona had declined Laura's offer of a summer job at her optometry office in favor of making sandwiches at Sara's SubClub, which was how she was spending her Sunday afternoon. Chip was playing Frisbee. Laura hated Frisbees – so uncatchable and impossible to throw. It was silly to have whole teams of people chasing a plastic saucer.

Almost as silly as juggling. Her failure to juggle had irked her. She knew she could eventually do it with practice, but she had wanted to do it then, in front of Winston. It was clear that her parents had delighted in Winston's juggling, which he had performed like a gift to them. Of course, she had been enthralled too, but now she remembered how her own gift to her father – the old home movies converted to video – had been received. He should have liked it more. They all should have liked it more. She should take it back, or at least crack the case so it would be unplayable when they came to their senses and realized what a gift she had given them. A gift that was lasting and tangible.

Juggling was ephemeral, a circus act. What was behind all that showing off anyway? What was behind *Winston*? Sure, he had practically become part of the family. It was the how and why of it that was baffling, and what she intended to discover. It couldn't be left to Josie, whose moroseness had driven her husband and son away for the summer. And Sara preferred to watch than to act. Besides, she was too busy making submarine sandwiches for a living. Laura was both embarrassed and secretly pleased at her sisters' low-skill occupations. She had lived up to her responsibilities as first-born by achieving the best career among the three of them. She got to wear a white lab coat; her name was embossed on a sign; she had business cards. She had once harbored even greater ambitions – something to do with live theater, being on stage under the lights, and sensing the breathing, rustling darkness that was the audience, before whom she would utter her lines convincingly and without fear.

◈ ◈ ◈

Tessie's tendency to shriek at the smallest upset had made Laura overly circumspect in her emotions. As a child, she had experienced a paralysis of sorts, a near-suspension of her senses. Fearful of creating a scene, she held herself in check, standing mute as an observer of disaster.

When Laura was in the first grade she was aware of certain things: that she wasn't in the popular group, but neither was she scorned by them; that she could aspire to ball monitor and line leader at recess, but not team captain in kickball. Still, she was a fairly confident girl, owing to her place in her family – first born. But with status came responsibility and expectations.

One afternoon she went to her parents' bedroom to look for Kleenex. She wasn't supposed to be there without permission, but it was just Kleenex she was after – and if she got a sample of her mother's lipstick, that would be a happy accident. She lingered at the dresser where her mother's cold creams, hairspray, and perfumes were a dusty jumble along with her father's cigarettes, a silver lighter that didn't work, and a box of matches that did.

She often watched her mother strike a match to light the candle to the Virgin Mary that stood on a shelf just above the dresser. Next to the candle was a vase of dead roses in dirty water. The yellow flame of the candle played at the edges of the slouching flowers. Laura watched with the knowledge that something bad was going to happen, that she would be a witness, and this filled her with dread. Still, she couldn't turn away. When she saw the shriveled petals flame and writhe, she wasn't sure if her mute inaction was due to a determination not to panic or a belief that if she ignored the danger, refused to acknowledge it, no harm would occur. She eyed a shiny lipstick tube briefly and then she turned her back on it and the burning roses and left the room.

She took a seat in the living room where her mother and sisters were watching *I Love Lucy*. No one turned away from the TV to look at her. And as Laura fixed her eyes there too, on Lucy who was big-eyed with guilt about something, she knew now she should have entered the room screaming, should have startled them all into frenzy and fear. But it was too late for that.

"Mommy," she said quietly, barely over the TV laughter. "There's a fire in your room."

Her mother's attention was still on Lucy's antics, and Laura wasn't sure if she should repeat herself. Maybe it wasn't something that called for urgency. But then her mother turned to her suddenly.

"What? What?"

She ran to the bedroom and Laura followed. From the doorway Laura saw her mother yank the bedspread from the bed and whip it across the room at the flames that had by now made a small bonfire of the shriveled flowers. As her mother smothered the fire, Laura could hear the knock and clash of perfume bottles and cold cream jars under the bedspread. When her mother was sure the fire had been extinguished, she peeled the bedspread back slowly, little by little revealing the destruction beneath: lids dislodged from bottles, jars rolling on their sides, lipstick tubes upended, charred bits of stem, and everything damp from the brown water of the overturned vase. Then her mother held up the bedspread to show Laura the hole blackened at the edges.

"What's the matter with you?"

◈ ◈ ◈

N*othing,* Laura told herself. *Nothing's the matter with me.* The memory still rankled. Hadn't she proved her competence and good sense over and over? And she would prove it again to Winston with her tennis racquet.

She was still gritting her teeth with purpose when she saw the Cadillac sail past her. Traffic was light for a Sunday so there was no mistaking the car for any other than Winston's. There was a passenger in the front seat, and at first Laura thought it might be her father. The alarming possibility of a kidnapping flitted across her mind. Her eyes went to the tennis racquet beside her, and she considered its weapon potential. She felt her adrenaline pump, felt overeager and a little bit silly as she accelerated until she was close enough to ascertain that the person in the car was not her father, but someone young like Winston and with a wild head of hair.

She continued to follow them, driving miles past her exit. Soon, Mex-Insur billboards cluttered both sides of the highway. They were going to Tijuana! She would go, too. It had been years since she'd been across the border. It had been fun when they were younger and would go just to vex their mother, who imagined horrors on every corner. After a while, when they'd collected their share of wool blankets, pottery, turquoise jewelry, and cheap margaritas, the border lost its fascination.

Now Winston was going. At first she thought she would catch up to them, join them, maybe show them around. She'd never seen Winston outside of the context of the family. This would be her chance to know something about him that no one else knew, to have him to herself, or nearly so. Then there was his companion to consider, a further point of curiosity. Who was this person? Who was Winston, for that matter? Better to just follow them, she decided.

She parked in the same dusty parking lot as they did, hunkering down in her seat until they had walked across the street toward the concourse that led across the border. She followed Winston and his companion at a safe distance, slowing or stopping to browse when they did. Even in her surveillance, she managed to buy some bracelets for Mona. She always bought gifts for Mona – bribes for affection. When she had to, she pushed her way past tourists to keep Winston in sight, not a difficult thing, really, since he tended to stand out in a crowd. Here though, something was different – maybe the light – and Winston seemed not to have the same grace or ease he displayed when he was among her family. She wondered if this had more to do with Winston or her family.

◈ ◈ ◈

When Winston and his friend disappeared into a narrow shop, Laura, fearing discovery, hung back on the sidewalk to wait. She was immediately set upon by a young man urging her to have her picture taken. "Souvenir," he said, and he motioned toward the donkey and cart on the corner, where another young man was fitting oversized sombreros to the heads of two pastel-clad ladies. It was tacky and touristy. Embarrassing. But for some reason, she did it. After the two ladies were assisted off the cart by one of the men, Laura clambered up, declining a helping hand. She didn't care who saw her. That is, she didn't care who among the general throng of vendors and shoppers saw her. Even perched above the donkey, she was still keeping an eye out for Winston.

The man handed her a sombrero. It had *Sexy* embroidered on its giant rim. She eyed it doubtfully, deciding that if it was a joke, she would make it a good one. But once the sombrero lay heavy on her head, she could not play the joke to its fullest, could not cross her legs or lean back on her elbows so that her small chest jutted forward. She slouched a little, hands clasped around her knees, and she looked past the camera as if by her gaze she could be lost amid the roil of traffic and pedestrians and diesel-colored air.

Relieved of the sombrero, she watched as the young man swished the photo paper in developer and then in fixer in shallow plastic tubs at the curb. He squeegeed the photo, inserted it into a cardboard frame, and presented it to her. "A special memory," he said as she inspected the soft blur of herself on the still-damp paper. She felt silly now to be holding the stupid souvenir and she stuffed it in her bag.

As she looked around to see if anyone was looking at her, she remembered that she was supposed to be on the lookout for Winston and his wild-haired friend. Surely, they would not have walked past her unnoticed. For a moment, she was gripped by the same panic she had felt when Mona as a child used to slip away from her at the grocery store. She scanned the street in both directions, darted into shops to inspect the customers, no longer discreet in her behavior, willing to be discovered by Winston, welcoming the prospect of a face-off. Laura stood on a street corner as tourists, street vendors, and beggars streamed around her. As she wondered where to look, what to do, she realized how she must look in her tennis clothes in the middle of downtown Tijuana. She was alone and no one knew where she was.

But she was a pragmatic woman. She had lost Winston, but she would not panic or berate herself. Though she wondered if she should blame Winston – what if he had seen her and deliberately ditched her? What kind of game was this boy playing? Hot with indignation, she looked around her one last time, but the crowd had thickened. It was the busiest part of the busiest day for tourists in Tijuana, and Laura decided to do what others everywhere around her were doing – shop and eat. But first, she would get her nails done.

◈ ◈ ◈

Laura shooed a fly away from the complimentary chips and salsa with a newly manicured hand. She had spent a lazy hour at the nail salon, and then another compulsively buying things she didn't really need, determined to make her trip to Tijuana worthwhile. A new leather handbag, a purportedly hand-woven tablecloth, and several blouses sat in thin plastic bags at her feet. She looked down at them – her feet – with satisfaction. When Laura declined color on her fingernails, the nail artist coaxed her to have a pedicure, and this time Laura acquiesced to polish. Inside her tennis shoes and sport socks, her toenails were painted lurid red. She crossed her legs and flexed her raised foot and smiled at the flamboyance hidden there, while admiring her hands – buffed but unembellished. Well-groomed, unostentatious hands were important in her profession, reassuring to her clients as she adjusted their glasses or demonstrated proper insertion of a contact lens. This was something she would have to mention to Sara, who allowed Mona to come to work with her fingernails painted blue or orange or whatever outrageous hue she happened to favor that day. Sure, she wore those latex gloves when she made sandwiches, lining buns with lettuce and cold cuts and cheese, but the gaudy color of her nails was insufficiently muted by the milky plastic. Painted nails and food preparation made for an unappetizing combination.

So did karaoke at an outdoor restaurant. Laura bit her taco and sipped her beer, squinting in disapproval at a man singing on the jerry-rigged stage in the middle of the plaza. She couldn't tell if he was being deliberately ridiculous or if his awful performance was in earnest. Both locals and tourists seemed to accept him as just another Tijuana sideshow. She angled her chair so she faced away from the stage. She hated to see people make fools of themselves.

She was seated at a small metal table sticky from grease and beer. She had eschewed the half-price margaritas for a Corona. She liked ordering it, saying its name, a kind of sexy growl. And she liked drinking from a bottle. It seemed somehow bold. A suitable finish to her afternoon. She eyed the plastic bags of purchases at her feet, and wondered how she would explain her day to Chip or if she would explain it at all. The whole thing seemed rather harebrained and impetuous, not to mention futile, having failed to uncover anything objectionable about Winston. She swallowed the last of her Corona and tucked some bills beneath the empty bottle. As the karaoke man finished his set to a few scattered handclaps, Laura gathered up her shopping bags and made her way over the cobblestone plaza.

Tired and eager to get back to her car, she had just quickened her pace when a familiar voice, made big and reverberating by a microphone, stopped her. She pivoted on her rubber soles, nearly losing her balance on the uneven stones. Though she was now a good distance from the stage, she knew immediately who was occupying it. But as she watched Winston perform, she realized she was not spellbound the way she had been when he juggled for them, not eager to imitate his skill, not envious of his inborn talent. While his voice was melodic and true, there was something pleading and painful about it, made all the worse by the indifference of the audience. Now she wondered – had her family somehow been duped by Winston, beguiled by a charisma that was of their own invention?

She hurried to the border gate, feeling the determination in her step, assuring herself that her eagerness to divulge what she had seen about Winston had nothing to do with her parents appreciating Winston's juggling act more than her own solid and substantial gift of a videocassette of memories.

19

THE SCENT OF LILIES

"We thought he was just sleeping." Tessie kept repeating. "We had no idea." She retold the story again and again as if on one more telling the ending might change.

On the way back from Las Vegas, the Filipino Seniors bus had stopped in Barstow for refueling. The passengers had disembarked, anxious to stretch their legs, use an off-bus toilet, and browse the trinket shop – and for those who still insisted on the habit, smoke. Everyone got off the bus because it was a chance to gossip with someone other than their seat- or aisle-mate. Tessie stood in line with Gladys Galang to buy sugar-free chewing gum. Gloria stuffed her purse with napkins and salt and pepper packets from the snack bar condiment counter. She had always packed them for Rey whenever he went fishing, and still collected them even though he hadn't gone fishing in a while. "I fall asleep and the fish laugh at me." Sometimes it was an annoyance, even an embarrassment, this tendency of his to fall asleep in the middle of some activity. But mostly they all had grown so accustomed to it they hardly noticed.

When they boarded the bus again and Rey was already seated and snoozing, his head resting against the window, Gloria just took her seat next to him, adjusted her small pillow behind her head, and took the stick of gum Tessie offered from across the aisle. The bus was quiet, everyone exhausted from the gambling, the trips to the buffet, and then the hours on the road back home. Gloria read *People* and Tessie read *Us*, sharing bits of celebrity news with each other. They traded magazines and then fell asleep themselves. When the bus pulled up to the community center, almost everyone was awake, or rousing themselves with a groggy awareness that they were home. Except Rey.

Gladys Galang had given Tessie a ride home after medics had declared Rey dead and an ambulance had dispatched the body to the morgue. Linda arrived straight from a country club dinner in a strapless cocktail dress to gather a crumpled Gloria.

Tessie broke down as soon as Josie opened the door to let her in. Josie led her to the living room, sat her down, and patted her back as she listened to the story. They were both in tears then, wondering how they would break the news to Johnny. When they looked up, there he was, standing in the hallway looking at them.

"Rey," was all Tessie could get out.

"I heard," he said, all emotion clamped out of his voice. He was unsteady as he turned around and walked back down the darkened hall.

Tessie was crying even harder now. "I can't believe he's gone."

Josie stopped patting her mother as she craned her neck to make sure that her father made it back to the bedroom. She wondered if he was crying. She wished her mother would stop her crying. She had staunched her own tears as if there were some sort of limit to the number of people who could shed them at once. Now that she sat nearly dry-eyed, she started to wonder if it all wasn't some awful mistake. Maybe Rey really had been asleep. They just hadn't given him a chance to wake up. If they had all just stopped being so impatient with him, everything would be all right.

"We thought he was just sleeping," Tessie said one more time, spreading her hands helplessly. Josie, remembering how she had roused Rey with the flash of her camera, wanted to shake her mother.

◈ ◈ ◈

It was their second family gathering in little more than a month. Only this one was in the echoing coolness of St. Michael's, with incense in the air that made it hard to breathe. They sat on the hard, straight-backed benches and held the program that listed the prayers for the service. The paper crackled, too loudly in the big church; when the organ played, they were all relieved by the music. The priest wore purple, a bright spot among the black-clad mourners, and when he sprinkled the coffin with holy water, the drops flew like little sparks of light. They proceeded to the sanctuary: Father Ramos and his altar boys, and then the pallbearers carrying Rey. The casket was closed, but everyone knew Rey was dressed in his best *barong* and some of his favorite things were tucked in at his side: his gardening trowel, some fishing lures, and – in a heartbreaking gesture – some salt and pepper packets from Gloria. Sonny had wanted to slip a hundred-dollar bill in Rey's breast pocket – a souvenir of his Las Vegas winnings. But Gloria objected, calling it wasteful, and Linda considered it tacky. Gloria ironed a handkerchief, scented it with Old Spice, and slid it into Rey's pocket herself, her hands trembling over her husband's dead body.

She followed behind the coffin, hunched in grief, supported on either side by Linda and Sonny. The twins followed in black jumpers and berets.

Josie looked at her parents in front of her. Johnny's suit hung loosely at his shoulders and seat, the extra fabric failing to hide his frailty. But it was Tessie who appeared to have been rendered brittle with emotion. Her head drooped under the old-fashioned mantilla she wore; her hands were clasped so tightly in front of her that Josie could see the jut of her shoulder blades through her black rayon dress. Johnny's hand cupped her elbow as if his own flimsy weight could keep her from collapsing onto the seat.

When Josie had heard that Gloria and Tessie had been reading celebrity magazines while Rey sat dead beside them she had been angry. She hadn't shown it and neither had her father. Only now she realized that her father hadn't been mad. He knew that this was how Rey had expected to go: quietly and unnoticed, almost a joke, a sight gag in a sitcom. Still, it was no consolation.

Winston, handsome in a gray summer suit, stood on the other side of Johnny. Josie had watched with interest and surprise as her parents clashed over whether to call Winston.

"He's not family," her father said, oddly adamant.

"Of course he's not," her mother said. "But he's a friend of the family." Then she added, "Right?" as if it were something she had forgotten and had to be reminded of.

Josie intervened. "He knew Uncle Rey. He should be told that he died." So Tessie had called him, and there he stood, nervous and solicitous. During the parts of the mass that required a change in elevation, the sitting, standing, sitting, kneeling that Josie believed was intended to keep people from falling asleep, Winston hovered within reach of Johnny's elbow. Otherwise, he stood slightly apart from her father. Winston was clearly saddened by Rey's passing, but Josie sensed something else in his demeanor – a tension in his neck, a faint bunching of the skin above his brow that showed even in profile.

Josie and her sisters had purposely sat behind him, though their taking a backseat to his charisma had been a given practically from the start. Today was different, though. Laura's revelation, a generous term for her weakly substantiated indictment of Winston as a phony, had put them all on guard. At first, they had laughed at her when they gathered for an emergency meeting after hours at her optometry office and she had revealed her secret pursuit of Winston across the border.

"You should've seen him," she insisted.

"But karaoke?" Sara asked, puzzled.

"He wasn't the same Winston we've been seeing all this time." She made some fluttering motion with her hand. "You had to be there."

"We'll just have to watch him," Josie said, her skepticism raised, unsure whether it was toward Winston or Laura, but nevertheless urged to vigilance as they sat amid the abundant display of eyeglass frames in Laura's office.

Now the three of them sat in church, their eyes focused as much on Winston's back as on the funeral service.

After the responsorial psalm and the reading by Father Ramos in his mumbling accent, Sonny stepped up to the lectern to eulogize his father. Sonny's voice never shook as he talked about Rey's quiet compassion, his big heart, his mischievous grin. It was only when he came to the end of his speech that his words took on a quiver. "Rey Bacaycay lived a happy life." Though Sonny had never been in the military, had never even been a Boy Scout, he saluted his father.

Josie had the urge to applaud. Instead there was just the sound of Sonny's heels as he made his way back to Gloria, whose shoulders were shuddering softly.

When Rey's family stood to receive communion, the rest of the mourners followed, including to Josie's surprise her parents, always so uncomfortable with the ritual of confession that they denied themselves the sacrament. Winston did not accompany them. Then on either side of her, Laura and Sara rose. Without really thinking about it, Josie rose too and stood in line with her sisters, all of them taking communion, unheeding of their detachment from the church and its rituals and requirements. The wafer stuck to the roof of her mouth, and she had to poke at it with her tongue to loosen it as she made her way back to her seat. She took her place in the pew behind Winston and knelt. She noticed a small strand of hair at the nape of Winston's neck sticking out slightly. Winston's short hair had begun to grow out. It was lovely hair, but this piece was rebellious, something wayward requiring gel or mousse or a pair of scissors. It was a disquieting imperfection, and Josie, swallowing the remnants of the wafer in her mouth, looked away so as not to be irked.

It was nearly noon when they arrived at the graveside, and the sun was high and hot above them in their black clothes. The heat was causing them to perspire, making foreheads shiny and upper lips moist. Father Ramos, still glittery in his purple vestments, offered a final prayer. Two young sailors in dress whites stood at sweaty attention. At some invisible cue, they began to fold the flag that draped Rey's casket, using crisp measured movements with their gloved hands. When they had tucked the flag into a thick triangle, one of them carried it over to Gloria, and as he laid it in her hands, he recited something in a low voice, a respectful drone, and for all its roteness, it was a deeply stirring moment. Then there was a click of a button and a taped version of "Taps" wavered in the air, its low notes defeated by the freeway noises down the hill. The pallbearers placed their gloves on top of the casket like so many limp doves.

◈ ◈ ◈

They gathered at Gloria's house. Walker had been charged with setting up extra tables in the garage and driveway to accommodate the spillover from the cramped living room and kitchen. Chip and Andy had picked up party-size pans of *pancit* and *lumpia* from the Filipino restaurant on Bonita Road, and they were in the process of arranging platters of food when the first mourners arrived.

It always amazed Josie how after a funeral, people could be so ravenous. And so social. Eating made them garrulous and gossipy, made them tell tasteless jokes and bubble with edgy laughter that bounced off the walls of the garage. Some even mugged for her camera, and she retreated, annoyed. At least she didn't have to feel intrusive taking pictures at a post-funeral gathering when her subjects were crossing their eyes and making rabbit ears behind each other's heads. She stationed herself on the porch in the corner next to the empty bamboo bird cage – a monstrosity that for years had housed Rey's rude mynah before it keeled over one night, hanging upside down in death. When Rey discovered it, he had to break off its feet to separate the bird from its roost.

From where she stood, Josie was perched above the family and guests, and she had a view of the driveway, the interior of the garage and the line of cars parked on the street. She panned the scene with her camera, settling here on Father Ramos making quick work of a plate of *pancit*, there on a gossipy exchange between two elderly women shielding their busy mouths with their napkins, and everywhere flies performing aerobatics.

She moved her camera's eye to the street where amid the station wagons and mid-sized sedans, Winston's Cadillac glinted hazily, its interior clouded with shadow from some mysterious source. Soon though, Josie realized they were not shadows but the bobbing heads of the twins, who were playing in the front seat, yanking the steering wheel and flipping the sun visors up and down. All afternoon Gloria had been exercising a sudden compulsion to oversee her granddaughters and had spent much of the afternoon hovering about them, stroking their hair or pressing their hands, seeking them out when they managed to escape her. Now Gloria, her black dress wilted, her hair staticky, stalked toward the Cadillac to retrieve the twins. Josie took her camera away from the scene, unwilling to witness her grieving aunt forcing her love on those little girls.

She welcomed the request of the two elderly women for something cold to drink. Something thirst-quenching, a beer would do, the old ladies said, so Josie went to the cooler to fish some bottles from the melting ice. After she had completed her deed of supplying alcohol to the aged, Josie again took up her post on the porch, just in time to see Winston slam the door to his car. He had freed himself of his jacket but looked no cooler for having done so. He stood a moment staring at the door as if trying to decipher something there, then he turned around and headed back toward the party, taking a seat at a nearly empty table.

Josie took the seat next to him. She noticed that Winston's smile was faltering, and the line above his brow gave him a look of distraction. "You look worried."

Winston loosened his tie.

"Like you lost the family silver in a craps game."

His smile teetered to a weak laugh, the kind meant to cover something up.

She remembered disclosing her own little secret about her phantom house-painting project, not that he could guess it had been a cover-up for her escape from her own home. She regretted it now – telling Winston about the painting, or rather the *not*-painting. It had been an impulsive thing to say, but for some reason she had felt safe saying it. He was outside the family, yet strangely inside it as well.

But things had shifted. Winston had changed. He had less confidence, and he had a dejected look about him. And now, even though all the other men had taken off their ties after the funeral, Sonny had changed into his Hawaiian shirt, and Father Ramos had divested himself of his robes, Winston, with his tie loose around his neck, looked slovenly and dislocated. A little jumpy.

She had never been one to inspire others to confide in her, yet she was aware of her sisterly tone as she spoke. "What is it, Winston?"

"I lost something."

Josie felt a pang at this sudden reminder of their loss of Rey in the midst of all the food and gossip. "Haven't we all?"

Josie looked around her, gestured with a napkin at the mourners who at the moment were not visibly mourning, but were eating, drinking, and chatting as if at any other party. Even her mother, relieved of the burden of her mantilla, had left Gloria's side and was in blithesome conversation with Pening Rocas, their old high-school classmate.

Winston was perspiring, and though nearly everyone else's forehead was shiny from the heat, Winston's sweat seemed to have a source other than the ninety-degree temperature. It bothered her to see him like this, looking uncomposed and almost desperate. And now suddenly speechless. Josie resisted an impulse to tug at his slack tie.

"What is it, Winston? What did you lose?" She made no attempt to hide her fierce need to know.

He pulled his handsome features tight.

Josie, curious now, waited. But Winston would reveal nothing, and she became angry at his stupid secret. *Suit yourself,* she thought. She brushed invisible crumbs from her lap and joined Linda on the porch, leaving Winston alone at the table. Linda, in a black sleeveless sheath and open-toed black pumps, wore her hair in a tight chignon. Her arms were crossed over her flat abdomen and she slouched, though not unattractively.

Her makeup was smeared a little under one eye. Josie put her arm around her cousin who had lost her father. After a while Linda put her arm around Josie, who lifted the paper napkin in her hand to wipe the mascara that ran from Linda's eye.

Josie remembered telling Lyle that Winston was her brother, a lie that amused her for its effect on Lyle as much as the advantage it bestowed on her. Presenting Winston as family meant presenting herself as connected to the grace and charm that was Winston, elevating all the de la Cruzes to a level they had not previously realized. But the charm of that lie was gone now.

Her acceptance of Winston into the family had been a pseudo-adoption, something make-believe. Never had the possibility of a blood connection occurred to her, and she refused the idea now. It was ludicrous to consider it. She thought of her collection of photographs and the temporary place she had granted Winston among them. Her hand itched to remove it now.

◈ ◈ ◈

By mid-afternoon, many of the non-family guests had left – neighbors who had waved to Rey as he took his turtle-paced walks around the block, or acquaintances at the pier where he used to fish. The family was more subdued now, with small groups sitting together talking quietly if at all. Johnny moved like a ghost through the house. Tessie and Sonny were in the kitchen sealing leftover fried rice in Tupperware and loading the dishwasher. Father Ramos, sated with *pancit* and *lumpia*, dozed in a living room chair. In the TV room, Gloria was resting on the couch, a wet cloth across her eyes, while the twins watched *Pretty Woman*. Johnny wandered into the bedrooms and then out the back door.

He sat on a rickety rattan bench pitched at the cusp of light and dark. At that time of the afternoon, the sun, just above the roofline of the house, threw a long slab of shade across the backyard. In a few minutes, the shade would overtake him, and if he sat there long enough, he could watch it swallow all of Rey's garden. Once a well-ordered grouping of vegetable and flower beds against a backdrop of vines, flowering shrubs, and a clump of small banana trees, the garden had in recent years gone largely untended except for a few favorites – zucchini, chili peppers, some persistent tomatoes. Everything else had either doggedly aggrandized itself or died. There was a sweet smell of rot.

Johnny hunched in his suit jacket, its bagginess giving his shoulders room to tremble from his soundless sobs. Sensing his world slipping away, he had grabbed what he could to hang onto, and he felt ashamed at how he had trespassed to rummage for it. Though he had loved Rey, it wasn't his death that was making Johnny hiccup with grief. It was Sonny's tribute, which continued to play in his head the way it had earlier echoed in the church, simple and clear. *Rey Bacaycay led a happy life.* It was true, and it was a rebuke of his own life. Rey *was* a happy man, never giving a second thought about why or how he ended up in America. Rey had understood that what he had in America was better than anything he would have had in the Philippines. While Johnny had understood it too, he had not lived that way, always feeling instead that he had not completely arrived, that he could not completely stake a claim and settle in, despite his house in Kimball Park.

Johnny put his face in his hands, not wanting to see or feel or think, and for a moment he was able to be distracted by the sound of his own breathing. But then he began to consider the absurdity in being soothed by the raspy signs of his deterioration. He took his hands away from his eyes as if to remind himself that, yes, he was still there.

When he looked up, the line of shadow had crossed over

him. Beyond the new demarcation between sun and shade, he thought he saw the leaves of the banana tree shiver. Before his eyes could adjust fully, Winston was kneeling beside him, unheeding of the dirt and weeds, his hand on Johnny's arm, a consoling gesture. They'd barely spoken since they'd buried the cat, and he was moved by the touch. Johnny broke down and divulged what he had pilfered, withdrawing it from his jacket: the feather from Rey's hat. But Winston seemed unable to appreciate its meaning, and this disappointed Johnny to tears.

Then Josie showed up, silently like a cat, territorial and wary, and he allowed her to lead him away, the rebuke he felt at Sonny's words still following him.

Inside, the kitchen was crowded. Laura and Sara sat on either side of Linda at the table, the three of them eating cold *lumpia*, their lips glossy, almost nauseating with grease. Paper napkins stuck to their fingers as they wiped their hands. Sonny was tying the ends of a garbage bag. Tessie was untying her apron.

Josie prodded him into their midst as if she were presenting evidence of some kind.

"There you are," Tessie said, and then they were all upon him.

Laura gave him her chair at the table, and Linda poured him a glass of water, and soon they had all arranged themselves around him, a vase of lilies on the table a fragrant embellishment to their union. He felt their need to shield and preserve him inside their somber, mute company.

"Hey, everyone, look over here." It was Sonny holding Josie's camera. "Scoot in a bit." Johnny felt everyone list toward him.

Just as they readied themselves for the camera, the kitchen door opened and they all turned at the intrusion. Sonny lowered the camera. Winston hovered on the threshold, looking at the assemblage before him, his eyes darting from the family, with Johnny in their midst, to the camera.

He held out his hand. "I'll take it," he said.

It was more than the helpful gesture so typical of Winston, the kind of thing that had charmed them from the beginning, the kind of thing they had come to expect. It was an admission of something: that he wasn't one of them.

Sonny gave him the camera and joined the picture.

Johnny was still blinking from the camera flash when a black blur in house slippers swept in front of the table. It was Gloria, disheveled from her nap, mourning dress bunched at her waist, coif flattened at the back and damp at the front from the compress she had held there, fretful hands clutching something to her chest. She waved it at them: Rey's hat, the silly green fedora.

"We forgot his hat. He would've wanted to wear his hat." Her voice, shrill and strained, suddenly dropped as she stared at the hat which she held at arm's length. She brought it closer and then let out a moan. "The feather's gone. Where's the feather?"

None of them had moved from their picture pose, but now Sonny broke towards his mother, who dodged him as if he were a mugger. Linda stepped to the other side of her, arms in a half circle to corral her. Gloria, with nowhere to go, stood and cried into Rey's hat, "I'm a widow." Linda and Sonny closed in on her and made soothing sounds into her hair.

The rest of them waited and watched. Winston still held the camera, both hands supporting it as if it were something burdensome. Johnny jiggled his knee under the table. He expelled a small cough to clear his throat, because his chest felt constricted despite the looseness of his jacket. Tessie patted his back, which made Gloria lift her gaze from Rey's hat. Gloria, competitive even when it came to grief, shouted at Tessie, "At least you get to prepare for Johnny's death." And then, appalled at her own words, she threw Rey's hat at her sister. It bounced off the shoulder of a stunned Tessie and tumbled underneath the table.

Tessie rose to her feet, perhaps to return Gloria's assault, or extend a gesture of sympathy, or make a huffy exit out the door. Whatever her intent, she never had a chance to make it known, since in her haste she bumped the table, upsetting the vase of flowers. Lilies sprawled in a puddle of water. While Tessie only stared, Gloria flung her torso across the table and spread her arms to encompass the lilies on the loose, her black dress soaking up the rivulets of water. Sonny looked around for help, stumped by his mother's hysterics, but Linda seemed to tire of them. She pulled up a chair, sat her mother in it, and patted her shoulder mechanically. Johnny, seeking safety, bent over in his chair, his jacket hunching at his ears to further shield him. He could see underneath the table. There, on the floor, was Rey's hat. He reached for it, pulled it into his lap, and sat back up in his chair.

Father Ramos, awakened by the commotion, stumbled sleepily into the kitchen. His appearance triggered a stream of confessions – or rather, revelations against others. It was tattletale time and everyone, it seemed, was game.

"Tessie ruined the lilies," cried Gloria, who herself was mangling the blossoms in her attempt to restore the bouquet.

"Winston lost something," Josie called out.

"Maybe he lost it in Tijuana," Laura said.

"She followed you," Sara confessed for Laura. Winston only tightened his grip on the camera, too bewildered to say anything. Johnny saw Tessie blanch at the disclosure.

"Spying?" she cried, indignant. "What if someone followed you around?"

Winston had a sudden fit of clumsiness with the camera,

recovering in time to cradle it into his stomach and keep it from crashing to the floor.

Before Johnny could even try to make sense of any of it, Sonny changed the subject, chiming in with his announcement that he had snuck a hundred-dollar bill into Rey's pocket, and that it was now secure in the coffin with him. Johnny silently cheered, while Linda, who had not ceased her mechanical pats to her mother's shoulder, now slugged Sonny with her free hand.

Father Ramos was imploring them for calm, and when they did hush, he made a quick exit. But it was not Father Ramos who had quieted the family. Gloria had by now gathered the damaged lilies, bunching the stems in her grasp. She rose, shrugging off Linda's hand, and held the flowers aloft. The scent of the lilies filled the air and bits of orange pistil dripped on the kitchen table. Petals threatened to abandon the stalk.

They were all fixed on Gloria, steeling themselves for her next act of hysteria, but Johnny's gaze was drawn to the flowers. Some distant thought snagged at the back of his brain. From within his trance, he saw Gloria wave her bouquet in his face, a gesture that Tessie clearly took to be a provocation. She reached out and yanked at the bent heads of the lilies, decapitating a few, and so began a tug of war between the sisters. Just as their children were about to intervene, they were all stopped short by a shout.

"Bunny!"

20

STALLED

A week had passed since his outburst and it was as if nothing had happened. Yet everything had changed. Johnny was in the car, parked in the driveway. He was in the driver's seat, a place he had not occupied for a while. He looked in the rear-view mirror at the street behind him. He could release the brake and the car would roll nearly all the way past the curb. And then what? He hadn't brought the keys. He couldn't start the engine and drive away. This was as far as he could escape.

He had wandered the house trying to avoid Tessie – not to avoid a confrontation, but to avoid her avoidance of one. After his explanation, which sounded feeble, but was as accurate as he could muster, she seemed determined to soldier on with as little emotion as possible, as if it all had been spent at the free-for-all after Rey's funeral.

He didn't remember much of what happened in the moments after he called Bunny's name. But he remembered the silence, no one wanting to look at anyone else. Rey's hat was in his lap and he surrendered it gently to Sonny, though it was still missing the feather that was concealed in his jacket.

Then somehow they were in the car, this old, big, unwieldy car. Josie drove them home, Tessie in front and him in the back, where he had banished himself. Tessie made small talk, forcing

Josie to participate by addressing questions to her about the weather, the price of apples, the weather again. And he, numb from the shambles of that endless afternoon, could only think about how Tessie had weeks ago asked for a new car. Of course, she should have one.

In bed that night, as they lay motionless, he staring at the ceiling, she on her side facing away, he did his best. It was an associative thing, he said, like when he did crossword puzzles. One word triggered another; one image translated into something new.

"There was just too much..." he broke off, shaking his head in the dark, remembering the barrage of emotions: Gloria's howling, his daughters' finger-pointing at who knew what, Tessie's attack on the lilies. "The lilies," he said. It made him think of the Philippines, the *sampaguita*, he told her. That was the connection for him.

"Okay," she said.

She left the house regularly now to look after Gloria, and while this seemed a reasonable and charitable thing to do, he felt cut off. They were back to where they had started, the gulf between them wider than ever.

He recalled that day when it was Winston's Cadillac parked here in the driveway, gleaming from having just been washed. He remembered sitting in the passenger seat, holding Bunny's admonishing letter. She was right: they each had their reasons for what happened that afternoon on her couch. They were reasons that had nothing to do with love or passion – at least not for each other. Would Tessie ever understand that?

His leg jiggled, hitting the steering wheel. When he could no longer fight off the urge, he reached under the seat, his fingers scratching at bits of trash until they gripped the familiar packet. He had stashed it months ago, when he still hadn't been convinced that he was really sick. He pulled the flattened packet from under the seat and inspected the contents – three bent and surely stale cigarettes and a torn book of matches. He extracted a limp cigarette and put it to his lips. Already the feel of it keyed him up. Despite the deadliness of that old indifferent habit, he wanted to revert back to it, to the nonchalance he used to have about inhaling the hot smoke into his blood. He lit up, sucked in the poisons, and for a fleeting, pleasurable second felt the friendly relief. Then came the wooziness, and he was strangling with a sudden collection of phlegm in his throat. He opened the car door, tossed the cigarette onto the asphalt, and heaved a gob of spit after it. He hung over the side, bent at the waist, catching his breath slowly, his eyes fluttering closed on the inhale. On one of his exhales, he opened his eyes to Tessie's feet, tense inside the crisscross strap of her sandals.

"I have to go to Gloria's," he heard her say.

He straightened himself slowly and eased himself out of the car, crushing the discarded cigarette beneath his slipper. When he looked at Tessie, she was staring at his foot, at the ferocious motion of it. He held the door for her as she slid in and adjusted the mirror. She pulled the door shut, out of his hands.

"We'll have to get that new car soon," he said stupidly.

She nodded and drove away.

21

A CHANCE TO TANGO

In Rey's garden, Tessie shaded her eyes with her hand as she scanned the fading plants. Tomatoes were cracked, their spilled juice dried in the wound. Overgrown zucchini, severed from the stalk by their own weight, rotted in the dirt. Flies swam in the hot air, lighting every so often on the spongy insides of a faltering blossom. Tessie stepped gingerly through the untended rows, her sandals scuffing the packed soil. The sun bore down on her neck and arms, and after only a few minutes, Tessie's interest began to wilt.

She spied the edge of the clay pot just in time to avoid tripping on it. The pot was buried to its rim, parts of which had broken off from wear. It had confined the growth of the mint, lack of water had dried it at its edges, and lanky dandelions had sprung up around it. She squatted, her toes spreading as she balanced on the balls of her feet to pluck a sprig of mint from among the weeds. She rose, gladdened by her find, and carried it into Gloria's kitchen.

She had been coming to Gloria's almost every day since the funeral to sit with her for an hour or so, to fix her a sandwich or just a glass of lemonade and listen to her talk softly of Rey's quiet exit, which she now deemed intentional in its unobtrusiveness. "Isn't that just like him?" Gloria seemed to have nearly, but not quite, gotten it out of her system. Just as Tessie had nearly, but not quite, gotten out of her system the shock of that afternoon when Johnny had shouted Bunny's name. It was the lilies, he told her. The smell of them. It reminded him of the Philippines. That was all.

Gloria had taken Tessie's side in the matter, and Tessie reciprocated by ministering to her sister's post-funeral adjustment. This was where her energy went, rather than confronting Johnny about his outburst.

She hadn't meant to come today, but Gloria called her, sounding anxious as ever. Though now as she poured Gloria's iced tea and garnished it with the freshly harvested mint, it occurred to Tessie that the anxiety in Gloria's summons had differed from the distress she had shown in the days immediately following Rey's death and funeral.

Tessie brought the iced teas into the living room. She had not garnished her own, wanting Rey's mint to adorn only Gloria's glass. Gloria sat on the couch, not slumped back into the cushions as she had on previous days, but on the edge, her knees touching the glass-topped coffee table. On the table were the condolence cards that had come in the mail. There had been no new ones in the last few days. Gloria seemed to take comfort in the neat pile that the old ones made. Between sips of her iced tea, she placed her glass on the table near the pile. She seemed not to notice the sprig of mint. Tessie bit her lip.

"I slept a little better last night," Gloria reported, as had become her habit when Tessie visited.

"Good. You look more rested."

"But I'm not, really. I mean, it's all relative, you know."

"Yes, relative to the day before, you're more rested," Tessie said, alarmed at the insistence in her voice toward her sister who had so recently lost her husband.

Gloria took a piece of the mint in her teeth as she sipped

her tea. She pulled it from her mouth and set it on the table, where it lay limp in a sliver of wetness. "What I mean is I don't think I can ever sleep the way I used to, now that I'm alone. I'm afraid. I hear things at night, so I turn on the light and I just lie there afraid."

"It'll get easier as time goes on." Tessie was ashamed at her use of this tired expression, used by people like her who had not suffered what her sister had suffered.

Gloria stared at the mint leaf on the table, though she seemed not to see it. "The funny thing is when Rey was alive, I never had these fears. But what could he have done if someone had broken in? He was an old man."

Tessie thought Gloria would cry now as she had done so many times in the last few days. But Gloria just sat with a crooked little smile at the thought of Rey protecting her against an intruder. Tessie remembered Johnny's valiant effort with the snake.

"He would have done his best."

"I know." Now she did cry, and Tessie moved onto the couch next to her and stroked her hair, which had not been set since the funeral. It was time to take her to the hairdresser.

Gloria finished her bout of weeping and the sisters pulled apart. Gloria, having relieved herself of the weight of her tears, now appeared almost refreshed, ready to move on temporarily to other topics. She shifted herself to sit sideways on the couch, facing Tessie. This made Tessie think of the times when they were teenagers and Gloria would assume her big-sister role and the confiding tone that was not altogether genuine. Even in this time of grieving, Tessie was not up to accommodating Gloria's self-importance.

"I'll get us some more iced tea."

On the kitchen counter, Tessie found a remnant of mint. She thought of the discarded sprig on the coffee table, and added this leftover piece to her glass. This pungent bit of Rey's quiet, scruffy garden.

When Tessie brought the refilled glasses back into the living room, Gloria was tucking an envelope beneath the pile of condolence cards. The envelope was letter size and conspicuous against the Hallmarks. Gloria took her glass from Tessie and after a few sips remarked. "That's Rey's mint, isn't it?"

"Yes, that's it there," Tessie said, pointing to the damp, stringy sprig on the table.

Gloria sighed. "I can't take care of that garden."

"It's okay. You don't have to."

Gloria sighed again. "I found a funny thing."

"Oh?" Tessie's hands went cold. She wanted to cover her ears with them, not wanting to hear anything bad about Rey. She didn't want to know that after a husband was in the grave, there were "funny things" to be discovered.

Gloria opened her mouth a few times, but when she seemed uncharacteristically unable to form any words, she instead reached for the envelope under the sympathy cards and handed it facedown to Tessie.

Tessie turned the envelope over and saw her husband's name written in delicate script. In the corner were the name and address of Bunny Piña. There was no stamp on the envelope that was dingy with handling. It was, she noticed now, unsealed.

"It was open when I found it." Gloria said. "I couldn't read it."

Tessie was about to feel grateful for this circumspection on her sister's part when Gloria confessed the reason. "It's in Tagalog."

Tessie didn't want to open the letter. She wanted to show her sister that a person's private correspondence was to be respected. But she couldn't help it. She unfolded the paper that might have been thick with fragrance once, but now smelled almost musty. She looked at the prettily inked words that made no sense to her.

"See?" Gloria said.

◈ ◈ ◈

It was too early to start dinner, but Tessie didn't want to sit. Her blood felt light and brisk inside her limbs; she tried to temper it by scrubbing the kitchen counters, making the tile gleam and her forearm ache. She had been moving about like this since returning from Gloria's. Johnny had been asleep in the bedroom when she got home and looked in on him, curled on his side, his arms tucked into his chest, a sock trailing off one foot.

She looked up at the shelf where the candle burned. She still couldn't believe she had forgotten about it that weekend – which now seemed so long ago. The day after she returned from Las Vegas, that first day after Rey's death, she woke after a shaky sleep and lay uneasily next to Johnny, whose breath rumbled with snores. There was something unnaturally dim about the room. At first she attributed it to the gloom that Rey's death had brought. But no, something else was missing. She began a sweep around the room with her eyes: first to the right, where the television gave a blank stare from its perch on the desk, and then left at the mirror above the dresser. There, she saw reflected nearly the whole of the room: the TV, the rumpled covers of the bed, the closet door that wouldn't close, and then finally the shelf with its coterie of saints – in the middle of which stood the burnt-out candle of the Virgin of Guadalupe.

Tessie had sat up in bed with a gasp, but then clapped her hand over her mouth, not wanting to wake Johnny. She slipped out of bed, careful not to yank the covers, and on hands and knees at the bedside reached underneath to pull out another Virgin of Guadalupe candle. She lit the candle, took the expired one from the shelf, and put the newborn flame in its place. She looked at Johnny, who had not moved, though his breathing had changed to a forced regularity.

The guilt she had felt then about her neglect was replaced now by the shock at hearing Johnny call out Bunny's name. They hadn't spoken of it, any of it – not the candle, not Bunny, not the time Tessie was devoting to Gloria. She hadn't wanted to.

Johnny was in the living room playing Scrabble by himself.

Winston had been Johnny's Scrabble partner all summer, but he had not visited since Rey's funeral, since the catastrophe in Gloria's kitchen. Tessie resented those days now – their Scrabble play. There had always been a hint of conspiracy to it, as there had been, in fact, to everything they did together. There was smugness in their laughter, their inside jokes, the way that sometimes Johnny gave Winston a friendly jostle to the ribs.

She was sure though that Bunny's letter explained it all. And where was it now, but in plain view? Well, practically. It was in her purse, which was in plain view on the end table near the couch where Johnny sat hunched over the Scrabble board.

Tessie took up a dust cloth, went to the living room, and began to skim her cloth across the hard surfaces there. She picked up her purse to dust the table top and set the purse back down, leaving it there, though she knew Johnny had no reason to look inside. She could only imagine his surprise at finding Bunny's letter there. What about such a discovery would be the most surprising to him? Tessie's possession of the letter, or its very existence? Did he know of it? Had he read it?

Tessie moved her dust cloth to the swan that so often had been shoved to the side to make room for board games with Winston. She trailed her cloth along the plastic ivy that meandered over the edge of the table toward the swirled pattern on the carpet, where she spotted a stray Scrabble tile. She picked it up. The letter B.

"Here," she said, holding it out to Johnny, who looked up, startled.

Tessie looked at his board in time to see not a crisscross of random words, but words made from a deliberate selection of letters. She saw *death* and *dying*, *cancer* and *snake*; she saw *candle* and she saw *Rey*; and then they were just a jumble of tiles because Johnny sent them skittering off the board with a swipe of his hand. She stood staring at the mess, feeling helpless. She was still holding the letter B. She placed it in the middle of the board. It formed a word all on its own.

Johnny sat, short of breath, as if winded from the blow he had delivered to the Scrabble tiles. As she watched the fragile shuddering of his shoulders, Tessie thought of the letter from Bunny. It made her angrier than ever that he was sick.

◈ ◈ ◈

"Anger is one of the stages," a woman in a Calvin Klein tank top told her in a tone that made clear to Tessie that they had already covered this ground. There were nods from the group. Though they all knew each other, they still wore nametags, badges of burden and sorrow.

Tessie knew it was a mistake coming to the support group, but after yesterday she needed an outlet for her feelings. Though she knew she might be grasping at air, she had come here hoping someone might tell her something that would set things straight again. She looked around the circle at the women, all of them with cancer-afflicted husbands. She couldn't remember the last time she had been among them, but she knew there had been a leader, a pixie-faced woman with a happy name who could rein in rude remarks.

"Where's the leader of the group?" Tessie asked.

"Melody's sick," the woman next to her said.

"We're self-directed today," the Calvin Klein woman said.

The women had formed a bond without her. They knew each other's names and the names and illnesses of the spouses. They were knitting shrouds for each other. And now in this self-directed meeting, Tessie was told she had missed the anger stage, so she got up and directed herself out of the room.

Tessie had not missed the anger stage. She had always been angry. She had just never known it. She marched to her car, and the ineffectual thumping of her rubber soles on concrete made the blood seethe behind her eyes. With every other step, she counted some instance in her life when she had not fully given vent to her anger: the time when she was eight and Gloria broke their mother's favorite lamp and blamed it on Tessie; when she was fifteen and could not have a quinceañera; when she was nineteen and became pregnant and everything was all wrong; when Winston came into their lives; when the snake invaded her sun porch; when her husband uttered another woman's name.

Now, as she slammed her feet into the pavement, what angered her was Johnny never having asked her where she went when she left the house. Of course she meant to keep it a secret, but if he had asked, she would have told him. He should've asked.

Today especially she wanted him to ask, so she could say, *Dancing. I go dancing.* And then she would say, *Winston knew.*

◈ ◈ ◈

Armida didn't appreciate late arrivals, and Tessie had never dared walk in late to dance class before, but this was her real therapy. She was determined to participate even though in her sneakers and sweat pants she was in sore violation of the class dress code. She slipped inside the door, pausing to survey the pairings, seeing that Armida was serving as Manny's partner as she shouted encouragement and directions to the other dancers. It was a cumbia they were dancing, and Tessie stood apart, her sneakers chafing against the old hardwood floor as she rotated her hips to the music. Sweat rose off the dancers and mixed with Armida's perfume and hairspray. The scent filled the room to its mildewed corners. This was the smell of dance, Tessie thought, all nerve and fire, the people on the floor striving to be one with the structures and rhythms of the music, because when that happened they blended with their partner and that was the point of it all.

The music ended. When Armida, her high heels tapping, went to the middle of the room to explain a new variation, Tessie slid into place opposite Manny, who winked nervously at her. She winced as her sneakers squeaked against the floor.

"Better late than never, Tessie." Armida looked with displeasure at Tessie's attire. Manny took a step forward as if to shield Tessie, and she was grateful to him for the gesture, though today she would not be daunted by Armida's omniscient eye. "It's '90s cumbia. Glamorous cumbia."

"I know," Tessie said. "Sorry." Her voice shook and she hoped she wouldn't start crying. She didn't want to have to excuse herself from a group for the second time that afternoon.

Armida clapped her hands together. "Okay, for today, all the glamour must come from inside." Armida laid her jeweled hands over her cleavage.

Glamorous cumbia was an important distinction for Armida, who always shared the history of the dances with her students. Cumbia was mostly popular with the lower social classes, Armida had told them. It had begun as a courtship dance among the slaves. "But it has evolved to this brilliance, this dance of hopefulness and freedom."

Armida punched the button on the stereo. "*¡Bailemos!*"

Dancing cumbia made Tessie feel young. She loved the simplicity of the dance, but she had always been inhibited about swaying her hips, moving instead in a way that was more mechanical than organic, originating from the outer hip rather than deeper in the muscles. She felt she was too old to allow the drumming of the music to attach so frankly to her pelvis. But somehow, the skirts she always wore made up for her anemic hip swaying. Today, though, in her sweat pants and sneakers, she felt a new freedom: she felt more open to the music and its compulsive backbeat. She felt her body relax and let the urgency of the percussion fill it. As Manny guided her through turns and crossovers, he held her hand lightly, touched the small of her back with quiet fingertips. Armida came to dance beside them and applaud. "*Eso es,*" she cried.

This is what it feels like to be understood, Tessie thought.

◈ ◈ ◈

Tessie and Manny were the only ones left in the café. The other dancers had gone home after a round of nachos. They were housewives and retirees, gone back to their ordinary lives after an afternoon of exhilaration brought on by congas and drums and insinuative saxophone. Tessie and Manny had stayed, not talking much now that they were alone, looking out the window at Armida in her dance studio across the street, giving a private tango lesson to a slender young man with a poetic profile.

Tessie sipped her pineapple juice. She would have ordered herself a Coke, but someone had ordered pitchers of the juice, apparently some sort of post-class ritual for the dancers. Caridad, the waitress, had greeted them, holding the pitchers aloft like prizes, "*Jugo de piña.*"

At the mention of *piña*, Tessie was reminded of what had driven her here. Across from her, Manny sat with his hands on the table, resting one on the other. They were large, burly hands, but his touch was surprisingly light when he guided her in dance. Then there was the last time she was here with him and the other dancers, when he had laid his hand on top of hers to prevent her from reaching inside her purse to pay her share of the bill. She remembered the cool weight of it on her hunched fingers that quivered at the contact. His hand hadn't lingered, and she had dug into her purse anyway, insisting on at least paying a few dollars for tip.

Manny drummed gently on the table with the fingers of his top hand.

"Do you need to go?" Tessie asked, hearing the anxiety in her voice, not sure what she wanted his answer to be.

"No. Do you?"

"No."

They went silent again as they continued to watch Armida tango with her student. Armida flung her leg up behind her, sending her turquoise high heel to jab the air, a graceful, subtle violence.

"You usually hurry off right after class," Manny said.

"Well, not today." Johnny might be expecting her by now, but today she didn't care. Let him wonder.

"I'm thinking of signing up for tango lessons," Tessie said, still watching the pair across the street.

"You'd be very good at it."

She had never considered dancing the tango. It was too dramatic, she thought. Overwrought. Was she really considering it now? She wasn't sure, and was only slightly ashamed of herself at having just wangled a compliment from Manny.

She looked at him and he lowered his eyes. He repositioned the decorative *molcajete* on the table, and Tessie followed his hand. It was ringless. Had he never been married? She knew he lived with his mother. Or, no, his mother lived with him. There was a difference.

"You'd be good at it, too," Tessie told him, though in fact

she wasn't at all sure he would be. He was not a stylist, more a journeyman.

"Really?" Manny grinned.

"Yes," Tessie said, and turned away again to watch Armida and her partner. He was propelling her backward, their torsos erect above their long, sweeping steps, Armida's calf parting the slit in her skirt.

Tessie wondered more than ever what Bunny looked like.

"Why don't we?" Manny asked her.

"What?"

"Sign up for lessons." He had turned his hands so that his palms faced upward, open to her.

It was tempting. But could she really slink and glide with such abandon?

Tessie sighed. "Tango is for the young people."

"Tessie," Manny said, moving his hand toward hers, "it's never too late to tango."

Tessie followed Manny's pick-up truck, wondering at her actions – how she put her hands in his, how in leaving the cafe with him, she felt the closeness of his body next to hers though they were no longer touching. She didn't have to follow him. She could turn anytime. Once, she allowed another car to move in front of her, but Manny pulled to the curb so she could catch up.

Manny stopped in front of a small house, worn but neat, not a tract home like hers, but distinct in its shape and features from its neighbors. The lawn was dry and brown, and closely trimmed. There were no flowers. Tessie was curious about the inside of the house, but Manny led her down the side of the house to the backyard which was taken up in large part by a small, flat-roofed structure painted to match the house. It was too large to be a tool shed or storage locker. Besides, there were windows with curtains and a welcome mat at the door.

"Sometimes I need my privacy," Manny told her as he unlocked the door and invited her to cross the threshold.

It was just one room with a kitchen along one wall and a combination of bedroom and living-room furniture occupying the rest of the space. It smelled of beer and jalapeños, but happily not of dirty laundry.

"You live here?"

"It's just a getaway. My mother likes to watch her telenovelas in peace."

He went to the refrigerator. "Would you like some wine?"

She told him yes, though she never drank in the daytime.

She met his glass in a silent toast, avoiding his eyes, looking at his feet, which she suddenly found to be comically large. How had she never noticed them before? She tracked their movement as Manny went to the stereo to put on some music. It was not a tango or a cha-cha. Not a meringue. Nothing fast or dramatic or hip-swaying. It was a decorous waltz. He held his arms out to her. Whenever they danced, she had always looked at his shoulders or his chin, the slight hook of his nose, or the gentle creases in his forehead. But now she looked at his eyes, large and dark, with small red veins at the corners and, underneath, little pillows of skin, signs of age that did not detract from the kindness that was there. There was something else she had not seen before because she had never looked. Loneliness.

She was overwhelmed with the sight of it, and she buried her face in Manny's chest. She knew nothing of this man, yet what she wanted at this moment was to lie down next to him.

Though the music still played, they were no longer dancing. She didn't know whose feet had stopped moving first, and now she felt she could only stand if she stayed there leaning into Manny. He must have sensed the sudden weakness in her legs, her immovable sneakers, because he scooped an arm beneath her knees and lifted her up. She felt her hip rest on the soft ledge of his belly. He carried her the few steps to the bed and she closed her eyes as he set her upon the bedspread, coarse from too many launderings. She lay quietly, arms at her sides, her feet in their sneakers pointed at the ceiling, and she barely breathed, wondering again what it was she was expecting to happen. The bed dipped when Manny, in a movement as deft as dance, stretched out beside her, his posture mimicking hers. The touch points of their bodies – the backs of their hands, the broad part of their thighs, the hard outer bones of their ankles – were slightly electrifying to her. The sensation spread throughout her body, intensifying. She began to breathe rapidly; her hands and feet tingled and became numb. She was gasping for air.

Manny scrambled to right himself, and the swaying of the bed further compromised her stymied breaths. She could not answer Manny's repeated shouts of "What's wrong?" She could not gather her wits to shout back at him to shut up. She squeezed her eyes tight and when Manny ceased to shout, when she knew he was no longer in the room, she knew that he had run to get his mother.

She forced herself to breathe deeply to move air back into the closed-off capillaries of her fingertips, the cool pads of her toes. She stumbled to the door, hurrying the blood back into her legs. As she made her way to her car, she fumbled in her purse for her keys. Her fingers grazed the onion skin of Bunny's letter. She knew where she was headed.

22

STEP BY STEP

Johnny was alone and growing impatient. He still sat at the kitchen table, though it had been over two hours since Tessie had left him with a bowl of fish soup and some boiled eggplant for lunch. She had snatched up her keys and purse and announced she was going out. He had stared at her barely combed hair and the oily smudges on the knee of her peach-colored sweatpants, but he hadn't questioned her. He couldn't, really, after the Bunny thing.

So here he sat. He had gotten up a few times, once to go to the bathroom, once to just wander around the house in search of – something.

Josie should have been home from work by now, though he knew that sometimes she lingered there, taking treats from her pocket and pushing them through the wires of the kennel to those hopeless animals. When his daughters were young, they had begged to have a dog. He had been adamant: no pet whose shit was bigger than a pellet, and it had to be confined to a bowl or a cage. So at various times the girls had a turtle, a hamster, and a rabbit, each of which succumbed to some grievous end. One of them (the turtle, it must have been) had been accidentally ground up in the garbage disposal. The hamster escaped from its cage and lived in closets and bureau drawers, shredding socks and underwear into nests until Johnny found its stiffened body, its fur giving off the odor of the poison he had laid out for rats. The rabbit – he didn't remember its death. For some reason that bothered him now.

There were fish bones at the bottom of his soup bowl. A piece of eggplant lay cold and slimy in a pool of sunlight that had angled its way into the dark-walled kitchen. Somewhere outside, a door slammed, jolting him inside the silent house. He uncrumpled his napkin and laid it across the dirty dishes, then decided to sit in the yard for a while, where even the sound of the nearby freeway could sometimes be like company.

Outside, seated in one of the redwood painted chairs, he closed his eyes and waited for the sounds of the neighborhood. But other than some distant wind chimes and the buzz of some flies, there was little activity. Even Hector's mad rooster kept silent. There was the constant whooshing noise of the freeway, but it was not a companionable sound after all. It was just the sound of life going on elsewhere, purposefully, with a destination.

He stuffed his hands inside the pockets of the cardigan he wore over his pajamas. The sun was high and hot, but his body warmed up slowly, and his feet were always cold. He had finally gone through his stash of untouched tube socks, so that now not a single pair remained coupled by the little plastic thread and wraparound sticker. He opened his eyes now and stuck his legs straight out so he could look at his feet, swaddled in the thick cotton and stuffed inside his house slippers. The socks made his feet look more substantial than he knew them to be. He drew his feet back so they were flat on the grass and began jiggling his knee up and down in that way that often bothered Tessie. Where was she anyway?

If he waited a little longer, maybe Hector would wander out his front door to stand in his yard and just stare off into the distance as he often did. Maybe this time Johnny would do more than nod and grunt hello. He wondered how Hector spent his days, whether he thought about dying.

The sun was starting to bother him, so he rose and dusted the seat of his pajamas. Instead of shuffling toward his own front door, he lifted the latch at the gate of the chain-link fence, running his fingers against the metal to steady himself as he walked the outside of his property to the unfenced crabgrass of Hector's.

Hector, the only one on the block who had left his house its original drab color (a chocolate brown that had faded to dirt), periodically painted his door, always a different color. It had been blue for the last several years, and streaks of it could be seen through the uneven overlay of orange applied just months earlier. Johnny stood there a moment, wondering what he was doing in his pajamas and cardigan on the doorstep of a neighbor he had barely spoken to over the years. He was about to withdraw his hand, which had been hovering indecisively at the doorbell, when the door opened. Hector's face nearly collided with his own. They each jerked backward, Hector alarmed and Johnny embarrassed.

Now Johnny regretted having come. If he had just waited in his chair in his own front yard a few more minutes, Hector would have come out of his house. They would have exchanged their normal abbreviated greetings from the safety of their respective yards. Now in these unfamiliar circumstances, they each paused to get their bearings, Hector looking at his own front door as if to verify that, yes, this was his house, and Johnny searching for a reason why he had left his.

"Do you have a can opener?" Johnny blurted.

"Yes," Hector said, waiting, as if Johnny were merely taking a survey of the neighborhood.

"I can't find ours," Johnny explained, slowly gaining some

semblance of self-possession and becoming curious about the inside of Hector's house. "Can I borrow yours?"

When Hector opened the door a bit wider, Johnny stepped inside. The Cabrera house was the mirror image of his own in its layout, but the similarity stopped there. The walls were gray for lack of cleaning, and the patterns on the couch were obliterated from wear. Rents in the carpet ran underneath the wheeled cart that held the smeary-faced TV. Through the sliding glass door that led to the patio, Johnny could see the rooster – a rumpled mound of feathers perched in the center of a rotting picnic table.

"In here," Hector called from the kitchen.

Johnny found Hector scrabbling through drawers and cupboards. Johnny, feeling guilty about the false request, was about to tell him not to bother, when Hector turned around. "You want some coffee?"

Johnny didn't, not here in this dingy, sad house, but he said okay. "Just a little."

Hector took two cups from one of the cupboards, all of whose doors still gaped open from Hector's quest for the can opener. He spooned instant granules into each, then filled them from a simmering pan of water.

"Sit down." Hector motioned with one of the cups, sending coffee drops in flight. When Johnny had done so, Hector pushed an uncovered bowl with crusted edges at him. "Sugar?"

Johnny held up his hand. "Doctor's orders," he lied.

Hector frowned. "You used to take sugar. And milk."

Johnny was taken aback. Short of his peering through the de la Cruz window at breakfast time, Hector could not possibly know that Johnny took a generous glop of milk in his cup.

Hector scooted the sugar bowl back toward himself, scuffing the table – which Johnny guessed hadn't seen a tablecloth in years. They sipped their coffee in silence. Johnny kept his eyes from wandering too much around the room, not wanting to invade Hector's privacy, not wanting to see any more of his dismal surroundings than necessary. He allowed himself to look only in the vicinity of Hector's head: behind it the exposed interior of the cupboards with mismatched and chipped dishes, dented cans of soup, and drippy bottles of soy sauce and Tabasco; to the left, the stove where the pot of water still simmered; to the right, the refrigerator, its sides streaky with handprints.

"Haven't seen your nephew around much lately," Hector said.

"He's not my nephew."

"Good-looking boy."

"Yes. No relation."

"He's gone, then?"

"Yes. Gone." Johnny felt only a slight pang at the word. There had been no real goodbye, nothing spoken, only felt. He withheld a sigh. He remembered then that Hector's family was gone, scattered like marbles. Searching for something to say, his eyes went to the dusty ceiling fan, to a faint handprint on the wall, to the flap of a wing on the patio table.

"Why do you keep a rooster?"

Hector shrugged. "In the Philippines, we always had a house rooster."

It seemed a silly, obnoxious way to remember one's homeland, but Johnny observed, neutrally, "It's not allowed here in the city limits."

"No one complains." Hector narrowed his eyes at Johnny. "What about you?"

"Me, no, I don't complain." Johnny sipped at his coffee which was grainy and acidic.

"No," Hector said, waving his hand to dismiss Johnny's

answer. "What is it that you keep to remind you of back home?"

Johnny, believing he'd left everything behind, shook his head.

Hector insisted, "There's always something, you know."

A small granule of undissolved coffee sat on Johnny's tongue. He let it rest there while he ruminated on Hector's question. He remembered the sack filled with small provisions for his journey that his mother had thrust in his hands the day he left. The mango and banana, the coconut. The photograph. How he had held the sack in his lap as he bounced in Leoncio's truck. How he had handed it to his father for just a moment at the check-in station. How, faced with the disorienting act of saying goodbye to his father, he found that he had, without quite understanding how, crossed to another life and failed utterly in saying goodbye. How he had irretrievably left the sack in his father's hands.

All those years later, when he went back, those things could not be recovered. Even given a slab of coconut to hold and smell and eat, he could not conjure the essence of what he had lost, until he saw Bunny. Floral, fragrant, flesh-and-blood Bunny.

When Johnny did not produce an answer, Hector lit a cigarette. Johnny flinched at the smoke. He turned his head away and noticed the can opener on the floor wedged beneath the refrigerator.

Hector stabbed out his cigarette and blew smoke down into his armpit. "Sorry." He covered the offending butt with a newspaper. "How are you feeling?"

Johnny had never discussed his illness with any of the neighbors, but he knew they knew. "I think I'm going to die from this, you know." He had never made this admission to anyone, except to manipulate his wife and daughters. Maybe he wanted to see how it sounded saying it to sad-faced Hector in his dismal house.

Hector looked at him. "Maybe not."

Hector had always had a somber face, and it seemed to have grown mean over the years as one by one his family left. But now, up close and in the stark emptiness of his house, there might have been in the grooves of Hector's shadowy face an entrenched calm.

"We all die sometime, eh?"

"Yes," Johnny said, for some reason taking this as his cue to leave.

As Johnny rose, Hector said. "I had coffee with you and your wife in your backyard once. Do you remember?"

Johnny smiled, trying to remember it, trying to imagine it, and wondering where Tessie was now.

"Very pleasant," Hector said. "Very pleasant."

He followed Johnny to the door. "Come back again," he said, having forgotten the stated purpose of Johnny's visit. After the door closed behind him, Johnny moved slowly down the walk, thinking he himself had forgotten something. When he reached his own door, he remembered the can opener on the floor beneath the refrigerator, and all the drawers and cupboards where Hector had looked for it still gaping open.

There had been no pictures in Hector's house. No family photos of his grown children, none from their childhood. Nothing decorative on the walls or tables or shelves. Johnny was relieved to be back in his living room with its hodgepodge of knick-knacks and plastic plants, though they were tiresome at times and reminded him of swap-meet wares, outdated and slightly soiled. At least there was intention behind it all: Tessie's determination to achieve a magazine-beautiful décor. It would never come close to that, he knew. Like his own inability to dance or carry a tune. Like Josie's attempts at photographic art.

They were all a little off the mark. Sometimes a lot, like the way Gloria could miss her husband's last breath at her very elbow.

He was sitting in his chair in the living room. The pillows were flattened from too much use, and a small hole had appeared at the tip of the armrest, where he had developed the habit of pushing his fingernail into the upholstery. He put his finger there now. As he dug through the soft stuffing, probing for the hard skeleton of the chair, his eye fell on the stack of videos. He scooted himself off the chair, and on his knees in front of the television, he rummaged through the stack until he found the tape his daughters had given him, the one Laura had made. He slid it into the VCR and sat there on the floor to watch up close.

At first he watched dispassionately, registering the way the camera had followed its subjects, the way *he* had followed his subjects since he had been the one holding the camera. How sometimes he pulled back and watched from a distance, not focusing on anyone in particular, but letting his subjects, his daughters, run into and out of the frame until there were only palm trees and sand in the picture or a set of empty swings. How sometimes he trailed after them, staying close until they were self-conscious and wary, then mad at the intrusion, and a small hand would smother the lens.

He drew his knees up to his chest, wrapped his bony elbows around his bony knees, and nestled his chin on the crisscross of his wrists. While he recognized the little girls on the screen, he could not quite connect them to his grown-up daughters. He stared hard, as if something would be revealed to him through sheer concentration. Sometimes he would lose his focus, and the images would start to blur – but then there would be a blip in the picture, or Tessie would appear, young and slim and impatient to be off-camera, and he would snap back, acutely attentive again. He began to tire, and was ready to close his eyes when he saw himself on the screen for just a moment. He lifted his chin off his knees, craned his neck forward, and waited to see if he would appear again.

It's somebody's birthday party – Concha's. Yes, there she is, sitting at a card table in the backyard, a birthday cake in front of her – no, not a birthday cake. The camera pans across the top of the cake. Happy Anniversary. Then Fredo joins Concha at the table, and now the camera pans around the circle of people. There he sees himself, standing next to Tessie. He's clapping while holding a cigarette between his thumb and forefinger.

Just when Johnny wondered who was holding the camera, Rey's face appeared on the screen in close-up. He had turned the camera on himself, angling it so his chin and nose were foreshortened and his grin was comically broad. Johnny smiled at this younger Rey who had years yet to live.

The camera was back on the family. Concha and Fredo were dancing, swaying side to side, Concha's low-heeled black shoes making small quick movements in and around Fredo's slow-witted feet. The spectacle of the pair made the family laugh and it made them want to join in. Children and grandchildren joined in, partners or no. Tessie grabbed Laura, and Josie and Sara pranced with their cousins. Johnny was astonished to see himself flick his cigarette away, step into the center of the concrete patio slab, and begin to do his own tentative dance steps, repetitive and awkward, his weight shifting rhythmlessly from one foot to the other. Just as he was going to step back away, Josie and Sara each grabbed one of his hands, and they continued their silly prancing, each out of sync with the other, Johnny in the middle. Against the background of the pharmaceutical music, they laughed at themselves in their awkwardness because they could sense that even in their inept dance, there was a kind of grace. And when the music ran out, they danced in silence, and that was lovely too.

Johnny began to fear how the dancing would end, when the moment of grace would peter out or be extinguished in an instant. He did not want to see that moment, yet he could not turn away. Mercifully, the footage cut abruptly to another scene, an outing at the zoo, to an assemblage of pink flamingos in a pond, and the image of the de la Cruz family dancing stayed intact.

How had he not remembered that moment in their lives?

Johnny rewound the tape and watched the scene in reverse, looking for clues to how it had come about, but finding none. Still, it had happened, and it was there on the tape, ready to play.

An hour had passed and still neither Tessie nor Josie had come home. He didn't want to be alone. He went to the bedroom to get dressed. Then he picked up the phone.

He'd never called a cab before, never had reason to. After he dialed, he wasn't sure what to say. "24 Acacia Street," he said.

He went outside and waited. When the cab pulled up to the driveway, he felt satisfaction at his ability to summon this ride. The driver, who was bearded and wore a turban, asked, "Where to?"

Johnny hadn't really thought he would go anywhere. Somehow he thought the mere act of standing there, waiting, would cause Tessie or Josie or someone to show up, and he would send the cab on its way. No one had shown up, though, and the cab was here to take him – where? He opened the door and slid slowly into the cab.

"Where to?" the driver asked again.

"Holy Cross Cemetery," Johnny said, pulling the door shut firmly, happy now that a destination had suggested itself. He settled back into the seat, watching the homes of his neighbors roll by. As the cab turned the corner, he twisted around to look at his empty house. He faced forward again and caught the driver looking at him in the rear view mirror. Johnny wondered if his head got hot underneath the turban, whether it was heavy and weighed him down.

"Everything okay?" the driver asked.

And though it wasn't and hadn't been in a while, Johnny nodded and said yes, everything was okay, because now that he was in the cab and headed somewhere on his own, he felt refreshingly unfettered, like a boy released for recess or a prisoner given parole. He had left a note on the kitchen table: GONE OUT. He liked its brevity and its resolve. He liked that Tessie would come home and find *him* gone for a change.

Seldom one for small talk, Johnny now felt an urge for conversation. Nothing long and involved, just a moment of civilized exchange.

"How's business these days?"

"Today, a little slow."

Johnny wondered if his driver was one of those immigrants who worked 80 hours a week, growing his savings to bring his family over from India. Johnny patted his pocket to make sure he had his wallet.

"And how are things with you?" The driver turned his turbaned head for a quick glance to the back seat.

"Same," Johnny answered. "Slow."

Johnny settled back in his seat, pleased at what they had in common. He was almost happy in the cab as it sped along on the freeway. It was clean, the seat belts were unfrayed and sturdy, and there was a touch of saffron in the air.

He looked at the nameplate on the dashboard.

"Surjeet," he said, "do you mind turning off the air conditioner?"

Surjeet, apparently accustomed to meeting his customers' requests, complied without question, and Johnny rolled down his window, letting the wind rush at his face.

◈ ◈ ◈

Winston sat in the Cadillac parked with its sleek nose facing the ocean. He had taken it through the car wash that morning, watched as the suds obscured the windows, darkening the interior of the car, closing him in. The scrubbers rumbled over the top of the car and then the jets of spray made a drumbeat. As the car shook, Winston had the sense that it was moving backward. He yanked at the hand brake only to find it was already secured. The car wash machinery was moving. He and the Cadillac were standing still.

It was time to move on, he knew. To let it go, whatever it was he had been chasing. But he couldn't leave without the letter, or at least without knowing what happened to it. He stared out past the sparkling hood of the Cadillac at the ocean. He had been sitting here most of the morning, trying to decide what to do. The parking lot had been nearly empty then, but now cars circled the lot. Winston stayed, stubbornly occupying his spot.

He opened the glove compartment again and tried to imagine how the letter might have made its exit the last time he saw the de la Cruzes. If any of them had it, he hoped it was Johnny.

He should've asked him then in Rey's garden after the funeral. Winston had gone there to think. The loss of the letter weighed heavily on him, and though he would have liked to have made a quiet exit along with the other non-family guests, he couldn't bring himself to leave yet.

He sat under the banana tree, its floppy, bitten leaves the only shade among the dusty snarls of vegetation. Though he took a bitter pleasure in this especially unkempt patch of garden, soon a parade of ants at his dress loafers convinced him to leave his shelter. Then Johnny appeared, taking a seat on the weathered bench at the edge of the garden. Winston would have stayed hidden, but the loss of the letter and the possibility that Johnny might have it persuaded him to come out into the open. He moved only slightly from the tree, enough for Johnny to look up. The sight of him startled Winston.

There was remorse in Johnny's eyes, and it made Winston hopeful. Though the blood pumped in his legs, he knew he could not rush at Johnny. He pushed his loafers into the dry, hard dirt to root himself.

"I didn't ask," Johnny said. "I should've. But I just took it."

Winston moved to Johnny's side, knelt in the weeds that sprang at the perimeter of the bench. "What, Johnny? What did you take?"

Johnny reached inside his jacket. Winston closed his eyes with relief, then he opened them and saw what Johnny had withdrawn: the feather from Rey's hat. Stupid, silly feather. Johnny was weeping.

"It's okay," Winston said, trying to console them both. The words wilted in the hot, dusty air.

◈ ◈ ◈

On the freeway, Winston drove with the windows down and the wind boxing his ears. He cursed the existence of the letter, regretted having shown it to Johnny, grieved that now it was lost, and resolved to find it again.

When he arrived at the de la Cruz house, Josie was on her knees in the front yard, bent over a wet dog. She appeared to be talking to the dog and didn't look up until Winston clanked the gate of the chain-link fence closed. She squinted.

"Hey, stranger."

Winston felt the word was intentional, meant to be wounding.

"Nice dog," he said about the raggedy creature she was rubbing dry with the beach towel he recognized as his own, lost since the Fourth of July.

"Well, at least he's clean." Josie stood back to admire her deed.

Winston knelt down to scratch the grey-at-the-mouth dog, which collapsed onto the grass with gratitude. Josie took a comb to its tail. Neither of them spoke, and there was only the sound of the dog's blissful breaths.

"I saved his life," Josie said. "For now."

"It's a good thing."

"The least I can do."

Winston looked toward the door.

"Nobody's home. Just me and our new dog." Josie corrected herself. "Well, old dog."

Winston stopped petting the dog and sat back on his heels. He didn't really want to be here talking about the dog, but he wasn't sure how to move the conversation forward or to make a graceful exit. His hesitation allowed Josie to take the lead.

"Did you find it? The thing you lost?"

Winston couldn't tell if Josie was baiting him. Did *she* have the letter? "No," he told her.

She gave the dog a vigorous pat. She seemed to be finished with the conversation.

"How's Johnny?" he asked.

"What was he like the last time you saw him?"

The last time had been in Gloria's kitchen with the thrashing of the lilies, the echoing of Bunny's name. Winston declined to answer.

The dog got up and ambled to the shade.

"I think he knows he's on his last legs," Josie said, her voice catching.

"Johnny's still got some fight in him."

"Winston. I meant the dog."

Josie bristled, even clenched her fists. "Of course my dad has fight in him. He hasn't given up. No one has," she said, her voice growing loud. The dog rose up on his old legs and stood by her side. Two against one.

He addressed the dog. "So, how do you like your new home?"

"He's not living here. He's coming with me, back to my house." She scratched behind a scraggly ear. "It's time to go back home, isn't it?"

Winston couldn't help it. "So your house is all painted now."

Josie looked at him as if he had delivered the final insult. "Go mind your own business, Winston."

Winston drove back to his place regretting too many words.

◈ ◈ ◈

When he pulled up to Bev's, he flattened the brake pedal into the floor so quickly that the Cadillac leaped to a stop. He stared at the porch, trying to make sense of what he saw, because there was Tessie, holding a drink in her hand and chatting with his landlady. They were both looking at him, looking as if they could wait all day if need be.

Though he had just come from the de la Cruz house, where he had expected to talk to Johnny if not Tessie, the fact that Tessie had sought him out where he lived made his hands sweat. He tried to remember what, if anything, he had told Bev about the de la Cruzes and why he was there. He had meant to be discreet, but whenever he joined Bev for her afternoon tea, which was how she referred to her glass of Lipton with a splash of vodka, his tongue would become loose and his emotions unencumbered, and he would let slip some reference to his parentless state. Bev, giddy with Smirnoff, would become inconsolably weepy, and Winston would be shamefully grateful that someone would shed tears for him. Since Rey's funeral, he had avoided the afternoon tea hour, not trusting himself to contain his urge to unburden himself of what he now admitted was guilt at inserting himself so earnestly into the de la Cruz family.

He wondered if Bev's loyalty to him could be so easily supplanted by Tessie's one visit. Or had there been others? Already they looked like best friends.

"Look who's here," Bev said, patting Tessie's arm as Winston came slowly up the walk.

"Would you like some iced tea, Winston?" Tessie asked before he had reached the porch steps. She raised her own glass slightly, but there was little that resembled hospitality in the invitation.

There was an extra glass on the tray and a fresh pitcher ready to be poured. Such preparedness was unlike Bev, who usually went running back into the kitchen for a second glass, even when Winston's presence at afternoon tea had been planned.

Tessie was already pouring. "You look thirsty."

She was right. His throat was dry. He took the glass from her hand, wrapping his moist palm around it. Why was Tessie here?

Both Bev and Tessie were looking at him as if he owed *them* an explanation.

"I saw your new dog," Winston said to Tessie.

"What dog?" Tessie looked alarmed, and Winston winced at his blunder.

"I saw Josie. It's Josie's dog."

"Well, she's not keeping it at the house."

"No, right." He sipped his drink to stop himself blathering on about Josie moving back to her own house. He sipped again. There was no vodka in his tea.

Tessie jiggled her glass, making the ice cubes knock against each other.

"Well," Bev said, springing to her feet, "You two have a nice chat." She went inside. On the other side of the screen door, she sat in her living room and turned on the TV with the sound on mute.

Tessie refilled her glass, and there was more clinking and scraping of ice as she set the pitcher back down.

Winston steeled himself. "Do you want to go inside and talk?"

Tessie rose, waited for him to lead the way, and as he trod past Bev's rose bush with its disorderly branches and end-of-season sparseness, he felt her step close on his heel. He felt chased and beleaguered.

"Very nice," Tessie said, as he held the door open and she had her first glimpse of how he had been living. Winston relaxed a bit at her approval. Over the summer, he had made inexpensive but aesthetic purchases at the Saturday flea market on the boardwalk: an indigo bedspread, a cotton weave throw rug the polished gray of wet sand, a sleek black obelisk of a lamp. He had covered the cooler that had stored Odette's sandwiches with a hand-printed sarong, upon which a few books and magazines rested. On the coffee table were arranged some seashells, small flat stones, and twists of driftwood, along with the picture of him in the middle of Bunny and Carlitos. He saw Tessie's eyes go to the picture. He noticed for the first time her appearance. Limp sweatpants in an unbecoming color, scuffed sneakers, and her hair depleted of curl.

He offered her a seat, but she was still looking at the picture.

"It's me and my parents," he said.

"Your parents?" Tessie asked. Her voice went shrill with the last word and Winston thought of Gloria and the scene in her kitchen after Rey's funeral. He hastened to affirm for her what Johnny had so categorically done for him.

"Yes, my parents," he said. "Carlitos and Bunny."

Tessie continued to study the photo, but Winston saw a

loosening of the muscles in her face, saw the panic drain away, heard the relief in her voice when she said, "I'm truly sorry about your parents."

Though there was compassion in Tessie's voice, there was also a hint of tiredness, irritation even, as if it were time to get things over with, which now made Winston impatient for things to happen. He was still extending his hand toward the chair he was offering, and now Tessie sat. Winston sat down too.

Still holding her glass, she sipped from it now. Winston could hear her swallow – and then she was choking. Tears shone in her eyes. Winston's grip tightened around his own glass of iced tea. He tried to move himself to react, the way he had done all summer, but all he could do was apologize.

"Tessie, I'm sorry."

"About what?" Tessie dabbed at her eyes with the back of her hand and looked at him with curiosity. "What are you sorry about, Winston?"

"Everything." He wanted to offer her a tissue, but he had none. He rose, wondering if he should run to the bathroom for toilet paper.

Tessie reached inside her purse, and Winston sat back down, grateful that she would come to her own aid. But it was not a tissue that Tessie withdrew.

"You took it?" Winston blurted, relief giving way to dread. "It was you?"

He shifted his position in his chair, trying to steady himself for whatever was to come, and as he moved, Tessie clutched the envelope closer to herself. She looked indignant. Winston realized he should have waited for her to speak first, that this was her show to run.

"I did *not* take it," she said tightly, in a finders-keepers tone of voice. "It just ended up in my hands."

She was silent then, looking around herself as if confused.

Winston tried to assess the strength of her grip on the envelope – whether it would give if he should suddenly pull at it, or whether there would be a tug-of-war. But her gaze came back to him and she slowly handed him the envelope, though her grip remained firm.

"I want you to tell me what it says."

Winston wanted the letter in his hands, but was loath to take it if it meant complying with Tessie's request. To urge the letter on him, she removed it from the envelope. His hands shook slightly as he unfolded the crinkly ivory paper that still after all this time retained a faint floral scent. He stared at his mother's small, ornamental handwriting.

"I don't read Tagalog very well anymore," he said.

"But you do read it." Tessie said. "You *have* read the letter, haven't you, Winston?"

It wasn't really a question.

Winston smoothed out the letter, thankful for the reunion, but also anxious now at what was being asked of him.

"Winston, you know I expect you to tell me everything that's in there."

"Yes," he said, looking down at Bunny's already familiar words, translating them silently to himself.

Seeing Bunny's words again, Winston could almost hear his mother's voice, brazen with plushy tonal shifts, capable of being mean and tender in nearly the same breath. The letter taunted, it scolded, and it judged – but it told the truth. Winston knew this. And though the letter had never been meant for his eyes, he felt as if the words were directed at him. *You remember Carlitos.* It sounded like a command. Deep down, he had known all along that Carlitos was his father. Perhaps it was the little bit of dreaminess he had inherited from Carlitos that had sent him on his trip down here.

"Well, what's it say?"

Winston took a deep breath to relax the muscles in his face and turned to Tessie. She was holding the picture of him and Bunny and Carlitos. In her other hand was the envelope. Both of them in her grasp like collateral.

"What's it say," she said again.

Winston pointed to the prettily inked pages. "I had a little trouble with some of the words."

"But you understand the jest of it?"

Winston had never laughed at Tessie's mispronunciations. He had found them endearing and delightful. But never so amazingly apt, which is why he was laughing, no, guffawing, uncontrollably now in Tessie's appalled face. Because, yes, he did understand the jest of it, how the joke was on him – just what had he expected by traveling down here in the Cadillac with Bunny's letter? He had brought this moment on himself, and now as he felt the laughter gurgle back down his throat, he saw Tessie's hand swooping from out of his peripheral vision, turned to meet it full on with his face, felt the slice of metal that was her ring connect with his cheekbone.

He had hoped to be knocked silly, stunned into incoherence, his speech slurred and incomprehensible. But Tessie had not slapped him; she was merely cupping one side of his face with her hand. Now she brought the other hand up so that his head was in the chapped vise of her fingers, and he could look nowhere but in her insistent eyes.

"You know you have to tell me the truth."

Winston nodded inside her clamped hands. She let go of his head and eased back into her chair, and he sat on the edge of his. In a halting voice, with his eyes studying the lithe script, his finger trailing each word, he read to Tessie only two lines from the letter: *...I'm living in the States now, not 100 miles from you and your family. Your sister gave me your address.* Then, his finger still picking out syllables on the page, he called upon the extemporizing gifts that had taken him twice to the finals of the state speech tournament: he reconstructed the hopeful and sentimental words Bunny had said to him after they arrived in Anaheim and the Matterhorn rose up in the pink-tinted smog. How they were in the States now, where they would make their home and their life, and pursue their dreams, the way Johnny had pursued his.

"Is that it?" Tessie asked.

Winston nodded, not wanting to look at her, not wanting to see whether she believed him or not.

Tessie lifted the letter possessively from Winston's fingers, folded it back along its softened creases. She picked up the envelope and began to slide the letter back inside.

Winston looked at her, at his fingers holding nothing.

Tessie pointed to the front of the envelope to Johnny's name. "It's his, you know."

Winston wondered if he should grab it from her and run. She was tapping the envelope in the palm of her hand as if daring him, he thought. Then he watched as she took the letter out of the envelope again. She put it back into his hands, clutching the envelope to herself.

"Keep it, Winston. Take it home with you."

Tessie left him then, and he was aware of the peach blur of her sweatpants past his window. Winston felt he had effectively been dismissed from the lives of the de la Cruz family. But he felt, too, that he *could* go home now. He looked at his mother's letter in his hands and at the picture of himself, his dead mother, and his missing father Tessie had left on the chair.

There was no reason to wait even a minute longer. He began to pack. Bev came over and watched.

"Will you be back?" she asked. She had on her pink Nike visor, pulled down over her eyes. The wrinkles at her mouth twitched.

Winston said no, he didn't think so. He put the last of his belongings – the letter, the picture – into Odette's cooler. Before he set off, he took Bev for a goodbye spin in the Cadillac, and then he was on the road alone.

He thought of the house in Anaheim. Only a short distance separated Bunny's house from the de la Cruz family. *Not 100 miles,* as Bunny's letter said. Not two hours' drive. He sped up, the Cadillac responsive to the resolve in his foot. He wanted to see the Matterhorn loom into sight. He wanted to deliver the gifts from Tijuana to Felix and Odette, to return the Cadillac and retrieve his motorcycle.

He would head to L.A. for his fall semester, swim laps in the pool at the apartment he'd share with Junior, make the Dean's List again. And then, maybe, sometime, he would do what he had failed to do when he was thirteen and had run away from Bunny – buy a plane ticket to Ireland. To see for himself the woolly sheep and green hills and stone castles. Not to find Carlitos. Of course not. *Never that,* he told himself, pounding the steering wheel for emphasis. Despite not having traveled very far up the freeway, he veered off to a rest stop, needing to take a breather, his fist aching.

◈ ◈ ◈

Josie hadn't named her dog yet. She wanted to name him Rey, but knew Gloria would not consider it an honor. Rey would have.

The dog had been called Rocky at the shelter, but the name was apt only if considered in the sense of *shaky or unsound.* His was a tentative, insecure nature and so did not merit the tough-dog connotation. Naming him Rey would have bestowed a bit of serenity, she thought.

But then, she had admired his behavior in Winton's presence, when he had risen to her defense. Perhaps Rocky suited after all. She snapped on a leash and led him out of the yard. He trotted next to her. It might have been companionship that kept him at her side. It might have been something else. She couldn't really know.

The park was packed with children, small boys lined up in rows, diving to the ground for hip-sagging push-ups and then springing to their feet to run in place, lifting their knees to knock their chests as their coach roared commands at them. It was the end of summer. The Pop Warner kids, their undeveloped bodies enlarged with pads and helmets, had replaced the Little Leaguers. The change marked the end of summer, which always made Josie a little sad.

She wondered where her parents were. She wondered if they would feel relief that she was moving back to her house, that her husband and son would be coming home soon after a summer of bonding without her. She wondered if they would refrain from disapproving remarks about her new dog. *Old dog,* she reminded herself.

She saw the green Buick coming down the street. *They really ought to replace that ugly thing,* she thought. She turned around to head back. Rocky obliged her when she tugged at his leash, and she heaped praise on him, which sent his tail into a mad sway. The Buick pulled past her at a speed incongruous with Tessie's normally staid driving. Alarmed, Josie quickened her pace. When she realized the passenger seat was empty, she broke into a run. Rocky bounded along beside her, and together they arrived at the driveway, panting and anxious.

Josie had barely caught her breath when she called out, "Where's Dad?"

"He's home." Tessie, already out of the car and in the front yard, turned around at the agitation in Josie's voice. "Where else would he be?" She glared distractedly at Rocky. "So that's the dog," she said, before hurrying into the house. Josie followed, regretting her harsh tone to Rocky as she ordered him to stay outside.

"Why weren't you home?" Tessie asked as she finished her tour of the house that was clearly empty of Johnny.

Josie sputtered, incredulous. "Why weren't *you* home?"

They faced off. Josie saw fear on her mother's face and knew that her own face showed the same thing. For once she felt a flash of sympathy between them. She reached for her mother's hand. It was impulsive, this touch, and if it caught her mother unawares, she didn't show it. They stood, clasping each other's hands. The moment had not yet begun to feel awkward when her mother abruptly disengaged her hand and pushed past Josie, leaving her to feel as if she'd been punched. Then she saw it too, the two-word note her father had left on the kitchen table: GONE OUT.

◈ ◈ ◈

At the cemetery, Johnny directed Surjeet to the east loop which sloped upward toward the chapel at the top of the rise. Twice he told Surjeet to stop, and he made his way slowly out of the car only to realize he was in the wrong place. The third time he told Surjeet to stop, he looked out the window first to survey the lay of the headstones and other markers.

"Is this the place?" Surjeet asked.

Johnny thought so, but wasn't sure. Still, he didn't want to be wrong again. Or at least he didn't want Surjeet to know that he was wrong. Johnny opened the door. "Yes, this is the place," he said, and if it wasn't, he was going to pretend that it was.

"Take your time. I'll stop the meter."

The graves sloped away from where he stood, the ground leveling off where a white fence wound a crooked course along a bluff. Below that ran the freeway. Johnny could hear its whoosh of cars. He stepped carefully, zigzagging his way around headstones, bouquets of wilting flowers, and every so often a spigot. Why hadn't he stopped to get flowers for Rey?

On the day of the burial, when they had all gathered here (at least he hoped it was here or somewhere near here) with the casket above the ground gleaming in the sun, the site had looked uniquely prepared for Rey. But now that he was in the ground, it was hard to locate landmarks that would lead Johnny to him. He was about to give up and pretend for Surjeet's benefit that he'd found it, bowing his head at the grave of Amelia Gonzalez, Beloved Wife and Mother, who had made her glorious exit in 1913. Then he recognized a large patch of clover shaped like the X-ray of his lungs he had seen when he had first gone to the doctor with his symptoms. He had stared at this clover at Rey's graveside service. He had tried to see a shape other than his lungs, the way his daughters used to look for pictures in the clouds, finding birds or galloping horses or sunflowers. Then as now, he only saw his lungs, and nearby was the stone with Rey's name on it.

Johnny was afraid to sit down, afraid he might have difficulty getting to his feet again. He sat down anyway and stayed there, knees bent, a sliver of shin exposed to the late afternoon warmth. He was quiet because he didn't believe in talking aloud to the dead. Then he slowly stretched out on his back, the rough grass tickling his neck and ears, his eyes closed against the high blue sky. He just wanted to feel what it might be like to lie here with the sun on his face, a light breeze hovering above him, and the sound of the freeway making noises like some great waterfall that poured itself into a river on its way to the sea. It was the sea he thought about now – how he had felt its pull when he lay in the sand on that Philippine beach as a boy. How it had delivered him to American soil. How he was not yet ready to rest in it.

When he opened his eyes, Surjeet was standing over him. "Everything fine?"

"Yes," Johnny replied. He allowed Surjeet to help him to his feet.

Back in the cab, Johnny felt suddenly tired, overwhelmed by the day's events – waiting for Tessie, sipping coffee with Hector, visiting Rey. It wouldn't do for him to fall asleep in the cab, where he might snore, babble, or drool, so he gave the driver Josie's address, which was nearby. The house was in an old neighborhood which Josie considered quaint and historic. *Vintage,* she said. *Old,* he thought. With bad plumbing. And lead paint. It was a good thing she was having her walls repainted.

"Right here," he told Surjeet as they came upon a little blue house with a low stone wall in front and a small bed of determined geraniums. Johnny pressed a squished bill into Surjeet's hand, hoping he wouldn't be offended by the immoderate tip.

Josie's car wasn't in the driveway, but he knocked at the door anyway. After a moment he dug inside the hanging basket of fuchsias until his fingers found the key. Inside he went straight to the couch and went to sleep.

◈ ◈ ◈

The four of them sat around the kitchen table. It occurred to Tessie that this is what their Sunday dinner table would look like after Johnny was really gone, not just GONE OUT.

"Maybe he went to a movie."

"Or a restaurant."

"Maybe someone saw him leave. Should we ask the neighbors?"

But they would not. How would it look, a wife not knowing where her sick husband was, grown daughters ignorant of their father's whereabouts?

Sara joked that they should put Josie's new dog on the scent, give him Johnny's pillow to sniff. No one laughed: not Tessie who was dismissive of anything to do with the dog, not Laura who considered jokes inappropriate to the moment, not Josie who secretly thought they *should* put Rocky on the scent and was indignant that the idea would be tossed off as a joke.

Sara's joke had put them at odds with each other. They sat leaden and silent. They could hear one another breathe. The air was as still as they were. Every so often one of them would glance at the broken clock on the wall as if expecting it to magically repair itself and start marking time again.

Tessie heaved a big sigh and roused them all from their inertia. Her daughters were slow to notice her tears, though Tessie did not hide her face, nor make any move to wipe the wetness from her cheeks. For a moment she wondered if her daughters might do it for her. She watched them look at one another. Perhaps they were spurred by something from their childhood, some impulse that urged them to open their limp hands towards each other. Josie and Laura, on either side of her, each took one of Tessie's hands. Sara took a hand of each sister. Now they were a circle. When had they done this before? Held each other's hands. They couldn't have only just invented it. It felt familiar and good and yet as Tessie began to recover herself, she loosened her hands from their clasp and dried her face.

"Josie, get that dog out of sight before your father comes home." Then Tessie went outside to sit in the front yard.

◈ ◈ ◈

In the backyard, Josie sat on the gritty bricks and watched Rocky explore the weedy disorder. He sniffed tired sunflowers and a dirt-caked garden glove, nudged a rubber ball with his nose. Every so often she tested his new attachment to her by calling his name and was gratified to see him trot back to her side – not immediately, and not devotedly, but still. She watched Rocky probe at the opening of the playhouse, backing away when he brushed cobwebs, finally inching his size and awkwardness inside the tight spaces – a blithe disruption of the dusty and derelict memories layered there. It was good to stir things up.

She called to Rocky and waited, but he didn't come. Disappointed, she stood and saw his tail working methodically back and forth, a pondering wag. He was behind the playhouse. She crossed the brick patio to find him pawing and snuffling at the dirt, and watched him dig to see what he would unearth.

◈ ◈ ◈

In the living room, Laura sat in her father's chair and tried to imagine where he might have gone. She remembered driving down the freeway in pursuit of Winston; she remembered the fleeting, absurd fear that he might have kidnapped her father. Wherever he was now, she was sure he was safe and that he would be back soon. Which meant, if she were going to act, she had to do it now. She pushed herself out of the chair and onto her knees to search the pile of videos. As she rummaged around, she considered how she might carry out her act of rebuke for the lack of appreciation for her gift. She could quietly steal it so that one day when her parents suddenly ached for the past on video, they would be left baffled and bereft when they couldn't find the tape; or she could smash it with her foot and leave it there broken on the floor like some sad, sloppy accident.

◈ ◈ ◈

Sara, alone in the kitchen, stood on the chair and lifted the clock from its place on the wall, leaving its bright yellow shape against the grimier hue surrounding it. She wiped the dust from its face and then turned it over, took a key from a small hollow, fitted it to a groove, and wound it. She liked the sound, mechanical and sure. She liked the motion, repetitive but with purpose. When she could wind no more, she stopped. The ticking began, and she felt a surge of triumph, as if she had resuscitated a comatose patient. She turned the clock back to its face to watch the hands move and saw with some disappointment that she had forgotten to set them to the correct time. It was late afternoon and the clock read just after nine. No matter. At least the clock was moving again.

Tessie sat in one of the two redwood-painted chairs. They had never officially been his-and-hers chairs, but somehow Johnny had always sat in the one on the right and Tessie in the one on the left. It was where she had sat when she commanded Josie to take her picture instead of snapping those dreaded still lifes; when she had watched Winston juggle so beautifully; when she had put her hand to quiet Johnny's jiggling knee so she could tell him she was going to Vegas with Rey and Gloria. She sat there now as she waited for Johnny to come home from who knew where.

But just for the sheer hell of it, she got up and moved to the other chair, becoming aware as she did so of the envelope – the one with Bunny's and Johnny's names on it – tucked inside her waistband. There were so many things she could do with it: leave it among Johnny's things for him to discover, put it under his napkin at dinner, pin it to the front of her shirt. Or she could bury it. Burn it. Tear it into pieces and swallow it. So many things she could do.

When Johnny woke in surroundings not his own, he was momentarily alarmed, but then remembered the cab ride there, his turbaned driver, his empty house. He went to the kitchen for a drink of water and found a depleted houseplant in the sink being sustained only by the faucet dripping slow brown beads onto the inside edge of the pot. Johnny, not usually one to minister to plants, was overcome by the sight of the drooping leaves. But even he, who knew little about plants, recognized this one might be saved. He watered the plant and then poured a glass of water for himself. It was only when he sat at the table to drink his water that he noticed what he had failed to see earlier: the unpainted walls of Josie's house. He was anxious to leave. As he reached for the phone, he thought how expert he was becoming at dialing for a cab.

Johnny cradled the plant in his lap in the front seat of the cab. It was the same cab that had brought him to Josie's. Surjeet had greeted him like an old acquaintance, holding the door open for him. "Home?" he asked.

Johnny was thankful at the sound of the word.

The driver eyed the plant. "Looks like you rescued that just in time."

Johnny said he hoped he had.

They drove silently, both of them looking at the road ahead. Later, when the cab turned the corner to Acacia Street, Surjeet said, "You're expected, eh?"

Johnny saw his house at the end of the street. Tessie was standing just inside the chain-link fence, her hand shading her eyes, her head turning, searching. His daughters' cars filled the driveway. He would gather them in the living room. *I have a surprise for you,* he'd say. He thought of the videotape set to play at the party scene, how he would push the button and they would all appear on the screen together. Dancing. *Remember this?* he would ask them. *Remember this,* he would tell them.

As the cab pulled up to the curb, Johnny watched Tessie's face, which at first showed only curiosity that a taxi would stop in their neighborhood. He leaned out the window, considered waving, but she'd spotted him now. He saw her relief, but it was not absolute, not without misgivings or blame or a slender but real impulse to turn away. Behind the chain-link fence, she stood atop the colored rock, her feet in sandals, so he knew the stony bed stabbed at her soles.

Surjeet ran around to the passenger side to help Johnny from the car. Johnny, clutching the nearly resuscitated plant, wanted to tell him he could make it on his own. But, in fact, he needed the support, because Tessie wasn't coming down to help him. She just stood there, listing on those rocks. Johnny leaned on Surjeet perhaps a little more than was necessary, feeling his excitement seep away, nearly forgetting what had triggered it.

The videotape, he reminded himself. *The videotape.*

As the anticipation began to build again inside of him, he felt a warmth pump through his chest and reach his ears, and he felt his eyes go bright and he turned to Tessie to persuade her of his sincerity. He saw her face loosen a bit, but then, as if she did not want to concede so quickly, she averted her glance, and it went tight and troubled. Realizing she was looking past him, he turned to see Winston's Cadillac coming down the street, its shiny grill flashing a steely grin; he knew now that Winston and Tessie had spoken.

Winston parked across the street as if observing some boundary, but when he walked toward them, it was with a self-possession that made Johnny recall Bunny at her best. Winston stopped at the driveway, looked first at Johnny, supported on Surjeet's arm, and then at Tessie behind the fence. There they stood, fixed for a moment in their geometry.

"What should I do?" Surjeet asked, taking away the question Johnny wanted to ask. Sweat beaded at Johnny's temples, and he shook his head to ease the prickle. His glasses dislodged and he lost his focus.

He heard Tessie ask, "Where have you been?"

He righted his glasses and located Tessie, still a bit blurry.

"Where were *you*?" he asked back, and he realized he was crying. He turned away, but there was Winston, so he looked at the space exactly between them, only to find Josie coming from the side of the house, looking grim and unforgiving, one hand grasping the collar of a keyed-up dog that strained against her hold, its trembling snout coated with dirt, its paw chafing at the cement. Though he knew the noise that followed – shouts from inside the house and thrown objects colliding – had not been set off by the dog's paw, he knew that all of the chaos was related.

A man could die, never having acknowledged his secrets, his betrayals, his regrets, and the world would not end. A man who was sick and whose death was surely not far off could not be blamed for conserving his energy for the business of surviving his last days.

He remembered how he had lain on the grass next to Rey at the cemetery, how the sun had warmed him, how the breeze had soothed him, how he felt he could really rest there on the hill above the freeway as the world went on without him. Now the energy left his limbs and he sank gratefully to the ground. His grip relaxed around the thing he was holding, along with the recognition of what it was. His eyes closed on their own. He felt Surjeet move behind him and gather him beneath the armpits. Then he was being grabbed at the ankles and levitated above the ground. He felt himself sway, and this feeling of being suspended, of hovering between consciousness and sleep felt safe and secret, and he willed himself to stay there so he would have to face neither the muddle of his life nor the disappointments of his dreams.

Through his wavering consciousness, he was aware of being transported across his front yard over the threshold of his front door around the coffee table to the couch, to its familiar sag where he could sink and settle. Sooner or later, though, he would have to open his eyes. Suddenly, he felt a cold weight across them. It took him a moment to realize he could lift it off his face, which he did slowly, peeling the wet cloth away to reveal a soft white movement above him.

"He's awake," someone said, a not unfamiliar voice, yet one Johnny knew was not part of his family.

He wondered where his glasses had gone. He squinted, and when the white cloud on the man's head translated itself into a turban, Johnny wondered if he were, despite the scratchy feel of upholstery beneath him, back at the cemetery with Surjeet trying to herd him back to the cab.

"Johnny?" This voice he knew: Winston calling his name.

Tessie was there now too, both of them looking down at him, neither of them graspable.

"My glasses," he said, which set off a general scrambling and jostling of objects, while he was left to hoist himself to sitting.

It was Surjeet who recovered the glasses and helped slip them on his face. Now he could see them all. There in front of him – his wife, his three daughters, Bunny's son.

"Everything okay, then?" Surjeet said.

No one answered.

Johnny liked having Surjeet in his living room, wanted more of his company, more of the harmless conversation of the cab ride. He longed for the cab ride. He sighed and nodded at Surjeet, who nodded to all of them and was gone.

Johnny became aware of a breathlessness in the room – at the hard work of all of them just being there. He noticed for the first time the disarray on the table and across the floor, videotapes scattered as if they'd been flung. He remembered the dog at Josie's side earlier and wondered where it had come from and where it was now. He turned to Winston, who seemed suddenly older, less boyish, no traces of the disquiet that had overcome him when they buried the cat. He looked at his daughters, but their faces said they would not answer to him until he answered to them.

"I have something to tell you," he said. He saw no softening of their faces, no reprieve in their questioning eyes, nor in the edgy, doubtful way they stood, which was, he realized, not unlike Tessie's. This alignment terrified him momentarily as the image of Hector alone at his kitchen table flared in Johnny's mind. Still, there was nothing to do but go on.

The room was quiet. He cleared his throat.

When Tessie sat down, he heard the rustle of paper and saw Bunny's envelope in the waistband of her pants. Tessie looked at it, removed it, and set it on a blank space of the coffee table. Johnny knew that even if Tessie were to burn it or bury it or scissor it to shreds, Bunny was with them to stay. Even Winston, whom Johnny was sure would soon enough drive away in the Cadillac, would never really leave their lives. But then, hadn't Bunny and Winston always been there in a way? Among the things he had lost, the things he had wished for but never gotten, the things he'd never wished for and gotten anyway.

Winston and his daughters were still standing.

"Sit down," he told them. He was not sure they would comply, but slowly they did, and as they repositioned themselves on a chair or on the floor, he groped feverishly beneath the debris on the table until he found the remote. He sat down on the edge of the couch between Tessie and Winston.

"Watch this," he said, as if he were about to perform an amazing feat. He aimed the remote, clicked on the video, and waited for the dancing to start.

ACKNOWLEDGMENTS 

My deep gratitude goes to the following organizations and individuals:

To 4Culture, Artist Trust, the Seattle Office of Art and Cultural Affairs, and the Bread Loaf/Rona Jaffe Foundation for grants and fellowships in support of my work.

To the Anderson Center for Interdisciplinary Arts, Atlantic Center for the Arts, and Hedgebrook for residencies in beautiful, nurturing spaces.

To past and present members of my writing group: Wendy Call, Alma Garcia, Allison Green, Jennifer D. Munro, and Sasha Su-Ling Welland – excellent readers, writers, and friends.

To Los Norteños Writers for offering community and to Kathleen Alcalá for her generosity and inspiration.

To Larissa Amir and Marie-Florence Shadlen who read and gave encouragement on an early version of this novel.

To Dale Alekel for always being a willing and eager reader of my work.

To Sara Crowe for all her effort on behalf of this book.

To Rick Simonson for encouragement and support.

To my writing teachers at the workshops I've attended over the years for sharing their talent and enthusiasm for stories.

To the editors at *Cha: An Asian Literary Journal* for opening a door and to Marshall Moore for inviting me in and giving this book his meticulous attention.

To my siblings Rose, Sandra, Joe, and Diana, and my mother Dolores for being there.

To Natalie and Ana for being in my life.

To James for everything.

CPSIA information can be obtained at www.ICGtesting.com
Printed in the USA
LVOW091605240812

295831LV00011B/120/P